THE
FRACTURED

PRAISE FOR THE JONATHAN QUINN SERIES

"Brilliant and heart pounding."—**Jeffery Deaver**, *New York Times* bestselling author

"Addictive."—**James Rollins**, *New York Times* bestselling author

"Unputdownable."—**Tess Gerritsen**, *New York Times* bestselling author

"The best elements of Lee Child, John le Carré, and Robert Ludlum."—**Sheldon Siegel**, *New York Times* bestselling author

"Quinn is one part James Bond, one part Jason Bourne."—**Nashville Book Worm**

"Welcome addition to the political thriller game."—***Publishers Weekly***

ALSO BY BRETT BATTLES

The Jonathan Quinn Thrillers
THE CLEANER
THE DECEIVED
SHADOW OF BETRAYAL (U.S.)/THE UNWANTED (U.K.)
THE SILENCED
BECOMING QUINN
THE DESTROYED
THE COLLECTED
THE ENRAGED
THE DISCARDED
THE BURIED
THE UNLEASHED
THE AGGRIEVED

The Excoms Thrillers
THE EXCOMS
TOWN AT THE EDGE OF DARKNESS

The Rewinder Thrillers
REWINDER
DESTROYER
SURVIVOR

The Logan Harper Thrillers
LITTLE GIRL GONE
EVERY PRECIOUS THING

The Project Eden Thrillers
SICK
EXIT NINE
PALE HORSE
ASHES
EDEN RISING
DREAM SKY
DOWN

THE ALEXANDRA POE THRILLERS
(with Robert Gregory Browne)
POE
TAKEDOWN

STANDALONES
THE PULL OF GRAVITY
NO RETURN
MINE

For Younger Readers

THE TROUBLE FAMILY CHRONICLES
HERE COMES MR. TROUBLE

THE FRACTURED

Brett Battles

A Jonathan Quinn Novel

THE FRACTURED
Copyright © 2018 by Brett Battles

Cover art copyright © 2018 by Robert Browne
Cover Images:
Cover image by Steve Halama © 2018 Steve Halama
Find Steve's excellent work on Instagram @steve3p_0

All rights reserved.

THE FRACTURED is a work of fiction. Names, characters, businesses, organizations, places, events, and incidents either are the product of the author's imagination or are used fictitiously. Any resemblance to actual persons, living or dead, events, or locales is entirely coincidental.

For more information about the author, please visit www.brettbattles.com.

CHAPTER ONE

NINE YEARS EARLIER
MARRAKESH, MOROCCO

JONATHAN QUINN SAT quietly in the back of the van, eyes on the video monitor, wireless earbuds in his ears. On the screen was the video feed from the body cam worn by the operation's team leader, Thomas Klopp.

"There's Canto," Nate said. He sat next to Quinn, keeping tabs on the feeds from cameras hidden around the neighborhood.

Quinn glanced at his apprentice's monitor. The upper left feed showed a street wide enough for only pedestrians and motorcycles. At the bottom of the image, a superimposed designation identified the location as being three blocks from the target's house. Maurice Canto was center screen, surrounded by four bodyguards, pictures of each having been in the briefing file. Based on Canto's known habits, an additional guard would be a dozen or so meters in front, and another the same distance behind.

Quinn toggled his mic. "Alpha's approaching."

"Copy," Klopp responded.

To Nate, Quinn said, "Locate the bodyguard on point."

"Checking." The images from different cameras flicked on the screen until Nate stopped on one. "There."

The lead guard was a block ahead of his boss.

"How did you miss him?" Quinn asked.

"I-I'm not sure."

"A slip like that could get someone killed."

"I know. I'm sorry."

By most measures, Nate was proving to be an excellent apprentice, but when mistakes like this happened, Quinn wondered if the kid would ever become a full-fledged cleaner.

Quinn activated his mic again. "Guard one is two blocks away, using route C."

"Copy," Klopp said.

Being a lookout was not a task Quinn normally took on. He was a scene cleaner, the person who scrubbed a mission location of all evidence of foul play. A job that, more times than not, included the removal of a body. But due to circumstances that the client—Albert Sanger of Stonewell Security Solutions—had described as "out of my control," the mission team was short-handed and Quinn had reluctantly agreed to the additional duties.

Like he and Nate had seen on the scouts they'd performed over the last two days, when the lead bodyguard reached the house, he brought up his phone and studied the screen to check the security cameras inside the house. These were the same cameras Quinn and Nate had tapped into the first night on the job, the feeds from which played on a third monitor in the van, between Quinn's and Nate's stations.

The guard completed his check a few seconds before his boss arrived. He shared a few words with Canto, and pushed a button on his phone.

A message flashed on the center monitor.

"Alarm's off," Quinn said into his mic.

"Copy," Klopp whispered.

Canto did not enter the residence right away. Instead, he and two of his bodyguards waited outside while the four others went in.

"Sticking to script," Quinn said. "Advance team's inside. Canto still out front."

Klopp clicked his mic once to acknowledge.

Via Canto's own security cameras, Quinn and Nate watched the men in the house split into two groups. One stayed on the ground floor, while the other pair started up the stairs.

Canto's place was a traditional, old-city home—several floors with open walkways all built around a central core open to the sky. Its age, however, did not mean it was rundown. Canto had clearly invested a lot of money renovating it, both in terms of style and security.

Like Quinn and Nate had seen before, the duo on the stairs went straight to the roof deck first. After they conducted a quick search, they descended to the fourth floor and took a fast but thorough look around. When they descended to the third level, Quinn switched his monitor to one of the rooftop cameras and said, "Cleared to position one."

Half a second later, Klopp and his four-man team appeared on top of the building behind Canto's. After quietly lowering themselves down the three-meter difference, they crept over to the top of the stairs.

"In position," Klopp said.

"I've got you on screen," Quinn replied.

On the center monitor, the two guards who'd been on the ground level went up one flight, where they were met by the two coming down. After a search of the floor and a short huddle, one pair returned to the ground floor while the other headed up again.

"Guard three and guard four heading back your way," Quinn said.

A click from Klopp.

As they'd rehearsed, Nate switched his screen to a feed from the ground floor, while Quinn activated the quad-box function on his, giving him shots from all four rooftop cameras simultaneously.

On Nate's monitor, the ground-floor guards walked over to the front door and let their boss in. The two guards who had been waiting outside with him remained where they were.

Some might call Canto paranoid, but the man had reason to be cautious. His position as a trusted adviser to the notorious arms dealer Janus Sideropoulos put a target on his back.

On three of the four cameras Quinn was watching, the other two guards stepped onto the roof, considerably more relaxed than they'd been on their previous visit. They didn't even realize they weren't alone until darts filled with Beta-Somnol—a fast-acting knockout drug—hit them. One was able to get his hand halfway up to the dart before he dropped to the deck. The other one didn't even try.

Quinn shot a look at Nate's monitor, but neither Canto nor the guards with him gave any hint they'd heard a thing. Canto had grabbed a bottle of something from a cabinet and was starting up the stairs.

Quinn said, "Canto's on the way."

"Alone?" Klopp asked.

"Alone."

"Copy."

On the third floor, Canto went to his office and shut the door behind him.

"Alpha in location three-one," Quinn said. "Guards one and two still on ground floor, guard one using the toilet, and guard two by the front door. No eyes on the stairs. You are free to move."

"Copy that."

Klopp led his team onto the stairway and down to the third floor. There, two of his men peeled off to keep an eye on Canto's office, while Klopp and the other two continued down until they were one floor above ground level.

"Status," he whispered.

"No change," Quinn said.

Klopp clicked his mic. He and his men then moved along the walkway, behind the half wall at the edge.

When they reached the optimum spot, Quinn said, "Stop."

The men complied.

"Guard two's standing near the front entrance," Quinn said. "It's a straight shot from there. If you move four meters ahead, you'll have your best angle on the door to the toilet. Approximately at your two o'clock."

Klopp left one of his men at the first position, and proceeded with the other to the second spot.

"Any movement at the toilet?" Klopp whispered.

"Door's still closed."

With a signal from Klopp, the man at position one rose just high enough to aim his dart gun and shoot. Guard two must have seen the projectile coming at the last second, because he tensed but couldn't avoid being hit. In a panic, he turned toward the front door, but the drug took him down before he could touch the knob.

The whoosh of a flushing toilet.

"Here he comes," Quinn said.

With no need to hide now, Klopp and his companion braced their weapons on top of the half wall and aimed them at the bathroom door. A moment later, the door swung open and guard one stepped out, his gaze on his crotch to make sure his pants were fastened.

Klopp's partner fired a dart into the guard's shoulder. This guy yanked the dart out before it could deliver its full payload, so Klopp pulled his own trigger, hitting the target in the thigh. The man reached for it but wasn't speedy enough this time, and kept heading down until he crumpled on the floor.

That was Quinn and Nate's cue.

Quick and efficient, they shut down the monitors and cleared everything from the central area of the van. Nate moved into the driver's seat, and Quinn the front passenger's. On previous missions, their spots had always been reversed, but the time had come for Nate to take on more responsibilities.

Quinn toggled his mic button. "Team two, ready?"

"Team two ready."

Team two consisted of the fifth and sixth men working with Klopp. They were positioned near Canto's building.

"Heading to you now," Quinn said.

"Copy."

Nate started the engine and navigated the ancient streets toward their destination. Unlike the narrow road Canto and his men had arrived on, the one in front of his house was wide enough for small vehicles, such as the undersized delivery van Quinn and Nate were in.

"Twenty seconds out," Quinn said into the radio.

As the van turned onto the target's street, Quinn and Nate caught sight of Canto's remaining pair of guards standing in the front-door recess.

Nate eased the van to a stop right in front of Canto's house, to avoid drawing any attention. Other than from Canto's bodyguards, of course. One of them slapped the side of the van and shouted for Nate to keep moving. Before he could make a second demand, team two moved into the narrow gap between the van and the building at either end, delivering the same Beta-Somnol fate that had befallen the guards' colleagues.

Quinn and Nate moved into the back of the van, slid open the side door and, with the help of team two, maneuvered the unconscious bodyguards inside. They then donned stocking caps, checked that their long sleeves were all the way down, and pulled on their rubber work gloves. With the tools of their trade in prepacked duffel bags slung over their shoulders, they exited the vehicle and team two entered.

Quinn nodded at Nate, who knocked twice on the house's front door, paused, and knocked once more. One of Klopp's inside men opened the door, and the two cleaners slipped into Canto's home. As soon as the door closed, they heard the van drive off. That whole operation had been accomplished in less than forty seconds, matching the best time from their practice the previous day.

Nate knelt beside the downed bodyguard near the door, while Quinn checked the one by the toilet. The man's pulse was slow and steady. A single dose from the darts would have been enough to keep someone his size unconscious for at least two hours, but this guy had been hit twice, receiving at least some of the first dose and all of the second. He'd likely be out for at least an extra hour. And boy, did he have a hellish hangover coming.

Quinn plucked out the dart from the guy's thigh and found the one the guard had pulled out on his own. After stowing them in his bag, Quinn glanced up the central opening toward the third floor. From his angle, he couldn't see much of anything, but knew Klopp and his team would be preparing to storm Canto's office. Once they had the target subdued, a second van would be called in, and Canto would be transferred into it in the same efficient manner as before.

Quinn and Nate's main job on the mission was not only to stage the house so that it looked like a kidnapping—not a stretch since that was exactly what it was—but to also plant evidence indicating the action had been perpetrated by Laurent Hájek, a rival of Janus Sideropoulos.

In one of the duffel bags, sealed in a special case, were partial fingerprints of known Hájek associates. Quinn and Nate would transfer them to a few select spots within the house. The trick was to leave just enough to convince Sideropoulos's people that their competitor was behind this. Too many prints—or too few, for that matter—and the scene would look like the setup it was.

Quinn rolled the guard over and tied his hands behind his back with the same kind of cord favored by Hájek's associates. Much less efficient than the zip ties Quinn and Nate usually used, but to each their own. After he'd bound the man's ankles, Quinn shoved him against the wall and headed over to see how Nate was doing.

"Klopp to Quinn."

Quinn clicked on his mic. "Go for Quinn."

"I need you up here. We have a problem."

"Copy." To Nate, Quinn said, "You good here?"

"I'm actually done." Nate zipped up his duffel. "You want me to come with you?"

Quinn nodded, and the two men headed up the stairs. When they reached the third floor, they discovered one of Klopp's men standing outside Canto's office.

"Your boss inside?" Quinn asked.

"Yes, sir," the man said, moving out of the way so they could enter.

The office was twice as long as it was wide, running parallel to the outer walkway. Shelves filled with expensive trinkets and treasures and old books lined the walls in a gaudy display of wealth. The spoils of blood money, Quinn knew.

A large, antique desk sat toward the other end of the room, and slumped over the top was Canto. By all appearances, it looked as if Klopp had achieved his goal, but if that was the case, Klopp and the three men with him would not have looked so uneasy.

"What's going on?" Quinn asked.

Klopp grabbed Canto by the hair and lifted the man's head. The Italian's eyes lolled dead in their sockets, and his mouth was surrounded by foam.

"The asshole killed himself," Klopp said. "I tagged him, but there was something weird about his expression as he fell down. I didn't think anything of it until I checked his pulse and realized he was dead."

Quinn walked around the desk to the other side of Canto. "Lean him back."

Klopp grabbed the dead man's shoulders and pulled him into a sitting position.

"Did you see him put something in his mouth?" Quinn asked.

Klopp shook his head. "His hands never got close to his face."

Glancing at Nate, Quinn said, "Flashlight."

When Quinn opened Canto's mouth, Nate shined his light between the Italian's teeth. One of the molars on the bottom right was broken. An old-school, fake-tooth suicide pill. He motioned for Klopp to take a look.

"Jesus. Is that what I think it is?" Klopp said.

"It appears to be."

"I thought those things were just Cold War fairy tales. Who would want one of those in their mouth?" He frowned. "Sanger is going to be pissed."

Quinn didn't care. Dealing with Sanger's reaction would be Klopp's problem.

The main thing Quinn needed to concern himself with was that he and Nate now had to get rid of a corpse. But, like any job he took, all the contingencies had been planned for.

The mission was essentially the same as far as Quinn was concerned. While Sanger and his friends at Stonewell wouldn't be able to extract any information from the dead man, they could exploit his disappearance and make Sideropoulos think his rival was gunning for him.

"We could use a little help," Quinn said.

"What kind of help?" Klopp asked. Op agents were seldom interested in assisting the cleaning staff.

"Tying up the guards on the roof," Quinn said. "Nate can give you the cord. Hands behind the back and ankles. And be sure to collect the darts and bring them back to me."

"That is not really our responsibility," Klopp said.

"No, but Canto's death is. Which has made my job more difficult. And don't forget, no one leaves until Nate and I leave."

Klopp grimaced but nodded and said to his men, "Sebastian, Carlos, take care of it."

The two men obtained the cord and left the room.

While Nate removed a body bag from his duffel and spread it on the floor, Quinn used paper towels and his special homemade solvent to clean the foam that had transferred from Canto's mouth to the desktop. He did the same with the foam still on the man's face. The towels were then put in a plastic trash bag. Next, Quinn wiped down the entire surface of the desk to remove any remaining foam particles and oil marks made by Canto's forehead and face.

He then grabbed Canto's right wrist, and set the dead man's hand down on the desk in a few spots the Italian would have normally touched. He checked to make sure a suitable amount of finger and palm prints had transferred effectively, and did the same with the left hand. That done, he zip-tied Canto's hands together and repeated the process with the man's ankles. This would keep the limbs from sliding around and throwing Quinn and Nate off balance as they carried him out.

He and Nate put Canto in the body bag and zipped it closed, after which Nate retrieved a handheld vacuum cleaner from his duffel and ran it over the desk and chair and surrounding area. Though both Quinn and Nate were wearing clothing that left little hair or skin exposed, it was best not to leave anything to chance.

"Point out everywhere you and your men have been in the room," Nate said to Klopp.

The op leader did so, and Nate vacuumed those areas, too. As he was finishing up, the two men who had gone to the roof returned.

"Any problems?" Quinn asked.

"We were only able to find one of the darts," one of the men said.

"What do you mean? Shouldn't it have been sticking out of a body?"

"Sorry, it wasn't there."

"You looked around?"

Both men nodded.

"It couldn't have just gotten up and walked away."

The man shrugged. "I don't know what to tell you. It wasn't there."

"It's got to be there somewhere. Nate."

"On it," Nate said.

UPON REACHING THE roof, Nate saw that the two unconscious bodyguards had been laid out next to the retaining wall. Klopp's men had followed directions in tying up the bodyguards, though Nate was less than impressed with their knotting skills.

He checked for the missing dart in the guards' clothing first, hoping it had gotten caught in a pocket or fold of fabric, but no such luck. He scanned the areas where each guard had gone down. There were a few potted plants, but none were hiding the dart.

He wondered if it might have blown off the roof, but there was no wind to speak of, and even if there was, the retaining wall would have kept the dart from rolling off.

"Quinn for Nate."

"Go for Nate."

"Any luck?"

"Still looking."

"We've got everything by the front door. Just waiting for you."

"Copy."

He checked under chairs, tables, and in the folds of the furrowed awnings that could be pulled over the seating area. The damn dart didn't seem to be anywhere.

But as he turned back to the stairs, he spotted something he'd missed before. The roof consisted of sections of different heights, imperfections from centuries of additions and repairs. A two-centimeter rise here, a five-centimeter drop-off there.

In the side of a drop-off near where one of the bodyguards had gone down was the open end of a pipe.

Nate got on his hands and knees and peered inside. The interior of the pipe was dark but something was in there. He shone his flashlight into the hole, then turned on his mic.

"Nate for Quinn. I found it."

QUINN RACED UPSTAIRS with the extractor from Nate's duffel. It was a long skinny metal tube that had wires running through it to control the claw at one end. The device was typically used to grab evidence that might have fallen behind or under a piece of furniture. Nate met him halfway down.

"Hurry," Quinn said, passing the tool to his apprentice.

When he rejoined the others downstairs, Klopp's expression had turned deadly serious. "We need to leave now."

"He won't be long," Quinn said.

"This is not a discussion. My scout picked up several of Sideropoulos's people heading in this direction. I've already ordered the van to come here."

As if to emphasize Klopp's words, the sound of a vehicle pulling to a stop outside could be heard. A moment later, someone knocked twice, then once.

"Quinn for Nate."

A pause, then Nate's voice, grunting, "Go for Nate."

"Abort and return to the first floor. Fast as you can."

CHAPTER
TWO

"ABORT?" NATE SAID. "I've almost got it."

"Give it up. Hostiles inbound."

Nate had the extractor in the pipe, its claw closed around the back of the dart. It had caught on something and was resisting coming out. Another tug, maybe two, and he'd have it free. He pulled again and felt the dart wiggle a few inches.

"Nate, did you hear me?"

Another pull. "I heard you, I'm just—" Whatever had been holding the dart gave way, and the extractor and dart shot out of the pipe. "Got it! I'm on my way."

Nate jumped to his feet and ran across the roof.

As he neared the stairway entrance, Quinn shouted, "Nate, stop! You'll never get here in time. Get onto one of the other roofs and stay out of sight."

Nate skidded to a halt. "Seriously?"

"Out of sight. Now!"

Nate whirled around and looked at the buildings that surrounded Canto's home. The building directly behind the place—the one Klopp and his men had been hiding on—was the only one higher than Canto's roof. Unfortunately, with no ropes or ladders, the three-meter wall might as well have been a hundred high.

The roofs to either side did not pose the same problem. From his and Quinn's prep work, Nate knew the one to the north was approximately four meters down. Doable, but at the risk of a twisted ankle or knee. The one to the south, however, was only two meters lower. He hurried to the edge and peered at the neighboring building.

It, too, had a roof terrace, but unlike the lounge chairs and sitting areas on Canto's patio, this terrace had been turned into a garden, where tables and shelves played home to hundreds of potted plants. Most of the area was shaded by portable umbrellas that had seen better days. At the back end was a small, doorless shed, and near it the opening onto the stairs that led down to the building proper.

No one was around, so Nate slipped off Canto's roof and onto that of his neighbor.

"We're away," Quinn said. "ETA on unfriendlies, thirty seconds. Tell me you're out of sight."

"Working on it," Nate said.

"Work faster."

Nate didn't have to do the math to know what was about to happen. As soon as Canto's colleagues entered the home, they would find the guards and immediately search the interior. Nate figured he had two minutes tops before they reached the roof.

As he weaved through the garden, he considered rearranging some of the junk so he could hide under one of the tables. But if the people coming were any good, that would be among the first places they'd check. For the same reason, the shed wasn't an option, either.

His best solution was to put as much distance as possible between him and Canto's place. He ran over to the next roof. It was only half a meter lower, so he hopped the small wall between them and raced across to the building on the other side.

A higher roof here, but not so high that he couldn't grab the edge and pull himself up. As soon as his gaze cleared the rim, though, he dropped back down.

Dammit.

An elderly man and two women were sitting at a table near the center of the terrace.

With no choice but to make do with the roof he was on, he whirled around and looked for someplace to hide. The terrace had a few chairs, a wooden table, and a covered counter that was too small to hide under.

He heard steps moving across the roof he'd just looked onto, heading in his direction. One of loungers must have seen him.

Cursing again, he snuck across to the stairway opening and moved down the steps until he was below roof level. The home he'd entered was similar to Canto's, a big open area surrounded by terraced levels where the rooms were. He could hear faint noises coming from somewhere below, but the floor directly below him was quiet.

From above, he heard a man's voice and then a woman's. Their conversation lasted for several moments before silence returned. Nate waited a handful of additional seconds before creeping up the stairs high enough to see the neighboring building. No one was there.

He turned toward Canto's place, peeking through the row of potted plants lining that side of the stairwell opening. He could just see the tops of some of the furniture above the edge of Canto's roof two buildings away. There was no sign of—

A voice, and then movement.

Never mind.

A man approached the end that overlooked the garden-terrace roof, holding a Heckler & Koch HK45 Tactical pistol—if Nate wasn't mistaken—its barrel elongated by a sound suppressor.

Another man joined the first, this guy at least a decade younger and a bit shorter. They shared a few words, then the older one motioned down at the garden. With a nod, the younger guy climbed over the edge and dropped down.

Nate groaned a silent *awesome*.

Younger Guy checked around the pots and, as expected, under the tables. He cautiously approached the shed and paused to the side before swinging into the opening, his gun ready.

Upon finding an empty hut, he looked back at his colleague and said something. It was loud enough for Nate to hear, but in a foreign language that sounded Eastern European. It certainly wasn't Arabic.

The partner looked past Younger Guy toward the roof

Nate was hiding on. For a moment, it felt like he was staring straight at Nate. When the man finally spoke, however, he called Younger Guy back to Canto's building.

The man leaned down to pull Younger Guy up. Just as they clasped hands, Nate heard another noise. This time, from below him.

He jerked around and glanced down the stairs. A middle-aged woman stood at the bottom, staring up at him as if she wasn't sure what she was seeing.

Then her eyes widened, and her mouth opened in part shout of alarm, part scream of terror.

Nate looked back at Canto's building. Younger Guy was hanging halfway up the wall, but both he and the older one were staring at Nate's hiding place. Nate whipped back around and raced down the stairs, saying in his broken Arabic, "Sorry. Sorry."

A door opened along the upper-floor walkway and a young man ran out. When he saw Nate, he grabbed a broom leaning against the wall and ran toward the stairs. He reached the bottom step at nearly the same moment Nate did, and swung the stick like it was an ax chopping wood.

Nate juked around the kid to the next flight down. He took the steps two at a time and was three quarters of the way to the next floor when the boy started down behind him.

With no one on the landing to block his way, Nate took the staircase to the ground level.

As he stepped onto the tiled floor, a wooden spoon flew centimeters from his face, and an older woman, screaming at Nate, ran at him as if planning on tackling him. He pivoted to his left and grabbed her as she went by, slowing her so she wouldn't crash into the stairs.

As he let go, he again said, "Sorry," and turned toward the front door.

Shouts rained down from above. Not the kid's voice, nor that of the middle-aged woman who'd first discovered Nate. This was a man's voice, commanding.

A bullet smacked into the floor a meter from Nate's foot.

Canto's people.

Nate jumped to the right, getting under the terraced floors, and ran toward the exit.

The door was an ancient wooden monstrosity, with an old-fashioned bar across it to hold it closed. Nate grabbed the bar but before he could lift it out, the kid was behind him, swinging the broom.

Nate dodged around one swing and ducked under another.

Frustrated, the kid sent the broom handle at Nate again, in a backswing.

Nate jumped out of the way again, but this time he grabbed the stick as it swung past and wrenched it out of the kid's hand.

The boy stumbled, then retreated when he realized Nate was the one with the weapon.

Nate held the broom menacingly in one hand, and used his other to shove the bar on the door out of the brackets, letting it fall with a clatter.

He feigned rushing at the kid—which sent the boy retreating across the room—and then tossed the broom to the side. He ripped his stocking cap off and pulled open the door. The temptation to keep running was strong, but his pursuers were still at least a floor away, and the last thing Nate wanted to do was draw attention from any of Canto's men who might be standing outside his house a few doors away.

Nate stepped onto the street, avoiding looking toward the Italian's building. Out of the corner of his eye, he noted two black sedans in front and a big guy in sunglasses guarding the door.

Nate turned in the opposite direction and walked down the street, increasing his pace with every step. Ten meters ahead was a cross street. If he could make it there before the two guys following him exited the house, he'd be free and clear.

"Quinn for Nate."

"A little busy right now," Nate whispered into his mic.

"Status."

"I have a tail."

"How? Where are you?"

"I'm dealing with it, all right? Just give me a few moments."

A pause. "Radio back the moment you're in a safe spot."

"Copy."

The street was sprinkled with groups of people. Where he could, Nate used them for cover, and where he couldn't, he stuck close to the buildings.

A shout from behind, angry, insistent.

Quinn lesson number 438: you don't always need to look back to know you're in trouble.

Nate started running a split second before a bullet slammed into the wall a forearm's length away. When he reached the corner, he swung onto the intersecting street.

The new road was one of the narrow ones, fit only for pedestrians and two-wheeled vehicles. There were few of either on it at the moment, eliminating his chance to blend into a crowd. The only option to get out of sight was to make it around the bend, twenty meters ahead.

He raced over the cobblestones, sure that at any second he'd hear another shout or boom of a gun, but he made it to the curve without either occurring.

This by no means meant he was in the clear. At best, he had a fifteen-second lead on the two who'd followed him from the roof. And they wouldn't be the only ones after him. By now they would have clued in their buddies at Canto's house, and the whole lot would be hot on Nate's trail.

He needed a busy road or a crowded market, anywhere he could disappear. As he ran, he looked around to get his bearings, and compared his location to what he'd memorized about the area. The biggest market was a quarter-kilometer away in the opposite direction.

He considered veering onto a path that would take him there, but Canto's friends were back that way, and Nate knew what only three of them looked like. He could run straight into any of the others without even realizing it. There was a smaller market on the next street up. He'd never been there and was unsure if it would be big enough to hide in, but it was better than nothing.

He plowed forward and took the first right turn. By comparison, the two-lane road felt like a superhighway. There were people here, and cars. And, best of all, the small market just down the street on the other side.

He weaved between vehicles to the opposite curb, where he slowed. Like before, he stayed in the shadows close to the buildings.

A stall alongside the road was selling caps and scarves, among other touristy things. Nate grabbed from the cart a Moroccan-style knitted hat and a blue patterned scarf.

He thrusted several bills into the merchant's hand. "Okay?"

The merchant looked at the money, and smiled. "Yes."

Nate shoved the hat on and wrapped the scarf around his neck. It wasn't his best disguise, but the goal was only to not stand out. He pretended to be interested in a sign hanging in a shop window and used the glass to check the street behind him.

The two guys from the roof were on the road, but they'd paused and were scanning the area.

They'd lost him.

Nate continued down to the market, and stepped into a street-side booth selling baskets and wooden toys and brassware. Using the merchandise as cover, he looked down the road again.

The big gorilla who had been standing in front of Canto's door had just turned onto the street and was heading toward the other two.

The booth's merchant said something to Nate, but Nate shook his head and tried to indicate he was just looking. The man persisted, so Nate thanked him and left.

He came to a booth-lined lane that ran perpendicular to the street, into a building. He turned onto it and stopped a couple of meters in, where he could still see his pursuers. There was no missing the agitation as the men talked. Younger Guy was the most animated, probably because the kid was getting most of the blame for losing Nate.

Nate was about to venture farther into the market when a black sedan like the ones he'd seen in front of Canto's building sped down the street and stopped in a cloud of dust next to the three men. Older Guy and the gorilla leaned into a window on the far side, while Younger Guy stood behind them, looking pissed off. After a few moments, the two men stepped back and a door swung open.

A man of average height emerged from the sedan, wearing large sunglasses that covered a good portion of his upper face, and a traditional keffiyeh headdress that covered his hair and mouth and neck. From the way the guy moved and held himself, Nate guessed he was late twenties to early forties, but he couldn't really see the guy's face. The only thing Nate had no doubt about was that this guy was in charge.

He was not, however, Canto's boss, Janus Sideropoulos, who was small and wiry. This guy was…average.

And given the very public dressing-down he was handing the three other men, he was clearly not happy.

Nate would have loved to watch the entire event, but knew this was the perfect time to get the hell out of there. Hoping there was a back way out of the market, he moved into the building, but the only rear exit was boarded up and there were no windows.

This place is more fire trap than market, he thought.

The aisle he'd entered took a ninety-degree turn near the back of the building, went on for twenty meters, then took another turn back toward the street, creating a U-shaped corridor of booths.

Nate took the second aisle back to the road and, as he neared the end, angled himself so he could check on the others again.

"Crap," he whispered, and quickly pulled back.

The men were heading for the market, the gorilla on a path that would take him to the aisle where Nate was. If Nate stepped out, he'd be instantly spotted, hat and scarf or not.

In less than thirty seconds, the same could be said if he stayed there in the aisle.

He headed back into the market, eyes out for a hiding place. Most of the booths were pressed against one another, using all the available space. There were a couple of gaps, though. One that led to the door he'd already checked, and another that gave access to the area where everyone was drawing their power from—a snake pit of cables running along a narrow space between the booths at the bottom of the U and the back of the building. Undoubtedly this would one day be the trigger for a fire that burned everything down.

Today, it would hopefully be Nate's salvation.

He slipped into the narrow gap, moving sideways to avoid ruffling the tarps at the back of the stalls, and scooted along the wall until he reached a slit between tarps through which he could watch the aisle.

For several seconds, he saw only locals and a few tourists strolling from booth to booth, checking out the wares. Then the gorilla strode into view. The guy stopped at every stall to scan it, pushing shoppers out of his way when necessary. The few who turned toward him as if they wanted to give him a piece of their mind quickly reconsidered.

Next came the keffiyeh-wearing boss. He, too, paused at each stall.

When he stopped at the booth directly in front of Nate, Nate felt the urge to pull back from the slit, but he held his place.

The man's gaze passed through the stall, taking everything in before he moved on.

Nate waited until the boss was two more stalls down before he continued down the wall. But all he discovered was the corner of the building, and the lack of a corresponding passageway leading back to the street.

"What the hell is going on?" Quinn asked.

Nate clicked his mic three times, letting his mentor know he wasn't in a position to talk.

"We're about three blocks from you," Quinn said, apparently having tracked Nate's phone. "Do you need assistance?"

What Nate wanted to say was *not yet*, but there was no code for that so he clicked twice for *no*.

"We'll stand by."

"ARE YOU CRAZY?" Klopp said to Quinn. "We can't just sit here." He shot a glance at the body bag holding Canto. "Not with *that* in the van."

"If you all want to go, go," Quinn said. "I can drive the van myself."

"Right. We'll just walk out," Klopp scoffed.

"Let's give him ten minutes."

A pause. "Five."

"Ten."

Klopp looked away and then back, his jaw tense. "Seven, but after that he is on his own. No renegotiating."

"Okay. Seven."

Quinn hoped it would be enough.

NATE CROUCHED IN the corner, facing the way he'd come. Little of the light from the market seeped into the passageway, so even if someone looked into the narrow space, he was confident they wouldn't see him.

He pulled out his gun and attached the suppressor. He didn't want to get into a gunfight with so many civilians around, but that didn't mean he could keep it from happening.

A minute passed.

Two.

Then three.

On one side of the slit Nate had been looking through, the tarp shook.

A voice on the other side, speaking what sounded like the same language Canto's friends on the roof had spoken.

A different voice answering, then light rushing into the back area as the tarp was pulled to the side.

Nate grabbed the tarp of the stall that backed into the corner, and just as the shadow of one of the men stepped into the narrow space, he pushed the cloth to the side and rushed into the stall.

The shout from the man who had entered the passageway boomed above the buzz of the market.

The corner stall's proprietor turned and spotted Nate.

Before the merchant could yell out, Nate raced into the aisle and shot a look toward the booth entered by the man who'd stepped into the narrow passageway. Younger Guy and the gorilla were there, waiting for their friend.

Head down, Nate sprinted toward the street. As he neared the exit, he turned on his mic. "Which direction are you?"

"Northeast," Quinn said.

Nate blasted out of the market and veered north.

"I'm coming in hot," Nate said.

"How many?"

"Two at the moment, but there's at least—"

A hand grabbed his shoulder and jerked him around.

It was the boss, and though Nate couldn't see the man's eyes, he could feel his glare. "Where the hell do you think you're going?" the man said in English, obviously seeing through Nate's flimsy disguise and guessing he wasn't a local.

Nate shoved him in the face, knocking off the glasses and dislodging the scarf across the man's mouth. For half a second, Nate had a good look at the guy's face—the thin lips, the too-wide mouth, and dark, piercing eyes, with a scar by the right eye that arced into his cheek like a comma or the path of a tear—and then Nate dipped his shoulder and twisted sideways, breaking free of the man's grasp.

The boss attempted to grab Nate again, but Nate pulled back and the man's hand missed him. Nate started to run, only to realize he'd been spun and was now heading back toward the market. From where the young guy and the gorilla had just exited.

They raced to intercept, herding him so that he would be caught between them and several cars parked at the side of the road.

Nate pretended he would try to sprint past them, but then made a sharp turn in the other direction and jumped onto one of the cars. He hopped off again on the street side to the blare of horns and shouts, but ignored them and hurried down the road.

As he turned west at the next intersection, Quinn was in his ear again. "Are you okay?"

"For…the moment," Nate replied between breaths.

"Are they still behind you?"

"Unfortunately."

"All right, here's what I want you to do."

After Quinn gave him instructions, Nate turned south at the next road and glanced back. Both Younger Guy and the gorilla were following, the former a good ten meters closer than the latter.

Nate continued running, turning again and again and again as he stuck to Quinn's plan. After the last change in direction, he slowed and looked over his shoulder. The seconds ticked by, until half a minute had passed without his pursuers showing up.

"I'm clear."

Quinn gave him the final directions.

Two minutes later, Nate reached the van.

As the van drove out of the city, Nate filled Quinn and Klopp in on the details of what had happened. When he finished, Klopp said, "Describe the man again."

"Which one?" Nate asked.

"The one who grabbed you. The boss."

"A few inches shorter than me. Not fat, not skinny."

"You mentioned a scar on his face."

"Yeah, like this." Nate traced a curved line on his own face. "Kind of like a comma."

"*Komma?*" Klopp said, miming the punctuation mark. "Like when you write?"

"Yeah. Exactly."

Klopp nodded, impressed. "That, my friend, was Christophe St. Amand."

"*St. Amand?* Seriously?"

Christophe St. Amand had also been part of the pre-mission briefing. He was Sideropoulos's right hand and enforcer. Not a lot was known about him, other than his reputation for being particularly brutal and a desire to remain anonymous. There were no known photos of him. Which made sense, giving the way the man had dressed to hide his features.

"You're lucky," Quinn said. "Rumor is, most people who come face to face with St. Amand don't live to talk about it."

"This, I can confirm," Klopp said.

The rest of the drive to their first stop was made in silence.

At an apartment building on the edge of the city, Klopp and his men transferred their gear into a couple of waiting sedans and said their goodbyes.

As part of mission prep, Quinn and Nate had picked out a location to dump any potential bodies, and by sundown, they reached it.

After removing Canto from the body bag, they dropped him into the pre-dug hole. Nate was instructed to drench the corpse in a special cocktail of chemicals that would accelerate decomposition, slopping extra onto the hands and face to make identification nearly impossible. Once the body was buried, they burned the body bag in a separate hole along with the trash they'd brought from Canto's home, and then mixed the ash with dirt and covered it up.

Nate groomed the dirt covering the holes to eliminate all visual signs of their existence. It was a special skill, one Nate had taken a while to perfect.

Quinn inspected the work and nodded. "Let's go home."

Nate couldn't help but think about Christophe St. Amand over the following months. He read all he could find about the man, which wasn't much, and pumped other operatives for whatever details they knew. All had heard rumors, but none had crossed paths with St. Amand.

As Nate's responsibilities on jobs continued to grow, his obsession with the scarred man diminished, and by the time Quinn made him his partner, Nate had stopped thinking about Christophe St. Amand altogether.

But that didn't mean he forgot.

CHAPTER
THREE

PRESENT DAY
WASHINGTON, DC

THE TAXI DROPPED Orlando off in front of the Smithsonian Institution at 10:06 a.m., leaving her nine minutes to reach the agreed upon bench on the National Mall.

It was a beautiful late May day, the temperature pleasant, the elm trees sporting new leaves, the tourists out in force in shirtsleeves, and a few even wearing shorts.

As she made her way to the meet, she covertly scrutinized the crowds, looking for anyone showing too much interest in her. This being Washington, she picked out several people she was pretty sure were intelligence agents. None gave her even the slightest bit of attention.

A break in a flock of tourists provided her with a quick view of the destination bench. Not surprisingly, the person she was meeting was already present. After a final scan of the nearby crowds, Orlando approached the woman. "Good morning, Misty."

Misty Blake smiled and stood. "Right on time as usual."

They hugged.

"Are you ready?" Orlando asked.

Misty took a deep breath, nodded. "As much as I'll ever be, I guess."

"You've got the materials?"

Misty patted the bag slung over her shoulder. "All set. Oh,

that reminds me." She pulled a clip-on badge out of the bag and held it out to Orlando. "You'll need this."

As Orlando attached the clip to her blouse, Misty clipped her own badge to the lapel of her business suit.

"Let's do this," Orlando said.

With Misty leading, they walked over to a staff-only entrance of the Smithsonian. There, a guard scanned their badges, searched Misty's bag, and waved them inside. A short hallway T-boned with a larger corridor. They turned left, strode past dozens of offices, entered a stairwell, and took the steps down to the basement level. A maze of hallways guided them deeper into the bowels of the museum. After what seemed like forever, Misty stopped in front of an unmarked door.

When she made no move to knock or open it, Orlando whispered, "Nervous?"

"Can you tell?"

"It's good to be nervous. This is a big deal. You just can't show them that."

"What if they don't react the way we anticipate?"

"Then I guess Quinn will have to break us out of prison."

Misty shot her a glance. "That's not funny."

Orlando almost said, "It wasn't meant to be," but instead replied, "Don't worry. You're going to do fine."

Misty smiled weakly, then closed her eyes and took a deep breath.

"Peter would be proud of you," Orlando said.

As Orlando had hoped, the words wrapped around Misty like a blanket of calm. Before he was killed, Peter had been not only Misty's boss at the old organization known as the Office, he'd also been her mentor and friend.

Misty knocked on the door.

CHAPTER
FOUR

THE NEXT DAY
SAN FRANCISCO, CALIFORNIA

JONATHAN QUINN DUG deep and pushed himself hard as he made the turn and began the final lap of his usual swim. When he reached the end, he performed another flip turn, but instead of swimming on, he spun so that he surfaced on his back, and let his momentum carry him until his feet dropped to the pool floor.

He looked at the digital clock on the wall. One hour and eight minutes. He'd done it in less time on a few occasions, but not by much.

After rinsing off the chlorine in the locker room, he pulled on his gym shorts, sweatshirt, and running shoes, and headed out to start the run home.

Orlando should be home now from her mysterious trip to DC. According to the online flight tracker, her plane had landed about the same time he'd headed for the gym.

He was anxious to see her. He didn't like spending nights apart, and the previous one had been their second in a row.

It also annoyed him that she wouldn't tell him why she'd gone east. They shared pretty much everything. But she'd been coy this time, saying he'd know soon enough.

He assumed it was about a job. That would be nice. He was ready to get back to work.

They had yet to take a paying gig this year. Instead their

time had been consumed first with the kidnapping of their kids while on vacation in Thailand, and next with the pursuit of those responsible for killing Quinn's sister, Liz, during the ensuing rescue mission. Work would be the distraction he needed. Not only to get a little relief from the pain of Liz's passing, but also to help him forget about the riff that had developed between him and his other partner, Nate.

Or was it former partner now?

Liz had been Nate's girlfriend, and to say he and Quinn had not agreed on how to deal with Liz's killer would have been a colossal understatement. In the end, it was Quinn's decision that ruled, and it was Nate who had walked away bitter and hurt.

When Quinn entered the house, he found Mr. Vo sitting in the living room, thumbing through a magazine. Mr. Vo and his wife had been with Orlando since she had lived in Vietnam. They helped around the house, cooking and assisting in taking care of Orlando's son, Garrett, and her and Quinn's daughter, Claire. They were more like live-in grandparents than hired help.

"She back yet?" Quinn asked.

Mr. Vo pointed at the ceiling. "Twenty minute ago. I hear her in office." The home office was directly above the living room, and it would be just like Orlando to head straight there and start working.

Quinn went down the hall to the kitchen and found Mrs. Vo sitting on a stool at the counter, cutting vegetables and watching *Game of Thrones* on her laptop computer. She had discovered the show the week before and had been binge-watching it ever since.

He grabbed a bottle of water out of the cupboard. "Did Jaime die yet?"

Without looking away from the screen, Mrs. Vo hissed, "Shhh," and waved a hand at him, telling him to go away. She had a thing for Cersei's brother, and Quinn never missed an opportunity to tease her about it.

"You know he's going to die at some point. *Everyone* dies on that show."

She grabbed a rag off the counter and threw it at him. "Get out!"

Laughing, he headed for the stairs.

"YEAH, I UNDERSTAND," Orlando was saying into the phone as Quinn entered the office. "If that's what it is, that's what it is…. Right. Goodbye."

As she hung up, Quinn hugged her from behind. "Welcome back."

She leaned her head against his shoulder. "Thanks. It's good to be home."

He swiveled her chair around and kissed her soft and deep. When their lips parted, he whispered, "I don't like it when you're not here."

She smirked. "Someone's in a sweet mood. Maybe I should go away more often."

"That's exactly opposite of what I just said."

She touched her forehead against his. "But I like what it does to you." Moisture rolled down the side of her eye. She pulled back, looked him over, then pushed him away. "You're all sweaty." He tried to kiss her again but she was having none of it. "Not until you take a shower."

"Aw, come on. Just one kiss."

"No."

He snickered and gave up the fight. "How was the trip?"

"Fine. Thanks."

"Did we get the job?"

"What job?"

"That's what this was all about, right?"

She smiled but said nothing.

"If you don't want to talk about that, how about telling me what that phone call was about. It didn't sound good."

Her smiled faded. "I was returning Helen's call."

"Helen called? Well, it's about damn time. Did she apologize?" Helen was the head of an organization, based right there in San Francisco, that had used Quinn and his team for several jobs, but there had been a falling-out in connection with Quinn going after the people responsible for Liz's death.

"No apology, and I didn't actually talk to Helen."

Quinn cocked his head. "Wait. You just said you were returning her call."

"When I asked for her, I was transferred to some guy in 'operations scheduling' named Jose."

"Okay. What did *Jose* want?"

"You're not going to like it."

"Just tell me."

"He said, quote, we are moving in another direction and your services will no longer be required. End quote."

"Our services will no longer be required? What the hell?"

"I told you there would be repercussions from London."

The targets Quinn and Orlando, their team, and several of their close associates had gone after were people Helen Cho's operation were interested in. This would have been fine if Helen had assigned them the mission, but they had been explicitly told to leave it alone. Quinn, however, was not about to let the people who had killed his sister roam free.

He had known Helen would be pissed, which was one of the reasons he'd given her the person who had pulled the trigger ending Liz's life. The assassin, though, was not the biggest target they'd captured. That distinction belonged to the people who had hired the killer. They were the trophies Helen wanted. Unfortunately for her, Quinn had already promised them to MI6.

It looked like Helen would never forgive them for that. At least she wasn't their only client. Still, Quinn preferred that he and Orlando chose who they worked for and who they didn't, so having it decided the other way around did not sit well.

"Any other good news?"

"Jose told me that he had been instructed to inform some of their sister organizations—"

"Sister organizations?"

"That's what he called them. He said he'd been instructed to tell them they should avoid hiring us, too."

"Did he inform you who these *sister* organizations are?"

"He's emailing me a list."

"Isn't that nice of him."

"Funny. That's exactly what I told him."

Quinn dropped into a chair. "So, do we have any job offers?"

"Fourteen, actually."

He perked up. "Now *that* is good news. What have we got?"

"I've already turned them all down."

"What?"

"Most of them were small ops offered by orgs we don't want to be involved with."

"Okay, but most is not all."

"There were three jobs from acceptable clients."

"And you turned them down, too."

"I did."

He narrowed his eyes. "Are we going on a vacation I don't know about?"

"No vacation."

"Then, what? You unilaterally decided we're retiring?"

"No retirement. Not yet, anyway."

"Orlando, what the hell is going on?"

Her lip ticked upward in the smallest of grins. "I've kind of committed us to something. A gratis job."

He stared at her in disbelief. "Gratis? You do recall that we haven't taken any paying work since last year, right?" While he was correct, the implication that they needed the money was not. If they wanted, they *could* have retired right then and there and lived out their lives in comfort.

"It's for a friend of yours."

"For the love of God, will you just tell me?"

"It's for me."

It was doubtful his brow had ever been as furrowed as it was at that very moment. "What are you talking about?"

"I have a job that I want to hire you for."

"We already work together. We're partners, remember?"

"We do, and we are. I guess it would be more accurate for me to say I'm hiring both of us."

Quinn closed his eyes and rubbed the side of his head. "Was it your goal to give me a headache? Because if it was, mission accomplished."

Orlando twisted back to her computer, opened her secure vid-chat software, and clicked on a number from her frequent call list. After two rings, a live image of Misty Blake appeared.

"Afternoon," Misty said. She was in Washington, DC, where it was already sneaking up on three p.m.

"Uh, hi," Quinn said, his confusion not lessened in the least.

"Why is his face all scrunched up like that?" she asked. "Is he okay?"

"He's fine," Orlando said.

Misty's eyes widened. "Oh, you haven't told him yet, have you?"

"I thought it would be better if we did it together," Orlando said.

"Tell me what?" Quinn said.

"The Office would like to engage our services," Orlando said.

This didn't help alleviate his bewilderment. "The Office doesn't exist anymore."

"Correction. The *original* version doesn't exist anymore," Misty said.

"Misty's reviving it," Orlando said.

The Office was the organization that provided Quinn most of his work until a few years ago, when Peter, its head and founder, had been killed. When that happened, the powers that be shut down the organization, and Misty, Peter's assistant, had been shuffled off to a series of menial federal jobs. Though she had gained tremendous knowledge about the espionage world thanks to Peter, as far as Quinn knew she had zero political clout to pull off being put in charge of her own intelligence operation.

"Are you saying the NSA is allowing you to restart the Office?" Quinn asked. Though the Office had been semi-independent, it was a government agency, under the oversight of US intelligence powerbrokers.

"They have," Misty responded. "And as a completely independent organization, I might point out."

"Come on. They would have never done that."

"Well, they have," Orlando said.

Misty smiled uncomfortably. "Peter had a collection of…um…I guess you would call it…uh—"

"Information," Orlando jumped in.

"Yes. Information. He kept it separate from the Office's records. I discovered it about a year ago."

"Blackmail material, you mean," Quinn said.

Misty shrugged. "I guess some might think of it that way." She smiled. "The NSA has agreed to officially part company with us, with the understanding that most of the work we do in the next three years will be routed through ACORT."

ACORT was a specially created, post-9/11 agency that operated mostly in the shadows as the NSA's rapid response arm, for both domestic and international issues, and primarily outsourced its work to independent organizations. The acronym stood for the Advisory Council on Organizational Redundancy in Technology, a cover name, meant to obscure the group's true purpose. Those in the know referred to it as either ACORT or the Council.

"You keep saying *us* and *we*," Quinn said.

"The NSA insisted on one condition for letting the Office go—that I needed to work with an experienced director of operations. They tried to push one of their people on me, but when I told them who I wanted for the job, they couldn't say no."

Quinn slowly turned to Orlando. "You?"

"Don't sound so surprised," Orlando said.

"I'm not surprised, per se. Of course you'd be perfect, but *we* work together."

"We do. That's not going to change. Though, if you're interested, I'm sure Misty and I can find a position—"

Quinn's eyes widened. "Oh, no. I am *not* interested in a management job. I like working in the field."

"And you will continue to do so," Misty said. "Though I could really use your mind for mission planning and analysis."

Quinn shifted his gaze between the two women. "You guys are serious."

"We are," Misty said.

"Think about it," Orlando said. "We're building an organization from the ground up. We'll be able to put it together however we think is best."

While Quinn knew Orlando also enjoyed working in the field, this bigger-picture stuff—the organizing, the setting up of systems, all the tiny details—was the kind of thing she dreamed about.

Quinn was not as excited to punch a timecard.

Reading his mind, Orlando said, "No one's asking you to jump in right now."

"Eh, that was pretty much exactly what you were just asking."

"What I mean is, you can work with us on a per-job basis for now. Later, if you think you'd like to help more, the opportunity will be there."

"You're saying *us*, too. Which tells me you've already accepted the position."

"I have."

"Isn't that something we should have talked about?"

"We are talking about it."

"I mean *before* you said yes?"

Her expression softened. "Probably. But the truth is, you wouldn't have been able to change my mind, and you would have ultimately supported my decision."

"Maybe, but I still would have liked to have been involved in the discussion."

"You're right. I'm sorry. I should have talked to you first."

He frowned and took a breath. "Just tell me this—doesn't this mean we have to move to DC?"

"Not sure if you've heard about it yet or not," Misty chimed in. "But there's this thing called the internet. Allows people to work from wherever they want."

"We're staying here," Orlando said. "For now, I'll work out of the house, and then find an office in the city."

"Helen isn't going to be happy having another operation in town," Quinn said.

"Good. Serves her right for cutting us off."

Quinn raised an eyebrow. "Correct me if I'm wrong, but she cut us off *after* you already committed to Misty."

"The timelines might be a little fuzzy, but we both know she'd been planning to dump us since we screwed her in London."

Quinn rubbed his hand over his eyes. "Tell me about this job I'm apparently doing for free."

CHAPTER FIVE

ROME, ITALY

THE SMELL OF wet earth and blood permeated the basement, the odor so strong that jars of vapor rub were kept at the top of the staircase for visitors to apply under their noses before descending.

The room was divided into two areas, by a thick plaster wall that extended from roughly the center point of the longer side of the room and stopped in the middle of the space, creating the dual alcoves known as Section 1 and Section 2. At the closed end of each alcove sat a sloped concrete slab covered in rubber, the angle allowing any liquids on it to drain into a spout at the back corner. Pipes would usher the fluid away and into the river fifty meters to the south. Powerful spray nozzles attached to flexible metal pipes hung above each pad to aid in the cleansing.

At the open end of the room was a row of two dozen hooks from which hung full-body rubber aprons. Four of the hooks were empty, their aprons in use by four of the five men at the closed-off end of Section 1. The fifth man, Baldo Kronig, didn't require the covering, as he was doing the bleeding.

Kronig, a professional courier, had made the mistake of allowing himself to be dispossessed of a package he'd been hired to deliver. Those who had taken the package had nearly killed him. It would have been better for him if they had.

"I don't know," he said, for what seemed the billionth

time.

Drake was a brute of a man, so when he twisted the plyers, he elicited more than a common scream from the captive. "You know who they are," Drake said. "They *paid* you to give them the box."

"No one paid me!"

"Give us their names, and all of this is over."

"I have no idea who they were!"

As Drake twisted the tool again, the skin around Kronig's nipple tore.

The man's scream was so intense, Drake and his colleagues winced. Not wanting to leave the job half done, the big man yanked the plyers, tore the nipple free, and held it in front of Kronig's face.

"Look what your refusal has done. This was not necessary." He removed the nipple from the tool and pushed it against Kronig's lips. "Open your mouth."

Kronig pressed his lips together.

"*Open* your mouth."

The courier shook his head.

"Then give us the names."

For a moment, the head shaking continued, and then the man said, "Uh…uh…it was…it was Dominique's men. I-I recognized one of them."

"From when they paid you?"

"Sure. Yes. From when they paid me."

Drake handed the plyers to one of his assistants, and then grabbed Kronig by the jaw and forced the man's mouth open. He tossed the nipple inside, pushed the jaw closed, and pinched the man's lips together.

"Chew, Mr. Kronig."

Kronig tried to spit the skin out but Drake's grip was strong.

"We know you are lying. Chew." Dominique would have never interrupted the shipment. She was way too smart for that.

Kronig stared back, terrified, his jaw still.

"Very well," Drake said. He nodded to his two other assistants.

One grabbed Kronig's shoulders and the other the man's head. Drake began moving the man's jaw himself. Drake could feel the squish of the meat through the jawbone. He moved the jaw again, and was able to catch the flesh one more time before Kronig swallowed the nipple whole.

When Drake's men let go of Kronig, the guy's head drooped forward.

Drake let the courier whimper for a few seconds, then grabbed the plyers and clamped the tool onto the man's remaining nipple.

"Who did you give the box to?"

But Kronig could take no more, and after Drake began to twist, the man passed out.

Drake slapped the courier a few times, but the man remained unconscious. Drake turned to one of his assistants. "Get the adrenaline."

Before the assistant could take a step, the sixth man in the basement, who'd been standing at the other end of the room, cleared his throat. "Don't waste your time."

Drake turned and said, "Very well, sir. What would you like us to do?"

The sixth man pushed off the wall. "He knows nothing. Dispose of him." He headed for the door.

Drake and his assistants stood silently until their boss was gone. Drake then grabbed a long, thin spike and stabbed Kronig through the heart.

When he pulled the spike out, he said, "You heard Mr. St. Amand. Dispose of him."

CHAPTER SIX

**TWO NIGHTS LATER
WESTERN OKLAHOMA**

QUINN SCANNED THE compound, first using the normal setting on his binoculars, then night vision, and finally thermal. The place was sprawling—a large main house and seven additional structures laid out in rectangular formation. The open area in the center was divided into a large parking lot, a playground, and a combo outdoor meeting space/eating area, complete with picnic tables and a couple of half-barrel barbecues.

At first glance, the place could be mistaken for a summer camp, or maybe a ranch-type resort. That was, if you ignored the eight-foot-high, barbed wire-topped, electric fence surrounding the property. The barrier was there because instead of playing host to kids and vacationing families, the compound was home to a private militia bent on toppling the US government, no matter which party was in charge.

Jackson Reed, head of the Clear Vision militia, had obviously valued sightlines over defensive positions when he'd chosen the location. On three sides the land was flat enough that his people would be able to spot anyone heading their way long before the intruders arrived. On the fourth side, the ground had been sliced up by thousands of years of flooding, creating an undulating terrain of ridges and dry gullies impassable by vehicles and nearly so on foot.

To improve their defenses, Reed's people had dug a

fifteen-foot wide, ten-foot deep trench just outside the fence. The only way over it was via the bridge by the main gate. According to the briefing, the bridge was removable and could be quickly dragged into the compound by a couple of trucks. If there was no time for that, remote control charges were apparently installed on either side that would drop the platform to the bottom of the trench. The waterless mote wouldn't stop a determined assailant for long, but it would buy the militia members time to arm up and prepare for a firefight.

The ACORT briefing document also noted a high probability that Reed's people were in possession of several surface-to-air rocket launchers. It seemed unlikely the militia was expecting anything like an air attack, though. The group had been keeping a low profile for the last few years, playing nicey-nice with the local government and generally not ruffling any feathers.

Intelligence indicated that would soon change. An informant on the inside—codenamed Sheepskin—had reported Reed was gearing up for something big. A *destabilizing event*. There were rumblings from other sources, too, but no firm information on what that event might be.

Without a better idea of Reed's plans, a full-scale FBI raid of the compound was off the table. But the government couldn't sit around and wait for something to happen. Hence ACORT's involvement. One of its analysts had come up with a brazen plan that would cut the militia's legs out from under it—if the plan is pulled off.

ACORT had been ordered by the NSA to give the mission to the newly reformed Office as a test of the reconstituted organization's abilities.

Orlando was overseeing the op. As for Quinn, though he was used to coming in on a mission after the fact and making everything look pretty, tonight he would be leading the team doing the dirty work.

He had roped in Steve Howard, Greta Sorenson, and Makoto Takahashi to serve on the team. They had spent nearly an hour hiking through the rugged terrain east of the compound, and were finally approaching the fence. It sat atop a rise ten to fifteen feet higher than Quinn and his team's position.

Orlando was in the getaway vehicle, parked in a grove of trees less than a mile on the other side of the buildings. With her was Marina Weeks, an experienced driver who had spent the last day going over every inch of road in the area. They would monitor events and move to the retrieval point once Quinn and the others gave them the signal.

Quinn checked his position on his phone before whispering, "This way."

He led the others through the craggy ground toward the base of the bluff the fence sat on. When they were within twenty yards, he checked the map again and slightly adjusted their course.

"Should be right over there," he said, nodding toward the nearby rise. "Hand signals only from this point." When the others indicated they understood, he clicked on his mic again. "Quinn for Orlando. We're going silent."

"Copy," she said.

The key to the raid was to get in and out without anyone knowing. If just one militia member picked up a hint of what was going on, the whole thing would be blown. Going through or over the fence was not an option, as there was too great a chance they'd be seen.

According to Sheepskin, however, the compound also possessed a secret entrance. Reed had apparently built it so he could leave the facility now and then without his people knowing. How the inside man knew about it, Quinn had no idea. He just hoped the info was true.

He crept along the edge of the rise until he spotted the round-topped rock and thicket of brush below it that he'd been told about.

When he found the crawl space under the bushes, he got on his hands and knees, motioned for the others to wait, and slipped into the overgrown tunnel. The crawlway ended at a five-foot-square cleared area covered by a rocky overhang. Though from other vantage points the ledge looked like a natural feature of the landscape, the steel support beams revealed it was manmade.

At the back of the overhang against the hillside was the promised door.

He clicked his mic once, signaling the others to come through, then moved up to the door. He found the fingerprint reader hidden behind a panel that looked like a rock, like Sheepskin had said.

From his backpack he removed a small container, pulled out the five latex finger caps, and placed each on the corresponding digit of his left hand. The caps came down just past the top knuckle and fit snuggly over his rubber glove. Each cap was embossed with the appropriate Jackson Reed fingerprint. How the prints had been obtained, he didn't know, but he guessed a guy like Reed probably had a police record somewhere.

Quinn placed his faux fingertips on the reader. A green light glowed beneath them. When it turned off, the door latch hummed and clicked. Howard gave it a pull, confirming it was open.

Quinn shone his flashlight into the inky black of the tunnel. As secret passageways went, this one was more 1849 gold mine than twenty-first-century supervillain escape pod tunnel, its earthen walls and ceiling supported every few feet by wooden arches.

Quinn pointed at Howard and Sorenson—signaling they were to come with him while Takahashi was to remain at the tunnel entrance—and moved inside.

The tunnel smelled dry and dusty, which did little to alleviate the sense it might collapse at any moment. As the inside man had indicated, the passage went basically straight under the compound for about a hundred and fifty feet before veering northwest at a forty-five-degree angle.

The section on the other side of the turn was only about half as long as the first part had been, and dead-ended at a concrete walled space, just wide enough for one person to stand in. On the left side, secured into the wall, was a ladder running into a shaft that went up a good fifteen feet above the passageway.

While Howard and Sorenson checked their weapons, Quinn transferred the packet containing a syringe of Beta-Somnol from his backpack into the pouch sewn onto the end of his sleeve. He looked over to make sure the others were ready before he headed up to the wooden trapdoor.

If Sheepskin had done as requested, the latch holding the door down would be unlocked, and the carpet covering the access point removed.

Quinn doused his flashlight and gave the door a push. No resistance. He slipped it upward until there was a narrow gap between it and the floor. The space beyond was dark and he could see nothing. He held the trapdoor in place, listening for signs of life. When he heard none, he pushed the door farther open.

Still not a sound. If there were others in the room, they would have ripped the door out of his grasp by now and shouted at him not to move, or at least turned on a light.

When the door had gone as far as it could, he climbed up two more rungs and stuck his head into the room. The black surrounding him was impenetrable. Not wanting to but having little choice, he switched on his flashlight and swung it around.

Sheepskin had said the tunnel would let out in a storage cellar. Sure enough, the hatch opened in the middle of an aisle between floor-to-ceiling shelves, packed with supplies.

He signaled the others to remain in the tunnel, climbed out, and crept to the end of the shelves.

A central walkway, with more loaded shelves on either side. The inside man had said the tunnel led to the cellar of the main house, the one Jackson Reed called home, and from all appearances, that was where Quinn was.

He returned to the hatch and waved Howard and Sorenson up.

According to Sheepskin, there were three exits to the basement—the trapdoor Quinn and his team had come through, the main exit via a stairway to the first-floor kitchen, and a hidden back stairway that went straight up to Reed's second-floor bedroom.

Quinn led the others to a pair of floor-to-ceiling cabinets

in the southeast corner that sat perpendicular to each other and to the walls, creating a squared-out notch.

Quinn scanned the shelves, picking out the items he was looking for. Then, in the sequence he'd memorized, he pushed two of the selected books back as far as they would go, and pulled out a third volume to the very edge of the shelf. Lastly, he slid an old ammo box inward until it clicked in place.

With a gentle tug, one of the cabinets silently swung out, revealing the spiral stairway.

Quinn went up first, then Howard, and, after shutting the cabinet behind her, Sorenson. They kept their pace slow to avoid creating any noise, but Reed had obviously been concerned with the same issue, as the stairs barely made more than the occasional soft creak.

Quinn killed his light when he reached the door at the top and turned the handle.

Once more, Sheepskin's information proved correct. The door opened behind a rack of clothes hanging in a large, walk-in closet.

They crept through to the main door and Quinn placed his ear against it. He heard a fan, probably a ceiling one, but that was the only noise.

He crouched, pulled out his phone, and attached a gooseneck, micro camera to it. He slipped the camera under the doorway. The picture that came back was filled with dark shadows so he switched the feed to night vision.

A dresser and some other kind of cabinet sat to either side of the closet door, while across the room, against the far wall was a king-sized bed. From the lumpy covers, it seemed someone was using it. The room was big enough to have a sitting area and a desk. None of the chairs were occupied, nor was anyone standing anywhere.

He pulled the camera back, dismantled the gooseneck, and stowed both. He and the others donned their night vision goggles.

Howard entered the bedroom first and angled to the left, gun out. Sorenson, also armed, went next and headed right. Quinn removed the syringe of Beta-Somnol from his sleeve pocket and followed.

Son of a bitch.

The bed was occupied, all right, but by two people. That put a real crimp in the plan of getting Reed and getting out without anyone being the wiser.

Conveniently, the larger of the two was lying on his back. Reed. His gray, military cut hair; thick, definitely not military approved beard; close-set eyes; and acne-scarred cheeks were more than enough to ID him.

The man's bedmate was a woman, small, facing away on the other side of the bed.

Quinn would have to spread the knockout juice between them. It meant Reed wouldn't be under as long, but they should still have more than enough time to get him to the van without the militia leader regaining consciousness.

Deciding it would be best to put the woman under first, Quinn circled the bed. As he leaned down, he froze.

She was wide awake and staring at him. Almost as alarming was the fact she couldn't have been more than sixteen.

She looked nervous, but not nearly as scared as she should have been at the sight of a stranger in the room.

"It's okay," she said. "He won't wake up."

Quinn shot a look at Reed, but the man remained on his side.

"He's drunk," she whispered. "He always sleeps like a rock when he's drunk."

Perhaps she was telling the truth, but that didn't undo the fact she'd seen Quinn. About the only thing he could do was prevent her witnessing the rest of the mission.

"You need to close your eyes," he whispered, raising the syringe. "This won't hurt. When you wake up, it'll be better for you if you forget you ever saw me."

He reached to pull the blanket off her shoulder.

"Don't," she said. "Please. I'm Sheepskin."

That stopped him dead. "You?"

She nodded. "You used the tunnel and came up the secret stairs. That was my idea."

She was Sheepskin, all right. Needing a moment to figure

out what he would do with her, he motioned for Howard to keep an eye on her and moved back around to Reed.

The militia leader didn't even twitch when the needle went in. Quinn gave him three quarters of the dose.

The syringe kit came with spare needles, so he switched out the used one before he returned to the girl's side of the bed. "I'm going to give you this," he said. "It'll knock you out until morning. That way no one will think you had anything to do with his disappearance."

She pulled back from him. "No. No, no. I-I-I can't stay here anymore. Please. You have to take me with you. You *have* to."

"That's…" He was going to say *that's not the plan* but couldn't bring himself to finish.

He glanced at Howard and Sorenson. Both looked as unsettled as he felt.

Son of a bitch.

The girl was just a kid, not that much older than Orlando's son, Garrett. What if the other militia members decided she'd helped in the leader's abduction, despite her being drugged? They'd kill her, probably rape her again first, and dump her body where it would never be found.

"Okay," Quinn said. "But you do exactly what we say. Understand?"

"Yes. Don't worry, I will. Thank you."

Quinn started to lift the blanket to help her up, but dropped it back in place when he realized she was naked. "Where are your clothes?"

She pointed at a door across the room. "In the bathroom."

"I'll get them," Sorenson said, and hurried through the doorway.

The girl bit her lip. "We need to get my sister, too."

"Your sister?"

"She's only thirteen. I-I-I can't leave without her."

Quinn hadn't thought his blood could turn any colder, but he was wrong. "Do they…use her like"—he motioned at the bed—"like this, too?"

Eyes welling, she nodded.

"Is it just the two of you?"

"There are seven others."

Jesus.

"I don't have enough people to get them out right now," he said.

"I know. But my sister…"

He grimaced. "We've already been here longer than we planned. After we get Reed out, I'll make sure this whole place comes down, and we free your sister and the others as quickly as possible."

"I can get her brought here. To the room. Please. I can't leave her behind."

Quinn knew he should say no, but he couldn't. "How would you do it?"

"I'll need my robe."

Sorenson, who'd reentered the room, said, "I've got it." She handed the robe to the girl.

Quinn turned away so she could put it on. "What's your name?"

"Vanessa."

"And your sister's?"

"Jordan."

"You can call me Jonathan."

"All right. You can turn back around now…Jonathan."

She was sitting on the bed, the robe on. It wasn't exactly sheer but it was close.

"Don't you have something…more?" he asked.

"He would expect me to be wearing this."

Trying not to think too much about what that meant, he said, "Who would be expecting that?"

"The guard at the bottom of the stairs. If I ask him, he'll have someone get Jordan."

"Won't he be suspicious?"

Her face twisted and she shook her head. "It…wouldn't be the first time."

Quinn had to force himself not to glance at Reed, afraid he might put a bullet in the man's head.

"Okay," he said. "We'll try it."

She smiled and jumped off the bed. "I'll be right back." She headed to the door and let herself out.

Quinn clicked on his mic. "Quinn for Orlando."

"Go for Orlando."

"We'll be bringing two extra passengers."

A pause. "Who?"

"I'll explain when we get there. In the meantime, have Misty arrange it so I can talk directly to the client as soon as we get out of here."

"They're going to want to know what about."

"Tell them I'm giving them the keys to the compound."

He could almost hear her raise an eyebrow as she said, "Okay."

"One more thing. Tell them they'll want to have a strike team assembled and ready to go before the sun comes up."

"Copy."

Vanessa returned seconds later.

"Any problems?" Quinn asked.

"No."

"How long will it take?"

"No more than ten minutes."

Quinn and the others used the time to transfer Reed into the body bag they'd brought. The bag was equipped with an oxygen cylinder and breathing mask, the latter of which now sat over the man's nose and mouth. They lowered the bag down the shaft into the main tunnel.

"You two head out," Quinn said to his companions. "I'll wait with the girl."

"Sure you don't want one of us to stay with you?" Howard asked. "We can get Makoto to come in and help with the body."

"It's okay. We'll be right behind you."

Howard started down the shaft to join Sorenson and Reed in the tunnel while Quinn returned to the bedroom.

Vanessa sat on the edge of the bed, her hands in her lap. After a glance at the spot where Reed had lain, she asked. "What will they do with him?"

"Ask him a lot of questions, I would think."

"Will they kill him?"

"I, um, I doubt that's part of their plan."

"I want them to kill him."

Her tone was so matter-of-fact that Quinn thought he'd misheard her. When he realized he hadn't, he nodded. If Reed was the child predator he appeared to be, Quinn wanted him dead, too.

When he heard steps in the hallway outside, Quinn moved to the wall beside the door so he'd be out of sight when it opened.

A faint knock, as if someone didn't want to be heard. Vanessa hurried over, but before she could grab the handle, Quinn motioned for her to relax.

The girl took a deep breath, cracked open the door, and peeked through. A smile appeared on her face. After she opened the door wider, a smaller, younger girl entered. Vanessa immediately closed the door again.

The younger girl—Jordan—looked warily toward the bed, but when she didn't see Reed, she turned to her sister, confused. That's when she noticed Quinn.

Her eyes flew wide, but before she could scream, Vanessa clamped a hand over the girl's mouth.

"Shhh," Vanessa whispered. "It's okay. He's a friend."

Jordan looked less than convinced.

"He's going to get us out of here," Vanessa assured her.

Jordan's skepticism faded a bit.

"I'm serious. We're leaving right now."

"What? Leave?" Jordan said, her voice muffled by her sister's hand.

"That's right. So, can I trust you to be quiet?"

A pause and then a nod.

Vanessa slowly lifted her hand away.

Shooting a weary look toward Quinn, Jordan said to her sister, "Where's Mr. Reed?"

"Gone."

"Where?"

"What does it matter? He's gone."

Jordan nodded toward Quinn. "Who is he?"

"A friend."

"I've never seen him before."

Vanessa locked eyes with her sister. "Do you trust me?"

"Yeah. Of course."

"Then you need to believe me. He's a friend and he's getting us out of here."

"Right now?"

"Right now."

For the first time, Jordan looked hopeful.

Vanessa glanced at Quinn. "We're ready."

There had been a handful of situations that made Quinn seriously consider putting his life at risk to root out an evil. This one had just vaulted to the top of the list. He wanted to storm out of the bedroom and kill every militia member he encountered.

But he held the urge in check, said, "This way," and led the girls into the walk-in closet.

CHAPTER **SEVEN**

AT AN ALL-NIGHT truck stop twenty miles southeast of the militia compound, Orlando purchased clothes for Vanessa and Jordan. Once the girls were dressed, they, Sorenson, Howard, Takahashi, and Weeks went into the truck stop to get something to eat.

Orlando and Quinn remained in the van and called Misty via video chat. Quinn had already briefed Misty over the phone as they drove, and now it was time to talk to ACORT.

"Give me a second," she said.

The screen froze momentarily. When it came back to life, it was split into two feeds, with Misty on the right, and Kyle Otero, director of ACORT, on the left. Quinn laid out what he had learned, much of the details coming from Vanessa and Jordan.

When he finished, he said, "If you don't move in right now, the girls who are still there will continue to be raped and abused. I can't let that happen."

"*You* can't?" Otero said.

"No, sir. I can't. If you are unable to do anything about it, my team and I will."

"Relax, Mr. Quinn. I share your concern. But to make what you request happen, I need more than just your word. I need to talk to the girls."

Quinn had been hoping to avoid that, but understood the necessity. "You'll need to hold for a minute."

QUINN PACED OUTSIDE the van, glancing every few seconds at the back door. At Orlando's suggestion, only she and Sorenson had remained in the van with Vanessa and Jordan, hoping that would make them feel less uncomfortable.

That had been nearly fifteen minutes ago. How much convincing did the director need?

"I'm getting a coffee," Quinn said. "Anyone want anything?"

A trio of shaking heads sent him heading to the truck stop on his own. He hit the toilet before grabbing a cup of coffee. As he exited the building, he saw the van's side door was now open. Of course, the moment he'd left, they'd finished.

Vanessa and Jordan were still inside the van with Sorenson. Orlando was standing outside with Howard, Takahashi, and Weeks. When she spotted Quinn, she walked toward him and met him halfway.

"So?" he asked.

"A team is being assembled. Should be in place before sunup, just like you asked. He has to run it through the FBI, though, so they're going to need a search warrant."

Quinn frowned. "We can't wait for a search warrant."

"He says he anticipates having it before the team is ready."

"Okay, good."

"In the meantime, he wants eyes on the place and we're the closest."

That made sense. If the raid went down at dawn, the militia would likely not have realized yet its leader was missing, but if it had, the place would be buzzing with activity.

"When they do go in, he thinks the FBI will be very interested in using that tunnel. Since you have the experience…"

"He wants me to be the guide." Not a surprise, either. "We'll need to find someplace to stash Reed and the girls."

"Already worked out. Marina and Makoto will take them to the drop-off point."

"Then how are we supposed to get back?"

She smiled.

AT TEN MINUTES after three a.m., a search and rescue helicopter picked up Quinn, Orlando, Howard, and Sorenson from the field next to the truck stop, and took them to a deserted intersection five miles from the compound. Other than a traffic light hanging above the crossroads, the only light came from a car parked on the other side of the intersection from where they were dropped off. When the helicopter was airborne again, the vehicle drove over.

The only occupant was the driver. He rolled down his window and said, "One of you Orlando?"

"I am," Orlando said, stepping forward. "And you are?"

"Agent Brills, FBI." He flashed his Bureau ID.

They shook hands.

"I've been instructed to take you wherever you want to go," Brills said.

The team climbed in, Orlando taking the front passenger seat, the others in back. She gave the agent directions to the best spot from which they could observe the compound.

Once they were on their way, Quinn asked the man, "How many more of you are here?"

"As far as I know, I'm the only one so far. But I've been told more agents will be arriving within the next few hours."

"Have you been briefed?" Quinn asked.

"The only thing I've been told was to pick you up." He glanced at Orlando. "Before I forget, Special Agent Alvarez would like you to call him."

Orlando punched the number into her phone as the agent recited it.

After a moment, she said, "This is Orlando. I believe you were expecting my call." She was quiet for several seconds. "Yes, that's correct…of course…. Yes….yes…. Text me the coordinates…all right. Yes…talk to you soon."

"What was that all about?" Quinn asked after she hung up.

"You and I are going to do the briefing." She looked back at Howard and Sorenson. "You two will have to keep an eye on the compound on your own."

"I think we can handle it," Howard said.

Orlando turned on Brills. "I understand you have some

long-range comm gear?"

"Yes, ma'am. It's in the trunk."

THEY DROPPED OFF Howard and Sorenson a quarter-mile from the compound's entrance, then Quinn, Orlando, and Brills proceeded to a sheriff's substation, six miles east of Reed's property, that was to serve as the assembly point.

On a normal night near four a.m., the station would have been a ghost town. But this morning the place was jam-packed with over a dozen deputies, nearly as many police officers, and five men wearing light jackets with FBI printed on the back in big, bold letters. When Quinn and Orlando entered, one of the agents, a forty-plus Hispanic man, extracted himself from the small group of law enforcement officers he'd been talking to and walked over to them.

"Ms. Orlando?" he asked as he neared.

"It's just Orlando."

"Alvarez. Agent in charge."

They shook hands.

"This is my associate, Jonathan Quinn," she said.

Alvarez shook with Quinn, then said, "Please come with me."

He led them into an office off the main bullpen area and shut the door.

"I've been told you're aware this action has come together in a hurry. I've also been informed you have special knowledge of Jackson Reed's compound, and are going to share that with me and the team."

Orlando nodded. "Quinn can give you actual specifics. He was in the compound a few hours ago."

Alvarez raised an eyebrow. "A few hours ago."

"I'm afraid we're responsible for the rush," Quinn said.

"How so?"

There were certain aspects of the earlier mission, specifically the abduction of Reed, Alvarez was better off not knowing about. The FBI worked within the confines of the law. ACORT and those who worked for them? Not always. So Quinn left out some details but did explain about the girls.

"There are seven others still inside, most underage."

"I'd been informed there were children there, but..." Alvarez's jaw tensed, anger and disgust leaking through his stoic FBI persona. "Wait here."

He opened the door and reentered the main room. When he returned, he was carrying a binder. He set it on a clear area of the desk and flipped the cover back. The top sheet was a satellite photo of the militia compound, in a protective covering. Alvarez pulled the photograph free and set it beside the binder.

"Do you know exactly where they're located?" he asked.

"There's apparently a common room where the girls are kept." Quinn studied the photo, and pointed at a building across the central courtyard from the big house. "Here."

"Are you confident in this information?"

"I am. But there's a good chance at least a few of the girls will be...in the rooms of some of the militia members."

A frown slipped across Alvarez's mouth. "Please tell me there's an easier way of getting in other than through the front gate."

"As a matter of fact, there is."

MEMBERS OF THE joint task force were in position by five a.m. Most of the sheriff's deputies and police officers were split among three roadblocks, sealing off outside access to the compound. The remaining local law enforcement officers, two FBI agents, and Orlando were stationed in a grove of trees, approximately a hundred and fifty yards from the militia's front gate.

Quinn, Alvarez, and the other eight FBI agents who'd arrived for the mission had worked their way through the rough land behind the compound to the tunnel door, where they met up with Howard and Sorenson.

The agents were all wearing bulletproof vests and armed with assault rifles. The three with extensive tactical experience were at the front of the line with Quinn and Alvarez. The other agents, save two assigned to guard the tunnel door, would be strung out behind the lead group, with Howard and Sorenson bringing up the rear.

Alvarez toggled his comm mic. "This is Alvarez. All teams set?"

Quinn and his friends had been issued FBI comm gear, and could hear the others reply in the affirmative.

"Camera check," Alvarez said.

One of the agents at Orlando's position said, "Nine feeds, five by five."

The agents in the main strike group were all wearing body cams, the feeds being transmitted in real time back to recorders and monitors at Orlando's position. Quinn understood the reason, but wasn't exactly comfortable with being taped by the feds during an operation.

"We are a go," Alvarez said.

The agents in front raised their weapons, while those behind shined their flashlights on the door. Alvarez nodded to Quinn, who grabbed the handle and pulled the door open.

Light beams flooded the tunnel, confirming the portion in view was unoccupied.

Another nod, and Quinn led the way.

When they reached the house, they left Howard, Sorenson, and three of the agents in the basement. Quinn escorted Alvarez and the remaining three men up to Reed's bedroom.

Everything was exactly as it had been when Quinn and the girls left several hours earlier, so it was safe to assume no one had visited since Reed had been nabbed.

Quinn approached the main door and eased it open. The hallway beyond was dim and empty. He silently indicated to Alvarez where the guard at the base of the stairs would be. Alvarez nodded and tapped the man nearest him to go out first.

Quinn moved to let the chosen agent pass through and then followed. There were four additional doors along the second-floor hallway, all closed. While Quinn and the lead agent continued toward the stairs at the far end, Alvarez and the others checked the rooms.

The last part of the hallway opened up onto a fifteen-foot-long balcony, which ended at the top of the stairs. Along the edge of the balcony was a wooden railing, supported by two-inch-wide balusters, spaced every half foot.

Through the gaps, Quinn and the agent could see a man walking across the room below, carrying a steaming bowl of something, and a glass of what looked like orange juice. The man continued to a chair by the base of the stairs and sat down.

If this had been one of Quinn's typical missions, he would have expected an ops team member to take the guard out with a quick kill shot, given there was no way to get down and subdue him before being seen. But there was that whole FBI and staying within the confines of the law thing.

The lead agent moved over to the end of the railing and aimed his suppressed rifle at the guard. Instead of pulling the trigger, he turned on his laser sight, planting a red dot on the side of the man's head. He moved the dot to the bowl in the man's lap. The second the guard saw it, the agent whipped the dot up to the man's chest.

The philosophy behind the agent's method was to make the target aware he had no control so that he would give up without a fight. But no one had informed the guard of that. He jumped to his feet and swiveled around, his hand going for the holster at his side as he searched for the source of the light.

Thup.

The bullet pierced the man's heart before the guard's fingers could even touch the grip of his pistol.

The agent descended the stairs, sweeping his weapon through the space for other targets. Quinn followed closely, with Alvarez and the other agents on his heels.

The guard turned out to be the only one in the main part of the first floor. There were, however, two bedrooms on the east side. In one they found a man in a shower and were able to subdue him without a fight.

In the other was another man.

Sleeping.

And not alone.

The girl with him might have been eighteen but Quinn doubted it.

Four agents surrounded the bed and pointed their guns at the militia member. Alvarez put a hand over the girl's mouth.

Her eyes shot open. Alvarez touched a finger to his lips, and pointed at FBI printed on the breast of his windbreaker. Her fear turned to confusion, tinged with the slightest hint of hope.

Keeping his hand on her mouth, Alvarez motioned for her to climb out of bed. As she did, the militia man stirred. Everyone froze.

"Where do you think you're going," the guy mumbled.

He reached out to yank her back, but Alvarez pulled her off the bed. She was naked, with bruises on her legs and torso.

The sleeper opened his eyes and started turning toward where the girl had been lying. When he realized others were in the room, and pointing guns at him, he stopped.

Quinn found a towel in the bathroom and draped it over the girl. "You're not going to make any noise, are you?"

She shook her head, and Alvarez withdrew his hand.

"Do you have clothes here?" Quinn asked.

She pointed at a pile against the wall. He went with her and held the towel up as a screen while she dressed. While they did this, Alvarez turned to the man in the bed.

"How many others in the compound?" he asked.

The man sneered at him. "Am I under arrest, Mr. FBI man?"

"How many?"

"Fuck you. Read me my rights or get the hell out of here."

The girl had finished dressing so Quinn tossed the towel on the floor. "Everything's going to be okay now. I just need you to stay here for a moment."

"Thank you," she said, about as sincerely as he'd ever heard the words spoken.

Quinn smiled and walked over to the bed, where Alvarez had made no progress getting the militia man to talk.

Quinn pulled out a few zip ties. "Turn on your right side."

"Screw you. I ain't doing nothing without my lawyer."

"I don't know if you noticed, but my friends here are all wearing body cameras. So, just for the record, are you saying you're resisting arrest?"

"I haven't been arrested," the man said.

"You are now." Alvarez signaled for one of his men to

recite the man's Miranda rights. When the agent finished, Alvarez said, "On your side. Arms behind you."

The man complied. Quinn jammed the man's wrists together, looped a tie around them, and zipped it closed. He flipped the man back over. Using another tie, he immobilized the man's ankles.

"Better," Quinn said, and turned to Alvarez. "Agent?"

Quinn gestured for him and his team to face away from the bed. Alvarez's eyes narrowed.

Quinn asked, "Would you rather we walked out there blind?"

Alvarez stared at him, then said to his men, "Eyes on me."

He made a similar gesture to the one Quinn had made. After the men—and the cameras strapped to their chests—had turned away, Quinn pulled out his SIG SAUER P226 and jammed the suppressor barrel into the man's mouth.

The man tried to jerk his head away.

"I'd keep very still if I were you," Quinn suggested. "You never know what might make my trigger finger slip."

The guy stopped moving.

Quinn leaned in close, and whispered so the cameras wouldn't pick it up. "I know what you're thinking. He would never pull the trigger. The FBI has all these guidelines and ethics and things like that. You're probably thinking that as soon as you tell your lawyer about this very moment, he'll be able to get any charges against you thrown out and you'll walk away.

"But, see, you're missing an important piece of information. I'm not FBI. I'm not even government. I'm a ghost." He shoved the barrel farther in, causing the man to gag. "I'm going to ask you the same question the nice agent asked you, and every time you don't answer or give me a response I think isn't true, you're going to eat a little bit more of my gun. And when I hit the back of your mouth, I'll start shoving it down your throat." He paused. "So, how many more of you sons of bitches are in the compound right now?"

Quinn waited until the guy tried to say something before pulling the gun out. "Repeat that."

"Twenty-three," the man said, his voice hoarse.

Though Vanessa and Jordan hadn't known how many were there that night, they said there were usually about forty men around, sometimes a lot more.

Before the guy could shut his mouth, Quinn shoved the barrel back in. "Try again. This time at least get it in the ballpark."

The man started talking again.

"Last chance. Lie again and you'll eat this whole thing."

The guy said, "Ah ont ah, ah ont ah," which Quinn interpreted as he chose to cooperate.

When he removed the barrel, the man started coughing.

"Water," the guy eked out.

"Answer the question and we'll think about it."

The guy mumbled something.

"Louder."

The same sounds again, volume unchanged.

Quinn stuck the muzzle of the SIG against the underside of the man's jaw.

"Last chance."

The man found additional energy and said loudly, "Forty-eight."

"Thank you." Quinn stuck a chunk of bedsheet deeply enough into the man's mouth that he'd have a hard time removing it without his hands.

Quinn turned to the girl. "He says there are forty-eight other men here—does that sound right to you?"

"I think so. Well, and the girls."

"Right. Do you know where all the men sleep?"

"Yes," she said, looking like she wished she didn't.

He turned back to the captive. The agents were facing the bed again so Quinn said to Alvarez, "You're going to want to turn back around."

"I'm not sure—"

Quinn stared at him.

Alvarez signaled his men to turn away again.

Quinn glanced at the girl. "What's your name?"

"Amy."

He leaned down next to the militia man again. "This is for Amy," he whispered, and then whacked the grip of his gun into the man's jaw.

GIVEN THE EARLY hour and the fact that the strike team had infiltrated the facility from Reed's secret tunnel, it took less than ten minutes to neutralize the forty-four militia members in the bunkhouses. With the three they'd already subdued, and Reed himself, they were still one member short. Either the guy who'd been with Amy had his count wrong or someone was missing.

As for the other girls, the team had found only one more among the men. The asshole who had her had tried to use her as a hostage, but a precision shot from one of the FBI specialists split the man's skull.

Once the men were secured, Quinn had Amy take him to where the girls were kept when they weren't "needed."

It was more of a large storage shed than a livable building. The two big doors at the front could be padlocked, but at the moment the padlock was missing and the chain hung undone.

Quinn motioned for Amy to stay back. He turned the handle and started to push the door in.

A gun boomed from the room, the bullet blowing a hole and the door open.

As Quinn dove to the ground and crawled away from the opening, he could hear people running toward the building from several directions in the courtyard behind him. A moment later, Alvarez was at his side.

"I think we found the missing man," Quinn said.

"Are the other girls in there?" the agent asked.

"One way to find out."

Quinn looked around.

Several cars were parked ten yards away. Most were built within the last twenty years and would be equipped with steering-wheel locks. One, however, was an old ragtop Jeep Wrangler that looked like it'd been built before such locks became standard equipment.

Quinn snuck over to it, and waved for a couple of

Alvarez's men to join him. He disengaged the Jeep's parking brake, and, with the others' help, pushed the vehicle as close to the building's entrance as possible. Quinn then went over to where Amy was hiding with another agent.

"I need your help."

Her eyes widened. "I'm not going in there."

"I don't want you to go in. Just over to the Jeep."

"Why?"

After he told her, she reluctantly followed him.

"You ready?" he asked her, after they were in position behind the Jeep.

"I guess."

"Go ahead."

She took a deep breath and said, "Katrina? Are you there?"

"Louder," Quinn said.

"Katrina! Can you hear me? Are you in there?"

No response.

"Try again," Quinn said.

"It's okay," Amy yelled. "No one's going to hurt you. You can come out."

Another moment of nothing before a girl called out, "Amy?"

"Yes!" Amy smiled. "It's okay. Everything's okay. The police are here."

Another pause, and then a yelp, and then, "Are they with you?"

"What happened? Are you all right?"

"Are they with you *now*?" This time the question came from a male voice—young, angry, and frightened.

Alvarez whispered to Amy, "Is there another way in?"

She shook her head. "There were windows, but those were already boarded when I was brought here."

"Where?" Alvarez asked.

"On the opposite side."

Alvarez radioed his men to go around and check.

"Goddamn it!" the guy inside yelled. "Are they with you?"

Quinn put a hand on Amy's shoulder before she could speak. He shouted, "Yes, we are." He turned to Alvarez, whispered, "Keep him talking," and crept around the Jeep to the doorway.

"You need to back off!" the voice said. "I've got hostages! If you don't, I will start killing them!"

"There's no need for anyone to get hurt," Alvarez said.

While Alvarez continued to engage the militia man, Quinn attached the gooseneck microcamera to his phone again, and slipped the lens low around the door into the building. The interior was dark, until he selected night vision. He was now looking at a single large, rectangular room, approximately fifty feet long by thirty wide, with six sets of bunks running down each long side. All were empty. Quinn couldn't see anyone anywhere. He moved the camera all the way to the floor to look under the beds.

Behind the farthest bunk along the wall where Quinn was looking, he could see several people huddled low to the floor. From that distance, it was hard to separate one person from another. He pulled the camera out.

With the closest bunk only a few feet away, he felt confident he could enter the room unseen. He crawled around the door into the room.

No gunshots. No shouts about his entrance. Only the continued conversation between the shooter and Alvarez.

Quinn reached the first bunk and checked underneath. There was just enough room for him to pass beneath without knocking against the metal mesh supporting the mattress.

"You don't want to piss me off!" the man shouted. "I swear, I'll start killing!"

"No one wants to piss you off," Alvarez said. "We want to work this out so nobody has to die."

Using the voices as cover, Quinn picked up his pace, and was soon passing under the second bed, and the third. When he reached the fourth, he stopped and took another look toward the end of the room.

There should have been five girls in the room, plus the man. They might all be there, but Quinn could discern only four. The two people nearest the corner were definitely girls, so he focused on the other two and waited.

"Why don't you let the girls go?" Alvarez said. "I know you don't want to hurt them."

"You know what? What I *want* is for you to bring me a car and back the hell away from the building!"

Bingo.

During the exchange, as the man made his request, the body on the far left had moved in rhythm with the words.

Quinn slipped under the fourth bed and halfway under the fifth. He stopped again.

Alvarez repeated his suggestion regarding the hostages, and the militia asshole told him what Alvarez could do with his suggestion. Once more, the body on the far left moved with the words, but Quinn didn't need that for confirmation. He could now see the person at the end was a man.

Quinn pulled out his gun and moved under the last set of bunks.

"There's a black Ford F-150 out there," the man shouted. "The keys are under the mat! If I don't hear it pull up in the next minute, someone's going to die!"

The hand holding the gun must have been on the bed because Quinn couldn't see it. The other hand was pressed against the floor, propping the man up.

"I'm sending one of my people to get the truck now," Alvarez said. "As an act of good faith, why don't you send out half of the hostages."

Quinn stopped when he'd gone as far as necessary.

"Get the fucking truck here and then maybe we can talk about—"

In swift, fluid motion, Quinn grabbed the man's wrist, shoved the suppressor into the asshole's groin, and said in a calm voice, "Drop the weapon."

Instead of complying, the idiot tried to twist away.

Quinn pulled the trigger.

A howl of pain and the clatter of a gun hitting the floor.

Quinn pulled himself out from under the bed, his aim never leaving the hostage taker. But curled against the wall and writhing in agony, the guy was in no position to do any more damage.

Quinn kicked the man's gun, sending it skittering across the room. He looked over his shoulder at the girls. There were indeed five of them, pressed together in the corner, terrified.

"It's all right," he said. "No one's going to hurt you anymore."

THIRTY MINUTES LATER, Quinn and Orlando were standing with Alvarez near the middle of the compound, ready to take their leave.

The place was swarming with FBI agents, who had continued arriving well after the festivities had concluded. So far, reports from the roadblocks said no media had shown up, but it would be only a matter of time. Undoubtedly, this would at first be reported as another Waco-style raid, but when the news of the sexual slavery got out, few would be able to fault the FBI's actions.

The girls had been taken away to a nearby hospital. The mental abuse they'd suffered would take a while to mend, if it ever did. Orlando had talked to one of the girls before an ambulance took her away. The girl had been "gifted" to the militia by her father, "in support of Mr. Reed's goals." Orlando had relayed the information to Alvarez, who assured her and Quinn he would look into each and every one of the girls' circumstances and take the appropriate actions.

"If you don't," Orlando had said, "we will."

Alvarez almost smiled. "I have no doubt of that."

They talked for several more minutes, then Quinn held out his hand. "Good working with you."

For the second time that day, they shook.

"I would say we appreciate the assist, but I feel like we were the ones doing the assisting today, not you. You're a handy man to have around, Mr. Quinn."

"Don't get too used to it," Orlando said, shaking Alvarez's hand. "The FBI can't afford us."

"That does not surprise me."

"Agent Alvarez?" an agent called from near one of the

buildings. "You need to see this."

"I'll be right there." Alvarez turned back to Quinn and Orlando, said, "Thank you again," and headed over to the other agent.

SPECIAL AGENT ALVAREZ was led to a small building along the south side of the compound. Like most of the other structures, it was two stories high, but its footprint was only large enough to accommodate three rooms per floor. This was one of the militia's bunkhouses.

Alvarez hadn't been in this particular structure yet, but it was much the same as the ones he had visited—bunks and footlockers and little else.

The agent who was escorting him took him to an open door in the ground-floor hallway, near the bathroom. Beyond it were stairs leading down to a basement. So far, all the buildings had basements, a survival necessity here in Oklahoma.

Alvarez followed the agent down into a single room that matched the size of the house above. In addition to the basement lights, three powerful crime-scene lights had been erected. Five agents were gathered near the lights, three on their knees looking at the ground, while the other two were pulling items out of a gear bag.

When one of the kneeling men saw Alvarez, he moved to the side to make room. Surrounded by a concrete footing embedded in the floor was a steel door.

"Anyone try opening it?" Alvarez asked.

"Yes, sir," the agent who'd moved said. "It's locked." He nodded toward the two men at the gear bags. "Beltre and Langer are about to check to make sure it's not booby-trapped, then we should be able to get it unlocked."

"Was it just sitting exposed like this?"

"No, sir. It was under that platform." He pointed at a weathered wooden platform leaning against the wall, next to four barrels.

"Who found it?"

One of the other agents stood. "I did."

"Thomas, isn't it?" Alvarez said. He had met him only that morning.

"Thompson, sir."

"Right. Sorry. What made you look under the platform, Agent Thompson?"

"The barrels sitting on it were all empty, and it seemed like a strange place to store empty barrels."

"Nice work."

Alvarez and the other agents watched Beltre and Langer scan the door. When the men declared there were no obvious traps, two others set to work disengaging the lock. On the other side of the door was a set of stairs.

Since it had been Thompson's discovery, Alvarez allowed the agent to go first. The stairs let out at a passageway that ended at another locked door.

Once again, Beltre and Langer did their thing and declared it safe. The lock was a stubborn one, but it finally gave way.

Flashlights flooded through the opening. Thompson was again the first to step through.

"My God," he said.

Alvarez moved to join him and found himself on a metal platform. He added his flashlight beam to Thompson's.

My God, indeed.

The room was massive. A hundred feet across and at least that much long. The floor was approximately six feet below the platform, and reached by stairs to the right. Nearly half the space was taken up by rows of wide metal shelving units, only a fraction of which were filled. No shelves in the rest of the room, just a wide area that played home to several crates and items covered by tarps. The items both on the shelves and in the open space were highly organized, giving the impression Reed's people were expecting to fill the remaining area with much more of the same.

The team descended into the room.

"Pair off," Alvarez ordered. "If you find something of interest, shout out."

Alvarez and Thompson headed over to one of the tarps, where Thompson used a knife to cut the ropes anchoring the covering to the floor. Alvarez pulled the tarp up and shone his light underneath.

My God was not an adequate exclamation.

Sitting on a wooden palate was a large, military-grade, turret-mounted gun. From the size of the mounting plate, Alvarez guessed it could be attached to anything from the bed of a pickup truck to the deck of a boat. Hell, even to a tank.

Reed's militia had been on the FBI's watch list as a potential domestic terrorist organization for a few years, but the threat they posed had been pegged as moderate at best.

There was nothing moderate about what Alvarez was looking at.

From somewhere else in the room came the call, "Agent Alvarez, I have something."

Before Alvarez could extract himself from the tarp, a different agent shouted, "I have something, too."

"Agent Alvarez, over here," a third said.

"I have something here, too."

"Me, too."

"Agent Alvarez!"

CHAPTER **EIGHT**

**THREE DAYS LATER
WASHINGTON, DC**

Misty walked through her apartment, weaving around the stacks of boxes containing her possessions, and making sure she hadn't missed anything. The movers would be here within thirty minutes, and the faster everything was loaded up, the happier she'd be.

Under Peter, the Office had owned several properties—scattered not only around the DC area, but also the world. ACORT had thought it'd absorbed them all when the Office was disbanded, but there were several ACORT hadn't known about. As Misty was shuffled from one mind-numbing government post to another, she'd kept track of the ones that hadn't switched hands, sure the error would be corrected.

Much to her surprise, all had remained unclaimed.

Upon the rebirth of the organization, she had—after disclosing the existence of the properties and receiving ACORT's reluctant agreement—reasserted the Office's claim on them. One of the locations, a neglected place known as the Farm, had once been used as a retreat for agents who needed to lie low. Misty decided it would be the perfect location for not only the organization's new headquarters but her home, too.

It wasn't really a farm, but rather twenty acres of rolling hills in the Virginia countryside, thirty-two miles outside DC. It had a four-bedroom main house, two smaller guesthouses, a swimming pool, a gym that came with a sound-mitigated gun range in the basement, and, most importantly, a dedicated and untraceable connection to the 'net. At the time of Peter's death, the connection had been the fastest available. Now, not so much. That would be one of the first things Misty would have her new chief technology officer take care of. Of course, she still needed to find the right person for the role.

Misty had plans for the other properties, too, but first things first. She had an organization to get on its feet. Though the new Office was off to a pretty great start, with the rousing success of the Reed mission.

Best of all, it had turned into a PR coup for the feds. The breakup of an underage sex-slave operation received near universal praise. And after Anderson Cooper scored an interview with one of the freed girls who'd recently turned eighteen, even those who would have normally criticized the FBI's heavy-handed action were tempered in their responses.

All that praise translated into genuine gratitude toward the Office. Misty's organization had already been retained for two upcoming missions, with promises of more to follow.

Someone knocked on her front door. She looked at her watch. The movers were early. That was fine. She was ready for them.

Only, when she looked through the door's peephole, the two men standing on her porch were the director of ACORT, Kyle Otero, and a subordinate of his named Cameron Washington. She opened the door.

"Sorry to drop by unannounced," Otero said. "But I'm hoping we can have a moment of your time."

"No problem. Please, come in." She stepped aside so they could enter. "Just so you're aware, the movers are due at any minute."

"Today is moving day, then."

"Yes, sir."

"Excellent. I'm sure you're looking forward to getting settled."

"I am." She motioned to the dining table. "Would you like to sit?"

"Please," the director said.

After they were seated, she said, "What is it I can do for you, Director?"

"Do you recall someone named Christophe St. Amand?"

A tickle at the back of her mind. She *had* heard the name before. Years ago. She closed her eyes and worked her way through her memories.

She finally opened her eyes and said, "He works for Janus Sideropoulos, right?" If she hadn't spent so much time out of the intelligence game, she might have been able to place the name faster.

"Worked," Otero said. "Sideropoulos was killed two years ago."

"I see. Then who does St. Amand work for now?"

"He took over the organization when Sideropoulos died."

"I take it that means he's the one who killed him."

For the first time, Washington spoke. "That hasn't been proven yet."

"True," Otero agreed. "But we believe that's the case."

Misty looked from one man to the other. "You still haven't told me how I can help you."

"Mr. St. Amand is, to put it lightly, a notoriously private person," Otero said. "There are no known useful photographs of him."

"How is that even possible?"

With a nod from the director, Washington opened his briefcase, extracted an eight-by-twelve photograph, and set it on the table.

From the poor quality, she could tell the image was a blowup of security camera footage. It showed a man from the chest up. At least Misty assumed it was a man. He wore large sunglasses, a medical mask over his mouth and nose, and sported a luxurious head of hair that hung low over his forehead and completely covered his ears and neck.

"Wig?" she said.

A nod from Washington. "There are dozens of images like this. Different every time. Sometimes it's another wig, sometimes it's a hat. A couple times even a hoodie."

"But always something over his eyes and mouth," the director added.

Misty pushed the image toward the men. "Okay. So, you have a man you can't identify. Is that the job? Find him and get a clean picture?"

"Actually," Otero said, "we believe you already know what he looks like."

Misty cocked her head. "Excuse me?"

"Not you exactly. Someone who worked with you."

"You're going to have to be a little more specific."

"Several years ago, the Office took a job from a different section of the NSA. On that mission, one of your agents came face to face with St. Amand. It's in the mission file."

When the Office was shut down, the NSA took possession of Peter's records, though Misty had hidden away a secret set in case she ever needed it.

"Which mission are we talking about?" she asked.

"The unsuccessful rendition of Maurice Canto."

Now she remembered. The subject had committed suicide before the abduction team could nab him. She also recalled the encounter with St. Amand, and which agent had been involved. But she asked anyway, "And who was the agent?"

"He is listed as B2. No name. We are hoping you can tell us who he is."

She was the one who'd typed up all but a handful of the Office's mission files, so she *could* tell them, but information was power, and as the head of a newly reconstituted agency, she could use as much power as she could get. "I would have to consult the database. There should be a conversion list that will—"

"There isn't," Washington said, annoyed. "We've checked."

"The conversion list is gone? It was there when you assumed control of our assets." A one-word lie—that should have been *until* instead of *when*.

"Are you saying you don't remember who it is?" Otero asked.

She snorted. "Do you know how many different missions

the Office ran, and how many agents worked with us over the years?"

"The designation is B2," Washington said. "Seems like that should be a very easy one to remember."

"Sorry to disappoint you, Mr. Washington, but designations were randomly generated from project to project. I should, however, be able to figure out who it is. Is the reason you want to find him because you're looking for St. Amand?"

"That's classified," Washington said.

"I ask because chances are, this agent will be more open talking to me than to you."

"Whether we are looking for St. Amand or not, whoever the agent is, he *will* talk to us."

"Or she."

"What?" Washington said.

"You said he will talk to us. It could be a she."

"Oh, for chrissake. The point is—"

The director put a hand on the other man's arm. "Yes, we are looking for Christophe St. Amand. And if you think your agent would feel more comfortable discussing the matter with you, that works for us."

Misty smiled. "What I was actually going to suggest was that you hire the Office to assist with the search."

In the exchange of glances that followed between the two men, Misty sensed this was a possibility they had already considered, and that Otero, at least, was open to it.

The director focused back on her. "*If* you are able to find the agent, then I have no problem with bringing you onboard for this."

"Then it's settled," Misty said. "Good to be working with you again."

She held out her hand to Otero, who, after a pause, took it.

"You already know who it is, don't you?"

She continued to smile but said nothing.

"Hold on," Washington said. "If you do, then you've just lied to a federal agent. *Two* federal agents, in fact. Give us the name and maybe we won't file charges."

"Take it down, Cameron," Otero said. "No one's filing

charges. The Office's assistance would be greatly appreciated."

"Thank you," Misty said. "Now, perhaps you should tell me what the rush is to find Mr. St. Amand."

"No one said anything about a rush," Washington said.

"You're not a very good liar," she said.

Otero said, "We have reason to believe St. Amand is in the process of moving large stocks of illegal weapons and munitions into the United States."

"How do you know this?"

"Ironically, your people are responsible for this coming to light."

"How so?"

"The Reed assignment. If your team hadn't insisted on an immediate raid, we would have still been in the dark."

"You found weapons at the compound," she guessed.

"Some, yes, plus space for a whole lot more." He looked at Washington. "Show her."

After a moment's hesitation, Washington pulled more photos from his briefcase and laid them on the table.

The first was a shot of a gigantic room, partially occupied by shelves and several different types of containers. The others were close-ups of some of the items that had been stored—guns, bullets, rockets, explosives.

"This was at the Reed place?" Misty said, astonished.

Washington nodded.

"And you were able to tie it back to St. Amand?"

"We traced one of the shipments through a series of shell corporations and then to a French exporter who we've long suspected of being one of St. Amand's fronts. In the process, we've discovered that there may have been other shipments, potentially several dozens, to places other than Reed's compound."

"You think there are more of these caches spread around the country?"

"That is the concern, yes."

She stared at him. "For what purpose?"

"That is one of the things we'd like to ask Mr. St. Amand."

"What about Reed?"

"He is the reason we are here today. Yesterday, he was told about the statutory rape and sexual abuse charges that were going to be filed against him. Late last night, he used a knife that had been smuggled in to him to slit his wrists, and was not found until early this morning."

"Who gave him the knife?"

"It's not important," Washington said. By his tone, she suspected this was a very touchy subject for him.

"The perpetrator has been dealt with," the director said.

Someone knocked hard on the front door. "The movers." She quickly gathered the pictures and stood up. "May I keep these?"

"Of course," Otero said. "We'll forward you whatever other information we think you may need."

"Thank you, gentlemen. You can be assured the Office will jump right on this."

Another knock.

"Coming," she shouted.

SAN FRANCISCO

ORLANDO'S PHONE RANG. On the bed beside her, she felt Quinn stir.

"Are you going to get that?" he asked, still half asleep.

Without opening her eyes, Orlando reached over to her nightstand and found her phone on the first try. In a voice far more awake than she felt, she said, "Hello."

"Time to get up. We've got a new job." Misty.

Orlando sat up, her eyes cracking open. "What time is it?"

"Eight thirty."

That translated to 5:30 a.m. there on the West Coast. Orlando shook some of the cobwebs from her mind. "A new job? I thought we agreed not to take anything without consulting each other first."

"You're going to like this one. Besides, it's really more an extension of a job than a completely new one." Misty filled her in on the visit she received from the director of ACORT.

"B2 is Nate, isn't it?" Orlando said. "I remember him and

Quinn talking about it."

Quinn turned his head and looked at her, an eyebrow raised, but she mouthed *later*.

"According to Director Otero, Nate is one of the few people alive who's seen St. Amand's face," Misty said. "We're going to need him on this one. You *can* get him, right?"

Orlando couldn't help but glance at Quinn, which got him interested again. "I'm, um, not sure."

"No Nate, no job. You've got to bring him in."

"If you'd asked me before you said yes, we could have talked this out then."

"My choices were either to take the job or give ACORT Nate's name and information. Would you rather I'd have let them deal with it?"

It might have been easier, Orlando thought. But no, she wouldn't have wanted Misty to do that. "Let me see what I can do."

"Make it fast. We need to get on this, like, yesterday."

Orlando sighed. "I'll do what I can."

"I…I know you will. I'm sorry I didn't consult you first. I won't do that again."

"Don't worry about it. I'll call you back as soon as I know anything."

"Thank you."

Orlando hung up and threw the covers back.

"What was that all about?" Quinn asked as she climbed out of bed.

"Just give me a few minutes."

In the bathroom, she stared into the mirror, her gaze unfocused.

The last time she'd seen Nate had been in the woods outside London, where they had captured the woman who had killed Quinn's sister—and Nate's girlfriend—Liz. In an act of clearheadedness, Quinn had put aside his need for revenge and decided the woman would be turned over to US intelligence. Nate was not as forgiving. If it had been anyone but Quinn who had made the decision, Nate would have ignored it and killed the woman himself. Instead, he had stormed off.

By the time Quinn and Orlando returned to California, Nate had moved out of Quinn's Los Angeles home. She had no idea where he'd gone. She'd sent out feelers to make sure he was all right, but no one had reported seeing him.

The only people she hadn't asked were Daeng and Jar. If Nate was still talking to anyone in her and Quinn's inner circle, it would have been one of them. But she didn't want to force them to choose sides, and had to trust that if Nate was really in trouble, they would let her know. She'd let the matter drop, hoping time alone would help Nate heal.

But now, if she didn't contact him, the heavies at ACORT would. Better the devil you know.

She turned on the shower as hot as she could take it and stood under the spray, letting the parts of her body that hadn't woken up yet work their way back to life. By the time she returned to the bedroom, Quinn was sitting on the edge of the mattress, dressed in workout clothes.

Before he could ask her again what was up, she said, "We have a new job."

"Okay. Um…shouldn't you be happier about that?"

"I am…I mean, it's not the job itself that's a problem."

"This should be interesting."

"Christophe St. Amand. Remember him?"

"Sideropoulos's bulldog. Or was."

"Right. He's the guy in charge now. We've been hired to find him."

"Okay. How hard can that be?"

"No one knows what he looks like. Apparently, he never goes in public without his face covered. ACORT also thinks he might be using one or more decoys pretending to be him."

"I remember the face-covering bit. He was doing that when we encountered him in Marrakesh. Well, except for when—"

There it is, she thought as Quinn stopped.

"Nate," he said.

"Nate. The feds know he's seen St. Amand's face. That's why they've hired the Office."

He was silent for several seconds. "I assume they don't

realize…"

"…that he's dropped off the face of the earth? No, they don't."

"Do we really need him? I remember he gave a description. That's got to be in the mission records."

"The records ACORT has contains only a very basic description. The raw data in the backup Misty has is more detailed. Maybe it would help, maybe it wouldn't. The larger issue is that if we try to do it without Nate and ACORT finds out, the Office will be ruined. Plus, ACORT would force Misty to hand over Nate's information and go after him themselves."

"Crap," he said. "Do we even know where he is?"

"Not a clue."

"Well, this day's off to a great start."

"Isn't it, though?"

CHAPTER **NINE**

**TWO WEEKS EARLIER
LAS VEGAS, NEVADA**

NATE SAT ON a cheap wooden chair in the middle of the sparsely decorated living room, watching the sun rise through a window in his apartment. He'd been up for two hours already. These days he seldom slept past four a.m., no matter what time he went to bed.

It had been nearly six months since his girlfriend had been killed in an empty lot in Jakarta, and just over a month since the people responsible had been captured or killed, but the intense sense of loss still clung to him as strongly as it had the night he held Liz's head in his lap after her life drained away. He'd been able to ignore the grief to a certain extent while he hunted her killer, but it had all come crashing back after Quinn had prevented him from exacting his revenge.

He had fled back to Los Angeles and cleared his stuff out of Quinn's house. At that moment, he'd wanted nothing more to do with his former mentor. He wasn't sure if that was still true or not.

He wasn't sure about most things these days.

His first thought had been to go south, to Mexico, or maybe Central America, or maybe all the way to the southern tip of Argentina. Tierra del Fuego. He spoke perfect Spanish. But no matter where he went in that direction, someone would eventually peg him as a foreigner.

What he really wanted, what he *needed*, was to go someplace he could blend into the woodwork and disappear. The US or Canada was his best bet, a big city where outsiders wouldn't be noticed. Places like Chicago or Vancouver or New York.

Or Las Vegas.

The city's main purpose was to cater to tourists from around the world. Thousands and thousands of new faces came and went every week. Apartment buildings filled with the ever-changing horde, people who saw no need to get to know their neighbors. The perfect destination.

Nate had sublet his apartment from one of the disillusioned who'd wanted to return to the East Coast. Or was it the Northwest? He couldn't remember. Nor did he care. The building was generic to its core. Tan and baked and barely noticeable. A dream killer on a street with more of the same.

In the nearly four weeks he'd been there, he had yet to see the people who lived in the units on either side of his. That was fine. Like them, he wasn't there to make friends.

In that first week, his daily routine had been to wait until the sun had fully risen and then go for a walk. Some days he would wander for a few hours, some days he'd go all day. Much depended on the weather. Mentally he may have been a mess but he wasn't suicidal, and when the thermometer began reaching triple digits, which it had started doing more regularly, he'd return to the apartment and stare at the walls until the sun went down, and then start walking again.

He had been there simply to exist. But after a while, Liz refused to let him fall into that pit.

You're better than this, she had said.
I know it's hard, but you need to do more than just be.
You need to live.

Soon his walks were no longer purposeless.

He watched the last bit of the sun rise above the lip of the valley, and then lifted out of his chair and left his apartment.

Today, he headed west toward the park that had become the latest fixture on his route.

LARSON PARK ATTRACTED a lot of early morning exercise buffs, running down its paths, doing pullups on the playground monkey bars, performing sit-ups in the grass. There was even a group of tai chi practitioners, their dance-like routines welcoming each new day.

Nate's interest was in the group of high schoolers who waited every day for their bus at the northwest corner of the park. Some talked and laughed together. Others seemed content to stare at their phones.

He stretched his legs on the bench that had become his normal vantage point and watched them. Right on cue, the kid he was waiting for appeared. He was a big guy, the kind a football coach would spot on campus and do everything he could to recruit.

What happened next was also a repeat. A wave of tension passed through the other kids as they realized the big guy was coming. Only one student seemed happy to see him. He walked over to greet the guy, while the others shied away.

It was like a live performance of the same script, with subtle variations from show to show.

The next cue went to the kid with the green backpack, a scrawny boy who couldn't have been more than fourteen. Unlike the students who took a few steps back at the sight of the big guy, Green Backpack slipped all the way to the rear of the crowd and tried not to be seen at all.

As the big kid laughed with his buddy and looked around, Green Backpack shifted his position to avoid the other's direct gaze. But Nate knew the effort was doomed. The big guy always noticed the kid.

"Marcos, come here," the big guy yelled.

Marcos—the green bag boy——didn't move.

"Come *here*," the big guy repeated.

Marcos took a tentative step forward, but it apparently wasn't fast enough for his tormentor. The big guy bulled toward him, growling, "You little shit," as the other students dodged.

From down the street came the rumble of a large vehicle. The bus was approaching, a few minutes earlier than usual.

This didn't stop the bully.

He shoved Marcos in the chest, sending him backpedaling into a tree. Before Marcos could skirt away, the big kid grabbed the front of his shirt and pressed him against the tree.

It's time, Liz whispered in Nate's head.

In the days he'd been here so far, he had just watched.

Do something, she said.

Nate jogged toward the boys, like just another person trying to stay in shape. A few feet before he reached them, he said, "Excuse me. Coming through."

The bully jumped back and whined, "What the hell?"

"Sorry," Nate said, smiling.

"Go around next time, asshole!"

Nate glanced over his shoulder and gave the guy a thumbs-up.

As he'd hoped, Marcos had taken advantage of the distraction and run toward the sidewalk, where the bus was pulling to the curb.

The bully turned to locate his mark, and muttered, "Shit," upon realizing he'd missed his chance.

FOR THE FIRST time, Nate made a second visit to the park on the same day, arriving that afternoon just after two.

He had changed into jeans and a baggy button-up shirt, and was wearing a floppy gardening hat and large sunglasses, making him look nothing like he had that morning.

While his outfit did help protect him from the sun, it did nothing about the heat. When he last checked, it was 101 degrees, and the forecast said the temperature would go up another few degrees before it would start heading in the other direction again.

He checked out the immediate neighborhood, then returned to his favorite bench to wait. When he saw the bus turn onto the road, he made his way to the corner from where the bully appeared every morning. From there, he watched the students disembark.

Interestingly, Marcos wasn't among them. The big guy was there, though. And that was all that was important.

The kid knocked his shoulder into a girl, and laughed as her books spilled onto the ground. When the bully turned to cross the street, Nate started walking down the road the kid was headed for, moving out of sight.

Three houses down, Nate turned up the walk and approached the front door. He had chosen the place on his earlier look around, as it appeared no one was home. He pretended to knock on the door in case neighbors were watching. After hearing the bully walk by, he headed back to the street.

A block down, the kid took a left, crossed the street, and entered an alley. Nate paused when he reached the cinderblock wall at the corner of the backstreet and casually looked around it. The kid was twenty yards away, walking lazily down the center of the road, clearly having no idea Nate was watching him.

The cinderblock walls continued down both sides of the alley, broken up only by gates and garages with wide, cream-colored, roll-up doors. All the gates and doors were closed.

Nate repositioned to a group of trash cans a couple of properties down, and knelt behind them.

The kid was about halfway to the next block. If he went all the way and turned, Nate would have to sprint to the end and hope the boy didn't turn down another street before he got there.

That ended up not being an issue.

Four houses from the end of the block, on the left side of the alley, the kid pulled something out of his pocket and aimed it at the garage. When the door had rolled high enough, the boy ducked under. Seconds later, the door reversed direction.

Nate waited until it was all the way down before walking over to it. According to the map on his phone, the garage belonged to the house at 34297 Celeste Lane. Nate placed a marker on the address.

You can fix this, Liz said.

"Is that what you want?" he whispered.

He knew the answer without her having to say anything.

He spent a little time scouting, then walked to the nearest

main road and caught the city bus out of the area.

HE WAS UP at four a.m. again the next morning. The previous night, before returning to his apartment, he had called Jar from a paid phone and enlisted her help, like he had twice the previous week. When he checked the server he had directed her to use, the expected message was there.

> 34297 Celeste Lane is owned by Samuel Pearson. Son's name is Samuel Pearson, Junior. Mother deceased. Solo car accident, seven years ago. Woman named Lani Davis lives with them. Unsure of relationship. Information on the other houses you asked about is attached. If you need anything else, let me know. Whatever you're doing, be careful.

Today, he left the apartment before the sun came up.

First task, another walk-by of the bully's house. Too early for any lights on inside. Nate did note the ten-year-old Honda Accord and the classic Dodge Charger parked out front that hadn't been there the previous afternoon. Since there were plenty of open parking spots along the street, it was a good bet the vehicles were connected to the house.

Nate headed over to the park, and bided his time running through a litany of exercises near his favorite bench. By the time the first of the kids arrived, he was stretching again.

He was hopeful Marcos had found alternative transportation or had at least decided to take a mental health day, but there the kid was, walking up the street, carrying the ever-present green backpack over his shoulder.

Nate wanted to tell him to hide somewhere until after the bus had arrived, but he couldn't chance Sam Junior seeing him interacting with Marcos. The encounter the day before would be easy to forget, but not if it happened two days in a row.

Right on cue, the bully arrived and began his daily reign of terror. The bus didn't arrive in time today to save Marcos from being shoved to the ground. Twice. When the bus finally came, the bully gave Marcos a final push before joining the others. Marcos waited until everyone else was onboard before he hurried over and climbed on. It looked like the driver said something to him, but the kid rushed past and slid into one of the seats near the front.

"Don't worry, kid," Nate whispered. "That's the last time."

BULLIES LIKE SAM Junior were seldom born that way.

Nate returned to the street where the bully lived and walked by the kid's house again. Both the Accord and the Charger were gone. He circled into the alley and hopped the cinderblock wall into the bully's backyard.

Whatever landscaping the place had once boasted had long been replaced by a field of dirt, decorated with piles of junk and trash, an old swing set with no swings, and a dying tree smack dab in the middle of it all.

Nate approached the sliding glass door at the back and peeked inside. A dim room filled with worn furniture. He put his ear against the glass. All was quiet.

An examination of the door revealed no contact points for an alarm system. That would make things even easier.

In one of the junk piles, he found a wire hanger and used it to disengage the lock.

He took a quick walk through the house and confirmed no one was home.

From documents found in boxes in the master bedroom, Nate learned the Dodge Charger belonged to Sam Senior and the Accord to Lani Davis. Given there were only two beds in the house, and one was in Sam Junior's room, Nate figured Davis was Sam Senior's live-in girlfriend.

Sam Junior's room was decorated with a mix of hockey posters and pages ripped out of *Sport Illustrated*'s swimsuit editions. The bed was unmade, its sheets sweat stained. In the corner was a TV, an Xbox console, and a stack of first-person shooter games. It wasn't hard to imagine the kid sitting in his beanbag chair every night, killing imaginary enemies while his homework went untouched.

Nate noted damage throughout the house—holes in the walls, broken doorframes. The results of violent outbursts, he guessed.

According to Sam Senior's papers, he worked as an electrician for a company that owned several hotels on the Strip, while Davis provided advice at Madam Kimberly's House of the Spirits under the name Madam Velina.

Posing as a manager from HR, Nate called Pearson's supervisor, who sloughed him off to an assistant, who informed Nate that Sam Senior usually worked the seven a.m. to four p.m. shift at the Tahitian Grand Hotel, and averaged less than two hours of overtime a week.

Next, Nate called Madam Kimberly's House of the Spirits and asked for an appointment with Madam Velina at five that evening. When he was told she was booked up until 6:30, he said that was fine and scheduled his appointment for then.

Since House of the Spirits was clear across town, and Davis would wait at least fifteen minutes before deciding her 6:30 wasn't showing up, it was unlikely she'd be home before 7:30 p.m.

Sam Senior, on the other hand, could be back as early as 4:20 if he drove straight home, or an hour or so later if he hit a bar first. Either way, there would be plenty of time between then and when the girlfriend showed up at the house.

NATE SPENT THE rest of the morning and early afternoon far from the part of town where he lived, running errands that included renting a Lexus sedan and purchasing a stylish set of clothes.

After changing into his new suit and putting on a wig in a gas station restroom, he returned to the park and hid a remote microcamera in a tree, pointing it toward the bus stop.

The previous afternoon, he had seen three houses with For Sale signs in their yard, all backing up to the same alley as the Pearsons' home. One was still being lived in. The others, however, appeared unoccupied. These last two were the other homes he'd asked Jar to investigate for him.

The information attached to her email that morning contained house specs, pictures of the interiors, the names of the firms handling each sale, and the master codes for the lockboxes in which the house keys were stored.

After driving by the empty homes, he parked in front of the one on the same block as the Pearsons', as it appeared the neighbors on either side of it weren't home. With his new over-the-shoulder briefcase that carried his purchases, he headed to the house, acting like a real estate agent preparing for a showing. At the front door, he input the master code into the real estate app he'd downloaded, and, just like that, he had the key.

The house had been staged with appealing furniture. He familiarized himself with the layout, and decided the full bath along the back would suit his purposes.

He removed a cloth tarp from his briefcase, refolded it so that it would fit perfectly over the window, and affixed it with duct tape. It wasn't an ideal sound barrier, but it would do an adequate enough job.

Plastic sheeting went on the floor next. He then laid more sheeting down the hallway, into the kitchen, and all the way to the back door. The house set, Nate exited the back door and walked over to the garage.

The door opened with the same key as the house. The garage was empty and had been swept clean.

He located the remote control for the roll-up door and pushed the button. The motor whirled to life and the door ascended.

Nate removed the bait from his bag and set it in the center of the garage. He headed into the alley and mimicked the path the bully had walked the day before. As he came to the open garage door, he glanced over and nodded to himself. The bait was clearly visible.

After mounting a microcam to the fence and aiming it down the alley, and placing a second inside the garage, he closed the rolling door.

IN THE HOUSE, Nate changed into his alternate outfit—a long-sleeved black turtleneck shirt, black jeans, and matching stocking cap. The cap would become a ski mask when he pulled it down later. After donning a double set of rubber gloves, he moved one of the dining room chairs into the bathroom, covered it with plastic, and sat down to wait.

Fifteen minutes prior to the school bus's usual drop-off time, he began monitoring the camera he'd left at the park. Good thing, as the bus showed up five minutes early.

Marcos was one of the first kids to disembark. He hit the ground running and was long gone by the time Sam Junior stepped off. The bully glanced at his now distant victim and laughed. Nate worried Junior might pursue Marcos, but as the bus pulled away, Junior crossed the street, heading in his usual direction.

Nate returned to the backyard and placed the second part of his honeypot on the ground, just outside the pedestrian door at the back of the garage. He hit the rolling-door button, watched it curl up into the ceiling.

From a hidden position in the backyard, he watched the alley camera feed on his phone.

The bully showed up right when Nate expected him. As Junior neared the open garage, the boy's gaze swung toward it. He continued for a few more steps, then stopped.

He'd seen the bait.

How smart are you, kid?

Junior stared into the garage for several seconds, and then looked up and down the alley. When he saw he was alone, he hurried into the garage.

Not too smart at all, apparently.

Nate switched to the camera inside the garage to see the kid crouching down and picking up one of bullets sitting next to the pistol magazine Nate had left on the floor.

The kid grinned, looked back toward the alley as if worried someone was watching him. Seeing no one, he picked up the magazine and turned it in his hand. From the top, he popped out another bullet and laughed with pleasure.

It was at this point he noticed the back door was also open, and that the gun the magazine likely fit into was lying just outside.

He rose and started walking toward it.

Guns and boys, like attracting magnets.

Nate pulled down the ski mask and donned reflective sunglasses. He removed the wet cloth from its Ziploc bag.

The bully barely stopped long enough in the doorway to make sure no one was in the yard. As Junior reached for the pistol, Nate slipped behind him and wrapped a hand around his face, placing the rag doused with homemade chloroform over the kid's nose and mouth.

Junior tried to rip Nate's hand away, but within seconds he slumped onto the ground.

Nate checked his pulse, then carried the kid into the kitchen and laid him on the floor. The kid should be out for several hours, but there was no sense in taking any chances. Nate zip-tied the boy's wrists and ankles and put a gag across his mouth, loose enough so that the kid wouldn't choke, but tight enough that if Junior tried to scream, it wouldn't be loud enough to be heard.

Task one completed.

NATE WAS SITTING in Junior's bedroom when the front door opened at 4:36 p.m.

He listened as Sam Senior walked in, stopped in the kitchen, and headed down the hallway.

"SJ, I told you to wash the fucking dishes when you got home! They had better be done by the time I come back out!"

The heavy steps marched into the master bedroom, followed by the sound of the door slamming shut.

Nate slipped out of Junior's room and tiptoed over to the master's door. From the other side, he could hear a drawer open and close, then a few more footsteps before things went quiet. Three minutes later, a toilet flushed and a shower started up.

By the time Sam Senior finished washing off, Nate was in the bedroom, leaning against the wall next to the bathroom door. The man stepped out with nothing but the towel he was using to dry his hair.

He gave his head one more wipe before turning to toss the towel back into the bathroom, only to find Nate standing in his way.

Jerking back, he shouted, "What the hell?"

Nate shoved the doused cloth over the man's mouth and nose.

Maybe the guy was tired from his day, or maybe his constitution was weaker than his son's. Whatever the case, the struggle he put up before he toppled to the floor was feeble compared to what Junior had managed.

NATE WRAPPED SAM Senior in a sheet and lugged him into the backyard, where he dumped the man in an old wheelbarrow he'd found in the garage. He performed a quick cleaning job on the house, removing any signs of his presence.

Once that was complete, he checked the alley. One of the neighbors had come home and was pulling into his garage. As soon as he was out of sight, Nate remotely opened the door to the garage of the house that was for sale, then wheeled Senior out the gate, down the alley, and through the doorway.

He carried Sam Senior into the bathroom and zip-tied him to the plastic-covered chair.

He sat on the edge of the tub to wait.

A MOAN SIGNALED the first sign of consciousness.

A minute later, Sam Senior's head swayed back and forth across his chest. When his eyes finally opened, they did so gingerly, as if each molecule of light might cut a hole in his retinas.

"Welcome back, Mr. Pearson," Nate said, his voice calm and low.

It took the man a few seconds to figure out where the sound was coming from. Once he did, he tried to move his arms, but they weren't going anywhere. "What's going on? Where-where am I? Who the hell are you?"

"No need to talk so loud. I'm right here."

"Screw that!"

Nate slapped a new rag of chloroform across Senior's mouth. The cloth contained a much lower dose than the first one, just enough to send his captive back to dreamland.

Five minutes later, the waking process repeated itself.

In a voice the man probably thought sounded tough, he

said, "Who are you? What are you doing in my house?"

"Oh, Sammy. You're not very observant, are you? You might want to take a look around."

Sam Senior took his eyes off Nate and scanned the room, his expression growing more and more confused. "Where the hell am I?"

"If I were you, I'd be more concerned about the why I was here, not the where. In fact, I'd be wondering if I was going to get out of here alive."

Sam Senior was one of those people who showed a lot of white around the irises when they opened their eyes wide.

"W-w-what?"

"I mean, come on. We didn't cover the room in plastic just for aesthetics."

For the second time, the man looked around, now noticing the plastic sheets covering everything.

"What…what do you want?"

"Now *that* is a more appropriate question. What we want is for you to pull your head out of your ass."

Sam Senior opened his mouth, but apparently couldn't think of anything to say.

"I'm sure you can understand that getting involved in petty lives such as yours is something we'd rather avoid," Nate said. "There are issues much larger than your dysfunctionality that our time is better spent dealing with. And yet, here we are. Having to deal with exactly that."

"What are you talking about? And-and who's *we*?"

"Do you really need me to spell it out for you?" Nate said nothing for a moment. "My God, you're an idiot. How do you think this town runs? On the good will of its citizens and the generosity of its employers?" Another pause. "When one of the corporations that runs Vegas has a problem that is best kept quiet, *we* are the ones they call. And you, Mr. Pearson, have become one of those problems."

Pearson's gaze drifted to the plastic, the full impact of what it represented hitting him. He looked back at Nate, his lower lip trembling. "I don't know what you're taking about. I didn't do anything. I swear."

Nate smiled. "I believe you have a son. Samuel Junior."

Anger flared across Sam Senior's face. "What did that little bastard do?"

Nate leaned back. "Interesting that you would turn on him so quickly. It explains a lot."

"If-if-if he did something, I-I-I'll make it right."

"We all have a responsibility to our children, don't you think? To make sure they have a good start to life."

"Um, yeah. Sure. Uh, of course."

Nate sneered. "Oh, come on, Sammy. If you really believed that, I doubt we'd be in this predicament."

"No. I…I bel—"

"Here's the thing. Vegas may feel like a big city most of the time, but it's really just a small town. You can never really be sure who your neighbors are, and how important they might be to someone in power. And, more pertinent to our conversation, you never know which school these important neighbors' kids go to. You know what's a common concern of most parents? They don't like their kids getting picked on."

"School? Did SJ do something at school again?"

"You're familiar with his behavior."

"I, uh, know he gets blamed for things that aren't his fault."

"I agree. But not quite in the way you mean it. Do you know whose fault they really are?"

A crease above Sam Senior's nose. "I'm not sure what you mean."

Nate walked out of the room, and returned with the chef blowtorch he'd picked up while running his errands. He turned on the gas and lit the flame.

"What are you going to do with that?" Nate's captive asked, showing the whites of his eyes again.

"I can think of a couple dozen possibilities right off the top of my head." Nate stepped closer to Pearson, the powerful flame pointing at the man's face.

"I didn't *do* anything!"

"Are you SJ's father?"

"Yes."

"You raised him?"

"Um, yeah. Of course."

"And how would you rate the job you've done to this point?"

"Hey, it wasn't easy. His mom went off and died when he was just a kid. Someone had to work and put food on the table."

"He's *still* just a kid."

"I mean younger, you know. Elementary school."

"So, your answer would be, not too good."

"No, I didn't say that! Given the circumstances, I did a great job."

"Evidence says otherwise."

"Fuck you and your evidence. I did fine. I can't help he's the way he is."

Nate shook his head in pity. "That's the worse answer you've given so far." He moved the blowtorch toward Pearson's face, and turned the knob to intensify the flame. "You most certainly could have helped."

Pearson leaned as far back as he could to get away from the heat. "Fine! Fine! I'm a crappy father. Is that what you want?"

"What we want is for you to fix this."

"O-o-okay, sure. No problem. I'll talk to him. I'll make sure he doesn't do anything again. I promise."

Nate smiled. "We know he won't do anything again, but I'm afraid your time to talk to him is in the past."

"What does that mean?"

"You are being given two choices. One, do everything we will suggest. Or two, argue with me, pay an immediate penalty for doing that, and then still do everything we suggest." He inched the flame closer. "Which is it going to be?"

"Jesus! Get that away from me! Please! I'll do whatever you suggest! I promise!"

Nate waited a moment before pulling the blowtorch back. "I'm impressed. Maybe you can learn new things."

"Yeah. I most definitely can. Just tell me. I'll do it."

"If there is even one little misstep, I will come back. You may wonder, how would we ever know that? Easy. For the next several years, we will know *everything* about you. We will know how you talk to your son, what you do to him, how you treat him. And if you make my employers unhappy, they'll send someone not nearly as nice as I am for a visit."

The color vanished from Sam Senior's face. "Tell me what you want me to do."

Nate turned off the torch and did just that.

When he finished, Sam Senior stared at him. "I don't have that kind of money."

"Then I suggest you find it. Get a second job. Take another mortgage out on your house. Sell your Charger."

St. Bartholomew's military boarding school in Maryland would not be cheap, and Sam Junior would hate it at first. In the long run, however, the distance from his old life and the discipline he'd learn would give him a chance at a more promising future than the potentially disastrous one he was heading toward.

Nate fiddled with the dial on the blowtorch. "Or would you rather argue about this some more?"

"No. I'll-I'll do it."

"When?"

"As soon as I can."

"Incorrect. You will pull him out of school first thing tomorrow morning. By next Monday, he will be attending St. Bart's. Tell me you understand."

Sam Senior nodded, looking as if he'd been hit by a truck.

"Say it."

"I-I understand."

"Excellent. Then our business is concluded."

Nate went over to the sink where his bottle of chloroform sat, and poured some onto the cloth he'd used previously.

"Please. You don't have to do this."

Nate did not honor his request.

NATE MOVED BOTH Pearsons into the garage of the house that was for sale, then removed all the plastic and made sure the place looked as pristine as it had when he arrived. After changing back into his real estate agent getup, he left via the front door and drove his rental car around to the alley.

Sam Senior went into the trunk, while Junior got a ride in the wheelbarrow back to his house, where Nate put him in his bed.

Nate drove Sam Senior out of town and dumped him about a hundred yards from the highway, half a mile from a twenty-four-hour truck stop.

The next morning, Nate was back at his park bench to witness the kids being picked up for school. When SJ hadn't arrived by the time the bus did, Marcos wasn't the only student who cracked a smile.

After Nate returned to his apartment, he hacked into the school district's system and found that Sam Pearson, Junior, had been withdrawn from school. The reason: relocation.

The following Monday, Nate checked the St. Bart's system and learned SJ had indeed been registered, and was expected to arrive the next day. That was one day later than the deadline he'd given the kid's dad.

He called Sam Senior's cell from a pay phone at one of the hotels.

"We are disappointed," he said in the same calm whisper he'd used during their face-to-face.

"I-I-I-I—"

"Our directions were for your son to start school today."

"He's on a plane *right now*. I just couldn't get a flight over the weekend. He'll be there in a couple hours. I promise."

Nate remained silent.

"They know about it," the man said, even more nervous than before. "Call them. SJ's starting tomorrow. Please. I tried!"

"We will check."

He hung up as the man continued pleading his case.

On Tuesday, Nate checked St. Bart's system again. As of that morning, SJ was officially in class.

Nate headed out on what he knew would be his last walk in Vegas. As perfect as the city might be to get lost in, it was time to find someplace new.

CHAPTER
TEN

**TODAY
ROME**

DRAKE LEANED INTO the open passenger-side window of the Mercedes and said, "They've just gone inside."

After failing to obtain any useful information from the courier, he and his team had intensified their hunt, finally turning up a clue from a low-level numbers guy with a grudge against his employer. That employer was one Carlo Bianchi, a bastard with a small-time smuggling operation that he thought was more important that it was. Apparently Bianchi had designs on growing his business, and thought he could hasten his expansion by cutting into St. Amand's interests. Taking the package from the courier had been the first step toward that goal.

Bianchi's problem was that he was aware of only a small fraction of St. Amand's business, and thought St. Amand was just a slightly bigger smuggler whom Bianchi—if he played his cards right—could absorb.

St. Amand glanced out the window at the building behind Drake. It was one of a dozen similar warehouse buildings in the area. According to Drake's sources, this particular structure served as Bianchi's main distribution center.

The numbers guy said St. Amand's missing package was being kept in a safe in a second-floor office, and that Bianchi was planning on going directly there upon returning from a trip to America. Drake had three cars waiting at Fiumicino International Airport when Bianchi arrived ninety minutes ago. Working in tag-team fashion, the vehicles had followed the smuggler to make sure his plan hadn't changed, while St. Amand, Drake, and the rest of their men waited near the warehouse.

"Do it," St. Amand said.

Drake lifted a radio to his mouth. "Go."

CARLO BIANCHI WAS feeling pretty damn good. His meetings in the States had gone better than he could have hoped, and he'd come home with a new business partnership that would increase his income by nearly a third. Even better, while he'd been gone, his subordinates had gotten their hands on one of St. Amand's messengers, and obtained a package containing a data stick and a hundred thousand euros in one-hundred euro notes.

He'd ordered no one to look at the stick until his return. Some people might call him paranoid, but he knew the biggest threats to success often came from the inside.

He was in the middle of a business call when his car arrived at its destination.

"I don't care," he said, wanting the conversation to be over. "We have an arrangement. One which *I* have lived up to. *You*, so far, have not."

The customer on the other end said, "But—"

"My representative will be there at noon tomorrow, which gives you over sixteen hours to get this situation fixed."

"But—"

Bianchi disconnected the call. He exited the sedan and headed into the warehouse, in the company of his first lieutenant, Luca. Inside, three more of his inner circle were waiting.

"Good evening, Mr. Bianchi," Salvador Necci said.

"Good evening."

"Welcome back. Sounds like it was a successful trip?"

Bianchi grunted. "I want to see that data stick."

"Of course," Elia Vicoli said. "It's in your office."

THE FIRST OF Bianchi's men to fall were the six watchers situated around the building, all receiving bullets to the head within a heartbeat of one another. Drake's team proceeded to the main door, where they used a key from one of the downed guards to disengage the lock. When everyone was ready again, one man pulled the door open and two others rushed in, shooting the pair of guards stationed in the hallway.

Six team members split off to deal with any other threats on the lower level, while Drake and the rest of his men headed upstairs.

The second-floor hallway was empty. According to the snitch, Bianchi's office was located at the far end, and the safe containing the data stick was inside.

They were about seven meters from the door when it opened and one of Bianchi's men walked out. Before he could raise an alarm, Drake pulled the trigger of his suppressor-equipped pistol and delivered a bullet to the center of the man's forehead.

The man hit the floor with a noticeable thump. Drake and his men rushed forward, ready to fire again if anyone came to check.

BIANCHI LET LUCA open the safe and retrieve the package.

The wooden box was about the length and width of a banker's box and half the height.

Bianchi lifted the lid and smiled at the stacks of euros inside. "You're sure it's a hundred thousand?"

"Counted it myself," Necci said.

Bianchi picked up one of the bundles. The bills were crisp and unused. "You're sure they're not counterfeit."

"Yes, sir," Vicoli said.

Bianchi flipped through it, the sound of money fluttering against itself one of his all-time favorites. Looking back in the box, he spotted an opaque plastic container about the size of three smartphones stacked on top of one another. He pulled it out and flipped open the top. The data stick sat inside, snug in a slot in the black packing foam.

He removed the stick and set the container on the desk.

Thump.

Everyone turned toward the office door.

"What was that?" Bianchi asked.

Luca pulled out his gun and said to Necci and Vicoli, "Check it out."

The two men drew their weapons and crossed to the door. It flew inward before they reached it.

Thup, thup, thup, thup.

Necci and Vicoli went down immediately, while Luca dove at his boss, knocking Bianchi to the floor and covering him with his body.

The sound of gunfire was replaced by that of pounding steps hurrying into the room.

A pair stopped a meter away, then—

Thup.

As Luca's body went slack, Bianchi felt something drip onto the back of his neck.

Someone grabbed Luca and pulled him aside. More hands latched on to the back of Bianchi's jacket and yanked him to his feet.

Nearly a dozen black-dressed men were crowded into the room, all but one holding assault rifles. The last man was the biggest of the bunch, at least a decade older, and holding a pistol at his side. He took a hard look at Bianchi before he unclipped a radio from his belt.

"Got him," he said.

A reply came over the radio. "On my way."

The man with the pistol motioned at two of the others, and said something to them in a language Bianchi didn't know. Something Slavic, perhaps.

The two men lifted the smuggler to his feet and shoved him into the desk chair.

Bianchi knew if he didn't find a way out of this soon, he'd be screwed. "Hey, there's over a hundred thousand euros in there," he said, nodding at the box. "Take it. It's yours. Let me go and I'll forget all about it."

The big man snorted but said nothing.

"I'm serious! Look for yourself."

The big man pointed his pistol at Bianchi's forehead. "Shut up."

"What's the harm in making a deal? We both win."

The man walked up to him and shoved the suppressor against Bianchi's cheek. "Do you not understand what *shut up* means?"

Bianchi swallowed with difficulty and nodded.

The big man pulled the gun back, but left it pointed at Bianchi's head.

From out in the hallway came the sound of someone approaching. A man entered, wearing sunglasses and a black scarf covering the rest of his face and most of his head. Though Bianchi couldn't see the man's face, the man's disguise was ID enough.

Whatever hope he had of getting out alive vanished.

ST. AMAND GRIMACED at Bianchi.

For all the trouble the upstart had caused, St. Amand had hoped the man would have at least some sense of defiance, perhaps even a little entitlement. But all the jiggling pile of meat could muster was the stink of fear and despair.

St. Amand opened the wooden box. "Has anyone counted this?" he asked in Italian.

"Not yet," Drake said.

"It's all there, Mr. St. Amand," Bianchi said. "I swear."

"I'm sure you'll forgive me for not trusting you." St. Amand signaled for Drake to have a few of the men make sure no money was missing, then he picked up the plastic container and opened it. The data stick was missing. "And this?" He tilted the container so Bianchi could see inside. "Is it here, too? Because I don't see it."

"Uh…" Bianchi scanned the floor. "It's around here somewhere. It fell in the confusion."

"Fell out of its box?"

Bianchi hesitated, then said in a contrite voice, "I…was holding it."

"I'm sorry. Did you say you were holding it?"

110

A gulp. "Yes."

"That is…disappointing."

St. Amand walked around the desk, his gaze sweeping the carpet. When he didn't see the stick, he hooked a shoe under the dead man lying next to the desk and flipped him over. The stick fell from a fold in the man's jacket.

St. Amand picked it up and examined it. "You're lucky. It looks undamaged. Of course, we won't know for sure until we check the data." He slipped the stick into his pocket, and leaned against the desk in front of the smuggler. "Now, tell me. What made you think you could steal something from me and not face the consequences?"

"We-we weren't the ones who stole it. We, um, found it. When I, uh, uh, realized what we had, I knew we had to get it back to you right away."

St. Amand raised an eyebrow. "Is that so?"

"Yes. You see, I just returned from America. I came straight here so my men could show it to me. I'd literally just realized it was yours when your men…came in."

"Just now."

"That's right."

"And how, exactly, did you realize it was mine? I don't believe my name is written on any of the banknotes. It's certainly not on the data stick."

Bianchi's expression cracked. "It was what one of my men said. They-they told me the person who had it before them said he'd taken it from you."

"So, what you're saying is that you didn't just realize it was mine. You knew it was all along."

"Well, I…I mean, I didn't want to presume."

"You're contradicting yourself."

"No. It's…um…"

Over at the box, one of the money counters said, "It's short three thousand."

The shock on Bianchi's face was genuine. "That can't be right. It was supposed to be all there! I was told it was!"

"Search the bodies," St. Amand said.

His men came up with 2,486 euros, over two grand of

which from a single man.

"You owe me five hundred and fourteen euros," St. Amand told Bianchi.

"My wallet's in my jacket pocket. You can have everything that's there."

"Yes, we can."

The wallet was where Bianchi said it would be. In it was six hundred and forty euros.

St. Amand counted out exactly five hundred and fourteen and put the money in the box with what was collected from the dead men. The rest he set in a pile in front of Bianchi.

"This is yours."

"You can have it. I…insist."

"I'm not a thief, Mr. Bianchi. I'm a businessman. The box you stole contained one hundred thousand euros when it was sent to me, so one hundred thousand is what I will take with me."

"I *didn't* steal anything."

St. Amand pulled out the data stick again. "And let's not forget this. It's what you were really after, isn't it? Probably thought it might help you take over my business."

"What? I would never even dream—"

"What do you think is on here?"

"I…I don't know." That was one of the first honest things the man had said.

"Of course you don't know. But I'll tell you. On this are schedules for upcoming weapons shipments being made by dozens of different manufacturers and military operations, from all over the world."

Bianchi brow furrowed. "Weapons?"

"Handguns, rifles, rocket launchers, drones, tanks." St. Amand chuffed at the man's look of surprise. "What did you think I do? Smuggle only mundane nonsense like you? I am at a whole different level."

"I…I didn't know. I'm sorry." Another honest answer.

"I accept your apology. But we still have a problem."

"If you think I'll say anything, I won't. I promise. No one will ever hear anything about you from me."

St. Amand patted the man on the cheek. "I appreciate that, but it's not what I'm talking about."

"Whatever it is, I'm sure we can find a solution."

"I already know the solution. But perhaps you'd like to know what the problem is first."

"Yes, of course. What, uh, what's the problem?"

"I can't have people who've seen my face walking around."

"But I haven't seen your face!"

St. Amand pulled his scarf down and removed his sunglasses. "Now you have."

Bianchi stared for a second, then squeezed his eyes shut as if he could erase what he'd just witnessed.

St. Amand held out a hand to Drake, who slapped a pistol into it.

"Stealing from others is a very nasty habit," St. Amand said.

He shoved the suppressor into Bianchi's mouth and pulled the trigger.

The smuggler fell off the chair. St. Amand handed Drake the weapon and the data stick. Drake would analyze the information and identify the shipments containing equipment St. Amand's clients needed. He would determine vulnerable points along the shipping routes where the equipment could find its way into their hands. Their American clients were champing at the bit for their orders and wouldn't wait forever. Something big was about to happen soon in the States, and St. Amand wanted to get as much money out of them as possible before it did.

St. Amand picked up the euro-stuffed box and headed for the door, leaving the money he'd set aside for Bianchi on the table.

He was a principled man, after all.

CHAPTER
ELEVEN

SAN FRANCISCO

IF ANYONE KNEW where Nate was, Daeng would, Quinn thought.

Daeng had returned to Bangkok after the events in the UK for a much deserved vacation. Quinn tried his friend's mobile phone but was sent directly to voicemail. When the beep sounded, instead of allowing him to record a message, a prerecorded female voice spoke in Thai and the line disconnected.

"Great," he muttered. Daeng's mailbox was full.

"What?" Orlando asked. She was sitting at her computer, searching for any digital trails Nate might have left.

"Not answering."

If he couldn't reach Daeng, maybe Jar knew where Nate was.

She picked up on the first ring. "Yes?"

"It's Quinn."

"I know that."

"Do you know where Daeng is? I'm trying to get ahold of him."

"If you want Daeng, you should call *his* number, not mine." Jar was not like most people. Hers was a nearly black and white world, based on logic. Casual conversation was lost on her.

"I have called him. But he's not answering and his

mailbox is full."

Jar said nothing.

"Do you know where he is?"

"Yes."

"Can you please tell me?"

"He did not say it was a secret."

Realizing his mistake, Quinn rephrased the question, "Jar, please tell me where Daeng is."

"He is at the temple."

"Wat Doi Thong?"

"Correct."

Wat Doi Thong was the same temple Quinn had gone to a few years earlier when he was recovering from an injury. It was the same temple where Nate had come looking for Quinn and met Daeng for the first time. Quinn had the number of the man who helped maintain the place.

"Thanks, Jar." He was about to say goodbye, but stopped. "You haven't been in contact with Nate since we all left England, have you?"

Silence.

"Jar?"

Another few seconds, then, "Yes."

"When?"

"Fourteen days ago."

"You contacted him, or he contacted you?"

"I feel very uncomfortable talking about this."

"Did he tell you not to tell me?"

A beat. "Not this time."

"This time? You've been in contact before?"

"I would not have said it like that if I had not been."

Quinn took a breath. Jar was a brilliant information specialist, and not bad in the field, either, but talking with her could be exhausting. "I need to get ahold of him. I know he doesn't want to talk to me right now, but it's important. If it makes it any easier for you, Orlando can be the one who talks to him. Do you know where he is?"

"He needs time. He is still in pain."

"We're both still in pain."

"I did not say that you were not."

"I know. Sorry." He took a breath. "Do you know where he is?"

"I know where he *was*, ten days ago. I do not know if he is still there today."

"Where was that?"

"Why do you need to talk to him?"

Now it was Quinn's turn to hesitate. "We need his help."

"For a job?"

"Yes."

"That does not seem like a very good reason to me. He wants to be alone. You can find someone else."

"If I could do this without him, I would. But I can't."

"You are sure?"

"I'm positive."

She was quiet for several seconds. "He was in Las Vegas."

That was a surprise. Vegas was only a short plane ride from San Francisco. "What's his phone number?"

"I don't know it."

"Jar, please. I know you must have—"

"He called me. *From* pay phone. That is what he said, at least. The number was scrambled. He had me store any information I gathered for him on a server belonging to one of the casinos."

"Information? He was working?"

"I…do not think so. Not like you mean."

"Then what was he doing?"

"I am not sure."

"So, you don't have *any* direct method for contacting him?"

"No."

Quinn thought for a moment. "Would you be willing to send me the information that you sent him? It might help me figure out where he is."

She didn't respond.

"I understand," Quinn said. "You feel like you're breaking his trust. But I promise you, I will not interfere with whatever he is doing."

"Why do you need *him* and not anyone else?"

Fair question. "I need his memory. He witnessed something the rest of us didn't."

"And it is important to know what he knows?"

"Very."

He heard her take a breath.

"All right. I will send it to you."

"Thank you, Jar. I appreciate it."

Orlando tapped him on the arm and whispered, "Don't hang up."

"Hold on," he said into the phone, then put a hand over the receiver. "What is it?"

"Let me talk to her."

Quinn put the call on speaker.

"Jar, it's Orlando."

"*Sawadee ka*, Orlando. *Sabaidee rue, ka?*"

"*Sabaidee, khob khun ka*," Orlando said. "I was only getting one side of your conversation with Quinn. Did you say you know where Daeng is?"

"Yes."

"Good. Can you do me a favor and get in touch with him? Tell him we have a job for him."

"Of course."

"Actually, it's for both of you," Orlando said. "If you're free, that is."

"I am always available for you. Where do you want us?"

"I'll get back to you on that. For now, get Daeng, pack your bags, and get ready to head to the airport."

"But send that information," Quinn reminded her.

"I am on it," Jar said and hung up.

After Quinn filled Orlando in on what he'd learned about Nate, he checked his email and found a message from Jar. He opened the attached documents.

They all concerned a person named Samuel Pearson. Check that, two people—Samuel Pearson, Sr., and Samuel Pearson, Jr., the latter a fifteen-year-old high school sophomore with multiple disciplinary entries on his record.

"Why would Nate be interested in these two?"

Orlando scanned the documents and shrugged. "No idea. But he was interested, apparently. And maybe he still is."

"Which I guess means I'm going to Vegas."

MIDWEST UNITED STATES

ON THE MORNING Nate left Vegas, he purchased a used Toyota Camry from Craigslist. It was gray with no dents or noticeable scratches. An innocuous car that would be forgotten moments after it was seen.

He had headed east, unsure of his destination, knowing only it was time to move on.

The incident with the Pearsons wasn't the first time he'd intervened in a problem since his self-imposed exile had begun, but it had been his most involved. He doubted he would have come close to achieving the same level of results with less effort, though.

You did good, Liz had told him after he left the Pearsons' house. Her praise was the only thing that really mattered.

He wound his way northeast, across the Rockies, where he spent two days in Denver before deciding it wasn't the place for him. The thing about Vegas was that whichever direction he looked, he had seen either the casino-filled artificial playground of the soulless, or the never-ending brown of the desert, the glare and the starkness excellent fits for his damaged psyche. In Denver, the mountains were a towering, ever-present wall in the west. Beautiful and majestic, the antithesis of where he had just come from. That kind of beauty had a way of fracturing shells like the one he'd built around himself. He wasn't ready for his to crack yet.

Onward, then. Farther east.

Kansas and Missouri were appealing, but his desire for anonymity still required a larger city than either state possessed.

He finally found what he was looking for five hours northeast of St. Louis.

Chicago, the sprawling, unofficial capital of middle America, contained more than enough people for him to lose himself among. He took a room at a pay-by-the-week hotel in a seedier part of town, and once more began walking the days away.

He wasn't looking to find another project. In fact, he told himself to avoid doing just that. But two weeks after he left Vegas, after he had given Sam Junior a chance to redeem his life, another project found him.

Help her, Liz said.

LAS VEGAS

QUINN ARRIVED IN the late afternoon, picked up his rental car, and drove straight to the address belonging to Samuel Pearson.

The house was located in an unimpressive middle-class neighborhood of decent-sized homes whose developer had clearly been working from a limited playbook. There seemed to be only four basic home designs, and three exterior color choices, all in the brown family. The majority of the houses looked well kept, though there were a few whose owners seemed less adept at maintenance than others. The Pearson house fell firmly into this latter group, as did the Dodge Charger sitting in front of it.

Quinn drove by the high school the son attended. It looked like any other high school in the desert—a bunch of separate one-story buildings spread out over a large piece of land. The school was several miles away from the Pearsons' place.

Tell me, Nate. Why the interest in these people?

He called Orlando and told her what little he'd discovered. "You come up with anything on your end?" She had promised to take a deeper dive into the Pearsons while Quinn was traveling.

"Get this," she said. "Right after Jar helped Nate, Pearson withdrew his son from high school."

"For what reason?"

"Relocation."

"The house still looked occupied to me. And I didn't see any signs that they were getting ready to move."

"Not the whole family. Just the kid. Turns out the dad

transferred him to St. Bartholomew's in Maryland."

"St. Bart's?"

"Yep."

That was too coincidental. A few years earlier, Quinn and Nate had worked on a mission connected to the school. A St. Bart's alumni, employed by a corporation with close ties to the CIA, had given a guest lecture about the pride of choosing a career in intelligence. The irony was that the man had been selling secrets to more than one foreign government for years. The corporation he worked for had uncovered the deceit and wanted to clean up the mess before their CIA overlords found out.

An assassin had administered the drug that killed the man in his sleep, and Quinn and Nate had done cleanup. During their prep work, they had learned everything they needed to know about the town, the hotel, and the school, even taking a tour of St. Bart's the day before the lecture. Though neither Quinn or Nate would have wanted to attend there when they were younger, they both came away impressed not only by the beauty of the school, but by its high rate of graduation and college placement.

Late May was a weird time of year to be transferring to St. Bart's. The spring semester would be nearing an end, and the shorter summer program would still be a few weeks off.

"Did he get a scholarship?" he asked. The tuition costs at St. Bart's, if he remembered correctly, was similar to that of a private university. And if the Pearsons' house was any indication, they did not have that kind of money lying around.

"According to the admission notes, Samuel Pearson, Jr., was enrolled on a special-circumstances basis."

"What does that mean?"

"Beats me. That's all it said."

"What about the money?"

"A five-thousand-dollar deposit was made the day before the son arrived, and there's a payment of twenty grand due by June fifteenth."

"That's coming up quick. Does the family have that kind of cash?"

"Barely."

Quinn looked out at a patch of open desert. St. Bart's was open to anyone, but it had a reputation for taking in troubled kids and putting them on the right path. From the records, the son seemed to fit that bill. Had Nate befriended the family and suggested the move?

"You still there?" Orlando asked.

"Yeah, sorry. Just trying to figure out Nate's connection to all this. He's not related to the family, is he?"

"I couldn't find any connection."

Nate never really talked much about his family. Of course, that didn't mean Quinn and Orlando were ignorant of their friend's history. Quinn had done extensive research on Nate's background before recruiting him as his apprentice. When Orlando had joined the team, she became privy to that information.

"I guess I could go have a conversation with Pearson," Quinn said.

"I've got a better idea. I had Jar send me the exact times of the calls Nate made to her, and was able to cross-check those against the database of pay phone usage in the city."

"There's got to be a ton of pay phones in this city." Vegas was unique that way.

"True, but not as much as there used to be," she said. "And people don't use them that much anymore."

"Are you saying you know which phone he used?"

"Babe, who do you think you're talking to?"

THE PHONE WAS located in the back of a place called Lucky Lynn's Saloon and Gambling Hall. It was one of the smaller establishments, a bar and grill on one side and the casino on the other.

When Quinn walked in, about a dozen people were in the gaming room, spread out between slot machines and the two Black Jack tables. He looked around, as if searching for the right machine to plop in front of. Near the center of the room, he stopped next to a slot machine and sent Orlando a text.

Cameras inside and out. Footage?

He continued to the back of the room.

Five phones lined the wall opposite the entrances to the restrooms. Foot-and-a-half dividers stuck out between them, giving some semblance of privacy. According to Orlando, the phone number of the one Nate had used ended with 2502. Quinn went straight to the one farthest from the gambling area. Above the keypad, under a plastic covering, was the phone's number, which—surprise, surprise—ended in 2502.

He picked up the receiver and punched in Orlando's number.

"Cute," she said, answering.

Quinn looked around. "It's about as secluded as you can get in this place."

"Makes sense."

"You see my text?"

"Yeah. Working on it right now."

"Call me on my cell when you're done. I'm going for a walk."

He left the building through the nearest exit and crossed the parking area to the public sidewalk. There, he looked up and down the street. It was a mixed neighborhood of fast-food places, gas stations, cheap motels, and forgettable apartment buildings. Had Nate been staying at one of the nearby motels? Or had he driven here from somewhere else in the city?

Normally, Quinn would have thought the latter, but Nate hadn't been here on a job, at least not as far as Quinn knew, so it was possible he had chosen convenience over tradecraft.

He returned to Lucky Lynn's, this time entering the bar and grill, where he ordered a chicken Caesar salad and a Three Weavers Expatriate IPA. Orlando called back not long after he started eating.

"He was definitely there," she said.

"You found footage of him?"

"I did. I'm running a bot through the casino's stored footage to see if he showed up any other times besides the calls we know about."

"Was he alone?"

"Appeared to be."

"What about the exterior cameras? Did he leave in a car?"

"No car. He was on foot every time."

Quinn perked up. Perhaps Nate *had* been staying in the area. "Did you see which direction he went?"

"He always arrived from the north, and headed back that way when he left."

"Please tell me you tried tracking him from there."

"I just started. I've got him to the streetlight at the end of the block so far, and have a search underway for other cameras along the road."

"I'll head that way as soon as I finish eating. Feed me whatever you learn as soon as you have it."

"Will do."

Quinn polished off the rest of his salad and headed outside. At the intersection Orlando had mentioned were two gas stations, a McDonald's, and a place called the Dream Along Inn. Was that where Nate was staying?

The double buzz of a text.

> Continue north to 7-Eleven.

Orlando had obviously seen him on one of the cameras.

He waited for the green light and crossed the road. The 7-Eleven was two blocks down. By the time he reached it, a new text had come in.

> Left at the corner.
> One block to Peaches' Market.
> Cross to other side of the street.
> Down one more block to KFC.

Right before he reached the chicken place, Orlando called.

"I have him on archive footage going straight ahead for another block and a half. But then he moved into a dead zone and didn't come out the other side."

Quinn started walking again. "Any side streets he could have gone down?"

"None in that area."

"What about cars? Maybe that's where he'd left his car and drove off."

"Already checked. He was in none of the cars driving out of the area in either direction."

"For what time range?"

"I gave him a twenty-minute window from the moment he disappeared."

Quinn had the urge to hurry, sensing they were close, but he made himself keep to a normal, pedestrian pace. When he reached the point where Orlando lost Nate, he stopped and looked around.

"Looks like about seven apartment buildings per side," he said. "No houses or empty lots. No businesses, either. He must have gone into one of the buildings."

"You can eliminate the first three you passed, and the one ahead of you on the corner. I've got all of those on camera. Also, I don't think it would have made any sense for him to have crossed the street only to need to cross back."

"I agree. So that leaves me with three buildings." He checked the time. It was a little after seven p.m.

"I can check property records and see who owns each place," she said. "It's possible I might even be able to dig up tenant lists."

"Don't waste your time. This time at night, I'm betting I should be able to find managers at home."

A pause. "Quinn."

"Yeah?"

"If Nate's there... don't be—"

"I know I screwed up before. I'm not going to be an asshole."

"I wasn't going to say an *asshole*."

"Are you sure about that?"

"I swear. Of course, it's what I would have meant."

"I love you, babe."

"Love you, too."

Quinn started with the nearest building. A directory at the entrance pointed him to apartment 201. He found it on the second floor, a metal plaque reading MANAGER under the apartment number.

A woman with a high head of coiffed hair answered, wearing a bright red thigh-length robe and a look of impatience. "Yes?"

"Special Agent Marsh," Quinn said, flashing the FBI badge he'd brought for this purpose.

"FBI? I don't know what anyone told you, but I—"

"Ma'am, have you seen this man?" He showed her a picture of Nate on his phone.

It took her a few seconds to process the request. When she finally looked at the screen, she said, "What's he done?"

"Have you seen him, ma'am?"

She frowned. "I don't think so. Maybe."

"Maybe?"

"He looks a little familiar…I think."

"Could he be one of your tenants?"

She looked up, shocked. "Good God, no. I know all my people, and he is not one of them."

Quinn slipped the phone back in his pocket. "Do you remember where you may have seen him?"

"I'm not even sure I did."

Quinn pulled out one of the business cards he kept with the badge and handed it to her. The number on it would route a caller to Quinn's phone, with an alert informing him it was from his FBI line. "If you think of anything, just give me a call."

The manager of the next building, an old guy in shorts and a Hawaiian shirt, didn't recognize the picture at all.

Quinn walked down the sidewalk and turned into the last apartment building. If he struck out here, too, then maybe all Nate had done was pass through the buildings to the other side. Perhaps the place where he was staying was on the next road or the one after that. Or maybe *that* was where Nate had parked his car.

The new building was a bland box, with open-air walkways on each of its three floors, shaped like a squared-off oval around a swimming pool in bad need of a cleaning.

Like the other complexes, this one also had a directory, only whoever had been in charge of maintaining it had either lost interest or quit, as few of the apartment numbers had names beside them, and those that did were missing letters. The listing for apartment 106 read M NAG R.

Stuck to the door of 106 was a Post-it note.

<pre>
         AVAILABLE RENTAL IS
          OPEN FOR VIEWING
           UNTIL 8:00 P.M.
              APT 315
</pre>

Quinn located the stairs and went up, assuming that's where he'd find the manager.

The door to apartment 315 was wide open, light from inside spilling onto the walkway. Voices drifted out, a couple of young guys and an older one. Quinn paused at the threshold and looked inside. The small living room and a shotgun kitchen were both empty so he knocked on the door.

From a hallway to the right, the older voice called out, "Be with you in a minute. Have a look around."

Quinn stepped inside. The only real selling point was a large window that offered a fairly decent view. He was looking out from it when the others entered the main room.

"The washer and dryer are on the first floor," the older guy was saying. "Feel free to take a look on your way out."

"Thanks," one of the younger two said.

"And get that application back quick. We're going to make our decision this weekend."

"We will," the other said.

As the two prospective tenants left, Quinn turned to face the older man.

"Evening," the guy said. "I'm Paulie Wilkes, the manager. It's a one bedroom, one bath. Back of the building and top floor, can't get more private than that. Security deposit's two grand, and the rent is—"

"I'm not interested in the apartment, Mr. Wilkes." Quinn pulled out the badge and held it up. "Special Agent Marsh, FBI."

"Oh, um, what can I do for you?"

Quinn showed him the picture of Nate. "Have you ever seen this man?"

The manager had barely glanced at the photo when his face scrunched up. "You're kidding, right?"

"Why do you ask that? Are you saying you *have* seen him?"

"Of course I have. That's Kyle McManus. You're standing in what was his apartment until a couple weeks ago."

"Mr…McManus lived here?"

"Don't tell me you didn't already know that."

"You're sure this is him?" He held the phone out again.

Wilkes took another look. "Yeah, that's him. No question."

"And you say he moved out two weeks ago."

"Uh-huh. Did he do something? Is that why he left?"

"No, sir. We just need to talk to him. Nothing more."

Wilkes looked skeptical. "You sure he's not a hired killer or something like that? He was really quiet. Kept to himself."

"Sorry to disappoint you. Not a hired killer. Did he give you any notice that he was leaving?"

"Not beforehand. Just stuck a note under my door when he left."

"Would it be possible for me to see it?"

Wilkes became guarded. "I don't know. Don't you need a warrant for that kind of thing?"

"Do you have something to hide?"

"No, of course, not. It's just…it's a private letter."

"Which you can choose of your own volition to share with the FBI."

The man appeared to undergo some kind of internal struggle before saying, "Fine. It's downstairs."

"After you," Quinn said.

Wilkes stuck a BE RIGHT BACK note on the door and led Quinn down to apartment 106.

"It's in my office," the manager said, and disappeared into a hallway. When he returned he was holding a folded piece of paper, which, after a slight hesitation, he handed to Quinn.

Mr. Wilkes,

An unexpected personal matter has come up that I need to attend to immediately. This, unfortunately, means I am vacating my apartment. I realize that by leaving so suddenly I've put you in a difficult position. As compensation for my premature departure, please keep the security deposit and the remainder of the three months' advance payment I made.

I apologize for any inconvenience.

Kyle McManus

Quinn recognized Nate's handwriting. It was clear why Wilkes had been reluctant to share it. If he were able to find a new tenant right away, he could collect double rent for a while, probably pocket the excess without the property owners finding out.

"Did he leave anything else?" Quinn asked. "A forwarding address, perhaps?"

"Nope. Just that."

As Quinn read the letter again, he could sense Wilkes's discomfort increasing.

"Look," the manager said. "I'm just trying to make a living here. It ain't easy these—"

Quinn held up a hand. "How you run your business is up to you, Mr. Wilkes. My only concern is locating Kyle McManus."

"Oh. Okay. Good. I mean, I understand."

"What day did he leave?"

"Wednesday before last. Well, I guess he could have split late that Tuesday night. I found the note when I woke up on Wednesday."

"And what time was that?"

Wilkes grimaced and mumbled, "About ten, I guess."

Quinn folded the paper and slipped it into his pocket. "I'm going to hold on to this."

"Is that really necessary?"

"I'm afraid it is."

Wilks nodded slowly, as if convinced Quinn was going to hand it over to the IRS.

QUINN FILLED ORLANDO in on what he'd learned, and then drove to the Aria Hotel, where she had reserved him a room. He was toweling off after a shower when she called back.

"I was able to track Nate to a housing tract in Spring Valley," she said. "No cameras after that point so I couldn't see where he went, but thirty-five minutes later, he drove out in a Toyota Camry."

"Anyone with him?"

"Nope."

"Were you able to get a look at the plates?"

"Yeah. The car belongs to a woman named Lorena Cheng, who, it turns out, lives four blocks from where I lost Nate."

"Did he steal it?"

"No. He bought it."

"Bought it?"

"I checked LVPD for a stolen-vehicle report first, but none was filed. So I set up a search for anything connected to the car and Ms. Cheng. Got a hit on her phone number. She'd been advertising the car on Craigslist. No record of the sale at the DMV yet, though. Which tells me Nate left town pretty much right away and didn't bother filing the papers."

"You weren't able to determine where he went?"

"Lost him in another area where there weren't many cameras. I have a bot searching Department of Transportation footage, but there are a *lot* of Toyota Camrys out there. And if he did leave town, there are several ways he could have gone without being videotaped."

"So I guess I just hold here."

"At the moment."

They said their goodnights and though it was still relatively early, Quinn crawled into bed. In his line of work, he had to grab whatever sleep he could, when he could. This time, *whatever* turned out to be just over an hour.

He grabbed his buzzing phone off the nightstand and

answered with a sleepy, "Yeah?"

"I hope you're still packed," Orlando said. "I have you booked on a plane to Chicago in two hours."

CHAPTER TWELVE

ROME

CHRISTOPHE ST. AMAND had only one philosophy, political or otherwise: If it benefited him, he was all for it.

Like many arms dealers, he was more than happy to supply both sides of a conflict. The longer animosities could be stretched out, the more money flowing into his accounts. His old boss, Janus Sideropoulos, had not been as good at that business practice, and far too often cash had been left on the table.

Removing Sideropoulos had been easy. The old Greek had trusted St. Amand. A touch of something in the old man's coffee to knock him out, a long plunge off an empty stretch of cliffside road on the Italian coast, and that was that. A tragic accident. In the aftermath, while everyone was still trying to come to terms with Sideropoulos's death, St. Amand was quietly taking control of the operation.

In his first eighteen months in charge, he'd had to fend off several rivals who'd thought they could take advantage of the change in leadership to muscle in on St. Amand's territory. But St. Amand had been planning his ascension for over two years. Case in point was the largely Bulgarian security force he and his primary lieutenant, Drake, had pulled together long before Sideropoulos was removed. St. Amand's mother had been Bulgarian, and he had exploited that connection to recruit a team of men from her homeland loyal to him, who spoke a language few others did. It had taken years for Drake to become fluent enough to speak to them in more than a few basic sentences.

It was also during this transitional time that he saw the true power of his anonymity. The masks had been useful when he was a security man; there was nothing scarier to someone than a visit from the mysterious St. Amand. Now that he was in charge, his enigmatic persona raised him to mythological status.

Customers and competitors alike were curious and fearful of the faceless man, sentiments he was more than happy to stoke with carefully placed rumors. To further confuse everyone, he had employed several faux St. Amands over the years to show up wherever he wanted them to, wearing the same disguises he did. The thing he liked best about this was that it allowed him to appear at meetings sans disguise and pretend to be a trusted St. Amand advisor.

At the moment, he was sitting unmasked in his private control room, watching one of the favorite aspects of his work.

There were ten screens of monitors in two rows of five, mounted on a curved steel framework. St. Amand's chair sat at the center of the imaginary circle they created, allowing him to swivel and face whichever monitor he was interested in. On the desk in front of him were a touch-screen control pad and a gooseneck microphone.

All the screens were dark except the bottom center one, which showed a sun-dappled road surrounded by jungle. The sun was not yet out in Rome, as it was 3:13 a.m. The image was from Indonesia, where it was after nine in the morning.

From what he'd been told, the road was usually humming with cars and trucks at this time of day. But thanks to army roadblocks at either end, it was currently deserted. A good thing, given the giant tree that had been toppled across it by St. Amand's men.

"Convoy ETA five minutes forty seconds." The male voice from the speaker belonged to one of the strike-team members.

St. Amand touched the control pad and leaned into the

mic. "I'm still only receiving the feed for camera A."

"Tovar? What's the deal?" Salah's voice. He was leading the operation.

"Sorry, Mr. St. Amand," Tovar said. "We had a bad cable. It's being replaced." A pause. "You should have picture any second."

After a beat, the remaining nine monitors flared to life. The majority showed shadowy shots of the jungle. These were the body cams worn by six of the team members. The remaining three were stable shots, like that of camera A. Two had different angles of the same stretch of road as A, while the third showed a different part of the highway, a kilometer away.

St. Amand activated his microphone again. "It's working now."

For the next few minutes, nothing. Then the first voice said, "Convoy ETA two minutes fifteen seconds. Passing camera D in thirty seconds."

St. Amand focused on the appropriate feed. Right on time, the first convoy vehicle—an armored truck with a manned machine gun mounted on the back—drove through the frame. This was followed by four identical semi-trucks pulling enclosed trailers filled with goodies. And at the back, two more machine-gun trucks. While St. Amand wasn't above paying for his inventory, securing requested items for just the cost of manpower, and perhaps a little bribery, was always his preference.

Another minute passed.

"ETA forty-five seconds."

The weaving body cameras all grew still.

Over the speaker, St. Amand could hear the sound of engines, faint at first.

"Thirty seconds...fifteen."

The sounds were louder now, St. Amand's speakers vibrating from the rumble.

"Ten. Nine. Eight..."

Right as the count reached zero, the gun truck at the front rolled into view on cameras A, B, and C, and stopped a few meters short of the felled tree. The big rig directly behind it appeared next and slowed to a stop. The others followed suit.

The machine-gun operator on the lead truck swung his gun back and forth before leaning down and shouting something into the vehicle. The passenger door opened, and a soldier in an officer's uniform climbed out.

His gaze moved along the length of the toppled tree. If it had been sawed down, he would have ordered the trucks to back out of there, but Salah's men had worked long and hard to expose the tree's roots and pull it down so that it looked like a natural event. The officer walked up to the trunk for a closer look.

"Team three, go," Salah said.

Team three—five men, two with cams—snuck out from a bush-filled gully beside the road and crept up to the last truck in the convoy. The team's sharpshooter put a sound-suppressed bullet into the head of the soldier manning the machine gun.

As the soldier slumped forward, the other team members moved up to the cab, two on either side. Though the vehicle might be armor plated, the windows were not bulletproof, courtesy of the general in charge of procurement who'd lined his pockets with the money saved from cutting that corner. The two men in the cab were clearly aware of this flaw, as they raised their arms the second they saw the guns pointing at them.

The soldiers were quietly removed from the vehicle and escorted into the jungle. Two of Salah's men took the soldiers' place in the cab, while the sharpshooter climbed onto the back of the truck, shoved the dead gunner onto the floor, and assumed the man's spot.

"Team three in position," the man in the driver's seat announced.

"Copy, team three," Salah said. "Team two, go."

Team two's takedown of the other gun truck at the back went as smoothly as the first hijacking.

"Team two in position."

"Copy, team two. Team one, go."

St. Amand turned his attention to the body cams worn by team one.

As expected, the officer who'd gone to check the tree had

followed the trunk up the meter-and-a-half slope at that side of the road, to the upturned roots. This took the officer behind some brush, hiding him from his colleagues' view. None of them saw the bullet pierce the back of his head, sending him flopping face-first into the hole the roots had been in.

One of Salah's men knelt next to the officer and stripped him of his uniform. This was passed to another man roughly the same size as the dead officer. The man pulled the clothes on.

A few moments later, the faux officer reappeared on cameras A, B, and C and approached the lead truck from the side, to avoid being scrutinized too closely. The only one who had any chance of realizing the man was an impostor was the gunner in the back. But the soldier was focused on potential trouble from the jungle, not on his commander.

The impostor pulled the cab door open and climbed inside.

Though camera A had a view of the truck's windshield, the reflection of the jungle on the glass prevented St. Amand from seeing what was going on inside.

But clearly everything went as planned, as several seconds later the impostor announced, "Team one, interior cleared."

"Copy, team one," Salah said. "Remaining teams, go."

As the remaining teams moved in on the four big rigs, team one's sharpshooter took out the lead truck's gunner.

Less than a minute later, everyone had reported in, and Salah announced, "Convoy secure."

The soldiers who hadn't been killed were stripped of their uniforms and tied up a few hundred meters off the road, while the dead were dumped into the gully.

The convoy moved out, with Salah driving the lead big rig.

The rest would be academic. Once they passed the next checkpoint, they would continue on the route the convoy was supposed to take for another thirty minutes before diverting northwest for the coast.

Arrangements had been made for several fishing boats to ferry the surface-to-air missiles, rifles, and other weaponry from the convoy to one of St. Amand's ships off the coast. The government patrol that cruised those waters had been well compensated for avoiding that section of the sea until long after the transfer was complete.

St. Amand didn't hang around to watch any of this. The hijacking had been the highlight, everything else was logistics.

He left the control room and called Drake. "The missiles have been secured. How are we doing on those drones?"

CHAPTER
THIRTEEN

CHICAGO, ILLINOIS

THE PRIVATE JET put Quinn in Chicago before sunrise, where he found the Audi A4 Orlando had arranged for him in the short-term parking structure. The engine hummed to life with the push of a button, and he was on his way into the city by five a.m.

He called Orlando once he was clear of the airport. "So, where am I going?"

"I've sent the info to the car's nav system."

Quinn toggled the switch that brought up the map on the dash screen.

"I'm looking at a big red square," he said, glancing at a shaded area about seven blocks per side.

"He's inside there somewhere."

"You couldn't narrow it down a bit more?"

"Is that a serious question or are you being cranky because you didn't sleep well?"

"I love you."

"So you keep telling me."

Traffic was mostly light as he drove into the city, and soon he was on surface streets, cruising the perimeter of Orlando's red zone.

The area in question was one of those formerly rundown sections of a city just starting to experience its hipster invasion. One didn't have to look too hard through the graffiti-tagged brick buildings and occasional deserted lot to see signs of the coming rejuvenation.

Quinn began systematically working his way through the neighborhood, scanning the parked cars for Nate's gray Camry. But not only was it one of the most common vehicles around, gray was apparently its most common color. Each time he spotted a potential match, he'd slow and get a picture of the license plate. So far, none were from Nevada, but he'd been expecting that. Nate had been well trained, and there was a very good chance he'd changed the car's plates more than once since he left Vegas.

Quinn sent the pictures to Orlando for her to check the plates against DMV records, see if any was a mismatch.

He was getting close to the end of the north/south streets when Orlando called.

"Got something," she said. "Photo number eight. Plates are for a Honda, not a Camry." She read off the number.

Quinn determined the picture had been taken three streets back, toward the south end. He turned at the next intersection and headed back. He parked a block from the suspected vehicle and walked from there.

Even if the Camry was Nate's, Quinn knew the vehicle's current location did not necessarily mean Nate was staying in one of the nearby buildings. Parking in the area was at a premium, so the spot could have been the only one available and Nate could be blocks away.

Another possibility, one that Quinn did not want to think about, was that Nate had abandoned the car and was now thousands of miles away. Whatever the case, first order of business was to ascertain if the Camry was indeed the one Nate had purchased in Nevada.

When Quinn reached the corner of the street the Camry was parked on, he paused to scan it. Two people, way down at the other end of the block. One was climbing into a beat-up old Buick sedan. The other was a jogger.

Quinn waited for the sedan to drive away before he crossed the street and continued toward the Camry. A few cars away, he checked the street again, this time glancing at the windows that looked down on it. No one seemed to be watching him.

He activated the camera on his phone, stepped into the road, and walked along the driver's side of the cars parked at the curb, as if he was going to get into one. When he reached the Camry, he slowed just long enough to get a photo of the VIN at the lower edge of the windshield. Though it was possible to change this out, too, it was a much more complicated job. The easier choice would have been to pop it off and leave it off, if you were really afraid of the car being ID'd. Whoever had changed the plates on this vehicle had apparently thought the extra step unnecessary.

As Quinn moved on, he texted the picture to Orlando. Less than thirty seconds later, his phone vibrated.

Bingo

It was Nate's car. The big question was whether he was still around or had dumped it and moved on. But that was something for Orlando to answer. Meanwhile, Quinn had to assume Nate was still here.

Quinn strolled the streets in the vicinity of the car, trying to think like Nate and see things the way Nate would have. Two and a half blocks away, Quinn stopped and stared at an old, ratty sign clinging to the side of an old, ratty building across the street.

THE GRANT HOTEL
Daily•Weekly•Monthly

"You're probably thinking your best bet is a private residence," Quinn had told his then-apprentice when they discussed emergency places to hole up. "In general terms, it is. But the kind of places you'd need are rare. First off, they have to be easy to get in and out of without anyone knowing you're there. Abandoned places next to other abandoned places could work. I like places that are for sale that are well hidden from their neighbors by landscaping, that kind of stuff. I would only use something in a housing tract if I had no other choice."

"Because of neighbors," Nate had said.

"Exactly. They're not going to like people they don't know hanging out in their neighborhoods. This is especially true in smaller cities and towns."

"How about rich neighborhoods? You know, where everyone stays to themselves and you can't see one place from the other."

"Now you're thinking. The thing is, though, in most situations, that's not going to be an option. If you need to hide out in a big city, my first choice would be one of those weekly hotels where you can pay in cash. The seedier the better. If they insist on seeing an ID, get out. You'll find somewhere they'll take your money without asking questions."

"Couldn't I just use one of my fake IDs?"

"Only as a last resort. You'll usually only get one chance to use an ID. Don't burn it if you don't have to."

"Got it. So sleazebag, no-ID-necessary hotels. I'm guessing they won't have room service."

From where Quinn was standing, the Grant Hotel looked to be a shining example of the sleazebag, no-ID type.

Quinn knew he couldn't just walk in and ask about his friend. Places like the Grant didn't like questions. The moment Quinn started inquiring about Nate, the desk clerk would likely play dumb, say he didn't know who Quinn was talking about. And using the FBI badge would probably make matters even worse.

Quinn continued walking around, in case there were other such hotels in the area, but the Grant was the only one within easy walking distance of Nate's car.

He called Orlando.

"I found a flophouse called the Grant Hotel. Doubt they keep records but still worth a check."

"I'll see what I can find."

The morning work shuffle was moving into full swing, and more and more parking spaces were opening up as local residents headed off. Quinn moved the Audi into a recently vacated space a block from the hotel. It was close enough that he had a good view of the Grant's front door, but far enough away that he'd likely remain unnoticed by anyone coming or going.

He killed the engine and settled in to wait.

THE PREVIOUS EVENING, when Quinn had been searching for Nate in Vegas, Nate had gone out in search of dinner in Chicago. But, as seemed to be happening to him a lot since his self-imposed exile, he found himself confronted with someone else's troubles.

At a dimly lit street corner, a woman, probably in her early thirties, was yelling, "Where is he?" over and over at two tough-looking, Caucasian guys. The woman was dressed in blue scrubs and had her hair in a tight bun, while the guys sported T-shirts that showed off the tattoos running down their arms and up their necks.

"Why you asking me?" the skinnier of the two men said.

"I know you know! Where is he, Damon?"

"You're crazy, you know that? Just go home. Get out of here. You don't want to make me angry."

The bigger guy stepped between Damon and the woman, but she quickly moved around him and grabbed Damon's arm.

"He's just a kid! If you don't tell me where he is, I'll go to the cops!"

"Get your hand off me, bitch!" Damon said.

His friend grabbed the woman and pulled her away.

"You think you scare me?" Damon snorted. "You don't scare me."

"If Brian isn't home in thirty minutes, I *will* go to the cops. And I know you don't want me to do that."

In the blink of an eye, Damon whipped out a gun and pointed it at the woman's head. Nate's hand automatically shot to the underarm holster he wasn't wearing.

If Damon had expected the woman to be cowed by his weapon, he must've been disappointed. She held her ground and stared defiantly at him.

People other than Nate might have silently gone the other way, or blended into the shadows and waited for everything to play out. But even if he hadn't had Liz's voice in his head telling him to do something, Nate would have acted.

He continued walking toward them, loudly scraping his foot across the sidewalk.

The two men's heads swiveled in his direction. The woman continued staring at Damon. Nate kept his gaze focused ahead, as if he hadn't noticed the trio, while actually watching their every move through the corner of his eye.

Damon tucked the gun in his waistband and whispered something to the woman. He and the big guy began walking rapidly down the other street. Nate half expected the woman to go after them, but she remained where she was.

As Nate neared, he could see she was shaking. He considered crossing over to see if she was all right, but he sensed she wouldn't appreciate a stranger poking into her business so he walked on.

When he reached the next intersection, he stopped and looked back. The woman had crossed to his side of the street and was walking in the opposite direction.

His stomach growled. The sandwich shop he'd been heading for was on the next block.

Help her, Liz said.

Nate clenched his fists and grimaced, then sighed and turned to follow the woman.

Four blocks south of the Grant Hotel, she entered a six-story brick apartment building. Nate walked up to the door and found it opened with a gentle push, the latch missing.

A hum from the elevator to the right indicated it was in use. A door next to it read STAIRS. Nate pushed through the door and raced up to the second-floor landing, where he paused only long enough to confirm the elevator was still moving. He did the same at the third, and again at the fourth, at this last hearing the clank and screech of the elevator door opening one more floor up.

He hurried to the fifth and peeked into the corridor. The scrubs-wearing woman was walking away from him. When she reached the second to last door on her left, she pulled out a key and let herself in. Nate waited to make sure she didn't immediately come back out before he walked down to the door.

Apartment 508.

He could hear someone moving around inside, but no voices. Apparently Brian was not home yet.

Nate left the building the same way he came, and stopped at the mailbox in the downstairs lobby. Some of the boxes had names on them. Apartment 508 did not.

He looked around to make sure there were no cameras, then used a credit card to dislodge the box's useless lock. Inside were a credit card bill and two medical bills—one from a Dr. Winston, and one from Chicago Memorial Hospital. Stamped on the outside of the doctor's envelope were the words FINAL NOTICE. All were addressed to a Kristina King. He guessed the woman had forgotten all about checking her mail when she returned, or she didn't want to think about what might be waiting for her. Given what he'd found, he guessed the second possibility was closer to the truth.

He returned the credit card and the hospital bills to the box, but held on to the envelope from Dr. Winston.

Back in his hotel room, he filled the pot from the cheap coffee maker with water and turned on the heating function. When steam rose from it, he held the envelope in the vapors, letting it loosen the flap.

Dr. Winston's specialty was oncology. The bundle of papers his office had sent concerned treatment for someone named Nancy Olsted. Though Ms. Olsted's diagnosis wasn't mentioned, it was obvious from the treatments that she had been in pretty bad shape.

Payment on an outstanding balance of $94,578 was nine months overdue. Nate checked the treatment dates. The last had occurred over ten months ago. Had the woman switched doctors? And why were her bills coming to Kristina King?

Nate set the bill down and looked out the room's only window.

This wasn't his business. He should just leave it alone.

"Where is he?" the woman had said.

"He's just a kid," she had pleaded.

"Where is he?"

Liz smiled at him from nowhere, gentle and understanding. *You know what you need to do.*

Nate closed his eyes. "Crap."

Thirty minutes later, he took the L to an all-night Fed Ex Express in a nicer part of town, where he used one of their computers to get onto the internet.

The name Kristina King did not generate a lot of hits, but a few was all Nate needed. The most important link he found was to a monthly newsletter from a Chicago-area trade school, the date two years previous. An article mentioned the then upcoming graduating class of dental hygienists. It was a small group, thirty-five in all, and Kristina King had achieved the highest marks. The woman pictured was the same woman Nate had followed to apartment 508. The couple of lines in the article directly related to King read:

> *Kristina is a native of Chicago, and lives with her son and mother. She looks forward to helping people maintain healthy teeth.*

Playing the obvious hunch, Nate searched BRIAN KING. There were several hits, but none were plausible as Kristina King's son. He tried NANCY OLSTED. The top hit was a short obituary that had run in the *Chicago Sun-Times*.

> Nancy Olsted, 57, passed away peacefully on July 6 after a long battle with ovarian cancer. Born in Boston, Massachusetts, Olsted had moved to Chicago with her family as a teen. She is survived by her daughter, Kristina, and grandson, Brian. Services will be held July 11 at Kaufman Mortuary.

While there was still plenty of missing information, this is how Nate saw the situation: a single working mom crushed under the emotional and financial toll of taking care of her dying mother, losing control of her son due to the strain.

Liz's voice, *You know what you need to do.*

Alive or dead, she would never have wanted him to walk away from a situation like this.

He sat back, his gaze unfocused. What he needed to do was help Kristina get her son back, and not just in the physical sense. But to do that, he needed to know more about the Kings, and to learn who this Damon asshole was.

No time to do all that, Liz chided him.

"I know," he mumbled.

He didn't know Damon's last name, and the guy would require some legwork first, but Nate could handle the asshole. What he needed was help with the Kings, and he knew exactly whom to ask.

He found a pay phone in the lobby of the Renaissance Hotel.

"*Sawadee, ka*," Jar answered.

"*Sawadee, khrap.* It's Nate. I know I've been asking a lot from you lately, but I need your help again."

"What can I do for you?"

He gave her what he knew about Kristina King and her family. "I need as much as you can find out about them."

"I will see what I can find. You should call me back in no longer than one hour. I will be unavailable after that."

"Permanently?" he asked, surprised.

"For a day only."

"Oh, good. You had me worried there for a moment. I'll be sure to call back before then."

"Nate…" She fell silent.

"What is it?"

The dead air continued for a moment longer, then, "Do not be late."

"I won't."

He hung up and headed to the L.

TEN MINUTES EARLIER
BANGKOK, THAILAND

JAR CONTRACTED THE groundskeeper at the temple, who contacted Daeng, who called her back via video.

"I assume this is important," he said.

"If you assume it, why do you need to say it?"

He smiled. "What's up?"

She told him about her conversation with Orlando, the

new job, and the subsequent email containing information about the flight to Italy they had been booked on, leaving that afternoon.

"There's no way I can get back there in time."

"That's not true. A helicopter will get you there in plenty of time."

"I don't think the monks have one of those lying around."

"Of course they don't. Unless that was a joke. Was that a joke?"

"Yes, Jar. It was a joke."

"It was not funny. I have sent a helicopter to pick you up. It should be at the temple in the next few minutes."

"You sent one."

Helicopters were rare in Thailand, and mainly the purview of the military. The one flying toward Daeng was operated by the army. Jar had asked her former employer, Christine, to use her contacts to arrange it. Christine was fond of Jar and even more fond of Daeng, so it had not been a problem.

"You said it yourself," Jar replied. "It's the only way you'll get to Suvarnabhumi on time." Suvarnabhumi was Bangkok's international airport.

"I haven't agreed to do the job yet."

"Shall I get Quinn and Orlando on the phone, so you can tell them no right now?"

A pause, followed by a chuckle. "I'll grab my bag."

Before Jar could respond, her mobile phone rang. She looked at the screen and saw an American number. "Hold on."

She typed the number into her search engine, and discovered it was a pay phone in Chicago.

"I think it's Nate," she said. "I'll put him on speaker."

"Wait, I don't want to get in the middle of this."

"Then don't say anything." She tapped ACCEPT and turned on the speaker. "*Sawadee, ka.*"

"*Sawadee, khrap.*" It was Nate. "I know I've been asking a lot from you lately, but I need your help again."

She typed the names he gave her into a new file. What he was asking for should be fairly simple, but there was another problem. "I will see what I can find. You should call me back in no longer than one hour. I will be unavailable after that."

She braced herself, expecting him to ask why, which would open up the whole can of worms about Quinn and Orlando, but his only concern was how long she would be unreachable.

When he said he would get back to her within the time frame, she felt the urge to come clean about the fact Quinn and Orlando were looking for him.

"Nate."

In the video chat window on her computer, Daeng was shaking his head vehemently and mouthing *no*.

She balked.

"What is it?" Nate asked.

She took a beat. "Do not be late."

"I won't."

After she set the phone down, she said, "I should have told him."

"If you had, he would have run again. At some point, Quinn and Nate need to confront each other. Better it to happen sooner than later, don't you think?"

"Because they need him for the job?" Jar said cynically.

A kind smile graced Daeng's lips. "The job is merely the vessel for the voyage."

"You have spent too much time at the temple." She thought for a moment. "I still do not feel good about this."

"Good. You shouldn't. It means you're growing. We will make a real human being out of you yet."

"Never say that again."

Daeng laughed loudly enough to almost drown out the sound of a descending helicopter.

CHAPTER
FOURTEEN

NATE WALKED THE streets between Kristina King's apartment building and where he'd seen her confront Damon. He was looking for the invisible watchers. These were people living near or at the bottom of the social ladder, the permanent flophouse residents and the homeless. Though most of society didn't see them, they saw most of society and knew more secrets than anyone realized.

The trick was getting them to talk. Nate was in luck. Damon proved to be a popular topic. There were those whose eyes widened with fear at the mere mention of his name, but others were willing to spill a little.

Nate would start conversations on a totally different topic, like "where are the best places to find food" or "do you know a safe place to sleep," then ease into something along the lines of "I saw these two guys a few streets over and didn't like the look of them." This would lead to him giving a description of Damon and his buddies, which would then bring about the a-ha moments from his unknowing informants as they realized who he was asking about.

And from that would drop the nuggets.

"You don't want to mess with them. They'll kill you, man."

"If you need to get high, thems your guys."

"See this scar? Damon did that. I ain't done nothing to him. That son of a bitch is crazy."

And, "You talking about Damon Cruise and Joey Kettles."

"Those don't sound like real names," Nate said.

He was sitting in front of a boarded-up building with a guy who went by the name Max. Nate's conversation starter this time had been half a Subway sandwich and a can of Budweiser.

"They're not," Max said. "They both grew up in the neighborhood. Back then they was just Danny Hawthorne and Joey Brenner."

"They grew up around here?"

"Sure did. Them the same age as my sister. Go to school together. Mean bastards then, mean bastards now."

The burner phone Nate carried with him in case of emergencies buzzed with the alarm he'd set. It was time to contact Jar.

"Thanks, Max. I appreciate it." As Nate rose, he pulled out two twenties folded inside a one dollar bill and handed them to the man.

He headed to a pay phone a block over and made the call.

"Any luck?" he asked.

"You were right about Kristina King," Jar said. "She is a dental hygienist. Based on the number of paychecks she deposits, she splits her time between at least four different offices. Three of them keep their work schedules on their servers, and even without knowing the fourth, I can tell you she is working seven days a week."

That would help explain why Kristina was having problems with her son. She likely left early and came home late. "Do you know how long they've lived in their apartment?"

"Moved in a month after her mother died. Before that, they had been living in the mother's house. It was sold to help pay the medical bills but it was not enough. Medicine is very expensive in your country."

"No kidding. Anything on the son?"

"Up until last year he was an above-average student. He had to switch schools when they moved. According to the records at the new school, he has not been doing nearly as well. He also has made several visits to the headmaster's office—"

"We call it the principal's office here."

"Okay, principal's office. There is no record of this

happening at his previous school."

"Any trouble with the police?"

"I have found nothing."

Which, of course, didn't mean there hadn't been any.

Nate heard what sounded like a distant PA announcement over the phone. "Where are you?"

A pause. "Suvarnabhumi."

"Meeting someone or going somewhere?"

"Both, actually."

That explained why she'd given him a deadline to call back.

"How long until your flight?" he asked.

"Seventy-one minutes, if we leave on time." The exactness of her answer was Jar in a nutshell.

"Then you have time to do another search for me."

"I have no idea if I do or do not. It will depend on the search."

He told her what he knew about Danny Hawthorne, alias Damon Cruise. "In his case I'm sure there are police records. At the very least, if you can get me an address, that would be great."

"I cannot promise anything."

"I know that. When shall I call you back?"

NATE CONSIDERED APPROACHING a few more people about Cruise, but in the end decided to stay near the phone. When the twenty-minute deadline she'd given him was up, he called again.

"Hawthorne is not a good man," Jar said. "He has been arrested seventeen times, and convicted five times for mister…um…mister—"

"Misdemeanors."

"Yes, that is the word. Petty theft and minor assault. He had been charged with mister meaner eight other times, and felony five times, but it says on each that the 'charges have been dropped.' I take that to mean they…disappeared?"

"That's exactly what it means. If he's been arrested, then they must have an address for him."

"Several, actually."

Nate snatched a flyer off the ground, pulled out a pen. "Give them to me."

"They are on the police records which I have loaded onto the server."

"I appreciate that. The problem is, I'm not going to be able to get to them for a bit, so how about we do this the old-fashioned way?"

She read off the five addresses. When she finished, she said, "He does not seem like someone you should involve yourself with."

"I'm not going to ask him on a date, Jar."

"This is not what I mean. I think you should not—"

"I know what you mean. And I appreciate it. Is that everything?"

"I only had twenty minutes."

"I know. And you did great. Thank you."

"Be careful, Nate."

"I will. Have a safe trip."

"Thank you."

"Nate again?"

Jar jumped at Daeng's voice. She had not heard him walk up. "Yes," she said, and slipped her phone into her pocket.

"I've been thinking. You should probably tell Quinn you know where Nate is."

Jar stared at him in disbelief. "If I'm not supposed to tell Nate about Quinn's interest in him, then I shouldn't tell Quinn about Nate's whereabouts, either. You said it before, we shouldn't get in the middle of this."

"That's not exactly what I said."

Over the speaker came the announcement for the imminent boarding of their flight to Rome.

"I guess it's too late, anyway," he said.

Jar frowned. "That is not true. If I were going to call Quinn, there is still several minutes before we would have—"

"Jar. I was trying to give you a convenient excuse."

DAMON CRUISE DIDN'T appear to live at any of the five addresses.

Hispanic families lived at two of the locations. A third one led Nate to an empty lot. According to mailboxes in the lobby at the fourth address, the specified apartment was occupied by someone with the last name Krieger. When Nate walked by the door, no light shined from the peephole, nor did he see any lights through the windows when he went back outside to check.

Number five was two blocks away. It had no name on the mailbox, but when Nate approached the door, he heard a TV on inside so he knocked.

Feet shuffled to the door. The pinprick of light through the peephole disappeared as the occupant looked through the viewer.

"Yes?" an older-sounding woman said.

"I'm looking for Daniel Hawthorne. Is he home?"

"Sorry. No Daniel here."

"Really? This *is* apartment three thirty-one, isn't it?" Nate leaned back as if checking the number again.

"I don't know what to tell you. No Daniel."

"Must have given me the wrong address. Sorry to have disturbed you."

Maybe Damon had lived there once, but it sure sounded like the woman didn't know who he was.

Nate decided it was time to introduce himself to the kid's mother and try to pull a little information out of her about her son. He thought his best tact would be to play the part of a private investigator, looking for a kid from Brian's school who'd run away. Even if she didn't invite him in, he could ask a few questions at the door that might flow into a discussion about Brian.

As he approached her door, however, he heard two voices coming from the other side—Kristina's, angry and curt, and a young male voice, feisty and defiant.

Had Brian come home?

The problem is larger than that, Liz said. *And you know it.*

She was right. If the son was involved with this Damon creep, then his life could continue to spiral down the drain until the kid either ended up in jail or the morgue.

The discussion on the other side of the door never quite reached the yelling point, but it got close. "Bad influence," and "throwing your life away," and "I taught you better than this" were rebuffed by "is not," and "it's my life and I can do what I want with it," and "you're never around to teach me *anything*."

Then a door slammed and silence descended.

Now was not the time for a visit. Nate headed to the elevator, ready to call it a night. As he pushed the call button, a door opened behind him and the same male voice he'd heard in the Kings' apartment yelled, "Hold the elevator!"

Nate glanced over his shoulder and spotted Brian King jogging toward him, his face tense. The boy was big for his age, nearly six-foot, and lean like a toothpick.

When the elevator arrived, Nate entered and pressed the hold button until Brian hurried in.

"Thanks," the kid said.

Nate smiled and pressed the button for the lobby.

Brian stared at the doors the entire trip down, anxious to get off. This allowed Nate to take a good look at him. Though the boy was tall, he was still a kid—the baby face, the hunched shoulders, the invisible robe of teenage angst.

The moment the doors opened, the boy shot out and across the lobby, stopping only long enough to pull the front door open. Nate followed him outside and down the sidewalk.

Brian's shoulders shook as he walked, his breaths coming in audible staccato bursts. The fury from his argument with his mom had turned to tears.

The teenage years were the worst, Nate thought, and doubly so for a boy whose life had been uprooted and whose only parent was seldom around. It was little wonder Brian had started down the path of self-destruction.

Nate trailed the boy through the neighborhood. Though he employed all his tricks for remaining undetected, none proved necessary as the boy was lost in his own world and never realized Nate was there.

Seven blocks from his apartment building, Brian swung around another corner. Nate increased his speed, but by the time he got to the intersection, Brian was gone.

Nate cursed under his breath and scanned the road.

If Brian had sprinted, he might have made it to the end of the block, but only just. And there had been no reason for the kid to sprint. Nate, who made a living at things like this, was convinced the kid hadn't known he was being followed.

The buildings on either side of the street were a mix of standalone structures that appeared to be used by small industrial businesses. A few of the buildings had parking lots beside them.

Nate headed down the block, looking between the buildings and into the lots. There appeared to be an open area behind the properties, separating them from those on the next road over. The area was about half the size of a football field and filled with weeds.

No sign of Brian.

By the time Nate reached the end of the block, he admitted to himself he had lost the kid. He opened the map on his phone and placed a marker in the middle of the block. On a hunch, he checked his current location against the list of Damon's addresses. The closest was number three, and that was the empty lot, four blocks away.

There was one more thing he could do before he called it a night. After taking the L into the city again, he found a late-night coffeehouse with computers for rent, downloaded the files Jar had found, and transferred them to his phone.

Back at the hotel, he moved the files to his laptop, and then lay in bed studying Danny Hawthorne/Damon Cruise's police record. Fifteen minutes in, he smiled, and silently thanked Detective Kelvin Martinez of the Chicago Police Department for being so thorough in his record keeping.

Nate had found Damon's weak spot.

The next morning, he woke early and headed out on what would appear to be a normal morning jog.

CHAPTER
FIFTEEN

LONDON, UNITED KINGDOM

ST. AMAND AND HIS entourage boarded his private jet at dawn, and flew two and a half hours northwest to London. Today, Claudio Lazzari, St. Amand's preferred double, was with them, as St. Amand himself would be playing the part of his own fictitious advisor, Antonio Becker. While this meant he didn't have to wear the paraphernalia that usually covered his head, it did not mean he wasn't in disguise.

Today's look consisted of a black, shoulder-length wig, foundation makeup four shades darker than his skin tone, dark brown contacts, steel-rimmed sunglasses, and motion picture-grade cheek prosthetics that both altered the shape of his face and covered the scar by his eye.

The first appointment of the day was at nine a.m. local time, in an office building near the new Globe Theatre, with a man named Louis Rolland. Rolland represented a West African rebel leader nicknamed Le Taureau, or The Bull. Le Taureau had designs on creating a new nation out of parts of Mali and Burkina Faso and Côte d'Ivoire, and had already made serious inroads in that effort.

St. Amand, who—unbeknownst to Le Taureau or Rolland—already helped supply two of the countries they were fighting, was looking forward to playing both sides. No matter who ultimately came out on top, the victorious side would be indebted to him. And the more people in powerful positions who owed him, the more the world became his to play with.

The limo pulled into a covered parking area next to the meeting location. With a nod from St. Amand, Drake and four men, who had been traveling in one of the two SUVs trailing the limo, entered the structure.

St. Amand studied his double. "The scarf is low on the right."

Lazzari adjusted the scarf. "My apologies, Mr. St. Amand."

"Don't let it happen again." This was said matter-of-factly, but his meaning was clear. If there was another incident, the man would no longer have a job. And a double's job, as had been made clear from the beginning, was for life.

Soon, Drake reemerged from the building and opened the back door of the limo. "Everything's ready."

THE MEETING WENT exactly as planned, and an agreement was reached on a series of new shipments, the first of which would arrive by the end of the month.

Meeting number two was across the river in the financial district. There was no set time for their arrival, as the client didn't know they were coming.

The office building was on Dukes Place, not far from the Gherkin tower. St. Amand entered with Drake, Lazzari, and two of Drake's men, and took an elevator to the eighth floor.

A tasteful sign next to the client's office read: MURPHY & COX, LTD.

The woman sitting at the reception desk in the exquisitely decorated lobby looked up as they walked in. "Can I help you?"

"Which way to David Cox's office?" St. Amand said.

"Do you have an appointment?"

"My dear, we don't need an appointment."

The welcoming expression on her face dimmed ever so slightly. "I'm sorry, but Mr. Cox is very busy today. Perhaps we could set up a time for you to come back."

Drake leaned over the desk, and allowed his jacket to hang open enough to reveal the gun in the holster under his arm. "We will not be coming back later. We will see Mr. Cox now."

She swallowed hard, her hand moving slowly off the desk.

"Don't," St. Amand said.

"I'm sorry?"

"The button you were going to push. I wouldn't do that if I were you."

She jerked her hand back as if she'd touched a flame.

"Now, please show us to Mr. Cox's office."

She looked at St. Amand, then at Drake and the others. "Of…course." She stood. "This way."

She led them down a long corridor to a door with a nameplate reading KENNETH COX, and looked back at them.

"Open it," Drake said.

The receptionist licked her lips and did as ordered.

The room they entered was not Cox's actual office, but that of his assistant. The woman was at least two decades older than the receptionist, and sported a dour expression that appeared to be permanently etched on her face.

She looked up as they entered. "What's going on? Marna, who are these people?"

"They're, um, here to see Mr. Cox."

The older woman looked at the men. "Well, I'm sorry. Mr. Cox does not see anyone without an appointment." Clearly, she was *not* sorry. To the receptionist, she said, "You should not have—"

She stopped as St. Amand and the others strode past her desk, toward the door to the inner office.

"You can't go in there," she said, trying to get in front of them.

Drake shoved her sideways, propelling her into her desk chair. She yelped in pain, and Marna rushed over to help her.

"The button," the assistant said, waving at her desk. "Push the button!"

Marna moved toward the desk, but one of Drake's men grabbed her before she could get there.

A lockdown button, no doubt. More and more executives were installing them.

Drake opened the door and led the others into the room.

Cox, who had been sitting on a couch reading a stack of

papers, jumped up.

"What's this? You can't just come in here like this! Pamela! Pamela, why are these—" Then his face drained of blood. "Mr. St. Amand?"

Lazzari crossed his arms and stared at Cox, unmoving. The real St. Amand and Drake approached the couch.

"Mr. Cox, you remember me, don't you?" St. Amand said.

"You're Becker."

"That's right. Though I prefer Mr. Becker." St. Amand smiled while lowering himself into the padded leather chair next to the coffee table. "Please, have a seat."

When Cox didn't move, Drake moved over to the couch, sat down, and patted the cushion next to him.

With considerable reluctance, Cox took a seat. "So, um, what can I do for you gentlemen?"

St. Amand closed the office door and walked toward the couch. "Mr. St. Amand is concerned."

"Concerned? About what?"

"About our communication problems."

"I wasn't aware we had a communication problem."

"Then you're saying there's been a banking error?"

"I'm sorry?"

"If there is no communication problem, then the only reason we haven't received the final payment for our last shipment to Oklahoma has to be a banking error, correct?"

Cox had been the broker who connected St. Amand to William Sandstrom and his ultraradical American militia network, which included Jackson Reed's Oklahoma organization.

"I, um, I meant to call you. There's been a…complication."

"What kind of complication?"

"Well, uh…see, the FBI raided Reed's compound. They confiscated his entire cache."

St. Amand looked at Drake.

"There has been nothing in the news," Drake said.

"I was informed by one of my contacts not long after it happened," Cox said. "So far the FBI's kept a lid on it."

"But you've known for, what? A few days?" St. Amand asked.

"Um, I would say more like a day, a day and a half at most."

"For a day and a half, then, and you didn't think it necessary to share this information with us?"

"Like I said. I was going to call you, but…it's a delicate matter. I wanted to gather more information first. Besides, there's nothing to be done."

"Nothing to be done? What about protecting ourselves from the potential exposure?"

The fear in Cox's eyes ratcheted up several notches. "There's no reason for you to be concerned at all. My-my-my contact said the search for the source of the weapons has reached a dead end. They can't find you. Your connection is well hidden."

"Is that so?"

"Yes. Definitely so. Definitely."

Cox was probably right on that point. Like everything else St. Amand did, the deliveries to the Americans were masked by a winding trail of fake companies nestled within other fake companies. A roadmap few, if any, could ever untangle.

"You had better hope you are correct." St. Amand stood. "If you would give me a moment, please."

"Um, okay. Sure."

St. Amand walked over to his double and pretended to speak quietly to him. Lazzari moved his head like he was listening. After several moments, St. Amand whispered, "Respond, five seconds."

Lazzari leaned his mouth up to St. Amand's ear and mumbled nonsense for the prescribed interval.

After he finished, St. Amand nodded and returned to the sitting area but remained on his feet. "Mr. St. Amand would like you to inform Mr. Sandstrom that the deals we had in place are terminated."

"What? No. You can't do that. We have an agreement."

"Had an agreement. What you have now is the FBI breathing down your client's neck."

"Wait. Please. Can't we talk about this?"

"There's nothing to discuss. You're not paying us nearly enough to compensate for the potential trouble our working together could bring us."

"If it's about money, let me talk to Mr. Sandstrom. I'm sure we can reach an accommodation you'll be happy with."

This was what St. Amand had been waiting for. Another desperate client who would be even more beholden to him in the future. Sure, there were risks, but St. Amand had been operating for years without any problems, and he didn't expect that to change now.

He walked over to Lazzari and exchanged more whispers, then said, "If Mr. Sandstrom is willing to discuss a change to the terms, Mr. St. Amand would be willing to meet with him in person tomorrow evening in Rome."

"Tomorrow evening? I don't know his schedule. He may not be able to make himself available that quickly."

"Then I guess our business together is complete."

St. Amand nodded at Drake, who stood, and the two men headed toward the door.

Cox jumped up. "No, wait. He'll, um, he'll be there. We both will."

St. Amand turned back. "No, Mr. Cox. You will stay here. Mr. St. Amand will meet with Mr. Sandstrom alone. No middle men. Or there will be no meeting at all."

Putting on as brave a face as he could, Cox said, "I'll let Mr. Sandstrom know."

CHAPTER SIXTEEN

CHICAGO

ACCORDING TO THE police report, Danny Hawthorne, aka Damon Cruise, had been arrested at the age of nineteen for possession with intent to sell. Due to a deal with the city attorney, Cruise's charges had been dropped in exchange for him giving up the name of his supplier. In the file, Detective Martinez had noted that Cruise had agreed to move in with his aunt until the trial was over, and to make himself available for more questioning if necessary. Once the verdict was read, his arrest would be expunged.

The item of most interest to Nate was the address Martinez had listed for the aunt, one Katarina Malinowski. It had not been on the list of Cruise's potential residences.

Nate found a pay phone near the apartment building and called the number in the report, wanting to see if the aunt was still at the same address. When a younger, male voice answered, "Hello," Nate wondered if Katarina Malinowski was another dead end.

"Good morning," Nate said. "My name is Tim Foster from Central One Bank. May I speak to Katarina Malinowski, please?"

"We're not interested."

"I'm not selling anything. I'm calling about some questionable activity on her account. Is she home?"

"Where did you say you were from?"

Nate grinned. He'd now heard enough to know the voice belonged to Damon Cruise. "Central One Bank. It's about her Visa card."

"Well, she ain't here. Call back later."

As Nate started to say, "Thank you," Cruise hung up.

It took Nate eight minutes to jog from the Grant Hotel to the block Katarina Malinowski's building was on, and another six to find a concealed spot from where he could watch the entrance.

For three hours, he watched residents leaving for work or school, with no sign of Cruise. Then, at 9:17 a.m., the front door swung open and there he was.

Nate let him get halfway down the block before he started to follow.

It was interesting, though not particularly surprising, that Cruise headed toward the same area Brian King had disappeared into the previous evening. Nate wasn't about to make the same mistake, and stayed close enough to see Cruise turn into one of the deserted parking lots.

From the corner, he watched Cruise cross the empty field behind the parking area to the back of an abandoned building on the next street over, and enter through the rear door.

Nate gave it a few minutes, then made his way around the edge of the field to the structure. The windows on the first two floors were all boarded up, while those on the upper three floors were broken or painted over or covered in grime or all the above.

Nate walked around the building to get a better sense of it. The only obvious way in was through the door Cruise had used. All the others, including the main entrance street side, were covered with plywood, like the windows. He did discover a not-so-obvious entrance on the side of the building, where another sheet of plywood hid a set of concrete stairs that led to a basement door.

Before he went through it, he needed to gear up.

QUINN WAS NOTHING if not a patient man. It was a requirement in his profession. Getting rid of bodies for a living often entailed waiting for the target in question to stop breathing, a timeline that did not always follow a plan. But this morning, as he sat in his car, watching the Grant Hotel for signs of Nate, he felt antsy.

The split between him and Nate weighed heavily on him. It was his fault. When Liz died, he had all but verbally blamed Nate. And then, when Nate was about to put down the woman who had shot Liz, Quinn had stopped him. It had been the right decision, but it was far from a satisfactory resolution for Nate.

And for Quinn.

He knew their coming encounter would not be an easy one, so he wanted to get it over with. He considered walking into the hotel and knocking on doors until he found Nate. But no matter which way he played it through in his mind, the meeting always ended with Nate slamming the door in Quinn's face. Better to approach him someplace public, where neither of them would want to make a scene. That, at least, would give them a chance at a conversation, however awkward it might be.

Quinn's stomach growled, reminding him he hadn't had breakfast yet. He grabbed his backpack off the passenger seat and rummaged around for the granola bars he kept in the front section. His hand had just encircled the foil wrapper when he noticed a jogger heading down the street, tucked up against the parked cars. The person was wearing identical clothes to the jogger Quinn had seen when he first arrived. It couldn't be the same person, though. It would have meant he'd been running for hours.

Quinn raised his camera and zoomed in on the jogger.

Well, I'll be damned.

It was Nate.

But he looked almost fresh, not like he'd been running the whole time. So what the hell had he been doing?

Quinn reached for the door handle but stopped himself. He would have to sprint to reach his partner before Nate arrived at the hotel. No way Nate would miss that. And as soon as he realized it was Quinn, he'd likely disappear into the building and Quinn might never find him again.

He let go of the handle and shot off a text to Orlando.

> He's definitely staying at the Grant.

Her response came almost immediately:

> You talked to him?

Quinn tapped the keyboard.

> Not yet.

He watched his friend enter the hotel, hoping it would not be long before he reappeared.

NATE TOOK A quick shower, pulled on a black T-shirt and jeans, and loaded his backpack with the items he thought he might need. He wished he could include plenty of other things, but the tools he'd been traveling with were limited.

The same four people who'd been in the small lobby when he returned earlier were still there when he left. Only the old woman with the cigarette-wrinkled face glanced at him. The others apparently couldn't care less.

The moment he reached the sidewalk, the back of his neck tingled, like it often did in dangerous situations. He stopped and scanned the street, wondering if Cruise or one of his friends had seen him snooping around and followed him back. But the few people he saw didn't set off any alarms.

He shoved the feeling into a mental box and started walking.

QUINN WAS SURPRISED when Nate came back out in less than fifteen minutes. His clothes were changed, and his hair damp. He was carrying a backpack over his shoulder.

Before Quinn could make any guesses as to where his friend was going, Nate stopped and looked around. Quinn was already sitting only high enough to peer over the dash, so slipping the rest of the way out of sight was simple and quick. He grabbed his phone, switched on the camera, and raised it just above the dash.

Nate was slowly turning his head, taking in the neighborhood. After a few seconds, his eyes passed over Quinn's car without pausing. Finally, he headed down the street in the same direction he'd come from earlier.

Quinn scooted back up, grabbed his own backpack, and exited the sedan.

Following Nate would be tricky. Quinn had trained him to be cautious, so even the slightest misstep could result in Quinn being discovered. Fortunately, he didn't need to do this on his own.

He donned his wireless earpiece and called Orlando. "Nate's on the move. I need you to help me tail him."

"Where is he now?"

"Approximately a block east of me," he said, knowing she likely had the location of his phone pinging on her screen.

"Hold on."

Quinn crossed over to the same side of the street Nate was on.

"He's still a block ahead of you?" Orlando asked.

"Yes."

"Then he's in a dark zone. If he keeps going straight, I should be able to get him on a traffic camera at the next intersection, though."

Nate continued down the street, walking casually but slightly faster than his normal pace.

What are you up to?

"Got him," Orlando said a few seconds later. "Depending on which way he goes, I should be able to track him for at least a few blocks."

Quinn eased back a bit.

Nate continued to the next intersection and turned right.

"We still good?" Quinn asked.

"Yep," Orlando said. "Don't fall too far behind, though. There are some dead zones coming up."

Quinn picked up his pace until he neared the intersection. "Am I clear to turn?"

"Yeah, go ahead. He'll be about three quarters of a block

away from you, on the other side of the street."

Quinn crossed the road before turning, so that they were on the same side. Two blocks up and one over, Nate crossed the road again and entered a new dead zone.

Quinn remained where he was for now, not wanting to draw unwanted attention.

Ahead a light turned green and a group of vehicles moved in Quinn's direction. Among them were a couple of delivery trucks. Quinn checked the other way, hoping for a break in traffic that would allow him to cross before the trucks blocked his view, but he was out of luck.

"I'm about to have a line-of-sight issue," he whispered.

"I'm on the camera at the traffic light," Orlando said. "I can't see him yet, but he should be coming into view any second."

Just as she said that, the first truck moved between Quinn and Nate.

"I don't have eyes on him," he said.

"Okay…I see movement about where he should…yeah, that's him."

Quinn let out a sigh of relief as the second truck moved into blocking position.

"Dammit," Orlando said. "Get to the other side. Now!"

"What is it?" he asked as he looked for an opening in the traffic.

"Nate just disappeared between a couple of buildings, and there are no cameras back there. I don't have him."

So much for worrying about horns.

Quinn ran into the road as the second truck passed, and zigzagged through traffic to the opposite sidewalk.

"Which way?" he asked.

"Head the way he was going. When you're at the spot, I'll tell you."

"There!" Orlando shouted as he came abreast of a neglected parking area.

He skidded to a stop and looked into the lot. "I don't see him."

"That's where he went."

Quinn moved cautiously along the building at the near side of the parking area, and paused when he reached the back corner. Behind the lot was a large field, at the end of which were buildings on the next street.

He was about to step into the field when he spotted Nate moving along the back of an abandoned-looking building, directly opposite the parking lot.

"I see him," he said, and described the building to help her ID it on a satellite image. "Wait, he just disappeared around the side, heading toward the other street."

"The building's in a dark spot," Orlando said. "But there are covered areas nearby. I should be able to pick him up again in a few moments."

Though Quinn wanted to rush across the field, he took a circuitous route along the edge of the clearing so he'd be less exposed, and came at the building from the opposite end of where Nate turned down.

"Anything yet?" he whispered into his mic.

"No," she replied, her tone worried.

He eased along the back of the building to the corner where he'd last seen Nate. He attached the gooseneck camera to his phone and slipped it around the edge. A twenty-foot gap filled with ratty, knee-high grass separated the building from the one next to it. Scattered along it were piles of debris, including what looked like an old air conditioning unit, lying on its side.

"He's not here," Quinn said.

"He hasn't shown on any of the cameras yet, either."

The only possibility left was directly in front of the building.

Staying in a crouch, Quinn moved down the gap to the front corner, and used the gooseneck camera to take a look street side.

"We have a problem," he whispered. "He's not in front of the building, either."

"Could he have gone around to the other side?"

Quinn frowned. "Maybe, but if that's where he wanted to go, he would have turned down that side in the first place. It's worth a check, though."

Concerned he'd be too exposed if he crossed in front of the building, he began retracing his steps to the back. Halfway there, his attention was drawn to a sheet of plywood he'd written off earlier as more debris. The thing was, the plywood was sitting on a concrete platform.

He slipped two fingers under the sheet and lifted it a few inches. Not a platform. The outer housing of a concrete stairwell. He raised the board higher, allowing more light to flow in. Not only was there a door at the bottom, but there were faint, partial footprints on the steps.

"I think he might have gone into the building," Quinn told Orlando.

"Why would he do that?"

"Hell if I know. Why did he come to Chicago in the first place? And what about the Pearsons in Las Vegas?"

He lifted the plywood out of the way and leaned it against the side of the building. He shined his flashlight on the nearest footprint. Though it was only half a shoe, there was enough of the pattern for him to recognize it.

"I've got prints here for Columbia running shoes. Bajada trail runners, I believe." Knowing this kind of thing was part of the continuous homework he did for his job. "Can you tell what kind of shoes Nate was wearing?"

"Give me a moment," she said.

While he waited for her, he descended the stairs and checked the door. It was unlocked.

He pressed his ear against it but didn't hear anything, so he pushed it open enough to stick his head inside. An empty room, about five feet square, with a dirt-covered floor and another doorway opposite his position. In addition to light indentations in the dirt that might be prints, there was an area of much thinner dirt, where most of the soil had been scraped away when the door had been opened. But not by Quinn, because the scraped section went farther than he'd pushed the door.

"Found a halfway decent shot of Nate's feet," Orlando said. "He's wearing Columbias."

"I'm going in."

TWICE ON THE trip to Cruise's building, Nate had felt he was being watched. The first time he checked, he saw a few people on the street, but no one he would have associated with Cruise.

The second time was right before he turned off the road toward the field behind Cruise's building. He'd looked around again—cars and trucks but no pedestrians.

He reached the plywood-covered basement stairwell a minute later. Flashlight in hand, he slipped underneath and descended to the door. The deadbolt was a little sticky, but he managed to work it free. A buildup of dirt on the floor provided some resistance as he pushed the door open. This told him no one had used the entrance in a long time.

Cupping his hand over his flashlight, he navigated through a small entrance room to a large, open area that he guessed took up the bulk of the basement. Though he walked as deftly as possible, he was well aware he wouldn't make it across the space without leaving some trace of his presence. There was too much dirt. If he felt it necessary, he could brush away any prints he left behind when he went back out.

From the big room, he moved into a long corridor, and found a set of stairs next to a pair of empty elevator shafts.

He took a few steps up the stairs and crouched there, ear cocked upward.

He could hear people moving around. Voices, too, and laughs. The noises were distant, either somewhere on the ground level far from the stairwell, or, more likely, from one of the upper floors.

He went back down to the elevator shafts. The one on the right still had an old metal door blocking most of the opening, but the one on the left was missing its door. He looked inside.

The only thing dividing the two shafts was what remained of the metal framing that had supported the elevator cars. A glance downward revealed the shaft continued for another four feet or so, to a concrete pad littered with trash. Above, the shaft was open all the way to the roof. *Almost* all the way, as here and there metal pipes and wooden boards protruded from the walls. There were two doors on each floor, one per shaft. The doors on the first three floors appeared to be intact, but at least one was missing from the fourth and fifth floors, the gaps allowing a little sunlight in.

He grabbed one of the support structure's crossbeams and gave it a gentle tug. The frame moved a bit but felt like it was still a few years from complete collapse. Nate didn't have a clear plan in mind just yet, but if he decided to take action, he knew the element of surprise would be key. So, instead of using the stairs, he swung into the shaft and began to climb.

He paused at each floor to check for the sounds. The higher he went, the louder they grew. Right below the open doors of the fourth floor, his path was blocked by a thick lead pipe that had fallen and become lodged precariously in the support frame. One bump and he was sure the pipe would crash to the bottom. With great care, he twisted around the obstruction, barely taking a breath until he was clear.

The voices were still coming from above. As he neared the fifth floor, he knew he had finally reached his destination.

He worked his way horizontally around the frame to get behind the elevator doors that were still intact, and peek through the slit down the middle.

Mattresses were scattered haphazardly throughout the space, and sprawled upon them were several men and women, some asleep, some in what Nate guessed were drug-induced trips. He didn't see Brian, so hopefully the boy had returned home. Cruise wasn't visible, either, but Nate could hear his voice, somewhere off to the right. The punk was cracking jokes with a few other guys, who laughed hysterically at every punchline whether it was funny or not.

Nate was looking at a drug den, with Cruise and his lackeys the den leaders.

Nate scooted to the back of the shaft until he could see the rest of the floor through the doorless side, and there was Cruise, surrounded by four guys around his age. On a portable card table next to them were a camp stove, small baggies filled with white powder, and at least twenty syringes lined up in a row, ready for use.

Perfect, Nate thought. He wouldn't even need to get his hands dirty. All he had to do was take a handful of covert photos and send them in an anonymous email to the police, with the building's address and the message that the party was in full swing. Cc: the FBI drug task force and the police would jump into action. Nate could then sit across the street and watch the show unfold.

He anchored himself and began snapping pictures. When he'd taken all he could from that angle, he moved around to get a good view of the mattresses. A girl on one of the closer bedrolls flopped onto her side and noticed him. She smiled and started to wave at him. Nate raised a finger to his mouth, and she clumsily started to mimic him, but then her head lolled back and her eyelids slid shut. When she didn't move again, he continued his documentation work.

After he had everything he needed, he moved back around so that he was hidden by the closed door, and composed the email. In addition to the general police address and the FBI's, he included the email addresses for Detective Martinez and the chief of police. In an hour, if not sooner, the building should be crawling with cops.

As he slipped his phone back into his pocket, he heard steps running up the stairs. One person, by the sound of it.

A few seconds later, Cruise said, "About fucking time! What took you so long? I'm starving."

"Sorry. They were busy." The new voice was younger and male.

"Give me that."

As the smell of hamburgers wafted into the shaft, Nate moved back around to where he could see Cruise and his friends.

The pit of his stomach clenched.

Standing with the older guys and holding several fast-food bags was Brian King.

So much for not getting my hands dirty.

QUINN MOVED THROUGH the basement, into a wide corridor, and over to where stairs led up to the ground floor. Before he placed a foot on them, he heard voices coming from inside the elevator shafts.

One of the big lessons his mentor, Durrie, had taught him, and he had subsequently taught Nate, was to, whenever possible, never leave anything of concern unchecked.

He crept over to the shaft and peered in.

The voices seemed to come from an open door on one of the upper floors. But the noise was not the most interesting thing about the shaft. That honor fell to Nate, who was two and a half floors up and heading higher.

Quinn dismissed the idea of climbing up after him. Whatever Nate was up to, Quinn didn't want to throw a wrench into it. At least not until he knew what it was first. The best thing he could do would be to position himself someplace from where he could offer aid if necessary, but otherwise stay out of sight.

He used the gooseneck camera to keep tabs on Nate's climb. When it became apparent the destination was the top floor, Quinn decided to get as high in the building as he could without anyone knowing.

He crept up the stairs to the first floor. Many of the walls were gone, creating a pillar-strewn open area from front to back and side to side.

Quinn was moving to the next flight when the door at the back of the building swung open in a splash of bright light.

He hustled back to the basement stairs.

The streak of light cutting across the room above the stairwell winked out as the door shut, plunging the first floor back into perpetual twilight. Upon hearing the new arrival walking rapidly in his direction, Quinn moved to the bottom of the stairs, ready to reposition deeper in the basement if necessary. But a few seconds later, the person headed up the stairs.

Quinn climbed back to the first level, arriving in time to see a pair of legs and youthful-looking sneakers. A younger man, Quinn guessed, maybe a teen. Using the guy's clunky steps as cover, Quinn started up the stairs.

Within only a few steps, he found himself engulfed in an

odorous cloud of greasy french fries and hamburgers. Ahead of him, the delivery boy kept going to the third floor, then fourth, and finally the fifth.

Quinn halted on floor four. The voices he'd heard were clearly coming from one level above and he had no desire to crash the party.

In addition to the aroma of burgers and fries, there was a new smell here, a mix of vinegar and something…medical. Since it had been a while since he last came across the odor, it took him a moment to place it.

Heroin.

Nate had been in a bad place for a while, but Quinn knew he wouldn't stoop to taking drugs. Besides, if he was here to buy, he'd be using the stairs. Was he attempting to take the place down?

Quinn looked over at the elevator shafts. Both doors on this floor were missing.

The drug trade, especially at the user level, was a messy, unpredictable business. Whatever Nate was planning, Quinn guessed it would be better if he didn't act alone.

He headed toward the shafts, thinking it was time for them to have a talk. But he made it only halfway there when something plummeted past the opening.

A fraction of a second later, the building shook with a loud crash.

CHAPTER
SEVENTEEN

NATE'S PLAN, IN its most basic terms, had been to keep Brian King from getting arrested on drug charges while he was still a kid. But now the cops were on the way and the boy was here.

Dammit.

Nate needed to get Brian out of there before the cops showed up. He needed a distraction. Fast.

He had the perfect one below him.

He climbed to the very top of the shaft, grabbed one of the many loose boards in the rafters, and, after taking aim, dropped it straight down. At first, it appeared as if the board was going to miss its target, but then the top end scraped against the lead pipe he'd contorted around earlier, breaking the pipe free and sending it tumbling down, banging and crashing all the way.

Several heads poked through the fifth-floor opening and looked down.

Nate had chosen a position in which it would have been very difficult for the men to see him if they looked up, but none did.

"Whoa!" one said.

"What the hell was that?"

"The goddamn building's falling apart!"

"Should we get out of here?"

"T-Boy, Brian, you stay here and keep everyone happy," Cruise said. "The rest of you come with me."

As soon as Cruise headed down the stairs, Nate climbed back to the fifth-floor doorway and peeked out. At the very edge of his view, he could see the profile of the man Cruise left behind, presumably T-Boy. Brian was not in sight, but he had to be there somewhere.

Nate eased over to the short expanse of wall between the two doorways and glanced around the edge. There was Brian, standing near the card table. Unfortunately, he was facing the elevators, and from the way his eyes widened, there was no question he'd seen Nate.

As the kid started to open his mouth, Nate swung into the room.

"T-Boy!" Brian called.

T-Boy looked at him. "What?"

Brian pointed toward Nate, but by the time T-Boy twisted around, Nate was only a few feet away.

"How you doing?" Nate said.

"What the fuck?"

T-Boy started to take a step backward and grab for the weapon tucked into the back of his pants. Nate smacked his palm into the bottom of the guy's jaw, preventing either of T-Boy's goals from being achieved.

As T-Boy swayed from the blow, Nate threw another punch into the side of the guy's head. T-Boy crumpled to the ground, moaning. In an instant, Nate was on him again, his arm wrapped around the guy's neck.

While he waited for the guy to lose consciousness, Nate glanced over at Brian.

Brian wasn't there.

QUINN HEARD THE men on the floor above him talking in the shaft doorway, and knew he had only seconds to hide before they came his way.

He moved behind the remains of a wall and pressed against it.

Feet pounded down the stairs onto the fourth floor, and continued down without slowing. As he peeked around the wall to make sure they were all gone, he heard the boy say something upstairs. Another voice spoke up, and then Nate's voice, followed by the sounds of a quick and decisive fight.

At the same time, someone ran across the upper room and onto the stairs.

He or she was undoubtedly heading down to warn the others.

Quinn hurried toward the stairs, reaching them as the runner turned onto the flight of stairs to the fourth floor. It was the delivery boy.

The kid was so intent on getting away that he didn't notice Quinn until he was almost on him. He tried to juke past Quinn but his momentum betrayed him, taking him right into Quinn's arm. Quinn locked it tight to the kid's chest and slapped a hand over the boy's mouth.

The kid struggled and screamed into Quinn's palm, but he had no chance of breaking free.

From above, Quinn heard someone else running toward the stairs. He lifted the kid off his feet and carried him behind one of the pillars.

THE MOMENT T-BOY passed out, Nate released his grip, grabbed the asshole's gun, and ran to the stairs.

He took the steps two at a time, hit the fourth floor, and turned toward the next downward flight.

"Nate!"

Nate jammed to a stop. For a full second, he thought he was seeing things.

"Quinn? What the hell are you doing here?"

His former mentor was holding on to Brian, the boy struggling in vain.

"I could ask you the same thing."

Nate could hear the faint sound of a siren. If it was heading in their direction, then the police were responding even faster than he'd hoped.

"We can talk about it later," Nate said. "We need to get out of here."

Quinn nodded at Brian "What do you want me to do with him?"

"He's coming with us."

Quinn raised an eyebrow but didn't ask anything else.

Nate held the gun so that Brian could see it. "My friend's going to take his hand off your mouth and you're going to stay silent. Understand?"

Brian nodded, his eyes wide.

When Quinn removed his hand, the boy kept his lips shut.

"Is there any other way down besides the stairs or the elevator shaft?" Quinn asked.

"I don't know. I've only been here a couple times."

"The stairs it is, then."

They reached the third floor and were descending to the second when they heard Cruise and his entourage coming up from the basement. On the second floor, Quinn, Nate, and Brian snuck into an alcove near the outer wall. Quinn put his hand over Brian's mouth again. Nate was pretty sure the kid wouldn't say anything, but it was the right move.

They waited until Cruise and the others had passed the second floor and were on the third before continuing down. The sirens were still several blocks away, but growing louder and more numerous.

When they reached the first floor, Nate headed straight for the back door. Though it was more exposed than the basement entrance at the side of the building, it would get them outside faster.

He paused upon reaching it to peek outside. With the coast clear, he led Quinn and Brian out.

Sirens blared.

"We have to hurry," Nate said.

"Sorry, kid," Quinn said to Brian, and threw the boy over his shoulder in a fireman's hold.

He and Nate raced across the field and into a narrow gap between two buildings.

Deep in the shadows, they stopped and looked back toward Cruise's headquarters. For a few moments, everything remained still, and then the back door flew open and two of Cruise's men rushed out, guns in hand.

They stopped thirty feet from the building, and had just begun scanning the clearing when two police cars raced through the parking area on the other side of the field, lights flashing.

Cruise's men sprinted back toward the building, but were a few steps shy of the door when more cops, these ones on foot, ran around the corner, guns drawn.

"Police! Drop your weapons! Hands in the air!"

The guy farthest from the door complied. The other one pointed his gun at the police and screamed, "Back off, you mother—"

A dozen bullets ripped through his body.

Nate leaned toward Brian. "You see that? He's probably the lucky one. Damon Cruise and his friends will be going to jail for a long time. Probably the rest of their lives. That's what happens to assholes like him. If we hadn't pulled you out, that would have happened to you, too. What I want to know is, if that's the kind of life you want, because if it is, we'll let you go right now and you can join them."

"No," Brian said. "No, please. Don't. I-I-I don't want that."

"Are you sure?"

Brian nodded, looking as if he was unable to say anything else.

"All right. Then I guess we'll take you home."

The boy didn't look happy with that choice, either.

NATE AND QUINN said little as they escorted Brian back to the apartment he shared with his mother. Given that it was late morning, it wasn't surprising that Kristina King wasn't home.

"What time does your mom get off work?" Nate asked.

"I don't know," Brian said. "Late."

"Do you have her number?"

"Sure, but…"

"But what?"

"She doesn't like me to call when she's working unless it's an emergency."

Nate stared at him. "And what would you call this?"

The boy looked away, saying nothing.

"Give me your phone," Nate said.

Brian reluctantly pulled it out of his pocket and handed it

over.

Nate pushed the home button and turned it toward the kid. "Unlock it."

"Come on. Do you really have to call her?"

Nate kept the phone where it was. Brian punched in a code and the lock screen disappeared.

Nate saw there were fifteen unanswered calls and just as many voicemail messages from MOM. Nate tapped CALL BACK.

The line rang four times before Kristina King answered. "Brian? Are you all right? Where are you?"

"Mrs. King, this is Special Agent Sloan of the FBI," Nate said.

"FBI? Oh my god, did something happen? Is my son all right?"

"He's fine, ma'am. He's with me…and my partner. We're at your apartment."

"Our apartment?"

"Yes, ma'am."

"Is…is he in trouble?"

"Actually, that's what we'd like to discuss with you. Is there any chance you can take an early lunch and meet us here?"

"Yes, of course. I'll leave right away. It's, um, it's going to take me a little while to get there. Thirty minutes…maybe forty-five."

"We'll be here."

NATE AND QUINN'S détente persisted during the wait, Nate not demanding to know why his partner was there, and Quinn not offering an explanation. The only time Brian spoke was to ask Nate if he really was an FBI agent. Nate showed him his counterfeit badge.

Twenty-seven minutes after the phone call, a key slipped into the lock on the front door. Nate, who'd been sitting at the kitchen table with Brian, rose, while Quinn turned from the window he'd been staring out of.

Kristina King hurried into the apartment and over to her

son. She ran her hands over Brian's arms and shoulders, her eyes searching him up and down. "Are you all right? You're not hurt, are you?"

Brian tried to squirm away. "Mom, stop. I'm...I'm okay."

Her hands still on his shoulders, she looked first at Nate, and then Quinn. "You're Agent Sloan?"

"I am, ma'am," Nate said.

"Oh. Whatever you think he's done, I'm sure there must be some kind of mistake. He's a good kid."

"Good kids don't hang around people like Damon Cruise."

Her face darkened. "Damon Cruise is an asshole. He trolls for kids like my son so he can groom them for his needs. You should be going after him, not Brian!"

"We couldn't agree more."

She blinked. "What's that mean?"

"Damon Cruise is no longer going to be a problem."

"I don't understand."

"Cruise and his friends were arrested this morning. I believe there is very little chance they'll see the outside anytime soon."

She stared at him. "Arrested? Are...are you serious?"

"Ask Brian."

She looked at her son.

His eyes were aimed at the floor.

"What do you know about this?" she asked.

"Nothing," the boy muttered.

"He was there," Nate said. "We pulled him out right before the raid."

"Raid?"

Nate looked at the boy. "Tell her."

Brian hesitated, then said in a quiet voice, "It's like he said. The police were all over the place. They...they shot Jayden."

"What?" Kristina said, horrified.

"The important thing here is that Cruise is gone and Brian is not being arrested," Nate said.

She stammered, unsure what to say.

"But even though Cruise is gone," Nate continued, "someone will move in to fill the void. Someone always does. Which means if you want to be sure Brian doesn't fall in with the wrong crowd again, you need to get him somewhere he'll have better opportunities."

"Excuse me?" Kristina narrowed her eyes. "I appreciate you keeping Brian from being arrested, but I don't need you lecturing me on how to raise him."

"I'm not lecturing. I'm simply stating facts. You are a single mother who loves her son, and are doing everything you can to provide for him. But in order to do that *and* pay off your mother's medical bills, all your time and energy is sucked up by work."

"How do you know about my mother's—"

"It's not your fault, but you're caught in a loop that you can't pull yourself out of on your own."

"Who the hell do you think you are?"

"The one who *can* pull you out."

She snorted. "Right. The FBI's running a help-the-needy program now, is that it?"

"Not everything I do is related to the FBI."

She groaned. "Oh, crap. I get it. You're in one of those fanatical religious groups, aren't you?"

"I am not."

"Some other kind of organization, then, something that sucks people in and tricks them out of what little money they have."

"Not that, either." Nate grabbed an envelope from a stack of mail on the kitchen counter, wrote the name Andrew Sawyer on it, and handed it to Kristina. "In the next two days, you will be receiving a call from this man. He'll find a job for you with one of the many dentists he works with. I suggest you seriously consider taking it. You will be doing what you trained for, plus will be making good enough money to not take on extra jobs. And, perhaps as important, it's a long way from here."

"I can't just take a job over the phone."

"Of course you can't. That's why you and Brian will be offered a chance to visit your future employer first. The trip will be paid for, as will your move if you decide to take the position."

"You can't be serious."

"I am."

"Who the hell are you?"

THERE WERE MORE questions and doubts, but Nate addressed each and every one. When he and Quinn departed, Kristina was, if not convinced, at least pondering the possibility of a better life for her son.

"Coffee?" Quinn asked when they reached the street.

Nate nodded. "There's no place good around here. Do you have a car?"

"I do."

They drove into a better part of the city and found a place called Alexander's Coffee House. Once they had their drinks, they took a table on the sparsely populated patio, where there'd be little chance of being overheard.

"So, who's Andrew Sawyer?" Quinn asked.

"I just made him up."

"And this job and move?"

"I'll work something out."

"And pay for it yourself."

Nate shrugged.

"You know she's not going to take you up on it, right?"

"She might."

"Yeah, some creepy guy comes into my house and offers me a too-good-to-be-true job, I'm going to believe him."

Nate said nothing.

"I know about the Pearsons in Las Vegas. How many others have you—"

"What are you doing here, Quinn?"

Quinn set his cup down. "I came looking for you."

"I figured that part out myself. How about being a little more specific?"

During his search for Nate, Quinn had thought of a million different ways to start this conversation. There was only one, though, that felt anywhere close to right. "I owe you an apology."

"For what exactly?"

"For so much."

Nate scoffed. "So, one apology to cover everything?"

"If I start doing individual ones, we're going to be here awhile."

"I've got no plans."

"Okay. To start with, I'm sorry for treating you like crap after Liz died."

Nate grimaced and looked away. "Perfect. You choose the one thing you don't have to apologize for." He shook his head. "What happened to Liz was my fault."

"It *wasn't* your fault. That's the point. When I found out she was with you, I should have had you send her away, but I didn't."

"And I should have never had her with me in the first place. But, okay, fine. How about we both take blame for that one?"

Quinn closed his eyes. "Blame doesn't matter, and that's not what I mean anyway. I should have never treated you the way I did. I was angry at myself, not you. You're my partner. You didn't deserve that."

"Was your partner."

"Still are, whether you want to admit it or not."

Nate said nothing.

"I'm also sorry about how I handled Katrine Dehler." Dehler was the assassin who had killed Quinn's sister.

"Are you saying you wished I'd pulled the trigger?"

"Yes. But even if we had it to do all over again, I still wouldn't have let you."

Nate stared down the street, lost in thought for several seconds. "I…I know it was the right call to stop me." He looked back at Quinn. "But if we did have it to do all over again, I would have ignored you and done it."

"I know."

They drank their coffees without talking. When Nate finished, he set his cup down and said, "Well, it's been nice catching up, but I have things to do."

"More Robin Hooding?"

Nate didn't laugh. "Tell Orlando hi."

"There's something else."

"Of course there's something else."

"We need you to come back."

Nate laughed. "There it is. The real reason you're here."

"It's the reason I'm here *today*, but the apologies, those were just as real, and were going to happen whenever we saw each other again."

"Fair enough, but I'm not interested in coming back."

"There's a reason we need *you* specifically."

"I don't think you were listening. I'm not available." Nate stood up. "There are plenty of others who can help you lug bodies around."

"It's not a cleaning job. We've been hired to find Christophe St. Amand."

Nate cocked his head. "St. Amand?"

"Yes. Turns out, you're still one of the few people on the planet who have actually seen his face."

"Why now?"

Quinn told him about the weapons shipments, and the possibility of something big brewing in the States that St. Amand was supplying. "He works out of Rome. Daeng and Jar are on their way there right now to scope things out. Orlando and I will be heading there soon. Without you, though, the rest of us will just be playing guessing games. If we can get him, whatever this thing is he's involved in will unravel."

Nate thought for a moment, then took a step back. "Sorry. I may be one of the few people who have seen him, but I'm not the only. Get one of the others. I'm not interested."

"Nate, wait," Quinn said as he rose. "That kid today. What you did probably saved his life. But that's just one person's. Stopping St. Amand will save a whole hell of a lot more."

"He's just like Cruise, though. When he's gone, someone will move in to take his place."

"And like Cruise, we can take St. Amand down right now. People will be alive who wouldn't otherwise be."

"I-I can't. I'm sorry. I just…can't."

Quinn followed him as he started walking away. "I know what you're really doing. These little projects of yours—they're for Liz, aren't they? Your way of trying to atone."

Nate picked up his pace without looking back.

"What do you think she'd say about St. Amand? She'd want you to help us, too. You know that."

Nate was almost running.

"Nate, please! Nate!"

When it became apparent his partner wasn't going to turn around, Quinn broke off the chase. He couldn't help but feel guilty for using his sister's name that way, but he also knew he was right. She *would* want Nate to help.

Obviously, Nate didn't see it that way.

IT TOOK ALL of Nate's will not to immediately break into a full-on sprint down the street.

By the time he reached the end of the block, he gave up all pretenses and started running. He didn't know this part of the city, but it didn't matter. He wasn't seeing buildings or cars or people or streets, only objects to avoid and paths to follow. He could have been in Los Angeles or Prague or Beijing, and it would have looked the same to him.

Blocks piled onto blocks, until he'd gone a mile, and then two, and then God knew how many. It wasn't until his legs began burning that he finally slowed. Without the intensity of the sprint numbing his mind, he could hear the words he knew had been echoing through his head all along.

He's right.

He tried to ignore Liz, push her words so far away they'd fall off a cliff and never find their way back to him, but he wasn't strong enough. He could never be strong enough against her.

He's right.

Tears flowed down his cheeks before he realized what was happening. He stopped and bent at the waist, a hand over his eyes. "I don't want to," he said between sobs. "I can't. Just let me do what I was doing. Let that be enough."

He's right.

"Is everything okay?"

Nate wiped his eyes and looked up. An old woman stood next to him, looking concerned.

"Are you hurt?" she asked. "Do you need help?"

He took a breath. "No. I'm okay. It's just…"

"Bad day?"

Bad year, he thought. The worst that ever was. "Something like that."

"The only way to beat a bad day is to keep moving forward," she said.

He almost laughed. As corny as the advice was, there was truth in it. "I like that."

She smiled. "See? Nothing's ever quite as bad as we think."

That, he knew, was not true, but he said, "Thank you."

She patted him on the shoulder and moved on.

Nate brushed away the last of the tears and scanned the street. Two blocks away, he could see a trestle for the L train.

"Is this what you really want?" he mouthed.

It's not a matter of want. It's a matter of what's right. Go.

He took a beat. "All right."

As he walked toward the train, he checked his phone for flight times.

A plane was leaving for Italy in just under three hours.

CHAPTER
EIGHTEEN

ROME

IT WAS EARLY evening by the time Daeng and Jar exited the arrival terminal at Fiumicino International Airport and climbed into their cab.

Orlando had sent them a text they received upon landing, with information on a flat she'd obtained for them, adding:

> Not the most luxurious place,
> but the photos look fine. Tourist
> season's starting up, so didn't have
> a lot of choices.

The flat was located off Campo de' Fiori, a plaza near the heart of the city, in a stone-sided building at least a hundred years old. Entrance was through a nondescript door along a narrow cobbled side street, ten meters off the plaza. From there, it was a long walk down a curved hallway and up a short flight of stairs.

Per instructions, they found flat 110 all by itself at the end of a short hallway offshoot. Mounted on the wall next to the ancient, formidable door was a very modern digital lockbox. Jar input the code they'd been given, removed the key from inside, and opened the door.

The flat was divided into two main rooms—an open living room/kitchen area at the front, and bedroom with an added loft in the back. The only additional space was a bathroom off the bedroom, with a shorter than average door that Daeng would have to duck to use. There were two beds in the bedroom, one in the lower space, and the other in the loft.

After they'd freshened up, they called Orlando.

"We're all set here," Daeng told her.

"Great. Is the place okay?"

"It'll work just fine. When will you guys be here?"

"Sometime tomorrow."

"That soon? Then Quinn found Nate."

"He did, but…well, things didn't go as we hoped. It looks like we're going to have to do this without him."

"How are we supposed to ID this guy, then?"

"Process of elimination. We have a pretty good idea where he operates. We'll just have to see who's there and start eliminating anyone who we're sure isn't him from the list."

"By we, you mean Jar and I," Daeng said.

"You're a smart man, Daeng. That's what I like about you."

"Appreciate the confidence. So where do we start?"

"The client gave us four addresses he believes are associated with St. Amand. I'd like you and Jar to make the rounds tonight, get the lay of the land. If you get the sense one or more of the places deserves a closer look, if it seems safe enough then go ahead and do it. But, no matter what, keep it low-key. We do *not* want to blow this gig before we get started."

"No making a mess of things. Got it."

"I'll text you the addresses. Anything else?"

"Gear?"

"Should be there waiting for you. You haven't seen it?"

"Hold on."

While Daeng scanned the living room, Jar went into the bedroom for a look around.

"Found it," she called a few moments later.

She reentered the living room, lugging a big black duffel.

"Where was it?" Daeng asked. It was way too big for either of them to have missed earlier.

"In the linen cabinet."

Jar set the bag down next to him.

"So, we're good?" Orlando asked.

Daeng unzipped the duffel and did a quick inventory of the contents. "We're good."

INCLUDED WITH THE flat were two Vespa motor scooters, stored in a central courtyard that had been converted into a parking area for the building's residents. Daeng and Jar donned comm gear, so they could talk without having to yell, strapped on helmets, and headed out.

The first address was a building a stone's throw from the Vatican. Like most of the structures in the city, it looked as if it would've been equally at home in the eighteenth century as in the twenty-first.

"Did you notice the cameras?" Daeng said after they'd driven by.

"Of course."

Jar had seen all seven of them, even though most people would never know they were there. The cameras were masked as stone ornaments, and distributed across the exterior of the building in a way that prevented anyone from approaching without being seen.

She and Daeng parked the scooters a few blocks away and walked back, blending in behind a group of Chinese tourists.

"Take some pictures," Daeng whispered.

"Of what?" Jar asked, not bothering to lower her voice. They were talking in Thai, and she doubted anyone around could understand them.

"Everything. We're sightseers."

It took her only a second to see the benefit of his idea. As tourists, no one would think twice about what she was pointing her lens at. She pulled out her phone and started taking random shots.

When they were a few buildings away from their destination, Daeng stopped and said, "Let's take one together."

He turned and held out his phone to get a shot with the building in the background. He put his arm across Jar's shoulders and pulled her to him.

This wasn't the first time she'd had to act cozy with Daeng, so she went along without protest. That did not mean she wasn't extremely uncomfortable. Touching—or any display of affection, real or faked—was not one of her strong suits.

"One more," he said, shifting their stance to get a different portion of the building in the shot.

When he finally let go of her, Jar took a deep breath.

"It wasn't *that* bad, was it?" he said, smirking.

"It was not too horrible."

He laughed softly as he brought up one of the photos he'd taken, and magnified it so that one of the cameras mounted near the top of the building filled the screen.

"HemiSource Ultra 7," Jar said, pulling from her encyclopedic knowledge of pretty much everything. HemiSource was a big player in residential security products in this part of the world. Its cameras were particularly popular with multi-residential buildings because of their incognito casings. Chances were, if they were using HemiSource outside, they'd be using the same vendor for any interior cameras and the overall monitoring system, as the company was big on providing all-inclusive systems. Its security software was robust, and not something an amateur could hack into easily.

"Give me a minute," Jar said.

Using her own phone, she tapped into the building's Wi-Fi network and plunged into the HemiSource operating system. If not for a mislabeled file on the building's end, she would have needed only half the ninety seconds it took her to break in.

She flipped through the interior camera feeds.

"Most floors are covered by three cams spaced evenly down each main corridor, with another near the elevators, and one in the fire stairwell."

"*Most?*" Daeng said.

"The top floor only has them in the stairwell."

Daeng raised an eyebrow, letting her know he thought that was suspicious. But she already knew it was suspicious. Anyone could see that.

Both Jar and Daeng took more photos as they walked by the front of the building, A glance through the pane of glass in the front door revealed at least one doorman/security guard stationed inside.

They turned down the next block and stopped out of sight. Daeng brought up a satellite image of the area, and he and Jar searched it for a way to reach the back of the building. There was space between the structure and the one behind it, but the only way into that space was to go through either of the buildings. Doing that would violate Orlando's "low-key" directive, so they decided to return to their scooters.

The next two locations on the list were similar, luxury-style apartment buildings, the first a half-kilometer east of the Spanish Steps, and the other right on Plaza Navona. Both were well covered by security systems that Jar penetrated without difficulty, and both had floors unregulated by in-house cameras.

"Maybe he moves around a lot," Daeng suggested as they drove to the final destination. "Hops from place to place, never staying in one more than a few nights at a time."

It was a reasonable assumption, but Jar needed more evidence before she could agree.

Unlike the other three locations, address number four was a five-story office building, near the Tiber river.

Though most of the windows on the upper floors were dark, the ground-floor lobby was all lit up. A guard sat at a desk, the flicker of a TV bouncing off his face.

Jar and Daeng stood on the sidewalk, just out of sight of the lobby, and turned to each other, like two people having a conversation. The only one doing the talking, though, was Daeng. He gibbered away in Thai about stuff neither of them cared about, while Jar used her phone to break into the building's security system.

The setup was marginally better protected than those she'd encountered at the residential addresses, and it took her a full three minutes to crack it. In the administrative database, she found a list of tenants. None was St. Amand. She could do some research when they returned to the flat, see if she could connect one of the names to the arms dealer.

After saving the information for easy access, she spent a few minutes probing the individual networks of each tenant. Most were simple to hack; two of the companies had no real security at all. She downloaded info on each business for later perusal. Out of the seventeen companies, four had systems that would require greater effort on her part to breach. That was also something she could do from her laptop back at the apartment.

Maybe the most interesting thing she discovered was that two of the lessees didn't seem to have computer systems at all. Perhaps the tenants had recently moved out, or not moved in yet. Being there and digitally unconnected was illogical to her, yet she couldn't dismiss the possibility the offices were in use.

Having accomplished as much as she could for the moment, she and Daeng took a walk around the block, creating a mental map of all the ways in and out of the building, and then headed back to the scooters.

As Jar was strapping on her helmet, a dark sedan, followed by an even darker SUV, drove past and pulled to the curb in front of the office building.

She propped her phone on the handlebars and activated the camera. She zoomed in just in time to record four men in business suits climbing out of the SUV.

"Daeng," she whispered.

"I see them."

The largest of the men walked up to the sedan while the others spread out, bodyguard style, along the sidewalk. After checking to make sure everyone was in place, the guy at the car opened the rear passenger door. Out climbed a fifth man in a suit. Unlike the others, he was wearing a hat, sunglasses, and a wide scarf wrapped around his face.

"That's got to be St. Amand," Daeng said.

Again, while Jar was inclined to agree, she wasn't ready to be definitive.

As the scarf-covered man stepped onto the sidewalk, he glanced in Jar and Daeng's direction. Though they were half a block away, it would have been hard for him not to have seen them. He said something to the big guy who'd opened the door.

The brute glanced toward Daeng and Jar and started walking in their direction, while Scarf Man and the others headed into the building.

Jar reached down to start her bike, but Daeng said, "No." He came around his scooter and leaned down next to her, putting his head almost on her shoulder. "Turn off the video and take a picture. Hurry."

She switched to picture mode and took a selfie of the two of them.

"Again," he said.

She could hear the man's footsteps as she pushed the button again.

"My eyes were closed," Daeng said, louder now. "Take another."

Jar snapped off another shot.

"Much better," he said.

As the man neared them, he said something in Italian. Jar was passable at French and Spanish and near fluent in English, but she had never learned Italian. Daeng had a decent understanding of it, but he ignored the man and said to Jar, in Thai, "One more, baby."

The guy spoke again.

Daeng finally looked at him, his brow creased.

"Don't speak...uh...*italiano*," Daeng said in heavily accented English.

"You can't take pictures here," the man said, also in English.

"Why no? Just take girlfriend and me."

Daeng looked at Jar and said in Thai, "Say something that sounds like you're a little confused and also upset."

"Okay. I'm a little confused and upset."

"Can you put a little more emotion in it?"

"I do not *like* to be called *baby*."

"That's better. Now put your camera away, but don't look happy about it."

She forced herself to frown as she shoved the phone back into her pocket.

Daeng turned back to the guy. "Sorry. Not know is a

problem. No more picture. Okay?"

The guy stared at him for a moment before nodding. "Good. I think it is better if you leave now, too."

"Leave?"

"Yes." The guy motioned for them to drive away.

"Ah, okay, sure. Sorry. We go."

Jar and Daeng started their bikes and pulled onto the road. As they drove by the building, Jar saw a light come on in the fifth-floor window at the far corner.

"Whose office is that?" Daeng asked.

Jar had been gifted with an excellent memory, so it took her only a few seconds to correlate the building's tenants to the floor plans. "Piazza and Campagna. They were listed as consultants."

"What kind, I wonder?"

Jar had no idea. Piazza and Campagna was one of the two businesses with no digital footprint.

ST. AMAND LOOKED up as Drake entered his office.

"A couple of Chinese tourists taking selfies," Drake said.

"You're sure?"

"Yeah. Didn't speak Italian and barely any English. They're gone now."

St. Amand nodded. "Good." He poured himself a whiskey from his bar and silently asked Drake if he wanted one.

"No, thank you, sir," Drake said. He never drank in the boss's presence.

St. Amand sat down behind his desk, took a sip, and set the glass down. "Let's give Mr. Cox a call."

Upon landing in Rome, St. Amand had received a text from Kenneth Cox requesting to talk to him.

Drake placed the call on his phone, switched it to speaker, and set it next to the glass. St. Amand recognized the voice of Cox's assistant when she answered. Her defiant tone from earlier was gone, and she put them right through to her boss.

"Thank you for calling me back," Cox said. "I trust the rest of your day has been pleasant."

"Mr. Cox, we are a bit pressed for time," St. Amand said.

"I suggest you get to the point."

"Of course. My apologies, Mr. Becker. I have been in contact with Mr. Sandstrom. He has agreed to meet with you tomorrow evening. He's working on transportation right now, but should be able to arrive by late afternoon. If you could tell me where you'd like to meet, I can pass that information—"

"We will contact Mr. Sandstrom directly with the location. You can tell him to expect a text when he arrives at the airport."

"Oh, um, okay, I guess that will work. I mean, of course that will work. Let me give you his phone number."

"We already have it."

"You already—"

St. Amand terminated the call.

To Drake, he said, "We'll meet at De Luca's. Make the arrangements."

"Yes, sir."

"And have Havel and Imrich follow him and make sure Sandstrom hasn't brought any fleas with him."

Sandstrom was not exactly an upright citizen, so who knew who else might be interested in him.

Drake nodded and turned to leave.

"One more thing," St. Amand said. "Have some samples available to show him. The fun stuff." He had no intention of cutting off the Sandstrom account. There was too much money involved. But he was not above making sure the man knew what he'd be missing if St. Amand did end their business arrangement.

"Consider it done," Drake said.

CHAPTER NINETEEN

WASHINGTON, DC

QUINN LANDED AT Dulles Airport at six p.m., and was greeted near the terminal exit by a man holding a sign with the false name Quinn's airline ticket had been booked under.

The driver was a true professional, and didn't try even once to strike up a conversation as he drove Quinn into the city. Quinn was grateful for that. His failure to convince Nate to join the mission lay heavy on his mind. After assisting his partner out of the tricky situation at the drug den, he'd been sure Nate would agree to help. But Quinn realized now that was never going to happen. The only thing that might bring Nate back was time.

The driver finally spoke after they reached the Four Seasons Hotel, saying, "Have a good evening" when he handed Quinn his bag from the trunk. Inside, Quinn rode the elevator to the top floor and located the room number he'd been given.

"Hi, babe," Orlando said after she opened the door.

He wrapped her in his arms and gave her a deep kiss, right there on the threshold.

Someone farther in the room cleared her throat.

Quinn let the kiss linger a moment longer. When their lips parted, he said, "I guess we're not alone."

"Nope," Orlando said.

Misty rose from the table where she'd been sitting as they walked into the room.

"Hello, Quinn," she said, hugging him.

"And here I thought you were the lucky one who got out of the business," he said.

"I didn't get out. I was forced out."

"Either way, you were out."

"Civilian life is not as…interesting."

He chuckled. "It's good to have you back."

"We were just going over the mission," Orlando said.

"Is there still a mission without Nate?" Quinn asked.

"The parameters haven't changed," Misty said. "St. Amand is still out there and needs to be identified. We'll have to do it without Nate's help."

"I thought Nate was the reason ACORT hired the…Office." He looked at Orlando. "Does that feel as weird to you to say again as it does to me?"

"A little."

"Nate *was* the reason," Misty said. "But no one ever explicitly said he was a must-have."

Quinn raised an eyebrow. "You're resorting to semantics already? You're going to be great at this job."

"I'm not resorting to anything. It's true."

"Have you at least told your clients he's not joining us?"

"Of course not. They've awarded us the job. How we accomplish it is our problem."

He held his hands up in surrender. "You're the boss."

"We're both the boss," Orlando said.

Quinn glanced at her. "I stand corrected." To both of them, he said, "Have we looked into locating someone else who's seen this guy?"

"I've been trying but no luck so far," Misty said. "Unless that changes, we'll have to make do with Nate's description."

"From a decade ago," Quinn said.

"Nine years," Orlando corrected him.

"It won't be impossible," Misty said. "We know how he dresses in public now."

Quinn snorted. "I looked at those photos. It's not even the same person in each. The difference is subtle, but it's there."

"One of them has to be him."

"Or not." He frowned. "Am I the only one who feels like you should level with the client? Without Nate we'll just be winging it."

"If we bow out of one of our first jobs since restarting, no one will ever hire us."

Passing on the job was probably the right thing to do at this point, but Misty's assessment wasn't wrong. And if the Office went away, Misty would find herself on the outside looking in again. Permanently this time.

He said, "Tell me we at least have a plan."

Misty perked up. "We do."

"Sort of," Orlando said.

"There's a chance your friends have already seen St. Amand."

It took him a second to realize what she meant. "Daeng and Jar?"

Orlando nodded, and showed him the video Jar had shot.

"It could be another decoy."

"It's possible," Orlando conceded, "but take a closer look at this."

Orlando replayed the footage, and fast-forwarded to the part where the man who might be St. Amand looked toward the camera and said something to one of the men with him. That man started walking in Daeng and Jar's direction. She hit Pause.

"See that?" Orlando asked. "He's giving orders. If he were a double, he wouldn't do that."

"He would if he was trying to act the part."

"I'm not so sure. This was an in-the-moment call. No one told him to give an order. If he was a double, wouldn't one of the others have given the command?"

"Play it again," Quinn said.

She let the video run a third time. She had a point.

"Okay. Say it *is* St. Amand," he said. "Then we can compare him to the earlier photos and eliminate the ones who don't match. And—"

"And then we can check the ones that do match," Orlando said, "to see if there are any identifying marks, maybe even exposed parts of his face."

"Exactly."

"What a great idea!" Orlando looked at Misty. "Thank God we have a man here now to solve our problems."

"You already thought of that, didn't you?" he said.

"Of course we already thought of that. The photos are being compared in my recognition program right now. Should have some results soon."

"I apologize."

"Tentatively accepted."

"So," Quinn said, "you still haven't told me about this sort-of plan."

NATE FLEW FROM Chicago to New York, where he caught an evening flight to Rome, arriving at noon the next day. At some point, he would have to contact Quinn and Orlando and let them know he was there, but that could wait. First, he wanted to see if he could get eyes on St. Amand. If that happened, he could deliver the information to his friends and be on his way without having to interact with them in any significant manner.

The problem was that Quinn hadn't given Nate specifics on where St. Amand was in Rome. It was a huge city with way more than its share of nooks and crannies where someone could lose themselves.

Nate wasn't completely at a loss, though. Quinn had said Daeng and Jar were on their way here so they should be in the city by now. Nate didn't want to approach them directly, but should be able to obtain their assistance without either of them knowing it.

He took a taxi into Rome, and had his driver drop him off at the small but upscale Kari Hotel, near the Trevi Fountain. Sitting in a quiet corner of the lobby, he pulled out his laptop. Several Wi-Fi networks appeared—a free public network, an easily hackable network for the hotel's guests, and two administrative networks that were likely just marginally more secure. He was most interested in one of the latter. It was designed to show up only on devices that had been network approved. Luckily for Nate, the software Orlando had designed automatically mimicked the appropriate data for these kinds of setups, and nothing was invisible to him.

He clicked the GO tab to start the automated hacking process, and received the message YOU ARE NOW CONNECTED TO KA_AD_PRV within twenty seconds. He inserted a reservation into the hotel's database under the name of Brandon Yates, for a prepaid, weeklong stay in a suite. The name corresponded with the Canadian passport he carried.

He opened the tracking app everyone on Quinn's team had. This allowed them to find the locations of the others' phones. It was because of this piece of software that Nate had abandoned his old phone soon after the mission in London.

He selected the SEARCH ALL option and waited while the request was processed. Soon a map of the entire planet appeared with four dots on it. Those representing Quinn and Orlando were in close proximity in Washington, DC. Daeng's and Jar's were also together, but only a few miles from Nate.

He pushed the information to his phone, then put away his laptop and walked up to the reception desk.

DAENG AND JAR'S task for the day was to get eyes again on the guy they assumed was St. Amand, plant tracking bugs on his vehicle and any others traveling with it, and see where the arms dealer went. And that all needed to be accomplished before Quinn and Orlando arrived that evening.

Daeng and Jar started that morning by making the rounds of the four addresses again. They'd seen nothing to indicate St. Amand was at any of them. They decided to stake out the office building.

They parked a couple of blocks away, where Jar spent a few minutes on her phone. When she slipped it back into her pocket, she said, "Follow me."

She led him into a building across the street and one over from St. Amand's place, and took Daeng up to the roof via the elevator and then a steep set of stairs.

Daeng saw why she'd chosen this building instead of the one directly across from St. Amand's office. Along the street side was a decorative façade that rose a good meter and a half above the roofline. It had holes through which they could watch St. Amand's building.

He peered through one of the openings, and discovered he could see into the fifth-floor window where they'd seen lights come on the previous evening.

He smiled at Jar. "Good work."

"I know."

NATE STOPPED A block and a half away from where the tracking app indicated Daeng's and Jar's phones were located. He tapped on Daeng's dot to open a pop-up containing additional information. What surprised him was that the dot was approximately six floors above street level. Also interesting was that the time elapsed since the last significant change was 36 minutes. Jar's pop-up revealed similar numbers.

Nate changed the map from graphic view to street view, and counted the floors of the building his friends apparently were in.

Check that. Not in, but *on*.

The building was only five stories high, which meant they were on the roof.

Nate moved down the street until he could see the building. A decorative wall of classically inspired carvings of gods and horses and chariots buttressed the roof. Yep, definitely a stakeout. The wall was the perfect blind to hide behind.

He crossed to the same side of the street as Daeng and Jar, hoping he could pick out what they were looking at. The building directly across from their roof appeared to be residential, and on either side of that were office buildings.

He scanned the area around him and found no good places to hang out, but that wasn't a big problem. With Daeng and Jar pinging on his tracker, he didn't need to stay in visual contact.

An internet search told him a café was four blocks away. He took one last look down the road, and headed off.

"I'M JUST SAYING, if you found yourself in that situation, what would you do?" Daeng asked.

He and Jar were at opposite ends of the roof's façade to give them a wider view of the street, talking via their comms.

"It is a stupid question," Jar said. "I would never find myself in that situation."

"You can't know that."

"Of course I can. It is fiction, and therefore it would be impossible for me to be in that situation."

"Technically, yes. But I mean a *similar* position."

"That was not the question. The question was whether I would have teamed up with Kylo Ren to defeat Emperor Snoke or not. The question is absurd."

"You know what I mean."

"No, I do not know. It is a story. How could I team up with someone in a *story*?"

Daeng took a deep breath. "The gist of the question is whether you would ever team up with someone who—"

"SUV approaching from the west," Jar said.

Daeng looked through the gap he'd been using. The vehicle was the same type as the one they'd seen last night.

"I count four inside," Jar said.

Daeng could see the driver and front passenger, but he didn't have the right angle to see into the backseat.

The vehicle pulled to the curb in front of the building, and the four men climbed out.

Daeng raised his binoculars. "Check out the driver."

"Yes."

The driver was the big guy who had chased them off when they were pretending to be taking selfies. Though Daeng hadn't gotten as good a look at the others last night, he was pretty sure the three men with the driver had been among them. The only one missing was St. Amand, or whoever had been wearing the scarf.

As the men entered the building, Daeng hopped to his feet. "Watch my back."

He hurried back inside the apartment building and hustled down to the ground floor.

When he reached the front door, he said, "Am I clear to enter the street?"

"I see movement in the offices but no one's at the windows. Go."

"Copy."

He pulled a tracker disk from inside his backpack, his keys from his pocket, then exited the building.

"Still clear," Jar said.

Pretending he was heading to one of the cars, he crossed the road on a diagonal path that would take him by the rear end of the SUV. As he neared the vehicle, he fiddled with the keys like he was looking for the right one, then dropped them so they skidded toward the SUV's rear tire.

Acting annoyed, he knelt down and grabbed them. When he started to rise again, he slipped the disk inside the wheel well, where it adhered to the side panel.

A second later, he was walking down the street again, toward a car that wasn't there.

NATE WATCHED THE dot representing Daeng descend to street level. Jar's dot remained on the roof. Once outside, Daeng paused, crossed the street, paused, and headed in roughly the same direction as the café Nate was in.

Nate's concern that he'd been discovered disappeared when Daeng turned at the next intersection and stopped.

Something was definitely up.

Nate signaled the waiter for his check.

JAR THOUGHT DAENG'S acting job was a bit over the top, but since none of St. Amand's people had seen his performance, she decided no harm had been done. She did, however, make a mental note to give him feedback when they had time.

She swung her binoculars back to the fifth-floor office. Most of the action she'd seen had happened out of sight, on the opposite side of the building. Every once in a while, though, she had seen movement through a doorway, and once, the driver had come into a street-side office, where he grabbed a hard-sided case and exited again.

Now there was no movement whatsoever.

She focused on the building's entrance, but nothing was

going on there, either.

"Status?" Daeng asked.

"Still inside," she said.

"Are you picking up the tracker?"

Jar opened the app and selected the ID for the bug Daeng had used. A red dot glowed on a map, right where the SUV was parked.

"We're good."

She looked back at the building and sucked in a surprised breath. "They're outside again."

The men were all carrying hard cases—two of them lugging a pair each, the other two transporting one per man. The cases were wide enough to hold a couple of footballs—the international kind, not American—and, with the exception of two of them, looked to be the length of a standard briefcase. The two outliers were over a meter long.

Jar lowered her binoculars and took pictures as the men loaded the cases into the back of the SUV.

"It looks like they're getting ready to leave," she reported.

"I'll follow them," Daeng said. "You stay on the roof until they're gone, then catch up."

"Copy."

As soon as the last case was safely inside, the men climbed into the vehicle.

"Affirmative on leaving," she said as the motor started.

"Copy."

The SUV pulled from the curb and headed down the street. When she could no longer see it, she texted Orlando the best pictures she'd taken and hurried toward the stairs.

BY THE TIME Daeng had his scooter on the road, the tracker app indicated he was five blocks behind the SUV. But Rome being Rome, his bike provided him the advantage of being able to maneuver around the traffic the SUV had to slog through. Soon he could see the vehicle a dozen car lengths ahead.

Deciding that was close enough for now, he settled into the flow and turned on his mic. "I have them in sight."

No reply.

"Jar? Do you copy?"

Silence.

He scanned for a break in traffic to turn and go back, but it was bumper to bumper. "Jar! *Do you copy?*"

A beat. "I copy. Sorry…I, um…I'll be there soon."

"Is everything all right?"

"Fine," she said quickly.

Ahead, the SUV had just turned a corner.

Daeng hurried to the intersection and swung onto the new road.

IT TOOK JAR four minutes to reach her scooter. She consulted her phone to get a fix on where the SUV and Daeng were, picked out a route that should put her on an intercept course, and pulled onto the street.

Three blocks down, as she rounded the corner to the right, she glimpsed someone hurrying down the sidewalk. She would have ignored him if not for the way he ran—with the slightest of hitches in his step—which seemed familiar.

She looked again, but he was gone.

Feeling a sense of unease, she slowed and turned back the other way.

"I have them in sight," Daeng said in her ear.

Though she heard him, she was trying to figure out where the runner had gone.

"Jar? Do you copy?"

The runner must have entered one of the buildings. She didn't have time to go searching. Besides, it couldn't have been who she thought it was.

"Jar! *Do you copy?*"

She turned the scooter around again. "I copy."

ACCORDING TO NATE'S phone, the nearest taxi stand was a couple of blocks south. He headed in that direction, thinking he needed to work on getting his own transportation as soon as he had some time.

The traffic light at the intersection ahead was green, but he didn't think it would stay that way for long, so he picked up the pace and made it across just in time. He was several meters farther down the sidewalk when he heard a scooter turn the corner behind him. As it passed by, he caught sight of the driver—a thin, tiny woman with black hair flying out the bottom of her helmet.

Jar! Crap.

He dropped behind the cars parked at the curb.

When he heard the scooter slow, he quietly chanted, "Just keep going. Just keep going."

Only instead of driving on, the scooter circled back and rolled slowly by his position. If Jar parked and got off, she'd find him right away.

After she turned back toward her original direction, he heard her say, "I copy. Sorry…I, um…I'll be there soon."

The scooter took off and vanished down the street. Nate checked the tracker to make sure she was gone, then got up and resumed his journey to get a taxi.

THE SUV STUCK to the main thoroughfares as it traveled past the Forum on its way into the eastern portion of the city. Daeng was able to keep the vehicle in sight, and hadn't needed to check the tracker for over twenty minutes.

When the vehicle turned onto a less crowded side street, he assumed they were getting close to their destination. Sure enough, ten minutes later the SUV stopped.

Daeng pulled to the curb just around the corner, long enough to don sunglasses and make sure his hair was all tucked under the helmet, and then turned the corner and drove by the SUV. The men were heading into the restaurant they'd parked in front of, a place called De Luca's.

Seemed odd to drive this far just for lunch. Unless, of course, the restaurant was close to their next destination.

Daeng would have loved to go inside, too, but having been seen up close the night before by the big driver, that was out of the question.

He parked his bike down the street, and perused the produce on display in front of a small market on the corner. He'd barely had a chance to move from the squash to the tomatoes when the restaurant door opened again. Three of the men emerged and headed for the rear of the SUV. As one of them opened the hatch, the driver stepped out of De Luca's in the company of an older man wearing an apron. Instead of joining the others, they stood near one of the patio tables, talking.

The older guy nodded several times, as if agreeing to whatever the driver was saying. The restaurant manager? Owner?

At the SUV, the men removed the six hard cases and carried them toward the restaurant. After a quick word with the driver, they headed inside.

So, not just a lunch stop.

The driver and the older guy shared a few more words and shook hands. The driver walked over to the SUV and climbed into the driver's seat.

Daeng eyed the restaurant, expecting the others to come out, but the vehicle's engine roared to life and the driver sped away.

Heading back to his scooter, Daeng clicked on his mic. "Daeng for Jar."

"Go for Jar."

"Where are you?"

"Parked a block behind you. My tracker shows the SUV moving again."

"Yeah, they just left."

"What were they doing here?"

He described what he'd seen. "I want to get a look inside the restaurant and see if I can figure out what's up, but..."

"But what if they remember you from last night?"

"Yeah."

"Then I will go."

He almost argued that the driver was gone, and was the only one who could ID Daeng, but he realized she was right again. Though it was unlikely the men who'd stayed behind would recognize Daeng, he couldn't be sure. Jar, on the other hand, had been facing away from the group when the driver told them to get out of there. None of them would know what she looked like.

"Are you sure you can handle it?" he asked.

"I go in. I order spaghetti. I eat. I leave. Yes, I can handle it."

"I'll be right outside if you run into any problems."

"That would be a waste of resources. You should follow the SUV."

Normally, he'd have done exactly that. But Jar, despite having gained quite a bit of field experience since January, was still learning. "I think it's better if I stay."

"Daeng, I will be fine. What if the SUV is going to where St. Amand is right now? We can't miss that opportunity."

"What if St. Amand is inside the restaurant?"

"Then we will have both possibilities covered, won't we?"

He snorted. "Okay, I'll go. But leave your mic on so I can hear everything you hear."

"Copy."

THE FIRST CABBIE Nate used quickly became uncomfortable with the many changes in direction Nate gave him. The man finally pulled to the curb and all but physically shoved Nate to the street. The guy behind the wheel of the second taxi was younger, and actually got excited at the prospect of not having an exact destination in mind. Of course, it didn't hurt that Nate had promised a hundred-euro tip.

The switching of cars and Daeng's head start meant Daeng had been at his stop in the eastern part of the city for nearly ten minutes by the time Nate arrived in the area. Jar had also shown up there, three minutes before Nate.

To be safe, Nate had the cabbie stop a block from Jar and two from Daeng. He gave the driver both the fare and the promised tip, and held up another hundred-euro bill. "Wait for me for fifteen minutes. If I don't come back, you can leave. Okay?"

"I'll wait twenty," the guy said. This was probably the most fun he'd had in ages.

Nate gave him the extra hundred and climbed out.

When he reached the intersection with the street that ran past the corner Daeng was on, he looked at the tracker again. Check that—the corner Daeng *had been* on. Nate's friend was on the move, at a pace that indicated he was using a vehicle again—a scooter seemed most likely, given that's what Jar had been riding.

Jar was moving, too, but her pace was walking, not driving.

Nate considered returning to the taxi and following Daeng, but he was curious as to what Jar was up to.

He moved to the grocery store at the corner where Daeng had been.

There was no need to check the tracker now. He could see Jar walking down the other side of the road, away from him. She passed a few buildings and entered what looked like a restaurant.

From the way she had walked up to it, the restaurant had been her destination.

Nate scanned the street. Not quite straight across from the restaurant was a bakery. He'd have preferred a café like before, but the place did have a few tables set up on the sidewalk, which hopefully meant there were more inside.

CHAPTER
TWENTY

A BELL RANG as Jar entered De Luca's restaurant. Two of the five tables in the front room were occupied, but not by the men from the SUV. Through an archway to her left, she could see into two additional dining areas, but both appeared to be unoccupied.

A stocky, older man wearing an apron stuck his head around the archway and said, "*Buon pomeriggio. Prego, si accomodi al tavolo che preferisce.*"

She understood the *good afternoon*, and though the rest of his words were a mystery, it was obvious from the way he gestured at the tables that she could sit anywhere. She chose the spot nearest the archway, taking the seat that allowed her a clear view into the back rooms.

The waiter returned a few minutes later with a menu, and asked her what she wanted to drink. At least, that's what she thought he asked.

"Water…um…*acqua*?"

"*Si, si.* Pellegrino?"

"*Si*," she said, and mangled her attempt at thanking him in Italian.

"*Grazie*," he corrected her.

"*Grazie*," she repeated.

He started to walk away.

"Wait. May I order, too?"

The waiter looked back.

She held up the menu, and gestured at him to write

something down.

"Ah, okay, okay," he said.

He nodded as she pointed at items on the menu, but by the time she finished he looked concerned. "Um…you…*mangi*…uh, eat. You eat?"

"Friends coming." She motioned to the other chairs.

He smiled and gave her a thumbs-up.

"Toilet?" she asked.

He pointed through the archway toward the back, and then headed toward one of the other occupied tables.

Wanting to remain mobile, Jar slipped a couple of the microcameras into her pocket and pushed her backpack under the table before heading to the back of the restaurant.

Her large order would buy her plenty of time, but she didn't want to be gone too long and cause the waiter to become curious. She decided to give herself five minutes, with the possibility of an extension if necessary.

Beyond the last of the additional dining rooms was a hallway that ran off to either side. A sign with the familiar man and woman toilet symbols pointed to the right. Past the toilets was another doorway. From the sounds coming from the other side, she guessed it was the kitchen. Down the hallway to the left was a set of narrow stairs that curved out of sight. She doubted the men had gone into the kitchen, which left somewhere upstairs as their possible destination.

She glanced back into the restaurant. The waiter was nowhere to be seen, and the only customer in sight had his back to her. Jar went left.

When she reached the stairs, she heard voices drifting down from the floor above. She pulled out one of the micro cams and stuck it in an unobtrusive spot with a view of the ground-floor hall.

Worried that the old wooden stairs might squeak, she placed her foot at the edge of the first tread and transferred her weight. A slight moan, but nothing earth shattering. Sticking to the sides of the steps, she worked her way up to the top, where she found a hallway that paralleled the one below.

There were several doors along the hall, the voices she'd

heard coming from behind one at the far end. The nearest door had been left open a few centimeters. The room was dark and quiet.

She carefully pushed the door inward, and found an unoccupied private dining room.

She continued down the hall and discovered two more rooms with identical setups.

She checked the time. She'd been gone for almost four minutes. She studied the hallway and found a spot to hide the final camera.

She had just finished securing it in place, and was contemplating walking down to the last door and listening for a moment, when she heard its handle turn.

With zero chance of making it to the stairs without being seen, she rushed into the nearest private dining room and hid behind the partially open door.

Someone entered the hallway and walked past her door. She recognized the man in the suit as one of those she and Daeng had been following.

She expected him to take the stairs down, but he stopped at the top and called, "Matteo!"

After a few seconds, someone shouted from below.

When the suited man spoke again, he did so in Italian, which didn't help Jar.

Another answer from below, then a *grazie* from the man at the top.

That, she got.

The man headed back down the hall. As soon as he reentered the room where he'd been and closed the door, she slipped into the hallway and descended the stairs.

 She was on the final few steps, seconds from making it free and clear, when the door to the kitchen swung open and her waiter walked out. He stopped the moment he saw her.

Jar smiled as she stepped off the last step and walked toward the opening to the public dining area.

The man's gaze flashed from her to the stairs and back, his eyes widening. He asked her a question that she guessed was some version of *what were you doing up there?*

She smiled again, said, "Sorry, I do not understand," and swung around the corner into the dining room.

"Stop," he said in English.

She turned to him, feigning surprise. "Is there a problem?"

"Uh...uh..." He said something in Italian under his breath. "You...stay."

He moved back into the hallway and shouted something she assumed was meant for the men upstairs.

Instead of remaining there, she continued to her table. It's what an innocent person would do.

More shouts in the back, a new voice joining the waiter's, and then the clamor of several people coming down the stairs. The other customers turned to see what was causing the noise.

Jar acted curious, too. When three of the suited men appeared at the back of the restaurant with the waiter, she innocently watched them for a moment until she remembered the comm receiver in her ear. It was small and consisted mostly of a transparent gel-like material, but it was not invisible. If one of the men saw it, they'd know what it was.

Using her menu as a screen, she pulled the device out and stuffed it into her pants pocket.

The men entered the front dining room and surrounded her table.

She looked up. "Can I help you?"

The guy in the middle, a thirtyish pretty boy, said in stilted English, "You. What you do up?"

She frowned. "I am sorry?"

He nodded back toward the stairs. "You go up. Why you go up?"

"Oh. You mean upstairs?"

"Yes. Up the stairs."

"Sorry, I thought the toilet was up there."

"Toilet not up there."

"I know that now."

Pretty Boy talked to the waiter, then turned back to Jar. "He say you not use toilet."

"I decided to come back and order food first. Is that a crime?"

"Crime? You police?"

"What? No. I am a tourist." She laughed. "Police. That is funny. Do I look like police?"

"Where from?"

"Excuse me?"

"You say tourist. Where from?"

"That is none of your business."

He said something in that other language, and one of his friends reached for Jar's bag.

"Hey!" she said, grabbing it before he could and standing up. "You cannot touch my stuff like that. Who do you think you are?"

"What your name?" Pretty Boy asked.

"That is not your business, either!" She looked at the waiter. "If this is how you run your restaurant, my friends and I will find someplace else to eat."

She whirled around and marched across the room. She was able to get the door open and take a step over the threshold before one of the men grabbed her arm and pulled her back.

"You not leave yet. Not finish talking."

"Let me go. I have not done anything!"

"My friend look in your bag. If everything okay, you can go."

"No! He will *not!*"

The man said something in his language again. One of his friends clamped onto Jar's other arm, then he and the first guy began forcing her toward the back of the restaurant.

Behind them, the bell attached to the front door dinged.

NATE TOOK ANOTHER bite of biscotti as he watched the restaurant across the street. Jar had been inside a little under ten minutes. Which meant only ten were left until Nate's cab drove off, if the driver gave Nate the full twenty he'd promised.

Nate reached for his coffee, but the door to De Luca's opened and Jar took a step out. Before she was all the way outside, someone yanked her back inside.

Nate jumped to his feet and hurried out of the shop. While his plan had been to avoid direct contact with his friends, it did not include staying idle if one of them got into trouble.

He pulled open the door to De Luca's and entered. Jar was being held by two men while a third was leading them deeper into the restaurant.

Going with the first thing that came to mind, he said, "Hey! What are you guys doing? Let go of my girlfriend!"

The procession stopped, and Jar and the others turned to Nate. There was no hiding the surprise on her face, but thankfully the men weren't looking at her.

Nate hurried over to her. "Sweetie, are you okay? Are they hurting you?"

Jar might not have had the best social skills, but she wasn't clueless. "They think I have done something, but I have not done *anything*."

"It's okay, babe. I'll take care of this." He looked at the man who had been leading the others and said in Italian, "Tell your friends to let go of my girlfriend."

"Your girlfriend?"

"Yeah, now let her go. Or I call the police."

The man grinned as if Nate had told a joke. When he spoke again, it was in an Eastern European language Nate didn't know.

The two men holding Jar loosened their grips but didn't release her.

"I said, let her go."

"Not until I know why she was upstairs."

Switching to English, Nate said, "He says you were upstairs and wants to know why."

"I already told him. I got lost."

Nate now understood what was going on. Thinking quickly, he came up with a plan. "Lost or poking around?" He sighed and shook his head. "Sweetheart, how many times do we have to talk about the fact that people don't like when others snoop around their places?" Switching back to Italian and taking a softer tone, he said, "I'm sorry. My girlfriend likes to see how things are put together. She's a student. You know, architecture?"

The man who'd been doing the talking narrowed his eyes.

"Study what?"

"Architecture. Designing buildings and that kind of thing."

It took a moment for the man to work it out. When he did, he looked at Jar. "She's an architect?"

Nate laughed. "No, not yet. She's still at the university."

To Jar, the man said in English, "He say you a student. What you study?"

"Architecture," she said as if it were a stupid question. The Italian words for architect and architecture were similar to those in English, so Nate had been confident she'd pick them up.

"This is why you go upstairs?"

She did an admirable job of looking uncomfortable. "Maybe…I am sorry. I just wanted to see how the building was laid out. See if it was a good use of space. Which, by the way, it is not."

The man seemed a bit unsure of what she'd said, but apparently it had been enough to convince him she wasn't a problem. He said something in the other language to his friends, and they let go of her.

"Next time you be careful where you go," the man said. "Now get out of here. Not come back."

Jar straightened her shirt. "Why would I come back? You have not been very—"

"Honey," Nate said, putting a hand on her back. "We should go."

Jar glared at the three men, and then marched past Nate toward the exit.

"Sorry for the misunderstanding," Nate said before following her.

He caught up to her on the sidewalk and put an arm around her back, in case the men looked out at them. She tensed and tried to pull away.

"Relax, it's just for show."

Though she stopped squirming, she didn't relax. "Why does everyone want to pretend I am their girlfriend?"

"What?"

"You did today. Daeng did last night. I am not a helpless girl who needs a man to save her."

"Whoa. No one said you were."

"I could have gotten out of trouble back there on my own."

"Without hurting someone?"

She looked the other way.

"Jar, you're one of the last people I would ever think of as helpless. But sometimes a little assistance is okay no matter who you are. Would you rather I'd have let you handle that yourself?"

Again, no reply.

"I didn't help out because you were a helpless girl. I did it because you're my friend."

She breathed deeply, then said, "Thank you."

"You're welcome."

They crossed at the corner and headed down the intersecting road. As soon as they were out of sight of the restaurant, Nate removed his arm from her back.

"What are you doing here?" Jar said.

"I was asked to come."

"We were told you said you would not."

He took a moment before answering. "I needed a little time to think about it."

They walked in silence for several moments.

"I am glad you are here," Jar said.

He smiled. "It's good to see you, too, Jar."

Jar reached for her pocket and pulled out her phone. There was a text on the screen. "It's Daeng."

"Is he okay?"

She tapped a reply. "It is nothing."

For the next several moments, she and Daeng traded messages. Finally, she put the phone away.

"You're sure he's not in trouble?"

"I am sure."

"Did you tell him about me?"

"No. Did you want me to?"

"I, um, I'm not sure yet."

"And that is why I did not tell him."

"Thank you."

She looked as if she was going to say something, but thought better of it.

"You want to tell me what you were doing in there?" he asked.

Jar was only partway into her story, of what had transpired since she and Daeng had arrived in Rome, when they reached her scooter. Nate hopped on behind her and had her drive him to where he'd left his cab.

Surprisingly, it was still waiting.

"Not going to need you anymore," Nate said. "But thanks for taking me around."

Looking disappointed, the cabbie handed Nate a business card. "If you need another ride, call me."

Nate glanced at the card and stuffed it into his pocket. "Thanks, Flavio. I will."

After the taxi drove off, Jar told Nate the rest of the story there at the side of the road.

"No idea what was in the cases they carried inside?" he asked.

"They were always closed."

"Why take them to that restaurant?"

"I do not know that, either."

He said nothing for several seconds. "I'm not sure if the place is important or not, but it would probably be a good idea for one of us to keep an eye on it."

"Or we could put up more cameras."

He raised an eyebrow. "You have cameras?"

"I have a full kit."

"Oh. Okay, good. We should definitely put up…wait, did you say more?"

"Yes. In addition to the ones I put in the upstairs and downstairs hallways inside the restaurant."

"You didn't mention that earlier."

"It was implied."

"How do you imply…you know what? Never mind. Let's get those cameras up."

DRAKE PULLED THE SUV to the curb in front of St. Amand's residence and called Manfred, the man he'd left in charge at the restaurant. "Is everything set?"

"Yes, sir." Something in Manfred's tone undercut his response.

"You don't sound sure."

Manfred hesitated. "There was a woman upstairs."

"In the room?"

"No," Manfred said quickly. "In the hallway, I think."

"You *think*?"

"Mr. De Luca caught her coming down the stairs."

"Did you talk to her? What was she doing?"

Another pause. "She was a tourist. I think she was just looking around."

"A tourist? How do you know that?"

"She was Asian and spoke English."

Asian? He recalled the couple from the previous night. "Was she alone?"

"Her boyfriend was with her."

"He was Asian, too?"

"No. Caucasian. He spoke Italian with an accent. British or maybe American."

Drake relaxed a bit. The couple outside St. Amand's office had both been Asian. "So, what happened?"

"I talked with them for a few minutes. They were harmless so I let them go."

Drake was silent for a moment. Chances were, Manfred was right and the woman was nothing to worry about, but Drake never liked leaving things to chance. "Do an electronics sweep and take another look around. When I call back, I want you to guarantee me that everything is buttoned up and ready."

"Right away."

MANFRED CONDUCTED THE sweep himself, starting with the meeting room. The only time he or one of the others hadn't been in it since their last sweep was when they questioned the woman, so, as he knew would be the case, he found nothing.

As he moved into the hallway, though, the digital meter

ticked upward for half a second before falling back to zero. He stopped, waiting for the meter to move again, but it remained in place. He tried walking over the same spot again. No blip this time.

The device had probably picked up someone's cellphone. It was supposed to screen out mobiles but that didn't always happen. He moved slowly down the hallway, his eyes glued to the screen. A bug would light the thing up, but other than a few normal-level twitches, the meter stayed quiet.

He checked all the other upstairs private dining rooms before heading downstairs, where he scanned the hallway, kitchen, toilets, and public dining areas. All came out clean. He texted Drake, letting him know everything was fine, and returned to the meeting room.

THE CAMERAS STAYED dark for five minutes after detecting a scanner, then only enough power came on to reactivate the sensor. When no scanner was detected, full power was restored, and the two cameras Jar had placed inside the restaurant went back online.

DAENG DIDN'T REALIZE Jar had turned off her comm until the SUV stopped next to a row of buildings in the Trastevere district. He had thought the silence was due to traffic noise drowning out the signal. Now that he was stopped, he realized nothing was coming through at all.

"Jar?" he said.

Dead air.

Was she in trouble? Had she been caught?

He should have insisted on staying.

He started the engine again, planning on returning to the restaurant, but before he could pull back onto the street, the driver climbed out of the SUV. As the big man moved around to the passenger side, three other suited men exited the building next to the vehicle.

One of the suited men was wearing a hat and sunglasses and scarf.

St. Amand. Crap.

"Jar," Daeng said again.

Nothing.

The driver opened the front passenger door and Potential St. Amand climbed in. The other two got into the backseat.

Crap, crap, crap.

Standard mission protocol dictated that he follow the target and let his fellow agent handle her situation herself. But this was Jar, and she was really no more than an apprentice.

He sent her a text.

> Your comm is off. Is everything okay?

At the SUV, the driver climbed in behind the wheel, and within moments was pulling the vehicle onto the road.

Daeng opened up the tracking software, activating not only the dot linked to the bug on the SUV but also the one for Jar's phone.

Huh. She wasn't at De Luca's anymore, though she was in the vicinity of the restaurant. Was that a good sign or bad? His phone buzzed.

A text from Jar.

> Was worried receiver would be seen. Everything is fine.

Okay, that was good news, but if everything *was* fine, then...

> Turn your comm back on.

Her reply came a few seconds later.

> Cannot now. Soon.

He tapped another message.

> Explain.

Her response:

Busy.

He started to type another message, but stopped. If she was busy, then his continued questioning could jeopardize what she was doing.

Reluctantly, he erased the message and zoomed in on the dot for the SUV. It had stair-stepped four blocks to the northeast. He attached the phone to the holder on his dash and took up the chase again.

CHAPTER
TWENTY ONE

ST. AMAND READ THE Sandstrom file again as Drake drove him through the city. It was always important to know everything possible about a client. For example, Sandstrom's many indiscretions over the years included nearly a dozen assault charges that had been dropped and subsequently expunged (though not as thoroughly as Sandstrom probably thought), a habit of sleeping with the wives of his subordinates, and at least two homicides that had been covered up by friends in law enforcement. There were also five other murders that Sandstrom was likely involved in.

St. Amand would never dream of blatantly using these facts in their discussions, but knowing them would allow him to subtly push some of Sandstrom's buttons if necessary.

He doubted it would come to that. The purpose of the meeting, as St. Amand saw it, was to ensure Sandstrom was well aware of St. Amand's displeasure about the situation in Oklahoma and how the news had been kept from him. St. Amand would use this to bluff about dropping the American and his network of militias as clients. By the end of the meeting, St. Amand was sure he and his organization would secure ten, or even twenty, million euros' worth in additional orders.

Sandstrom could easily afford it. He had the backing of some heavy hitters, including a handful of billionaires who felt a shake-up to the status quo was both necessary and inevitable. St. Amand had a feeling they couldn't care less about

Sandstrom's goal of carving out his own nation, dedicated to his homogeneous ideals. The billionaires probably had the same racist thoughts, but *their* goal was purely monetary. Instability creates chaos, and from chaos comes order. Strong, iron-fisted, dictatorial order. Whoever that dictator was, he would need these same financial backers to help him craft economic policies that cared little for regulations and standards, and more about profit.

St. Amand didn't really care about any of their goals except the chaos part. And, dear God, there would certainly be that. The great America in flames. He couldn't wait to see that headline on BBC World News.

He looked out the front window. Traffic was particularly bad this afternoon. If it kept up like this, it would be another thirty minutes before they reached their destination, and then another good hour to get to De Luca's. But that was fine. Time had been built into the schedule to make sure they arrived at the restaurant well before Sandstrom did.

St. Amand looked back at the file and flipped the page.

"HAVE YOU BEEN driving around this whole time?"

Daeng tensed in surprise at the sound of Jar's voice. In rapid fire, he asked, "Where are you? Why did you turn your radio off? Did something happen?"

"I turned it off to avoid one of St. Amand's men noticing it."

"How close did you get to them?"

"Close enough."

"What the hell happened?"

Ahead, the light turned red, stopping the SUV.

"Unimportant. Everything is fine."

"That doesn't make me feel any better." He weaved the scooter around the waiting cars to the front of the line, where all the other motorbikes had congregated.

"How you feel is not my problem. You have not answered *my* question."

"What question?" He thought back. "Oh. No, the SUV stopped to pick up St. Amand in Trastevere. We've been heading across the city since then."

"He's in the SUV now?"

"Yeah. I mean, I think it was him. He was wearing the scarf again, and—"

A scooter edged into the spot next to him.

"You are not a very good spy," Jar said, looking over at him.

Daeng stared back. Not at Jar, but at the person sitting behind her.

"Hey," Nate said.

Playing it as cool as he could, Daeng said, "I was under the impression you weren't joining us."

"I couldn't leave you hanging, now could I?"

The other scooter drivers revved their motors in anticipation of the green light.

"You guys hang back a little," Daeng said. He gave Nate a small smile. "Good to see you."

"Good to see you, too."

The light changed, and traffic surged forward.

QUINN AND ORLANDO left Washington on a private jet just after midnight. With them was Steve Howard, a freelancer they often used. While Howard did not know what St. Amand looked like, he was a skilled operative. Misty had remained in Washington, to coordinate things from that end.

Their pilot was able to shave almost an hour off the typical flight duration, landing them in Rome right after three p.m. local time.

As they taxied to the terminal, Orlando called Daeng and put him on speaker. From the background noise, it was clear their friend was driving.

"We just touched down," Orlando told him. "What's going on?"

"I'm following an SUV carrying the guy we think is St. Amand."

"You saw him again?"

"Yeah, he got in about forty minutes ago, and we've been working our way slowly to the northeast since then."

"Any idea of your destination?"

"Haven't a clue."

"Is Jar with you?"

There was a pause before Daeng said, "She is," and told them about a restaurant they'd seen some of St. Amand's men enter with several large cases. "We have cameras on the place, and last time we checked the men were still inside."

"Should we rendezvous with you? Or…?"

"Without knowing where we're going, you could be driving around in circles. Probably best if you head for the apartment. The key's in the lockbox. If things change before you get there, we'll let you know."

"Sounds good. Stay safe."

TEN MINUTES NORTH of the Spanish Steps, the SUV pulled to the side of the road.

Daeng and Jar eased to the curb. The driver, the man in the scarf, and the two men in the back of the SUV exited their vehicle and entered a very familiar building.

"Break into the cameras again," Daeng said to Jar.

"Again?" Nate said.

"That's one of the buildings we checked out yesterday. Supposedly has ties with St. Amand. Well, I guess not supposedly anymore."

"I am in," Jar said, looking at her phone.

Daeng and Nate huddled around her. Onscreen was the inside of the elevator the four men from the SUV were riding.

Nate pointed at the man wearing the scarf. "That's the guy you think is St. Amand?"

"He fits the known descriptions," Daeng said. "But you're the guru, right? Is it him?"

"He could be almost anybody with that damn thing covering his face."

The men exited the elevator on the fourth floor.

"No cameras in the hallways?" Nate asked.

"On the other floors, yes," Jar said. "But not on that one."

"Interesting. Who lives here?"

"The thinking is that St. Amand moves around between

residences," Daeng said.

"So today is switch day?"

"Seems possible."

Nate studied the building. "Were you able to get inside?"

"Didn't try. Wanted to keep a low profile." Daeng looked at Nate. "Um, I got a call a few minutes ago. Quinn and Orlando have just landed."

Nate nodded, but said nothing.

Daeng studied him for a moment. "I'm glad you're here."

Eyes on the building, Nate said, "Yeah, well, not sure I feel the same yet."

"It doesn't matter what you feel now. You'll know I'm right soon enough."

"Daeng, seriously, I'm not ready for one of your philosophical trips right now."

"Don't worry. I'm saving that for later."

"I doubt I'll be ready for it then, either."

"All I'm saying is that it's good for you to be among friends."

Nate took a deep breath. "Maybe."

NATE KNEW DAENG had his best interests at heart. In fact, he knew Daeng was right. For a long time now, Quinn and Orlando, then Daeng and most recently Jar, had been Nate's family.

But he didn't want to hear it. He preferred to remain in the cocoon he'd created, where the only way he could hurt was by doing something to himself. If he spent time with Daeng and Jar and Orlando and Quinn—especially Quinn—those walls would crack. He wasn't ready for that yet. He wasn't sure he'd ever be ready.

Thankfully, Daeng let the subject drop.

After a few quiet minutes, Jar said, "They are coming back down."

"All of them?" Nate asked.

"Plus one."

The feed from the elevator cam showed five people descending. The new member of the group had hair long enough to drape over his shoulders. Like the others, he was wearing a suit. The angle of the camera made it difficult to see much of his face.

As the elevator neared ground level, Jar switched to a camera covering the lobby. The men exited and walked through the room, this time the lens showing their faces.

The new guy was older than the men whose faces weren't covered, probably in his late forties, early fifties. He had high cheekbones and wore wide, wire-rimmed glasses. Something about him seemed familiar to Nate, but what and why, he wasn't sure. He *was* sure about another member of the group.

"I've seen him before," he said, pointing at the largest man.

"That's the driver," Daeng said.

"He was in Marrakesh with St. Amand," Nate said, recalling the brute who had chased him.

"Anyone else?" Jar asked.

Nate frowned. "I'm...I'm not sure."

When the men walked out of the building, Jar switched to one of the exterior cameras. The angle was almost straight down and didn't help with identification, but at least Nate and his friends could continue to observe the men without having to look at them.

As the group approached the SUV, one of the men ran around and got into the backseat on the other side. Potential St. Amand climbed into the back on the passenger side, followed by another man, putting Potential St. Amand in the middle. The brute went around to the driver's seat, while High Cheekbones climbed into the front passenger seat.

Nate grimaced. He'd been hoping to see enough of the scarfed man's face to ID him as St. Amand. That would have wrapped things up, and he could have been off to...well, anyplace else.

The SUV drove off.

Daeng opened the cargo area under the seat of his scooter, pulled out a small cloth bag, and tossed it to Nate. "Put these on."

Nate reluctantly pulled out the comm gear and donned the

earpiece. "Gee, thanks."

Daeng closed the compartment and climbed onto his bike. "Shall we?"

AT FIRST IT seemed as if the SUV was heading to the office building. But thirty-five minutes in, it passed the last chance to turn west and continued south apace.

Not too much farther on, Daeng said, "They must be heading to the restaurant."

"Jar," Nate said, "let's you and I get ahead of them and get there first. Daeng, you continue to follow."

"Okay," Daeng said. "I'll tell Quinn and Orlando to meet us there."

"Yeah, I guess."

"Let us know when you are getting close," Jar said.

She sped through the next light as it turned red, leaving Daeng and the SUV behind.

Daeng used the pause to call Orlando.

After he gave her the address, she said, "Got it. Where did you guys put the gear bag?"

"Closet by the bathroom."

"Thanks."

"Orlando," he said.

"Yeah?"

"Nate's here. He's with Jar."

Silence.

"Did you hear me?"

"Yes. Okay. I just…okay. Thanks for letting me know. See you there."

As Daeng disconnected, he had the ridiculous thought he'd betrayed Nate. He was going to be so glad when things were back to normal. Well, nothing would ever be pre-Liz's-death normal again, but at least whatever the new normal was going to be.

Unless the way things were now *was* the new normal.

Dear god, he hoped that wasn't true.

JAR PARKED THE scooter in the same spot she'd used earlier,

and she and Nate made their way back to the roof where they'd planted the remote camera relay.

The first thing they did was to review the footage the outside cameras had recorded while they were away. Jar played everything at high speed, slowing only when someone was coming or going from De Luca's. St. Amand's men appeared four times. Smoke breaks, and never more than two at a time. In every instance, the men went back inside.

Jar brought up the feeds for the interior cameras, and discovered the anomaly almost right away. "Looks like they did not completely believe us."

"What do you mean?"

"Not long after we left, the auto shutoff function was activated on both cameras."

She showed him the last few seconds before the feed when dark, when the door to the room at the far end was starting to open.

"How long were they off for?"

"One cycle."

"Then they only made one sweep."

"So it would seem."

She let the remaining video play, again at high speed. Most of the incidents when the men left the room matched the times they appeared on the outside cameras. When the playback reached the end of the prerecorded material and switched to the live feed, all four men were back in the room.

Nate retrieved his phone and touched the screen. "Daeng's six blocks away."

She glanced over and saw he had his tracking app open. Daeng's was the only dot on it. Since Nate didn't have the ID info of the bug on the SUV, she checked the app on her phone and saw the vehicle a block ahead of Daeng.

"Four minutes away," she said.

Nate looked around. "I'm going to see if I can get a direct view from up here."

He popped to his feet and moved across the roof, toward the buildings that faced De Luca's restaurant. Jar picked up the relay and followed.

There was a two-meter gap between the building they were on and one that fronted the same street as the restaurant. After a quick examination, Nate backed up several meters from the edge.

"What are you doing?" she asked.

"What do you think I'm doing?"

Without waiting for her to respond, he sprinted across the roof and launched himself over the gap, landing on the other side with plenty of room to spare.

"Stay there," he said. "I'll come back after they've gone inside."

He headed for the front edge of the building.

Jar looked at the gap. She'd jumped farther before. She'd just never done so over a five-story drop. She had no intention of being left behind, though.

She stuffed her phone in her pocket, removed her backpack, and set it and the relay against a vent, where they'd be in the shade. She ran as fast as she could and shoved off a good ten centimeters shy of the gap.

There was a moment around the halfway point when she wasn't sure she'd make it, but then her foot landed a finger's width beyond the edge on the other side, and her momentum propelled her the rest of the way to safety.

She snuck over to where Nate was lying at the street side of the roof, and stretched out next to him.

"Nice jump," he whispered. "Though I would have deducted a few form points on your landing."

"Is that supposed to be funny?"

He smirked. "You do know this means you're going to have to jump back, right?"

"Obviously. I am not stupid."

"No, you are far from that."

From their new position, they had a clear view of the street. The restaurant was across the road and to the right a couple of buildings. There were more people walking around than earlier in the day, plus several more parked cars. The curb right in front of the restaurant was empty, though, thanks to a few traffic cones that prevented anyone from using the spots.

"How are the guys upstairs doing?" Nate asked.

Jar reconnected her cell to the relay and held it so they both could see the screen. The door at the end of the upstairs hallway was open, but no one was in view. Jar switched to the lower corridor camera in time for it to show two of the men exit into the dining area.

She looked up in time to see the men step outside. One was the guy Nate had talked to, and the other was one of the men who'd been holding Jar. After waiting for an elderly couple to pass by on the sidewalk, they proceeded to the curb and moved the cones out of the way. They stood on the sidewalk, side by side, facing the road.

Jar switched her phone to the tracker. "Thirty seconds."

Right on schedule, the SUV turned onto the road and pulled up in front of the waiting men. One opened the back passenger-side door, while his partner opened the one in front. The first to emerge was High Cheekbones, then a bodyguard from the back and the man in the scarf. The other bodyguard exited on the far side and came around.

Once everyone was on the sidewalk and the doors were shut, the driver moved the SUV forward to the end of the coned-off section and climbed out. As this was happening, the others entered the restaurant.

"Cameras," Nate said.

Before he'd even finished saying the word, the feed from the lower hallway was playing on her phone. Soon, the men moved into view. The camera had an excellent angle on each man as he passed.

When the man in the scarf walked through, she said, "There's a bit of ear showing."

"Mark it."

"Already done."

She switched to the upper hall feed. This camera saw only the backs of the men's heads, though it did catch more of the semi-exposed ear. She marked this also.

The men entered the room at the far end, but the door stayed open until the brute joined them.

"Audio?" he asked.

She turned up the sound, but the camera was too far away, especially with the door closed, to pick up anything. After a few seconds, she turned it down again.

"Too bad you couldn't have placed it closer," he said.

She raised an eyebrow. "And if I had, I would have never made it to the front door, and you would have never seen me, and—"

Nate held up a hand. "I know. It wasn't a criticism. Just a wish."

"Wishes are wasted energy."

"Jar…"

When he didn't go on, she said, "What?"

"Nothing." He looked back at the street.

For a few moments there, the old Nate had peeked through, but he'd turned maudlin again. He'd been up and down since making his unannounced appearance. She wanted to help him but had no idea how. People were…hard.

"Daeng for Jar."

Jar clicked on her mic. "Go for Jar."

"I have you on a roof. Is that right?"

"Correct." She explained how to reach their position, and turned to Nate again.

His eyes were glassy, as if he was looking at something entirely different than what was in front of him. She moved her hand over his shoulder, letting it hover, uncertain if giving him a reassuring touch was the right thing or not. Her fingers opened and closed in indecision. She decided to go for it, touching him lightly at first, then letting the full weight of her hand rest on his shoulder.

He blinked and glanced at her, and for a moment it looked as if he might cry.

"I-I might not be the best person to help you," she said. "But I want you to know that I am here if you need me."

A tear rolled down his cheek as he smiled. "Thanks."

"You are my friend, Nate. You do not need to thank me."

For some reason, this drew a chuckle out of him. It did not feel mean spirited, however.

"And you're my friend, Jar. And I'm glad for it."

He held her gaze. She didn't know if she should look away, or smile, or what, so she simply stared back until he wiped his eyes.

"Don't tell the others," he said. "I have a reputation to keep."

"I would not think of telling—oh, that was a joke."

"Yeah. But, also, don't tell them."

"I will not."

"Thanks." He nodded at her phone. "Let's take a look at that exposed ear, shall we?"

IT WAS SURPRISING to Nate how easy it was to fall back into his old self. As he and Jar watched the men, he'd switch to full operations mode.

He studied each man's face as they passed the ground-floor camera, and was once more struck by the older guy with the high cheekbones. It was something in the eyes. Nate was sure he'd seen them before. As for the scarfed man, the partially exposed ear was interesting, though Nate couldn't remember noting much about St. Amand's ear back in Marrakesh.

He'd been honest when he told Jar his comment about getting the camera closer was not a criticism but a wish. And when she'd replied that wishes were a waste of energy, he'd almost joked, "Jar, so is being too serious."

But it had stuck in his throat, and made him realize he was acting like his old self. Then it dawned on him he hadn't thought about Liz since he hopped onto the back of Jar's scooter.

He couldn't help but feel like he'd almost forgotten Liz. Like he'd been on the verge of purging her from his mind. Of course, he could never do that, but the idea of it was enough to shake him to his core.

I'm sorry. I'll never do that again.
You will, and it will be okay, Liz replied.
Don't say that! Please, never say that!
A hush.
I'm sorry, he thought.
I know.

When Jar's hand touched his shoulder, it was almost as if Liz herself was doing it. He knew how hard it must have been for Jar to do what she did. And despite himself, his heart lifted.

They watched the ear footage again, Nate having her loop it over and over again, but no matter how much she replayed it, nothing about the scarfed man's ear stood out for Nate.

They had just switched back to the live feed from the restaurant's upstairs hallway when they both heard a thump on the roof behind them, signaling the arrival of Daeng. But then three more thumps followed.

Nate looked back.

Daeng was there, and so were Quinn and Orlando and Steve Howard.

Quinn crawled up next to him. "What's the situation?"

Fighting dryness in his throat, Nate said, "They're upstairs in a room above the restaurant. Jar's got a camera in the hallway outside it."

Orlando took the spot next to Quinn, while Daeng and Howard stretched out on the other side of Jar.

"Did you get a good look at them?"

"Decent enough."

"And?"

"I have no idea if the guy in the scarf is St. Amand or not. No way to tell unless we get him out of that garb."

Quinn looked at the building. "Anyone have any idea what they're doing here?"

"It has to be a meeting that has something to do with those cases they brought in," Daeng said.

"Sure, but what's in those cases?"

Nate shrugged. "This guy's an arms dealer. So, weapons, right?"

Quinn glanced over at Jar and Daeng. "You guys saw them carry them in. Did the cases look heavy?"

"Not particularly. Most of the guys carried two at once."

"Maybe it's samples," Orlando said. "One or two of each item, probably in fancy protection to keep them looking pristine."

"Yes," Jar said. "I agree with Orlando. That is the most

logical answer."

"If that's true," Quinn said, "and they brought them to the back room of a restaurant—"

"Upstairs room," Jar corrected him.

"Right, upstairs room. That must mean they're meeting with a customer, right?"

"Or a supplier," Howard offered. "The samples could be to show him what they're interested in."

Quinn said to Jar, "You're sure the only people in that room right now are St. Amand's?"

"Unless someone else has been in there all day and not left, I am positive."

"Which means the person or persons they're meeting with aren't here yet." Quinn said nothing for a moment. "Is the restaurant open right now? I mean, to anyone?"

"Yes," Jar said.

"What I'm wondering is if there's any way for us to still get a microphone close enough to that room to listen in."

"I would *not* try going up the stairs again," Nate said.

"What's below it? Can we get a mic on the ceiling and listen in through the floorboards?"

Jar shook her head. "The room is directly above the kitchen. Any one of you who goes in there will be questioned."

"Also, kitchens are noisy," Daeng said. "Doubt the mic would pick up much of anything other than that."

"Hold on," Orlando said. "What we really need is something *in*side the room, right?"

"Right," Quinn said.

"Then why don't we have someone who has access carry a bug inside for us?"

"A waiter?" Howard asked.

"I'm not talking about a waiter. I'm talking about the client."

"Okay," Quinn said. "What would be the plan?"

"Has anyone noticed people coming in any other way than the front door?"

"No," Jar said.

Nate and Daeng shook their heads.

"Good, then that's most likely the way the client will enter. We plant someone in the restaurant. Whoever it is waits until we tell him the client has arrived. Then, as the client walks through, our inside man gets up to go the bathroom, bumps into him, and sticks him with a bug. I mean, you know, unless someone has a better idea."

"I like it," Quinn said. "Who's got the bugs?"

"I do," Jar said.

"Okay, good." Quinn looked around at everyone. "We can't send Jar because she's been inside already."

"Same problem for me," Nate said.

"What are you talking about?"

"There was a little…misunderstanding with St. Amand's men this afternoon. I had to go in and smooth things over."

"Are you serious?"

"It was my fault," Jar said. "They thought I was trying to spy on them."

"What happened?"

"Like I said, I smoothed it over," Nate replied. "By the time we left they weren't worried about her anymore."

"Are you sure?"

"Pretty sure."

Quinn frowned. "Are we looking at any residual fallout?"

"I'd be shocked if there was," Nate said. He could feel someone staring at the back of his head and figured it was Jar, wondering why he hadn't mentioned the electronics sweep. But there was no sense in making Quinn more uncomfortable.

"Okay," Quinn said. "Then you're out, too."

"And me," Daeng said. "I had an exchange with one of them last night. A few of the others might recognize me, too."

Quinn stared at him, then Jar, and finally Nate. "So, what you're saying is that we haven't even been on this job for twenty-four hours and yet all three of you have already been exposed. That's fantastic."

"You probably shouldn't go, either," Orlando said.

"And why is that?"

"It's possible some of them were in Marrakesh nine years ago. St. Amand definitely was."

"And the big guy," Nate said. "The driver."

"Even more reason," Orlando said to Quinn. "I know it's not likely any of them saw you, and even if they did, they probably wouldn't remember you, but we can't know that for sure."

Quinn took a breath. "Okay, I'm out, too. I guess that just leaves you and—"

"I wouldn't send Orlando," Daeng said.

"Dear God, why not?"

"Well, they ran into me and Jar last night, and Jar today. I don't know if you've noticed, but there aren't a lot of other Asians walking around this neighborhood. A third one, a *second* in the restaurant today, might come off as suspicious."

"That sounds…"

"Racist? Yeah, I know. Welcome to our world."

"Fine. I guess there's only one choice."

They all turned toward Steve Howard.

"Please tell me you've never had any contact with these people," Quinn said.

"Not as far as I know."

"How are your sleight-of-hand skills?" Orlando asked.

"Haven't done anything like this in a while, but shouldn't be a problem."

"Then congratulations, you're the lucky winner. Hurry up and get over there before this person shows up." Quinn pulled a fifty-euro note out of his pocket and held it up. "Dinner's on me."

Howard pushed himself up, grabbed the bill, and said to Jar, "Bugs?"

She pointed back across the roof. "In my bag on the other side of the jump, front pocket."

He headed for the gap.

Three minutes later Nate and the others watched Howard cross the street and enter the restaurant.

Nate began scooting back from the roofline.

"Where are you going?" Quinn asked.

"Someone should be down there, in case something goes wrong." Nate climbed to his feet.

"I'll go with you," Daeng said.

Quinn said, "No. I'll go."

Oh, yay, Nate thought.

QUINN FOLLOWED NATE across the roof, over the gap, and down to street level.

"There's a market up at the corner," Nate said. "We can hang out just around from it."

"Okay."

Nate led him down the street and stopped short of the intersection with the street the restaurant was on.

"Should be good here," Nate said as he leaned against the wall.

Quinn nodded.

An awkward silence fell over them. Quinn tried a million times to say something and failed just as many. On the millionth and first attempt, he eked out, "Thank you."

Nate made no indication he'd heard.

"For coming, I mean," Quinn went on. "I didn't…"

Silence again. Finally Nate said, "Don't worry about it."

Quinn couldn't tell if what he said was meant to open conversation or cut it off. He decided to bull forward. "I just wanted you to know I appreciate it."

"I said, don't worry about it."

Meant to cut it off, Quinn realized, but it was too late to stop now.

"I do worry about it. I worry about it because you are an important member of our team."

Nate frowned, but said nothing.

"I worry about it because…because you are one of my…friends."

"Yeah, well—"

"I mean, one of my best friends."

That stopped Nate.

"We're both grieving, Nate. But we shouldn't be using that to push each other away." Quinn hesitated. "Liz wouldn't want us to do that."

Nate stared at Quinn, his eyes turning glassy.

Quinn worried he'd gone too far, that his friend was going to pull back into his shell and disappear.

But Nate nodded, once, and looked back out at the street. Though Nate didn't see him, Quinn nodded, too.

CHAPTER
TWENTY TWO

THE GULFSTREAM G650ER private jet landed at Fiumicino International Airport at 4:52 p.m. The plane, owned by American billionaire Stewart Morrison, had ferried several members of Morrison's company—Moste International—to Rome for a surprise visit to one of its European affiliates.

That was the story, anyway.

While the site visit would indeed take place, the trip had actually been put together so that William Sandstrom could enter the country quietly and under an assumed identity. Everyone on the plane had been told that Sandstrom—traveling under the name Harvey Dennison—and the two people accompanying him were from the West Coast office and in Italy on business unrelated to theirs. Only Morrison and a couple of his most trusted associates knew the truth. Though no one would have guessed it from Morrison's public face, he was one of Sandstrom's biggest financial backers.

With Morrison's substantial resources, and that of a few others, Sandstrom had worked tirelessly to create a network of militia organizations across the US who thought as he did, and had begun the process of equipping those organizations with the tools they would need in the coming uprising.

The raid of Jackson Reed's compound in Oklahoma had been a big blow, but so far not a fatal one. Sandstrom had done everything in his power to make sure the FBI's discoveries did not lead them to any of the other associated organizations. His one miscalculation had been choosing to not inform Christophe

St. Amand of the incident. He had hoped to have everything contained long before St. Amand learned anything. He would never make that mistake again.

His hope now was that he hadn't completely scuttled the relationship with his largest supplier by far. If that were to happen, it would set his plan back at least a year, if not more. But he wasn't coming unprepared. He had a plan he was confident St. Amand would jump at.

The other passengers were in a giddy mood as they exited the plane and entered the terminal dedicated to small-jet service. Sandstrom and his associates, Marlon Johnson and Dean Holt, inserted themselves into the mix as everyone lined up to get their passports checked. Johnson was Sandstrom's top advisor, while Holt was his good-for-little son-in-law, brought along mainly to carry the large briefcase Sandstrom hoped would help turn the coming meeting in his favor. As promised, their documents were scanned and stamped and returned without incident, and the briefcase went unchecked.

They were met by a trio of men holding signs outside Immigration, two reading MOSTE INTERNATIONAL and the other DENNISON. The latter sign holder led Sandstrom and his people to a dark passenger van with tinted windows.

As soon as they were on their way, Johnson said to the driver, "How long?"

"Much traffic now," the man replied. "An hour and fifteen minutes. Maybe a little more."

Either way, they wouldn't reach the meeting until after 6:30, which would already be thirty minutes later than planned.

"Let them know," Sandstrom said to Johnson.

As Johnson sent the text to St. Amand's people, Sandstrom settled back in his seat and closed his eyes.

IMRICH KYSELY HAD dropped off Havel Zima at the private jet terminal thirty minutes before Sandstrom's plane touched down. Most of St. Amand's security force was Bulgarian, but the two men were from Slovakia and always worked as a team, since they could never make heads or tails of what the others were saying.

While the plane was in the air, Havel had witnessed the arrival of three empty passenger vans. When the drivers had gone into the terminal, Havel took a jaunt into the parking area, confirmed one of the vans had the same plate number as what Drake had told him to look for, and then headed back inside.

The terminal itself was sparsely populated—a couple of groups making their way to the waiting area for flights, a pair of women at a ground transportation information desk, several others at a passenger check-in counter, the usual security guards and other terminal personnel, and the drivers of the three vans standing outside Customs and Immigration.

Having seen everything he needed to, Havel was pulling out his phone to let Imrich know it was time to pick him up when two men entered the building.

Americans.

Havel could spot their innate sense of entitlement a million miles away. But they weren't tourists. An air of authority clung to this pair like a second skin.

The men walked directly to the check-in counter and spoke to one of the attendants. She nodded several times and picked up a phone.

Havel wandered toward the counter, staring at his phone like he was checking his messages.

"Ah, okay," the woman said in Italian. "Thank you." She hung up. "The plane should be on the ground in ten minutes."

"Thank you. We appreciate your help," one of the men said. His Italian was very good, but it had the accent of an American.

Havel's eyes were still on his phone when the men turned. He snapped a couple of pictures, waited several seconds after they walked by, and followed.

The men headed toward the door. The moment they stepped outside, Havel increased his pace. When he reached the exit, he spotted one of the men getting into a car in the parking area. Presumably the other man had already climbed inside.

Havel waited just inside the door to see if they left, but the car stayed where it was.

The plane should be on the ground in ten minutes, the

woman had said.

That was the same time Sandstrom's plane was due.

A bit past the ten-minute mark, Havel's phone buzzed with a text. It was from Drake and had been sent to both him and Imrich.

> Sandstrom's plane has landed.

Havel called Imrich and had his partner pick him up. They waited at a turnout area from where they could see both the parking lot and the terminal.

Seventeen minutes later, a small group of people walked out of the terminal and into the parking area. A few minutes after that, the van with the matching plate number began moving.

Havel trained his binoculars on the sedan he'd seen the two Americans enter, and started counting. When he reached thirteen, the sedan backed out of its spot and headed to the exit, where the van was waiting for a gate to rise and let it out.

He called Drake. "You were right. It looks like our friends have picked up a tail."

DRAKE WAS DISMAYED, though not surprised, by Havel's information. The possibility of someone following Sandstrom was the reason Havel and Imrich were there in the first place.

"You're sure Sandstrom doesn't know about it?" he asked.

"I think not," Havel said. "They made sure they were out of sight when Sandstrom arrived."

"What did they look like?"

"Hold on. I'll send you pictures."

A few seconds later, Drake's phone vibrated. This was why Drake liked Havel and Imrich so much. They were thorough and efficient. He checked the pictures, but had never seen the men before. He did recognize their look, however. Law enforcement, or perhaps military. He forwarded both photos to one of his subordinates, with instructions to identify the men.

"I want you to stop that sedan as soon as an opportunity

arises. It needs to be subtle, but I don't want them getting anywhere near De Luca's."

"We're on it."

Drake hung up, thought for a moment, and made a call. "I need you to coordinate an emergency transfer. And it needs to happen in the next twenty minutes."

AS FBI LIAISON officers assigned to the US embassy in Rome, Francisco Ross and Oren Barham typically spent most of their time coordinating and consulting with Italian authorities on various issues. While this proved to be interesting at times, both men were itching to get back to the States, where they would be more visible to the higher-ups and thus increase their chances at promotion.

Occasionally they'd receive calls from American field offices, asking for their assistance on investigations that had spilled into Ross and Barham's neck of the woods. Most of the time, this would involve tracking down witnesses no longer in the US and interviewing them. Rarer were the calls like the one they'd received earlier that day.

A tip had been received that a man on the FBI's watch list was making a clandestine trip to Rome on a private airplane, scheduled to arrive later that afternoon. A picture of the man was sent, along with instructions to follow and observe only.

This felt like real work, and both men jumped into the task with gusto.

At the private aircraft terminal, they confirmed the plane was about to land and returned to their car, where they watched the building's entrance for the suspect.

"That's him," Barham said, as the man from the picture exited the terminal thirty minutes later with three others.

"I concur," Ross said. He texted the agent in the States that the tip had been correct.

Barham and Ross watched the group get into a van with tinted windows a couple of rows over. When it moved, Barham waited a few seconds before he started the engine and pulled out of their spot. They exited the lot, two vehicles behind the van.

As they drove out of the airport, neither man noticed the car parked off to the side. But even if they had, they would have thought nothing of it. There had been no mention, in the phone call or subsequent email, of any other parties who might have been interested in the subject.

"MR. SANDSTROM?"

Sandstrom slowly opened his eyes. There hadn't been enough time for him to fall asleep, but he'd been close.

"There's been a change of plans," Johnson said.

Sandstrom sat up, thoughts of resting forgotten. Before he could ask what his assistant meant, Johnson held out his phone so Sandstrom could see the text. "From Mr. St. Amand's contact person."

> You are being followed. It will be taken care of, but we feel it would be prudent for you to switch vehicles. Please instruct your driver to proceed to this location:

In a bubble below the text was a map with a marker denoting the new destination.

Sandstrom glanced out the back window at the crowded, two-lane divided highway. "Which one?"

"They didn't say."

Sandstrom turned back around. They had taken precautions to ensure their departure went unnoticed, but apparently the safeguards hadn't been enough.

"Maybe St. Amand's playing games with us," Holt suggested. "Keep us on our toes."

Sandstrom frowned. "Why the hell would he screw with us? We're a client."

"One he's not happy with."

"If he was going to do something, it would be after we meet, not before."

If Holt hadn't been married to Sandstrom's daughter, Sandstrom would have fired him on the spot. Not the first time he'd had that thought.

"Should we follow the instructions or return to the

airport?" Johnson asked.

God only knew how long Freedom Day would be delayed if they missed this meeting. The deal with St. Amand needed to be shored up now so that the supply lines would be in place in time. "We do as they say."

WHILE IMRICH MANEUVERED their sedan close to the Americans' car, he and Havel discussed several options for stopping the others. Once they had their plan, Havel studied the map and picked out the best location for the diversion. Imrich worked his way through traffic until they were directly in front of their target.

"Any time now," Havel said.

Imrich smiled. "Hang on."

Havel was sure that in an alternate life, Imrich would have driven Formula One race cars or stunt cars. Imrich had an instinctive feel for anything with an engine. It didn't matter if it was his first time behind the wheel of a specific car or not. Within minutes he would master it better than anyone who'd ever driven the vehicle.

That's why Havel was not the least bit nervous when Imrich sideswiped a delivery truck.

"WHOA! WHOA!" ROSS yelled as his hand shot out to the dash.

The car in front of them had veered into a truck in the next lane, then ricocheted back in front of them, and begun to spin.

"Slow down!"

His words came too late.

HAVEL MAY NOT have been scared, but he wasn't stupid. He gripped the handle above the door with both hands to avoid sliding into Imrich's lap.

With expert precision, Imrich tapped the brakes, giving their sedan just enough momentum to smack into the front of the Americans' sedan.

Everything became a blur of movement, dancing to a soundtrack of screeching brakes and twisting metal. When the spinning finally stopped, Imrich and Havel's car was sitting diagonally across the highway, blocking all lanes.

Havel blinked twice, took a deep breath, and looked around for the other vehicle.

The Americans were several meters away, their car lying on its roof against the right-side guardrail. Havel could see one of the men dangling upside down in his seat. The other man wasn't visible. People from vehicles behind the mess hurried toward the accident. The majority headed toward the flipped car, while a trio of men approached Havel and Imrich's sedan.

One of the men peered through the broken passenger window. "Are you all right? Anyone hurt?"

Other than a few dull aches and pains, Havel felt fine. "I'm okay." He looked over at Imrich. "You?"

Imrich nodded. "Am okay, too."

"What about the people in the other car?" Havel asked, acting concerned.

"I'll check. You should probably stay in your car until help arrives."

"Good idea."

As soon as the man was gone, Havel texted Drake.

The tail has been removed.

The Good Samaritan returned a moment later.

Apparently the men in the sedan had not fared as well as Havel and Imrich. The driver had apparently broken a couple of ribs, and done something to his left arm that didn't look good. His passenger was unconscious. Which, the Samaritan told them, was probably a good thing given the compound fracture on his leg.

When Havel had another free moment, he texted this information to his boss as well.

THE TRANSFER FROM the van to an SUV that would serve as Sandstrom's new ride was accomplished in an efficient manner.

Not long after they were on the road again, Johnson received a text from St. Amand's people. The car that had been tailing them was no longer a problem. Sandstrom was relieved, though the fact there had been a tail at all was still troubling, and made him wonder if he had a leak in his organization who had passed on his travel plans to someone, probably law enforcement.

Just over an hour later, the SUV stopped in front of the restaurant where the meeting was to take place. Two men who had been standing at the curb opened the passenger-side doors.

Johnson exited the front seat, while Sandstrom and his son-in-law climbed out the back.

A third man standing nearby turned out to be someone Sandstrom had met.

"Good to see you again, Mr. Sandstrom," Drake said, holding out a hand. "Welcome to Rome."

"Thank you," Sandstrom said as the two men shook.

"I hope you're hungry," Drake said. "De Luca's is one of Mr. St. Amand's favorites."

"I am." Sandstrom motioned toward the entrance. "Shall we?"

Drake raised a palm in front of Sandstrom. "One moment, please."

He nodded at one of the men with him. The man removed something from his jacket that looked like a cellphone.

"This will only take a moment," Drake said.

The man holding the device stepped in close and started to move it downward. The thing was obviously some kind of bug detector.

"Wait a minute," Sandstrom said, taking a step back. "You don't trust me?"

"It's not a matter of trust, Mr. Sandstrom," Drake said. "This is standard procedure. No scan, no meeting."

Sandstrom grimaced, but stepped forward again. "Fine. Let's get it over with."

Scan Guy resumed where he'd left off, then knelt and checked the front of Sandstrom's pants.

When he finished, he said, "Please turn around."

Sandstrom turned to face the SUV. After he was determined clean, Scan Guy moved on to Johnson and Holt.

Both were also cleared.

"Wonderful," Drake said. "Please, follow me."

ORLANDO, JAR, AND Daeng had spread out across the roof to concentrate on different parts of the street—Daeng on the restaurant, Jar on the road to the right, and Orlando the road to the left. Daeng was the first to spot something of note when three of St. Amand's men had stepped outside and taken up positions near the curb, similar to the guys who had been waiting when St. Amand arrived. Daeng reported that one was St. Amand's driver.

Ninety seconds later, Orlando clicked on her mic. "Potential vehicle." An SUV had turned onto the section of road she was watching, and was heading toward the restaurant. When it slowed and angled toward the curb, she said, "Looks like this is it."

Two of the waiting men opened the SUV's curbside doors. Orlando saw three men climb out. Two looked to be in their mid-thirties, one of whom was carrying a large, accounting-style briefcase. The third man was older, late fifties at least. She took pictures of each.

One of St. Amand's men, the big guy, stepped forward and shook hands with the older man. Instead of leading them inside, though, he signaled one of his associates. That man pulled something out of a pocket and moved it up and down the older man's body.

"Dammit," she said. "They're doing a bug check."

In a hushed voice, Howard asked from inside the restaurant, "Do I abort or still go?"

Orlando thought for a moment. The scan meant St. Amand was very cautious. Perhaps this initial check would be it, but what if they performed a second one inside? The cameras Jar had placed in the hallways had auto shutoff capabilities. Howard's bug did not.

But there was a way to make this work, one that would also buy them some extra insurance in case of a second check.

"Still a go," she said. "But not any of the people who just arrived. You need to tag one of St. Amand's men. The big one if you can. As soon as you do that, get the hell out of there."

"Copy."

The other two who had arrived with Sandstrom underwent the scans, then everyone headed for the restaurant door.

"Here they come."

DRAKE LED SANDSTROM and the others into De Luca's.

The front dining room was three-quarters full. A few of the customers looked over to see who had come in, but none let their gaze linger.

"This way," Drake said. He walked toward the archway leading into the other dining areas.

He was halfway across the front room when a man sitting at one of the tables rose. The guy hadn't been facing the door so when he turned to leave, he nearly crashed right into Drake.

The man grabbed Drake out of reflex. "Excuse me."

Drake whirled on him and grabbed his arm. "What are you doing?"

"Sorry. Lost my balance."

Drake looked the man up and down, and then he reached down to make sure his wallet was still in his pocket. "Be more careful," he snarled, and started walking again.

THE MOMENT THE men walked into the restaurant, Orlando sent the photos she'd taken of the new arrivals to Misty, with the note:

> St. Amand appears to be meeting with
> these people right now. Can you ID?

Over the comm came a thud and a soft expulsion of air, followed by Howard saying, "*Scusami*."

A few seconds later, the restaurant door opened and Howard stepped outside.

In a whisper, he said over the comm, "Done."

Quinn's voice came next. "Nate and I are around the corner, to your right and across the street."

"On my way."

Next to Orlando, Jar plugged a pair of headphones into her phone, placed one of the buds in her own ear, and offered the other to Orlando.

On Jar's screen was the video feed of the camera from the upstairs corridor. The audio, however, was from the bug Howard had put on St. Amand's driver. The hallway remained empty for a few seconds before the men walked into camera frame and headed down the hall to the door at the end.

When the driver reached the room's entrance, he opened it and said in a voice that came through the earpiece crisp and clear, "Please come in."

CHAPTER
TWENTY THREE

MISTY HAD BEEN at her desk since six a.m., waiting for news from the team in Rome. She received her first text from Orlando at around ten, right after their charter jet landed.

Since then, she'd heard from her head of operations two more times, the first informing Misty that Orlando, Quinn, and Howard were heading to the apartment, while Daeng and Jar were following the man they suspected was St. Amand.

The second text said the team had met up near a building the presumed St. Amand was inside. There was also this little tidbit:

Nate is here.

Misty had no idea how that happened, but the relief she felt from those three words was immense. Even if Nate didn't contribute anything to the effort, she could now honestly tell her client he had been part of the mission. She wanted to ask for details but refrained, knowing that could wait until the current action had concluded.

At noon, she retrieved last night's leftover Chinese takeout from the kitchen and ate it at her desk, not wanting to miss something important. Turned out there was enough time to eat before Orlando's fourth message arrived, just after Misty had polished off the final egg roll.

The text contained several pictures and the request for Misty to ID the men in the shots.

She looked them over first, but none were familiar. She uploaded the images to the Office's facial recognition system. In less than a minute, the program returned a hit on the oldest of the three men.

> NAME: William Sandstrom
> CITIZENSHIP: USA
> AGE: 63
> KNOWN WHITE SEPARATIST
> FBI WATCH LIST
> LAST KNOWN LOCATION: Rome, Italy

"Huh," she said to herself.

A white separatist on the FBI watch list. Jackson Reed had been a white separatist on that same list. That couldn't be a coincidence. The FBI knew Sandstrom was in Rome, but not that he was there to meet with St. Amand. If they had, she was sure Kyle Otero at ACORT would have let her know to keep an eye out for him.

Her computer bonged with another hit. She assumed it had to do with one of the other men, but she was wrong.

> ALERT ISSUED FOR WILLIAM SANDSTROM
> LAST KNOWN LOCATION: ROME, ITALY
> ANY INFORMATION REGARDING HIS WHEREABOUTS SHOULD BE GIVEN TO SPECIAL AGENT HARI MORRAY.

The alert had been posted only ten minutes earlier. Misty called one of her contacts at the FBI, and learned that two agents who had been following a suspect in Rome had been seriously injured in an accident. The contact didn't know who the suspect was, only that the person got away.

Misty texted Orlando.

> Older man is wanted. Name William Sandstrom. American. White separatist. Apparently threw off his FBI tail on way to your position. Agents injured. Would be helpful to find out what meeting is about.

Orlando replied within moments.

> Would an audio recording do?

Misty:

> Well, sure. You have ears inside?

Orlando:

> We're a full service outfit.

Misty:

> Don't tell Quinn, but I think I love you.

Orlando:

> Oh, I'm telling him.

Misty called Otero.

Fifteen minutes later, she had new instructions for her team.

ORLANDO AND JAR listened as the men in the room greeted each other and engaged in small talk, everyone, interestingly enough, talking in English. Since they had obviously met previously, no names had been mentioned so far. That was unfortunate.

Since Orlando had heard and seen St. Amand's driver speaking in the hallway, it wasn't difficult to pick out his voice among the others. The three new men were also easy to identify from their American, or perhaps Canadian, accents, with the slightly gravelly voice most likely belonging to the older guest.

She assigned the temporary ID St. Amand Thug Number 1 to the other voice dominating the early conversation. He was the deeper slow talker who spoke with the slightest of accents; she could narrow it down only to Eastern European. Every once in a while, other voices would speak up but not enough to warrant distinction yet.

The casual talk continued until after the food was brought in by two waiters, seen via the hallway camera, who had to make four trips before everyone had a meal. While the service was going, a text arrived from Misty with information about the older guest.

William Sandstrom.

Orlando had never heard of him, but that wasn't surprising. Though she and her colleagues did the occasional domestic job, most of their work was done outside the US.

Also not surprising was the fact Sandstrom was in the same business as the pedophile they'd taken down in Oklahoma. ACORT was worried something was going on. And now she was listening to what could turn out to be confirmation of that.

The next several minutes were filled with the sounds of silverware knocking against plates, a smattering of innocuous conversation, and the occasional smacking of lips.

"Would you care for another helping?" Thug 1, the deep, slow talker.

"No, thank you," Sandstrom said. "Mr. St. Amand, I noticed you're not having anything."

Orlando and Jar shared a look, then Orlando toggled her mic. "Just had confirmation that St. Amand's in the room."

"Copy," Quinn said.

Over the earbud, Thug 1 said, "Mr. St. Amand prefers to eat alone. But he does not want that to prevent others from enjoying a good meal."

Because he doesn't want to take his stupid scarf off, Orlando thought.

"Can I interest you in some dessert?" Thug 1 said. "They have a wonderful tiramisu here."

"None for me, thank you."

"Nonsense. You don't want to leave without at least trying it. Paolo, tell Matteo to bring some up for everyone."

"Right away," one of the unassigned voices said.

Seconds later, one of St. Amand's men exited the room and walked down the hallway.

"Thank you for the meal," Sandstrom said. "And for seeing us."

"Of course," Thug 1 said.

"I'd like to say right off, I am *deeply* sorry that you were not immediately informed about the trouble in Oklahoma. There was miscommunication on our side. I had thought Cox had told you what happened, and he had thought we wanted to keep it quiet. Let me just be clear. We would never consciously choose to keep that kind of information from you. We consider you a vital partner. Yes, our goal is ambitious, but it is achievable. With your help, Freedom Day will occur in less than eighteen months."

And there it was, Orlando thought. Proof.

"And without our help?" Thug 1 asked.

"I'd rather not even consider that an option."

"But it is an option. While we appreciate your apology, the fact remains that we were kept in the dark. Something like that could have been very dangerous for us. How do we know it won't happen again?"

"Because I'm telling you it won't, on my word of honor."

Orlando could hear a couple of whispered voices, but not what they were saying.

Thug 1 spoke again. "Mr. St. Amand knows your words are said honestly. But what of Mr. Cox? Will he follow through on your desires?"

"Mr. Cox will no longer factor in any of our interactions. You will be dealing directly with me."

More whispers.

"You have given us much to think about," Thug 1 said.

"Let me give you something else to think about."

"Please, we'd like to hear whatever you have to say."

"Perhaps…"

For a few seconds, the only noises were squeaks from chairs.

Thug 1 then said in Italian, "Clear the room."

On the hallway camera, the meeting room door opened. St. Amand's men exited, leaving the driver, the man Jar said had been in the front passenger seat of St. Amand's van, and the scarf-wearing man in the room.

Sandstrom said, "Dean, Marlon."

His companions appeared in the doorway. They talked for a moment, their voices too far from the bug for Orlando to pick out any details. When they finished, one stepped outside while the other stayed in the room and shut the door. The guy in the hall crossed his arms and stood at the room's entrance, like a bouncer not in the mood to let anyone in.

"So, Mr. Sandstrom," Thug 1 said, "what else should we be thinking about?"

Orlando's phone buzzed with a text, but Orlando only glanced at the screen before putting the cell back down. Whatever Misty wanted, it could wait a few moments.

"We appreciate all that you've done so far," Sandstrom said. "You've been instrumental in supplying so many in our network. But our requests so far have been small in comparison to what will be needed on Freedom Day, and though that's still a little while off, we believe the time has come to start building our stockpiles and planning future supply lines."

"You understand why we may be a bit skeptical," Thug 1 said. "After all, you'll be going up against the best trained, best equipped military in history."

"We think that is a false assumption. Granted, there will be elements of that which we will encounter, but it is our belief large numbers of their forces will refuse to engage us, and a good percentage of them will even join our cause."

Orlando and Jar shared a look.

"Is he talking about the US military?" Jar asked.

"It sounds like it."

"Would the soldiers do that?"

"Not a chance in hell." There might be a few defections, but nothing close to the numbers Sandstrom was implying.

Another round of whispers ensued, then Thug 1 said, "You have our attention. How much equipment are we talking about?"

Orlando heard a sheet of paper being unfolded.

"This is just a working document. Our needs will continue to grow the closer we get to when we finally act."

A moment of silence, then Thug 1 again. "This is a very impressive list. It will not come cheap."

"We wouldn't expect it to."

The sound of something heavy being set on a table, then the clack-clack of briefcase locks opening.

"This is merely a show of good faith," Sandstrom said. "There's two hundred fifty grand here. If you agree to keep us as your clients, before I leave this room fifty million dollars more will be transferred into whatever account you would like."

The room went quiet.

"One moment," Thug 1 said.

The whispers returned, lasting longer than the previous instances. When they stopped, Thug 1 said, "Your terms are acceptable."

"Excellent," Sandstrom said. "I can't tell you how happy that makes me."

"We, too, are pleased. We had hoped that we could work out our differences. In anticipation of that, we have brought some samples of the latest tech, which has recently come into our possession. May we show you?"

"Of course."

More items thumped on the table, heavier than the earlier ones. For the next ten minutes there was talk of uses and specs and anticipated results of nearly a dozen weapons. To say it was creepy to listen to would have been an understatement.

At the end, items were added to Sandstrom's list.

"We look forward to a long and *healthy* relationship," Thug 1 said.

"Thank you for giving me the time to explain our position," Sandstrom said, not hiding his relief.

On the hallway camera, three people carrying desserts walked down the hall to where Sandstrom's man stood at the door. A moment later, they were let into the room, and talk turned to dessert.

Orlando flipped on her mic. "I think this thing's going to be over soon."

"What was the meeting about?" Quinn asked.

"Food and hurt feelings. Oh, and that part where St. Amand's people agreed to sell Sandstrom at least fifty million dollars' worth of arms and ammunition." Her phone vibrated, reminding her of the message she'd received.

"Is that all?" Quinn said, with a smirk in his voice.

As she grabbed her phone, she said, "Actually, no. Sandstrom also admitted to being linked to Jackson Reed, plus whatever this big thing is they're planning, they're calling it Freedom Day, and it's supposed to happen in about eighteen months. And I've got to say, St. Amand? Not a big talker."

She opened the message.

"That's all recorded, right?" Quinn asked.

When Orlando didn't reply right away, Jar said, "Yes. All recorded."

"We should probably send a copy to—"

"The mission just changed," Orlando said. "Where are you guys?"

"Around the first corner north of the restaurant, west side. What's going on?"

"I'll tell you when I get there." Orlando waved Daeng over, then pulled out Jar's earbud and held it out to him. "Listen in with her and keep me updated. And I want to know the second they leave that room."

"Will do," Daeng said.

"Jar, make a clip of the audio to this point and send it to me. And both of you be ready to move as soon as I tell you."

"What is the new mission?" Jar asked.

"Target acquisition."

Orlando pushed up and headed across the roof.

ST. AMAND WAS seldom shocked, but there was no other way to describe his reaction to Sandstrom's fifty million-dollar offer. He'd thought he'd be lucky to get just a quarter of that.

He leaned over and whispered in his double's ear. "Consultation mode number one."

Claudio Lazzari nodded and sat back in his chair. He then leaned toward St. Amand—playing the part of right-hand man, Antonio Becker—and whispered nonsense words.

Real St. Amand nodded several times and turned to Sandstrom. "Your terms are acceptable."

For the first time since he'd arrived, Sandstrom smiled. "Excellent. I can't tell you how happy that makes me."

St. Amand then showed Sandstrom the samples Drake had brought. Sandstrom's eyes grew wide at the display, especially at the high-tech grenades and ultra-light night vision goggles. He placed orders for several of the items.

A knock on the door announced the arrival of dessert.

"Perfect," St. Amand said. "Please tell them to bring it in."

QUINN, NATE, AND Howard met Orlando as she exited the building.

"We'll walk and talk," Quinn said, to avoid drawing attention if they gathered in one spot.

They headed away from the street where De Luca's was located.

"So, what's the change?" Quinn asked.

"We've been ordered to grab Sandstrom," Orlando said.

"Sandstrom? What about watching St. Amand? Do we just forget about him now?"

"No, we're to keep someone on him, too. But our main focus will be Sandstrom."

"It's that crash, isn't it?" Quinn asked. The US government, like pretty much every government around the world, was not fond of having its people messed with.

"Misty didn't elaborate, but that would be my guess."

"Are we even prepared for a grab?" he said.

Daeng, who with Jar had been listening over the comm, chimed in with, "We have half a dozen Beta-Somnol syringes back at the flat."

"What about darts?" Nate asked.

"No, just the syringes."

"Forget about the Beta-Somnol for now," Quinn said. "It would take too long to get it. Nate, you should stay on St. Amand, since that's why you're here."

"Yeah, I agree," Nate said.

"Jar, you'll stay with him."

"Copy," Jar said.

"The rest of us will follow Sandstrom and see where he's going. If he heads to the airport, ACORT can call in a favor and have him detained before he gets on his plane. If it's somewhere else, then it will be on us to deal with him. How does that sound?"

"Good by me," Orlando said. "So, what do we have for transportation?"

"Jar and I have scooters," Daeng said. "But we'll need to leave one for her and Nate."

"Two of us will have to take a taxi, then," Quinn said.

Nate shoved a hand in his pocket. "Oh, hold on." When he pulled it out again, he was holding a business card. "I had this cabbie earlier who doesn't mind winging it."

"Call him and see if he's nearby," Quinn said. "Daeng, come on down. You and Steve can ride the scooter. Orlando and I will—"

He stopped when he noticed Orlando grimacing at her phone.

"Everything okay?"

She glanced at him. "There's been another change of plans."

"We're *not* grabbing Sandstrom?"

"Oh, no. We're still doing that."

"Then what's the change?"

"Actually, it's more of an addition."

MISTY'S COMPUTER DINGED, signaling the arrival of an email. The sender's address was a string of numbers and letters in no obvious pattern. It was the subject line that caught her attention: ORLANDO WANTED ME TO SEND YOU THIS. Attached to the email was an audio file. From the size it had to be at least thirty minutes long. Written in the message section of the email was a time code and the words: The good stuff begins here.

It must be from the Sandstrom-St. Amand meeting that was taking place. Misty ran the file through her virus-detection app before playing it, starting at the point indicated.

Within forty-five seconds, she hit Pause. Right there, in

clear English, was an offer by Sandstrom to pay fifty million dollars for God only knew how much weaponry. As much as she wanted to continue listening, she couldn't sit on this.

She composed an email to Otero at ACORT, noting the same time code, and sent off the audio file. She resumed playing, and made it to where dessert was about to be served when her phone rang.

"Mr. Otero," she said upon answering. "I take it you've sampled the file."

"Your team deserves a raise," he said.

"I'll be sure not to tell them that."

"Has this meeting ended?"

"As far as I know, it's still going on."

"I take it you've listened to this."

"Not much more than the part I flagged for you."

"Then I'm sure you will agree this is a clear and present danger to our country and our mission has escalated far beyond just grabbing Sandstrom."

"If you're saying we need to hold off on taking Sandstrom, I need to contact my team immediately."

"No. That is still on." He paused. "How good are your people?"

"They're my best. I would trust them for anything I needed done. They are well respected, highly accomplished, and completely dependable."

He paused. "Your people are in a unique position to stop this whole thing in its tracks, and prevent the countless deaths a protracted FBI investigation might incur."

"Isn't that what taking Sandstrom would do?"

"Likely, but to guarantee success, we would like your team to obtain his supplier, too."

"St. Amand?"

"Yes. Can they do it?"

"Of course they can. But I want to make sure we're clear on the fact that the US government is sanctioning the kidnapping of an American citizen *and* a foreign national *on* foreign soil?"

"What the US government is taking action on is an

imminent threat to our nation."

"I need written authorization for my files before I inform my team."

"Check your inbox."

She looked back at her computer as it dinged again. The message was from Otero, a full authorization for the rendition of William Sandstrom, Christophe St. Amand, and any associates picked up due to the action.

She saved a copy in a secured file and said, "We'll get right on it."

CHAPTER
TWENTY FOUR

MISTY'S NEW ORDERS meant Quinn's initial plan of having everyone but Nate and Jar go after Sandstrom had to be adjusted. It was decided Quinn would stay with them, while Orlando, Daeng, and Howard dealt with Sandstrom.

Nate's cabbie friend had indeed been nearby. When he arrived, Nate leaned into the passenger-side window.

"Thanks for coming," Nate said.

"I knew you would call," the taxi driver said. His smile faltered a bit upon seeing the others on the sidewalk. "I cannot fit all of you."

"Not all of us. Just three of my friends."

"You, no?"

Nate shook his head. "Don't worry, though. You'll have just as much fun as we had earlier." He turned to the others. "All yours."

The cabbie's look of disappointment vanished when Orlando climbed into the front passenger seat.

"What's your name?" she asked in Italian.

"Flavio," he replied, grinning. "Where can I take you?"

"Just down the street for now. We're waiting for someone else."

"Another passenger?"

"No. Someone we're going to follow."

His face brightened even more. "Okay!"

During the exchange, Daeng and Howard had installed themselves in the back. Flavio drove off, leaving Quinn and

Nate on the sidewalk.

"Jar, status?" Quinn said.

"Sounds like they're finishing up dessert."

"Time to come down."

"Copy."

He looked over at Nate. "So, where are the scooters?"

THE TIRAMISU WAS consumed with pleasure by everyone except Lazzari, who once again was not partaking.

When they were through, St. Amand said, "Is there anything else we can do for you?"

"At the moment, I can think of nothing, but I'm sure that will change," Sandstrom said.

"When it does, contact Mr. Drake. He'll pass everything on to us."

"Okay, then. I guess that's everything but the transfer. If you give me your account information, I can get things moving."

In less than ten minutes, St. Amand received confirmation of the fifty million sitting in his Cayman Island account.

"Thank you for the meal and your time." Sandstrom pushed back his chair.

Within seconds, everyone was on their feet.

Lazzari said, "I'm so glad you were able to join us. Let us know when you are in Rome again."

"Thank you," Sandstrom said. "Though I doubt it will be for some time. There's much work to do."

Lazzari came around the table and walked with Sandstrom across the room. "Yes, I imagine you will be quite busy." When they reached the door, the double said, "I'll leave you here. Have a pleasant trip home. You'll be hearing from us soon."

Sandstrom held out his hand. "I look forward to it."

The two men shook, and Drake said, "One of my men will walk you out." He opened the door and called down the hall, "Manfred, please see Mr. Sandstrom out."

Manfred came up the stairs and over to the doorway. "Right this way."

Drake waited until Sandstrom and his men had descended

out of sight before closing the door.

Now that the three men were alone, Lazzari said, "How was I?"

"You were excellent as always," St. Amand said.

"Oh, good. I'm so glad to hear that. I always wonder, you know."

"We'll be leaving soon. If you're going to eat, you should do it now."

Lazzari's eyes lit up. "I'm starving." He retrieved a covered plate of food from the serving table and carried it to where he'd sat during the meeting. After removing the scarf, he dug in.

St. Amand and Drake sat at the other end of the table. "I need you to figure out the logistics for their first shipment and have it to me by noon tomorrow."

"No problem."

"And if they're willing to part with fifty million dollars so quickly, then there should be a lot more we can pull out of them. I'd like to see some ideas on that, too."

"Yes, sir."

"OKAY, FLAVIO, GET ready," Orlando said.

She was monitoring the feed from the camera focused on the outside of De Luca's, and had just witnessed Sandstrom and his two companions being escorted to a waiting SUV.

As the vehicle pulled into the street, Orlando said, "Remember what we talked about. Close but not too close. And no sudden moves."

"I understand," Flavio said. He looked at his side-view mirror. "Is that them?"

Orlando glanced over her shoulder and saw the black SUV heading their way. "That's them."

When the cabbie reached to shift the transmission, Orlando touched his arm.

"Let them go by first," she said.

"Oh, um, all right." He moved his hand back to the steering wheel, gripping it.

"Flavio, take a breath."

His chest expanded as he sucked in air. If the exercise relaxed him, it wasn't by much.

The SUV drove by.

"Okay, now," Orlando said.

Flavio veered into the road.

Orlando had told him they were private investigators from America, following someone suspected of committing a crime. When he asked what the crime was, she had told him she wasn't at liberty to say specifically, but implied it was scandalous. This had solidified his desire to help.

The SUV headed east through the neighborhood, before switching onto one of the major roads heading north.

Though Orlando knew the answer, she asked Flavio, "Is there any reason they'd be going this way if they were headed to the airport?"

"Fiumicino? No. This is not the way."

She glanced back at Daeng, said, "Let Quinn know," and returned her gaze to the SUV.

She was pleasantly surprised by Flavio's shadowing abilities. She'd had to tell him only a couple of times to adjust his position. The tension he'd been wearing was gone, too, replaced by a wide smile and a glint of excitement in his eyes.

Not long after they passed the Colosseum, they turned east again.

"They could be heading to Roma Termini," the cabbie said. Roma Termini was Rome's main train station.

That would be perfect, Orlando thought. The station would be chaotic and provide plenty of chances to nab Sandstrom. And if for some reason they didn't get the opportunity there, they could follow him onto a train and take him wherever he got off.

But it soon became clear the SUV's destination was not Roma Termini, when the SUV stopped in front of the St. Regis Hotel, northwest of the station.

"Pull over right here," Orlando ordered.

Flavio whipped the cab to the curb.

"You guys stay here. I'll be right back," she said and grabbed her backpack.

"I cannot stay here," Flavio shot back. "No parking."

"Okay, then drive around the block until you hear from me."

She climbed out and shut the door.

At the hotel, the SUV's driver had opened the passenger doors, and Sandstrom and the other two men were climbing out. The moment they walked into the building, Orlando headed after them.

Fronting the hotel were three giant open doors that led to an enclosed area, where no more than three cars could be parked. Beyond this were steps leading up to a revolving door into the hotel. As Orlando passed through the nearest streetside door, Sandstrom's group reached the revolving one. She slowed her pace until they were inside, and then increased it again.

By the time she was through the revolving door, Sandstrom was being led to a reception desk by a smiling hotel employee.

Orlando took a seat on one of the couches in the lobby area, to the left of the central walkway, and pulled out her laptop. In moments, she'd broken into St. Regis's network and worked her way into the registration records, where she found no reservation for anyone named Sandstrom.

At least he was smart enough not to travel under his own name, she thought.

Finding out his alias would have been a pain in the ass if he hadn't been checking in right at that moment. All she had to do was monitor which names were being switched from pending to guest.

Three names, two rooms. Owen Miller and Jared Jones would be sharing a room, while Charles Wright would be alone in the one next door. Orlando noted the room numbers, brought up a layout of the hotel, and found where they were located.

Across the lobby, Sandstrom and his colleagues finished up at the desk and were escorted to an elevator. Orlando waited until they'd started up before she inserted the guest names Noah and Anna Perry into the St. Regis system, assigned them the room closest to Sandstrom's, and marked them as already checked in.

Next, she called Daeng. "Send Steve in here, then go get the gear bag. Call me when you're heading back and I'll tell you where to find us."

"On it."

She stood as Howard entered the lobby and met him halfway. She had already texted him her plan, so he was prepared when she frowned at him and said, "Did you find it?"

"I don't know what happened to it," he said in a very convincing, defensive husband-esque tone. "I'm sorry, all right?"

The attendant approached them. "Is there anything I can help you with?"

Annoyed, Orlando said, "My husband here lost our key."

"I must have left it in the restaurant," Howard said.

"That's not a problem at all," the attendant said. "What room?"

"Three twenty-seven," Orlando replied.

They walked over to the reception desk, where the attendant explained the situation to the clerk, who keyed the room number into a terminal. "Mrs. Perry?"

"Correct."

"May I see your ID, please."

"Of course." Orlando set her backpack on the counter and made a show of hunting around inside. Her false passports were all in the same special pocket, five sets, each from a different country with a different alias. She grabbed her Anna Perry American passport and handed it to the woman.

The receptionist checked the passport against the hotel records and handed it back.

"Could we get two more keys? You know, just in case he loses his again."

"Of course."

AS QUINN, NATE, and Jar waited for St. Amand to leave, Jar said, "There's something you should hear."

She minimized the video feed from inside the restaurant, making it a small box in the corner, and, since no one was around them, played on speakerphone the audio from the bug.

"You'll be hearing from us soon," a male voice said.

Jar paused it. "That is the one we thought was St. Amand."

"*Thought*?" Quinn said.

"Just listen." She hit Play again.

A different voice. "I look forward to it."

"Sandstrom," Jar whispered.

On the recording a third voice said, "Manfred, please see Mr. Sandstrom out."

"The man speaking is St. Amand's driver," Jar said.

The closing of a door was followed by several seconds of silence, then the first voice they'd heard spoke again. "How was I?"

"You were excellent as always."

Jar hit Pause. "This is the man who did most of the talking during the meeting."

"The guy with the high cheekbones?" Nate asked.

"Yes, I believe so."

Quinn motioned for her to resume the playback.

"Oh, good. I'm so glad to hear that. I always wonder, you know."

"We'll be leaving soon. If you're going to eat, you should do it now."

"I'm starving."

More moving around, then High Cheekbones began talking in Bulgarian, something about a shipment and noon tomorrow.

Jar hit Pause.

"Keep playing," Quinn told her.

"You understand this part?"

"A little bit," Quinn replied.

"What language is that?"

"Bulgarian."

She let it play.

The conversation was between High Cheekbones and the driver, and seemed to be about the deal St. Amand had made with Sandstrom. Quinn gleaned nothing new from it.

"Okay, that's enough," Quinn said.

Jar stopped the playback and enlarged the feed from inside the restaurant's upper hallway. It had remained empty the entire time they'd been listening.

"Those two were talking about the deal," Quinn said. "But the guy who is supposed to be St. Amand wasn't even involved."

"That first part when they were talking," Jar said, "what the man with the scarf said, made me think he was only acting. But English is not my first language so maybe I am wrong?"

"I don't think you are. Nate, how about you?"

Nate stared at the road, lost in thought.

"Nate?" Quinn said.

Nate turned to Jar. "Can you bring up pictures from when the guy in the scarf arrived at the restaurant?"

She searched through her phone and brought up one of the photos. Nate enlarged it.

"I'll be damned," he whispered.

"What?"

"When I saw the guy with the high cheekbones earlier, he seemed familiar. I thought maybe he was in Marrakesh or maybe I'd seen him on another job." Nate chuffed and pointed at the screen. "He was in Marrakesh, all right. *That's* St. Amand."

"You're sure?" Quinn asked. It was a reasonable assumption given what they'd heard, but there had been no proof to that effect on the audio.

"He's wearing prosthetics on his face that cover up his scar, and that wig he's wearing doesn't help, but it's him. If I had just run into him on the street and I wasn't looking for him, I would have never made the connection. It's a good disguise, but that is him."

Quinn had to give St. Amand points for being clever. Using a decoy to act as him, and then playing the part of an underling himself? It was a pretty ingenious way to observe an adversary—business or otherwise.

"They're moving," Jar said.

On the screen, the driver, the faux St. Amand, and the real one were moving down the hallway toward the stairs. Quinn mounted Daeng's scooter and put the key in the ignition.

Over at the other bike, Nate said, "I'll drive."

He made a move to get on but Jar blocked the way. "You will not."

"I have more experience in these kinds of situations."

"Really? Have you been driving one of these on the streets of Bangkok since you were ten?" She stared at him, daring him to top her.

"Fair point." He motioned for her to take the front spot.

Quinn and Jar drove the scooters to an intersection a block and a half north of the restaurant and pulled to the side, idling. Jar put her phone into the mount on the tiny dash and studied the screen.

"They are getting into the SUV," she said. "It is the same one they arrived in."

"The one with the bug," Nate said.

"Correct. There is a fourth person with them. One of the guards, I believe."

Nate looked over at Quinn "Front and back rotation?"

Quinn considered the suggestion. "We'll let them get going first, then we'll do it. Which position do you want to start with?"

"We'll take front."

"The SUV is leaving," Jar said.

Their eyes were all on the intersection when the black SUV drove by. When the tracker showed the vehicle was two blocks away, they took off.

Jar and Nate sped ahead, their job to casually work their way in front of the SUV. Quinn, traveling at a slightly more leisurely pace, would approach the vehicle from behind and maintain at least three car lengths between them.

The unofficial convoy wound through smaller streets before turning north toward the heart of the city. Thirty minutes later, the SUV entered another quiet neighborhood.

"They appear to be going to the building where they picked up the impostor," Jar said over the comm.

"How sure are you?" Quinn asked.

"If they turn right at the next corner, they will be only fifty meters from it."

"Keep going straight, then. Don't turn after them."

The SUV did indeed turn right.

When Quinn reached the intersection, he rolled the scooter to the curb and watched the SUV do the same, in front of a building toward the middle of the block. The driver and the man in the scarf exited the vehicle and walked toward the entrance, leaving behind the man with the high cheekbones and the other guard.

If Nate was right, and High Cheekbones was St. Amand, Quinn was staring at a nearly perfect situation to grab the asshole.

"Nate, where are you?" he asked.

"We're waiting down the street."

"Get back here. Fast."

"Something wrong?"

"Just the opposite."

CHAPTER
TWENTY FIVE

ORLANDO HAD TAPPED into the hotel security system and been keeping tabs on the fourth-floor corridor since right after she and Howard took possession of their room. The only traffic had been a young couple from down the hall leaving for a night out, and Daeng's arrival. Sandstrom and the two men with him never left their rooms.

The gear bag Daeng had retrieved contained, among other things, zip ties, a gooseneck camera, listening devices, and the syringes of Beta-Somnol. Daeng had taken two of the listening bugs and attached one each to the doors of Sandstrom's and his associates' rooms.

Surprisingly, the room the two men were sharing went quiet first. For a good twenty minutes beyond that, a TV could be heard playing in Sandstrom's room. There was the occasional sound of movement, and once the flush of a toilet.

Finally Sandstrom, too, seemed to have gone to bed.

Orlando decided to give it an extra ten minutes. During that time, she created video loops from the footage of the two security cameras in the hallway, and inserted them into the system so that anyone watching would think the hallway remained empty.

When the allotted time had expired, she, Daeng, and Howard went down to the associates' room. After removing the bugs, Orlando used an electronic lockpick to disengage the lock. While she was doing that, Daeng and Howard hoisted high above their heads the blanket they'd taken from their room, and created an alcove of semidarkness around the doorway.

Orlando turned the handle and pushed the door inward. The only sound from inside was snoring from one of the men. How the other guy slept through it, Orlando had no idea, but he couldn't have been awake or he would have reacted to the opening door.

She slipped inside. Daeng and Howard followed, and, in an unrehearsed dance, maneuvered the blanket inside and shut the door, while keeping much of the hall light from flooding in.

The snorer sputtered when Daeng pushed the needle into his arm, his eyes fluttering open. Before he could yell out a warning, Howard slapped a folded towel over his mouth, and held it there for the few seconds it took for the drug to send the man back to dreamland.

The secret as to how the other guy could sleep through his buddy's snores was earplugs. This was also the reason he didn't hear Orlando and her friends gather around his bed. He, too, only woke up when he was pricked with the needle. But unlike his roommate, he put up a decent struggle, and it took both Daeng and Howard to restrain and muzzle him so that Orlando could finish administering the drug.

They left the men in the beds and returned to the corridor, where they repeated their previous procedure on Sandstrom's door. Unlike the others, Sandstrom seemed to sense their presence as they neared his bed.

Pushing up on an elbow, he said, "Is someone—"

When his gaze landed on Orlando, he threw his covers back and tried to get out of bed. Daeng and Howard grabbed him from the other side before he could do more than roll on his hip. Sandstrom was strong for someone his age, but not enough to fight them off, and they were able to pull him back down without too much effort.

Since there was no need for secrecy anymore, Orlando turned on the reading lamp. "Hold him still."

Sandstrom's eyes widened at the syringe. "What is that?"

"It doesn't matter. You won't remember."

As she moved the needle closer, he began thrashing. "No!

You can't do this! My men are right next—"

Howard shoved a pillow over Sandstrom's mouth.

"We've already paid your men a visit," Orlando said.

Confusion in the man's eyes, then anger again.

"Relax. This isn't going to kill you."

He shouted something like *bullshit* into the pillow.

"Mr. Sandstrom, there are way too many people who want to talk with you first. But look on the bright side—you get to sleep the entire flight home."

She plunged the needle into his arm.

Daeng and Howard held on to him until he stopped moving.

The easy part was done. Now they had to get the three unconscious men out of the St. Regis without anyone knowing.

APPEARANCES WERE EVERYTHING in maintaining the ruse that Claudio Lazzari was the real St. Amand. Though it was unlikely anyone had Lazzari's apartment building under surveillance, one could never be too sure.

That was the reason Drake always escorted Lazzari up to his flat. Christophe St. Amand, the scarf-wearing gun-dealing enigma, would travel nowhere without a bodyguard, after all.

The real St. Amand waited in the SUV, checking email on his phone. A few minor orders from existing customers, a report from one of his researchers on a potential new client, and the daily message from his lead accountant, listing payments received and worldwide bank balances. In other words, nothing pressing.

He looked out the window at the stone buildings fronting the street. It didn't matter what time of day it was, Rome was always beautiful. The old mixed with the even older, set across rolling hills that had seen more significant history than most places ever would. He couldn't imagine living anywhere else. He'd been born in Brussels, attended boarding school in England, and spent large chunks of time in Paris and Prague, but none were better than Rome.

Drake exited Lazzari's building. As he crossed the sidewalk and started to circle around the front of the car, St.

Amand caught a flash of light in the side mirror. He glanced over his shoulder. A scooter was motoring down the road.

Those damn things were one of the few drawbacks of the city. They were both ubiquitous and annoying. If there was ever a movement to ban them, he'd do all he could to support it.

He turned back around and settled into his seat, looking forward to getting home.

MOVING LOW AND quiet, Quinn crept toward the SUV. Fifteen meters from the vehicle, he found a place to hide that still afforded him a good view of the building. He removed his gun, checked the sound suppressor, and stared at the entrance, waiting. The timing had to be just right for his plan to succeed. If they were off by even a few seconds they would miss the opportunity, and very likely tip off St. Amand that someone was after him.

The moment he saw the driver walking across the building's lobby, he whispered into his mic, "Kill the cameras."

A beat, then Jar said, "Cameras down."

The area in front of the building was now a dead zone.

The door opened and the driver walked out. When the man reached the sidewalk, Quinn said, "Now."

From back around the corner, he heard the rumble of Jar's scooter and tensed, ready for his own cue.

NATE SAT AS far back on the tandem seat as possible, a light hand resting on Jar's back to help maintain his balance as she swung onto the street where the SUV was.

Ahead, the driver was starting to go around the front end of St. Amand's vehicle. By Nate's estimation, he and Jar would arrive too early. He was about to say as much to her when she eased up on the accelerator.

The big guy glanced at them as he came around the driver's side of the vehicle, but since Jar was keeping the scooter near the center of the road, the man paid them little attention.

As soon as he looked away, Jar veered toward the SUV. Nate jammed his left foot on the exposed section of the seat in front of him, waited until he was almost abreast of the man, and launched himself off the motorbike.

The driver whirled around, but by then it was too late. Nate smashed into him and knocked him down.

Though the driver was big, smacking his head into the cobblestones prevented him from fighting back effectively. He slapped haphazardly at Nate, threw a couple of punches that missed entirely, and tried at least three times to shove Nate off.

As this was going on, Nate heard a lot of noise behind him—running and suppressed gunshots and doors opening. Then Quinn's voice over the radio. "Jar. Coming your way!"

Nate was too occupied to worry about what Quinn was talking about. The driver seemed to remember he had a weapon and started to slip a hand under his jacket. When Nate saw the metal grip, he jammed his prosthetic leg hard into the driver's groin, earning a screech of pain.

As the driver writhed, Nate grabbed the gun and pressed the muzzle under the man's chin.

"*Per favore*," the man eked out between groans. "*Per favore!*"

Nate eased back on his prosthetic a bit, and said in Italian, "If you relax, I'll take it all the way off."

The man made a valiant effort but was unable or unwilling to fully comply, so Nate left the leg where it was.

He toggled his mic. "Driver down." When no one responded, he said, "Quinn?"

Nothing for a couple of seconds, then Quinn said, "Copy. Driver down." It was clear from the sound of his voice that he was running.

"Everything all right?"

"Not exactly."

"Where are you?"

"Down the block...to the north."

"I'll be right there."

"We've got this. Just bring the SUV."

"Copy." Nate said to the driver, "Sorry about this."

He swung the pistol's grip into the side of the guy's head.

THE MOMENT NATE jumped off the scooter, Quinn sprinted to the SUV, reaching the open driver's door as Nate and the big man hit the ground.

He leaned into the vehicle, gun first.

"Everyone stay nice and calm and no one gets hurt."

St. Amand, still in his disguise, sat unmoving in the front passenger seat. His bodyguard, however, rocketed against the back of the driver's seat and reached around the side, trying to grab Quinn's pistol.

Quinn leaned just out of reach and pulled the trigger twice, sending the bullets through the seat and into the bodyguard's chest. The man fell back and tilted against the door, dead.

Quinn turned back to St. Amand, but the arms dealer was halfway out the door. Quinn could have easily put him down right then and there, but that would have put a crimp in the whole bring-St. Amand-in-alive thing.

Cursing under his breath, Quinn extracted himself from the SUV. St. Amand was almost to the door of the apartment building, which was the last place Quinn wanted him to go. He fired another shot, the bullet flying just past St. Amand's right shoulder, into the stone façade. It achieved the desired effect, as St. Amand took a hard turn to the left and raced down the sidewalk.

Quinn activated his radio. "Jar. Coming your way!"

WHEN MANFRED MADE his play to get the gun from the man who'd leaned into the SUV, St. Amand pulled the handle and shoved the door open. He hurried out of the vehicle toward the building, knowing he had a much better chance of survival if he could get inside. As he ran, he felt along the hem of his jacket, searching for the emergency beacon sewn into the lining. When pressed hard enough to break the outer shell, a signal would be sent to everyone in his security team, transmitting his location every ten seconds.

Before he could find the beacon, a bullet flew past his ear and pierced the building near the door. He jerked sideways, the hem dropping from his hand, and headed down the street, hoping he could find someplace to gain advantage over his pursuer.

He glanced over his shoulder. The gunman was about seven meters back. The fact he was that close and hadn't shot St. Amand meant the man wanted to take St. Amand alive. Which meant St. Amand had a much better chance of getting away.

He swung around the building at the corner.

Sitting across the sidewalk, two meters in front of him, was a scooter. There was no way to stop in time, so he tried to go around it but he was moving too fast.

He somersaulted over the bike and whacked his back hard against the sidewalk, knocking the air out of his lungs. For several seconds, he felt like he'd forgotten how to breathe. Then his breaths returned in long and deep and painful pants.

When he finally became aware of his surroundings, he realized a small Asian woman was standing over him, pointing a gun at his heavy chest. Next to her was the intruder from the SUV.

"Nice job," the man said.

"Thank you," the woman replied.

The man flashed a smile at St. Amand. He pointed at his own forehead, above his right eyebrow. "You're bleeding a little, Mr. St. Amand."

Because St. Amand was still coming out of the shock of his fall, it took a few moments before he realized the man had called him by name. St. Amand had never seen this guy before. Even if the guy had seen him, he shouldn't have known what St. Amand looked like.

His pulse quickened. That wasn't good. He could still get out of this, but only if he maintained control.

Using a tone even weaker than he felt, he asked, "May I get up?"

The man nodded. "Nice and easy."

St. Amand pushed himself into a sitting position, then slowly rose to his feet and straightened his jacket. As he did, his hand found the emergency beacon.

Snap.

NATE PUT THE driver into the SUV's rear cargo area, stripped off the guy's jacket and shirt, and used the latter to tie the man's hands together.

As he closed the hatch, he turned his mic back on. "I've got the SUV secured. Where are you?"

"Great. Bring it here. We're at the corner to the north."

He hopped into the driver's seat, cranked the key. "On my way."

"Great," Quinn replied. "We're to the right, just around the corner ahead of you."

"Copy."

When Nate turned the corner, Jar signaled him to pull to the curb. As soon as he stopped, she opened the back passenger door.

Her expression sour, she reached in and pushed the dead bodyguard into a sitting position. "There is blood on the seat. Could you have not killed him, perhaps?"

"Hey, talk to Quinn. That one's not on me."

She went over to where Quinn was standing with St. Amand, and the two of them escorted the arms dealer to the vehicle.

"Get in," Quinn said.

St. Amand started to crawl into the backseat, but stopped at the sight of his dead employee.

"Get *in*," Quinn repeated.

St. Amand did as instructed. Quinn moved in beside him and closed the door, while Jar took the passenger seat in front.

"Let's go," Quinn said to Nate.

Nate punched the gas. "Where are we going?"

"North," Quinn said. "Remember that private airfield off the highway to Florence?"

Nate remembered. The job had been about six years earlier, and involved the elimination of a double agent. The airfield was about a hundred kilometers north of Rome, near the village of Attigliano about two hours away, given the half hour of Rome traffic they still had to drive through.

Nate adjusted their course.

"Jar," Quinn said, "could you keep an eye on our friend

here a moment? You can shoot him in the knee if he makes a move."

Jar twisted in her seat and pointed her gun into the back.

"Best if you stay still," Quinn said to St. Amand.

Glancing back and forth between the rearview mirror and the road ahead, Nate watched Quinn rip the cheek prosthetics off the arms dealer's face.

Once finished, Quinn said to Nate, "Well?"

Nate looked at the prisoner again. Now there was no missing the comma-shaped scar touching the corner of his eye.

"It's him, all right. Can I go now?"

"Funny."

St. Amand stared at Nate in the mirror, his eyes narrowing. "I know you."

"I wouldn't say you *know* me, but we have crossed paths."

"When?"

"I'll just let you figure that out on your own."

The man's eyelids squeezed together until he was looking through slits, but he said nothing.

Quinn pulled his phone out of his pocket. "It's Orlando. Jar, are you okay with keeping an eye on Mr. St. Amand?"

"Absolutely."

Quinn accepted the call.

ORLANDO, DAENG, AND Howard moved Sandstrom and a bag containing his laptop and false passport into the room his men had been using, so they could deal with all three of them in one place. Orlando then instructed Howard to obtain a vehicle, and Daeng to scout the best way out and find a laundry cart or something similar to transport their unconscious prisoners.

While she waited for them to return, she called Quinn.

"Any luck yet?" she asked.

"You can relay to the boss, St. Amand *and* his driver are safely in our possession."

"I am the boss, remember?"

"I meant the other boss."

She rolled her eyes. "Any problems?"

"One casualty. A bodyguard who thought he was

Superman. We'll have to dispose of him at some point. How are things on your end?"

"Targets obtained. Just waiting for transportation. We didn't have to kill anyone."

"I'm happy for you. Remember that airfield north of Rome we used on the Ossani case?"

"I do," she said.

"We're heading there. Thought it would be a good place for Misty to send in someone to pick us up."

"I agree. I'll check with her and let you know the arrangements."

"Thanks. Don't—"

A loud jumble of noise over the phone.

"Quinn? Quinn!"

She realized the connection had been lost. She called again but was immediately sent to voicemail. She hung up and tried again. Voicemail again.

When a third attempt achieved the same result, she left a message. "What the hell happened? Call me back."

She opened her tracker app. Quinn's and Jar's phones were registering at the same spot, toward the north end of Rome. Neither was moving. She yanked her laptop out of her bag and searched for security cameras in that area, but the closest was a block and a half away.

"Dammit."

She took a deep breath. She could do nothing for them at the moment, so she needed to stay on task.

She texted Misty.

> Subjects apprehended. Extraction needed.
> Suggest airfield used on Ossani mission.
> I believe designation is KA14. We should be able
> to get there within approximately two hours.

Misty's reply came four minutes later.

> Excellent! Coordinating extraction
> with ACORT. Likely soonest six hours.
> Will update you when confirmed.

Unable to help herself, she checked the tracker again. Quinn and Jar were now several blocks apart, Quinn's dot moving at a much slower speed than Jar's.

Orlando thought maybe now she could find a camera they would be on, but as she hunted for one, someone rapped on the hotel room door twice, and twice again.

"It's me," Daeng said from the hallway.

She hurried over and opened the door.

Instead of a laundry cart, he had brought a bellman's luggage cart. On the platform sat a large cardboard box.

"This is the best you can do?" she asked.

"You're more than welcome to go look yourself," he said.

She stepped to the side. "Bring it in."

Daeng wheeled the cart through the doorway and over to the nearest bed.

"Did you locate the loading dock?" she asked.

"The dock won't work. Too many people around there. I did find a service entrance in the back that opens on an alley. Steve should be able to pull right up to it."

"Is there enough room for his vehicle to stay there without drawing attention? We're going to have to take these guys down one at a time."

"There is, but I don't think we need to worry about that. I located a storage room half filled with tables and chairs, not far from the exit. We transfer everyone down there, and when Steve arrives, transfer them straight out. It'll get us on the road a lot faster."

"What if someone from the hotel needs a table or a chair?"

"Everything's dusty. I bet it will be another week before someone goes in there. And nobody should walk in at this time of night. But if you'd feel more comfortable, we can just make the trips once Steve is here."

She glanced at Sandstrom and the others. "All right. We'll try your plan."

They started with one of Sandstrom's companions, and quickly learned the best method was to set the box on its side. That way it was easier to get the bodies in an out. Plus, they could turn the box so that the flaps that opened could be held closed by the bars on the luggage cart.

They wheeled the cart into the hallway and over to the service elevator. Orlando checked to make sure there was no camera inside before they headed down. While Daeng pushed the cart through the ground-floor hallways, Orlando deactivated the cameras, and reactivated them again once she and Daeng had passed the coverage area.

Soon, they reached the storage room. Orlando scanned it and determined it was as Daeng had promised. They transferred their unconscious cargo onto the floor behind a stack of tables. Orlando was tempted to stay there to deter anyone who might need to use the room, but things would go a lot faster if they both did the loading and unloading. They went back to the room together.

They took the other associate on trip two and deposited him on the storage room floor with his friend. When Orlando and Daeng were returning for Sandstrom, Orlando's phone vibrated. The caller ID read: HOWARD.

"I'm three blocks away," he said after she answered. "Should be there in a couple minutes."

She relayed the info about the alley. "Wait there until we come out."

"Got it."

Once they had Sandstrom transferred into the box, they loaded in all the men's computers and identifications. Daeng used a hotel towel to wipe down all the surfaces he and his team may have touched, while Orlando did the same thing in Sandstrom's room.

The cleaning completed, they pulled on their backpacks and began their final trip. When they reached the ground floor, Orlando pressed the button that held the door open and Daeng pushed the cart out.

From somewhere out of sight, a voice in Italian said, "Excuse me!"

Daeng glanced over his shoulder, whispered, "Problem," and started pushing the cart toward the back hallway at double speed.

Orlando stayed in the elevator, pressed against the front wall so she wouldn't be seen.

"Sir, sir. Excuse me."

She heard steps hurry by the elevator. Only one person.

She pulled a Beta-Somnol-filled syringe from her backpack and slipped into the hallway.

Ahead, Daeng was about to pass through a door leading into the corridor that paralleled the rear of the building. Five meters behind him was a man in the suit worn by hotel management.

As Daeng used the cart to push the door open, the hotel man said, "Sir, you can't go in there." Daeng didn't stop.

As the door started swinging shut, the hotel employee broke into a jog. He caught the door before it closed all the way. Using the sound of his heavy steps as cover, Orlando closed the gap between them and passed through the doorway a few seconds after he did.

Finally, he seemed to sense someone was behind him. As he started to turn, Orlando stuck the needle into an exposed portion of skin between his shoulder and neck.

"What? What is…"

He swooned, a hand going to his head.

"What did…what did…"

Orlando caught him before he collapsed to the floor, and activated her mic. "You're clear, Daeng, but I could use a little help."

Daeng was back in seconds. He threw the man over his shoulder and carried him around the corner into the back hall, past the waiting cart to the storage room.

Taking over pushing duties, Orlando guided the cart all the way to the service exit.

"Steve, do you read me?" she said.

"Loud and clear."

"Are you in position?"

"Yeah. Right outside."

"First passenger coming out to you now."

By the time she'd maneuvered the box so Sandstrom could be pulled out, Daeng had rejoined her. Together, they lugged the would-be terrorist outside.

Howard had commandeered a Mercedes delivery van that had a seven-digit number painted on the back but no other markings. Except for a few sealed boxes, the inside was empty, so Sandstrom—and his associates a few minutes later—fit in nicely.

Orlando made a final trip into the hotel and stuffed three hundred euros into the unconscious manager's pocket. As she headed back to the van, she pulled out her phone, intending to give Quinn another try, but saw a text from Misty.

> Extraction set for Airfield KA14 2:00 a.m.
> Let me know if that'll work for you.

The rendezvous time was a little less than four hours away. Just enough time, with a little padding, to get there. She tapped a reply.

> We'll be there.

She climbed into the van and tried Quinn's cell again. Voicemail.

"Where to?" Howard asked as he drove away from the hotel.

Orlando opened her tracker. Quinn and Jar were even farther apart now. "Do you know where Piazza Euclide is?"

"North, right?"

She nodded. "Head that way. Fast."

CHAPTER
TWENTY SIX

QUINN WAS ABOUT to tell Orlando not to forget to have Misty send someone to the apartment Jar and Daeng had been using to give the place a good cleaning, when a sedan sped out of a side street and smashed into the rear of the SUV.

The crunch of metal and whoosh of inflating airbags. A side bag smacked into Quinn and knocked the phone out of his hand.

A pair of bags plastered Nate in the driver's seat, preventing him from correcting the spin they'd been sent in.

As the front end swung around, it crashed into a car parked at the side of the road. The SUV vaulted into the air. It hit the ground and rolled onto its roof before it finally stopped moving.

If not for the dead bodyguard acting as a cushion, both Quinn and St. Amand would have slammed directly against the ceiling that was now below them.

As it was, they were piled on top of each other—dead man, then St. Amand, then Quinn.

Quinn reached under his jacket, pulled out his gun, and looked around. "Nate. Jar. Are you okay?"

They were both hanging upside down, held in place by their seatbelts.

Nate blinked a couple of times and mumbled, "I'm okay."

Jar looked unconscious.

The windows along the driver's side were all crunched down to half their normal height. No chance Quinn and the others were getting out that way. Thankfully the other side, with the exception of the glass, was intact.

"We've got to go," Quinn said. "Now!" He poked St. Amand in the ribs with his gun. "Follow me."

He crawled out of the SUV and scanned the street. Since he couldn't see the car that hit them, he guessed it was on the other side of the wreck. He peeked over the top—or rather, bottom—of the vehicle.

A BMW sedan sat diagonally across the road twenty meters away, the front end a snarled mess. The remnants of expended airbags hung in the window, and the two men they had protected were now moving fast toward the SUV. One was holding a gun, while the other was pulling his out. If Quinn had been harboring even a remote possibility that this had been a random collision, that thought was gone now.

He placed the suppressor end of his pistol under the SUV. When the men raised their weapons, Quinn pulled his trigger twice.

The first bullet dropped the guy on the left. The second was slightly off its mark and caught the other guy in the shoulder. The guy yelled out and rushed toward the cars at the curb for cover.

Quinn got another shot off before the guy disappeared from sight, but he couldn't tell whether or not he hit the guy.

He ducked and looked inside the SUV. Nate had freed himself and was trying to do the same for Jar. St. Amand had barely changed his position.

Quinn yanked on his foot. "Hey, asshole, I'm only interested in keeping you alive if you come with us. If you'd rather stay, I'll kill you now. Your choice."

St. Amand hesitated no more than a second before he started backing out of the car.

Quinn spotted his phone lying against the dead bodyguard's leg. "Hold on. Grab that phone first."

St. Amand grabbed the device and crawled the rest of the way out.

"Hand it over," Quinn said.

As St. Amand handed him the phone, a bullet hit the front

of the SUV.

"Hey, idiot," Quinn yelled. "You shoot again and the next bullet goes into your boss's head." When a follow-up shot failed to appear, Quinn looked at St. Amand again. "How did they find us?"

The man shrugged. "Lucky, I guess."

"Give me your phone."

"I don't have—"

"Give me your goddamn phone."

St. Amand reached into his jacket and retrieved his mobile. Quinn snatched it out of his hands, removed the battery, and broke the SIM card.

"Anything else?"

"What else could I—"

"On the ground, facedown. Hands above your head."

St. Amand complied. Quinn placed a knee above the prisoner's kidney and the gun on the back of his head, then patted the man down.

When he felt the disk in the man's jacket, he said nothing and continued the search, removing St. Amand's wallet, a wad of cash, and the asshole's shoes before letting him sit up again.

"Your jacket," Quinn said.

"What about my jacket?"

"Take it off."

"Go to hell. I'm not taking it off."

Quinn placed the gun against the man's shoulder. "I hope you've enjoyed the ability to raise your arm up and down, because it'll be a while before you can do it again."

He had every intention of pulling the trigger. St. Amand must have sensed this, because he said, "Fine, fine. I'll take it off."

The man removed his jacket.

Quinn nodded at the SUV. "Toss it inside."

St. Amand looked even less excited about doing this.

Quinn nudged his shoulder with the weapon. "Now."

St. Amand tossed it in on top of the dead man.

"Thanks," Quinn said. In the distance, he heard the first of what would soon be many sirens.

"Nate, hurry up. We've got to go."

"Jar's belt is stuck."

Quinn pulled out his pocketknife and thrust it inside. "Here. Cut her out."

A vehicle braked to a screeching stop on the other side of the SUV.

Quinn looked over the top again.

The new vehicle was a clone of the one Quinn and the others had been riding in, and was stopped next to the BMW. As the doors flew open and several men climbed out, a voice from the sidewalk yelled a warning in Bulgarian. The men from the SUV raced around their vehicle, out of sight.

"Nate, time's up. Reinforcements are here!"

"I got her down. I just need you to help me get her out."

Keeping his gun trained on St. Amand, Quinn did what he could to guide the unconscious Jar out the window. As soon as she cleared the frame, Nate hustled through.

"Can you carry her?" Quinn asked. "Or should I?"

Nate, his face bloody from a cut on his cheek, said, "I'll do it. You lead the way."

Quinn grabbed their prisoner by the arm. "All right. On your feet but keep low. Time to show me how much you want to stay alive."

AS DRAKE REGAINED consciousness, he could hear someone talking, and realized after a moment the man was speaking in English on the phone. But try as Drake might, the fog and pain rattling through his head made it impossible to understand anything.

The next thing he knew, he tumbled through the air and was banging off walls. After he finally came to rest, he lay there for a moment, stunned, before he opened his eyes.

He was in a vehicle. More specifically, lying on the ceiling of a vehicle, the backseat hanging above his head.

Voices again, and movement off to his side. He turned his head, and saw several others lying on the ceiling, too. The dim night made it difficult to know exactly how many. He tried to call to them, but discovered there was something in his mouth.

He reached up to pull it out, or tried, anyway. His hands had been tied behind his back. He closed his eyes and breathed deeply through his nose, trying to build up strength. When he opened his lids again, all but one of the others were gone. The one that remained appeared to be unconscious.

The next minute or so was a blur of scattered gunshots, shouts, more movement upfront, and the sound of running.

In the subsequent quiet, Drake's head cleared a little. He now remembered being jumped, and realized he must be in the organization's SUV.

"Anyone inside, not to move." Like the phone conversation before, these words were in English, but this time clearly said by a non-native speaker.

A shadow passed the window near Drake's head, and he heard the crunch of glass under a shoe.

A beat later, a flashlight beam lit up the pavement outside a broken window closer to the front. When it swung inside, it illuminated the unconscious man, and whoever was holding the light cursed. Drake saw he'd been wrong. The other guy in the vehicle wasn't unconscious. He was dead.

When the beam landed on Drake's face, he squinted and turned his face away. He tried to talk but was again stymied by whatever was in his mouth.

"Mr. Drake?"

A hand reached in and pulled the offending object from Drake's mouth. Drake coughed several times, then croaked, "Get that damn light out of my eyes!"

STAYING LOW, QUINN guided the others on a path that allowed the wreckage to mask their escape. As they neared the intersection, Quinn checked over his shoulder, and saw the reinforcements were now circling around the upside down SUV.

Giving up all attempts of staying hidden, he pulled St. Amand, shouted, "Go! Go!" and ran.

He took them left at the corner, and scanned ahead for a hiding place. There were no good ones. The best they could do for now was to increase the distance between them and St.

Amand's men, so that when a good hiding place did turn up, they could get into it without being seen. The problem was, St. Amand appeared to have realized this, too, and definitely wasn't putting his heart into running.

"In case you forgot," Quinn said, "the only way I'm leaving you behind is as a corpse. And I'm *very* close to leaving you behind."

Before St. Amand could respond, flashing red lights began bouncing off the buildings on the next street up.

Quinn pulled St. Amand between two parked cars and onto the sidewalk, Nate, carrying Jar, right behind them.

"Down," Quinn said, a split second before the first of three police cars turned onto their street.

Crouching, they used the parked cars as a shield and continued forward as the cars rushed by in the other direction. The moment the last car passed, Quinn jerked St. Amand up and started to run again.

As they took a right at the intersection the cops had come from, Quinn once again checked behind them. The first of St. Amand's men was a good twenty meters back, which was almost exactly the distance to the next intersection. If they could get around it before the others showed up, they would have a chance of shaking their pursuers.

Passing through a dark spot between streetlamps, Quinn almost missed the misaligned sections of sidewalk. He was forced to stutter-step to keep from tripping.

"Watch out," he called back to Nate.

The warning came too late. Nate caught the tip of his toe on the obstruction, and down he and Jar went, crashing onto the sidewalk.

Quinn clamped down on St. Amand, intending to go back. But Nate jumped to his feet and said, "Keep going. We'll catch up."

Quinn didn't want to leave his friends behind, but there was nothing he could do to help that Nate wasn't already doing.

He pushed St. Amand forward. "Run!"

NATE WAS PRETTY sure he'd cracked a rib during the car crash, but he'd had worse injuries in tougher situations. The good thing was that Jar was light as a feather, so he was able to carry her without too much trouble.

When Quinn said, "Watch out," Nate had looked at the ground ahead. Maybe if Jar wasn't partially lying across his chest, blocking his view, he would have seen the deviation in the sidewalk. But he was flying forward before he realized what had happened.

He had enough awareness to twist sideways right before he landed so that he was the one who hit the concrete and not Jar. Instead, her ribs bounced off his head before she rolled off him, stopping a meter away.

Ignoring the new pain in his shoulder and that of the rib injured in the car crash, he scrambled to his feet and leaned down to grab Jar. When he realized Quinn had stopped, he told him to keep going and then attempted to pull Jar straight up.

But his shoulder screamed that it was not down with that plan.

He tried again, only this time he maneuvered her into a sitting position, and tucked his good shoulder into the bend of her waist before he lifted her. This method was not without pain, either, but his body didn't completely reject the idea, and in short order he was on the move again.

Running brought its own version of torture, as each shift of Jar's weight sent a blast of fire down his arm and across his chest.

Ahead, Quinn and St. Amand reached the intersection and turned right, disappearing from sight. Ignoring his pain as best he could, Nate tried to increase his speed, but the fall had also zapped much of his strength. Instead of the gap between him and Quinn closing, it was the one between him and St. Amand's men that was decreasing.

As he neared the corner, he knew his and Jar's best chance of escape lay not with following his partner but in going in a different direction and splitting their pursuers. Nate still might not be able to outrun them, but he would have a much better chance of taking two of them out than he would with all four. When he reached the intersection, he sprinted left.

Nate could hear his pursuers shouting at one another as they approached the turn. A few seconds later, he glanced over his shoulder and saw his gambit had paid off. In fact, he'd hit the double bonus. The pair coming after him did not include the speedy guy who'd been leading them.

About thirty meters ahead, a chest-high wall stuck out from a building, all the way to the edge of the sidewalk.

Perfect.

He pushed himself as hard as he could, then swung around the wall and deposited Jar on the ground. Moving to the front edge, he pulled his gun out and aimed at the first of the two men. He took a breath, let it half out, and pulled the trigger.

The gun didn't fire.

"Crap!"

He checked the chamber but couldn't see any obvious problems, so he aimed and pulled the trigger again. Still nothing.

Something must have happened to it in the crash.

He glanced at Jar. Even without his messed up shoulder, there was no way he could pick her up and get moving again before the others reached them.

He flipped the pistol around, holding it like a hammer, and hunkered down against the wall. What little plan he had involved jumping the first one who came around the wall.

But the men had apparently noticed his problem with the gun, and instead of coming right at the wall, they took a wide arc out into the street, so that when Nate finally saw them, they were too far away for him to do much of anything. They were more than close enough, however, to use the guns they were aiming at him.

One of them said something in Bulgarian. The other translated in heavily accented English. "Drop it."

The worst death is one that can be avoided. Another Quinn lesson, in the live-to-fight-another-day vein.

Nate tossed the pistol on the ground and raised his hands.

The men cautiously walked toward him. One pulled a radio off his belt and said something into it. When the reply came, Nate recognized the name St. Amand but nothing else.

The man spoke into the device again, then another reply, this one short.

The English speaker motioned at Jar. "Dead?"

"No. But she needs a doctor."

The man chuffed. "Turn around and hands behind back."

Nate did as directed.

THE BLOCK QUINN and St. Amand veered onto was a short one, and Quinn was sure they could make the next turn without being seen. The only question was whether Nate and Jar would reach them in time.

He led St. Amand across the road to the corner and looked back to check on his friends.

For half a second, he thought they hadn't reached the road yet, but then he spotted them going the other way. The only explanation was that Nate was giving them both a better chance to get away.

Quinn yanked St. Amand around the corner.

"I…cannot…run…forever," St. Amand said between breaths.

"Shut up and run."

A block away was an intersection filled with cars going in both directions. A busy road, probably filled with pedestrians, too. In normal circumstances, Quinn would have welcomed the opportunity to lose his pursuers. But in this case, it would also provide St. Amand the chance to make a scene and get away.

It was time to find someplace to hide.

Several of the nearby buildings had porticos along the ground floor. A few were lit, but the majority were in shadows. Quinn picked one and guided St. Amand to it, hustling him down to the very end of the portico where the shadows were deepest.

"On the ground," he ordered. "If you even breathe loudly, I'll kill you."

"Then *you* will be the dead man."

"Don't look so smug. You're not even close to the first person who's said that to me. Now get down and shut up." He shoved his gun on St. Amand's shoulder until the man complied.

Steps on the street now, running, but not as fast as before. Quinn sensed they were unsure if they'd gone the right way.

A voice crackled over a radio. Bulgarian again. Quinn picked out the words *found* and *man* and *woman*.

The lead chaser raised a radio to his lips and asked if St. Amand was one of them.

"No."

The chaser spoke again, something about a vehicle, then clipped his radio on his belt and continued down the road with his colleague. Once they had moved out of earshot, Quinn relaxed a little.

St. Amand smirked. "Your friends are dead."

Quinn replied, "If they are, then so are you."

He pulled out his phone to text Orlando for assistance, but the screen was filled with cracks and remained black.

He cursed.

Nate and Jar would be in real trouble if someone didn't help them soon. Without a way to quickly get ahold of Orlando, the only someone was him.

"On your feet," he said.

He hauled St. Amand to the building's entrance. It was locked, but the latch was easily released with a card from St. Amand's wallet.

Quinn shoved the man inside.

The ground floor of the building appeared to be divided into over a dozen separate office suites housing small businesses. He guided St. Amand down the hallway. Most of the doors had nameplates beside them, but two had only mounts and no actual plates.

Quinn picked the lock of the one farthest from the building entrance. As he had hoped, the office was not being rented. From the mess, it looked to be in the middle of a refurbishment, but he was positive no one would show up before morning.

Perfect.

He ushered St. Amand into an interior room that didn't share walls with any of the other rented spaces.

"What is this?" St. Amand asked. "We wait here until your

other friends pick us up?"

"Not *we*," Quinn said.

He whipped his arm around St. Amand's neck and squeezed hard. A part of him wanted to keep going after the guy lost consciousness, but that wasn't the job. Quinn lowered St. Amand to the floor, then hunted for something to tie him up with.

Within all the junk lying around, he found several pieces of wire. He tied up St. Amand's wrists and ankles, and connected them behind the asshole's back. He then tied a piece of old curtain between St. Amand's teeth as a muzzle. On the floor of one of the larger rooms, he found a piece of paper and a broken pencil and used them to write a note. He stuck it in St. Amand's front pocket, leaving the paper hanging out a little so it wouldn't be missed.

Lastly, he put his phone in the same pocket as the note. Even though the screen wasn't working, Orlando should still be able to track its location. If not…well, St. Amand had better hope nothing happened to Quinn.

He headed outside and ran toward the intersection where he'd seen Nate and Jar going in the opposite direction.

When he reached it, he juked to his right, into the shadows of the building on the corner. The SUV the reinforcements had arrived in was sitting on the left side of the road, three quarters of a block beyond the intersection, facing the wrong direction. All its doors were open, and lit up by its headlights was Nate being roughly led to the vehicle.

Quinn clenched a fist. Perhaps if he moved in close enough, he could take out St. Amand's men without accidentally hitting—

The crackle of a radio, coming from somewhere behind him and moving closer.

Seconds later a man moved through the darkness down the road.

Quinn searched for a second person, but the walker appeared to be alone.

A garbled voice on the radio, followed by the shadow raising something to his featureless head and saying something

Quinn couldn't make out.

Quinn crept over to the sidewalk side of the parked cars, and found a gap between the vehicles wide enough to pass through without rubbing against either one. When he reached the street-side opening, he paused and listened as the shadow approached and then passed his position.

Silently, Quinn moved into the street behind the man, matching him step for step. The moment he was close enough, he threw a choke hold around the guy's neck.

St. Amand's man grabbed at Quinn's arm, trying to pull it loose, while twisting his body back and forth.

Quinn pressed his gun into the small of the man's back. "I pull the trigger and you never walk again."

The guy apparently knew enough English to understand the threat. He stopped twisting, and while his hand remained on Quinn's arm, it wasn't trying to dislodge it anymore.

The man huffed several times, in a mix of anger and fear.

"Don't fight it," Quinn said.

The guy ignored the suggestion, but within seconds, Quinn was dragging his unconscious body into a recess for rubbish containers at the end of the building closest to them.

Quinn used the man's tie to bind his hands together and secure them behind his back to a pipe along the bottom of the building. He took the guy's wallet, phone, and radio.

After shoving a wadded up paper sack into the man's mouth, Quinn hurried back to the intersection and crouched at the same spot as before. As he'd hoped, the SUV was still down the street, only now all the doors were closed.

In his hand, the radio barked again.

"STEFAN, WHERE THE hell are you?" Georgi asked from the front seat.

No response.

"Stefan?"

More dead air.

"Again," Drake said. He was sitting in the backseat, rubbing his wrists where they'd been tied, trying to ignore the throbbing pain in his ribs, the sting of the cuts on his face, and the pounding headache that still clouded his mind.

Georgi clicked the mic button. "Stefan, respond."

Still nothing.

"Who's with him?" Drake asked.

"Neno." Georgi raised the radio again. "Neno, are you there?"

A second passed. "I'm here."

"Isn't Stefan with you?"

"We split up. I'm supposed to meet up with him in three minutes."

"Where?" Drake asked.

Georgi relayed the question, and Neno gave him the location.

"Tell him we'll meet him there." Drake turned to Nikola in the driver's seat. "Let's go! Let's go!"

WHILE QUINN DIDN'T catch everything that was being said, he understood enough to get the gist. Including the part about a guy named Stefan, which, not so coincidentally, matched the name on the ID Quinn had taken from the man he'd just put to sleep.

As soon as it became clear the SUV was about to leave, he whipped around, searching the street for a vehicle he could appropriate. On the sidewalk, tucked against the next building down, was a trio of motorcycles.

He sprinted over and hotwired an old Yamaha with a cracked seat and a nearly full tank of gas. Two tries and he had the engine purring.

By the time he was on the road, the SUV had moved out of sight. He knew which way it had been headed so he flew down the street, checking each intersection he passed.

Three down, he spotted the SUV's taillights nearly ninety meters away. As he turned the corner, the vehicle took a left and moved out of sight again. He cranked the accelerator, reached the intersection within seconds, and caught sight of the SUV again.

He started to speed up more, but when the SUV swerved toward the curb, its brake lights glowing, he slowed. The back passenger door swung open. A man ran out from the shadows and jumped inside.

The aforementioned Neno, apparently.

Even before the door closed all the way, the SUV sped back onto the road.

Quinn leaned low over the handlebars and jammed on the gas, matching their speed.

AS NENO WAS getting into the SUV, Nikola asked Drake, "Where to?"

Drake had been thinking about that since they picked up the two hostages now lying in the cargo area.

He was pretty sure the unconscious woman was the one with the Asian guy who'd been taking pictures outside Mr. St. Amand's office building the night before. That pissed him off.

There was something vaguely familiar about the other guy, too, but he couldn't put his finger on what. He felt confident, though, the guy would know where Mr. St. Amand was being taken. Drake needed someplace quiet where he could pull the information out of the guy. Ideally, he would have taken his prisoners to his fully outfitted basement workroom where he'd questioned the courier a few days earlier, but it would take them over an hour to get there. He needed someplace closer.

When it came to him, he smiled.

"Bianchi's warehouse," he said.

CHAPTER
TWENTY SEVEN

"IT'S JUST UP ahead," Orlando said. "That building with the arches along the ground floor."

"I see it," Howard said.

Orlando checked the tracker as the van neared the building. Quinn's dot was glowing from somewhere inside, same as it had been now for nearly fifteen minutes. She tapped the dot and brought up the precise location information. The phone was transmitting from the back half of the ground floor, toward the east end.

With no place to park, Howard flicked on his hazard lights and stopped as close to the building as he could get. Orlando scanned the street for anything suspicious.

"Seems quiet," Daeng said, propped between the seats.

Orlando switched on her comm. "Quinn?" She waited, but the radio remained silent. "Drive around until we call you," she told Howard, and looked at Daeng. "Let's go."

She opened her door and hopped outside, Daeng right behind her. The moment they were clear of the van, Howard drove off.

The street was indeed quiet, the only sounds those drifting on the breeze from a busier road in the distance.

Orlando motioned for Daeng to stay put and approached the building alone, in case the calm was a ruse. She reached the door and did a visual check before trying the handle.

Upon hearing the latch release, she raised an eyebrow.

She pulled the door open and slipped inside. A small,

deserted lobby, with a directory of businesses on one wall listing each company's suite number. Straight ahead was the staircase to the upper floors, and right before that was a corridor running left and right.

She crept up to the hallway and peeked in both directions. Not a soul in sight.

She returned to the entrance and waved Daeng in.

The tracker app led them down the hall to the last door on the right. Orlando jiggled the doorknob. Locked.

She pulled out her lockpicks and solved the problem. Before pushing the door open, she and Daeng pulled out their guns and checked that the suppressors were securely attached.

Orlando turned the knob again and gave the door a push. As it swung inward, they saw the place was not in use.

Orlando could hear nothing.

She and Daeng moved inside. The tracker pointed them to a small room near the center of the office suite. Instead of Quinn, they found Christophe St. Amand lying on the floor, hog-tied and unconscious.

Daeng reached him first, and pulled a phone and a piece of paper out of St. Amand's pocket. On the paper was written the letter O. "I'm guessing this is for you."

Orlando took it and opened the note.

> N and J have been taken. Doing what I can to get them back. Stick to the plan and take this package and the other ones to rendezvous. Will catch up as soon as I can.
>
> Q

"That son of a bitch," she muttered.

"Quinn?" Daeng asked.

She handed him the note and turned on her mic. "Orlando for Steve."

"Go for Steve."

"Circle back. We've got more cargo."

AFTER ST. AMAND WAS deposited in the back of the van, Orlando injected him with Beta-Somnol and then crawled up front, where Howard waited in the driver's seat.

"Nate and Jar are in trouble and Quinn's gone after them," Orlando said. "I think Daeng and I should go help him, but that means you'll be making the run on your own. You okay with that?"

"Of course."

"I'm hoping we'll be there before the plane arrives, but I can't promise anything. You just need to make sure you're at the airfield well before two a.m."

"Got it," he replied.

"If you even have the smallest suspicion that you're going to run into trouble, call me immediately."

"I will."

She hesitated. "I'm sorry. We shouldn't be leaving you alone like this."

"Yes, you should. And don't worry. I'll be fine."

She leaned over and gave him a hug. "Thank you." When she released him, she turned for the passenger door, but stopped. "Here." She handed him a kit with two syringes and some spare needles. "Give each of them half a dose when you get to the airfield. That should hold them until long after they're in the air."

"Will do. Now get out of here and find the others."

"Thanks, Steve."

She climbed out of the van and joined Daeng on the sidewalk. "We need to find a ride."

Knowing they would need something that could carry the whole team save Howard, they settled on a BMW X3 SUV. Orlando hacked into the car's computer, disabling its alarm and tricking it into thinking her phone was an authorized key.

The dot representing Jar on the tracking app led them northeast, into an industrialized area on the outskirts of the Italian capital.

"Take a right at the next street," Orlando told Daeng, "and slow down."

Daeng eased back on the accelerator and made the turn.

Small factories and warehouses sat along either side of the road. Here and there, floodlights illuminated empty parking lots beside the structures.

Orlando switched on her comm. "Orlando for Quinn."

Like with his phone, there was no answer.

She looked back at the tracker. Jar's dot had remained static for the last ten minutes.

"Next intersection, go left," Orlando said. "The place is forty meters from the corner, so keep our speed steady and don't look around. At the intersection after that, go left again and we'll find someplace to park."

Orlando switched from the tracking app to her camera, and placed her phone against the door with the lens above the window frame. As they turned the corner, she hit the Record button and faced forward.

When they drove by the building, she tried to pick up what she could out of the corner of her eye, but there was little lighting and nothing stood out.

At the next block, Daeng turned again and pulled into a darkened parking area. Orlando stopped the recording and played the footage.

In the dim area next to the target building sat an SUV, very close to what appeared to be an entrance. The vehicle looked unoccupied, and no one was around it.

She shoved the phone into her pocket and activated her comm again. "Orlando for Quinn."

Same as before.

"Orlando for Quinn."

Still nothing.

"All right," she said to Daeng. "We'll walk from here."

As she reached for the door handle, a quiet, strained voice said over the radio, "Orlando?"

"Quinn?"

"No...Jar. Where...where am I?"

"Are you okay?"

"I...I do not know. We-we were in a—"

A muffled whisper from a different voice. Then Jar saying, "What?" and the other whisperer again. "Orlando. On the comm," Jar said. "I...I think so. Hold on."

Movement and grunts and a muttered "Ouch."

"Orlando?"

This voice she recognized immediately. "Nate. What's going on? Are you all right?"

"She hears you," Jar said.

"This is Jar's comm," he explained. "Mine fell out in the crash. We're tied up, so I can't take her earpiece."

"Crash? What the hell happened?"

Jar repeated the question.

"Later," he said. "Have to be careful they don't hear us."

"We've tracked Jar's phone to a warehouse at the north end of the city. Do you know if that's where you are?"

"We're in a building big enough to be a warehouse. They brought us into a store—" His volume dropped. "Someone's coming."

"Hang tight. We're going to get you out." She glanced at Daeng. "Let's get moving."

They exited the sedan and sprinted across the street.

QUINN KILLED HIS headlight soon after the SUV entered a quiet area of warehouses and businesses. But the light wasn't the only thing that could give him away. With no other traffic, the sound of the motorcycle's engine carried far. So, even driving dark, he maintained a large gap between himself and the others.

Every time the SUV turned a corner, he sped up so that he wouldn't lose them, and then let the gap grow again once he had them back in sight.

The plan had worked fine for a while. But the SUV turned again, and when he'd raced to the corner and looked down the intersecting road, the vehicle was gone.

Had they seen him? Were they hurrying out of the area on some other road? Or doubling back to surprise him from behind?

Before he could even guess, the red glow of brake lights spilled out from a gap between buildings on the right side of the road.

Quinn killed the engine and rolled the bike off the street, around the side of the building at the corner, where it wouldn't be seen easily. He then snuck along the front of the building toward the lights.

He was a bit over halfway to the gap when the lights went out. He tensed, ready to race back to the bike if the SUV reappeared. When several seconds passed without it showing up, he continued on until he reached the corner of the building. He crouched down and peered around it.

The SUV was parked beside the next building down—a warehouse, with a loading dock toward the back large enough to accommodate at least half a dozen trucks.

The hatch of the vehicle was open, and several people were standing nearby. Included among them was the driver Nate had knocked out when they apprehended St. Amand. One of the men reached into the back and pulled Nate out. Quinn's partner had his hands tied behind his back. Another man removed Jar, who still looked unconscious. The entire party entered the building.

Quinn waited to make sure everyone was gone before he slipped around the corner and crossed over.

As he'd guessed, the door to the building was locked. But warehouses had dozens of ways in.

Before he went searching for one of them, he pulled out his knife and cut the sidewalls of all four tires.

He jogged over to the loading dock, dismissing the roll-up doors as an option. Even if one had been unlocked, opening it would have created way too much noise. What he was interested in was the stack of crates at the near edge.

He climbed onto the top, jumped up, and grabbed the edge of the roof. He pulled himself over the lip and surveyed his new surroundings. The roof was divided roughly into thirds—the flatter section he was on, and the arching two thirds that made up the rest. Vents and pipes were scattered across the flat side, and dominating the remaining roof were long and dirty skylights, spaced every four meters. He had hoped to see an entrance to a stairwell, but there was none. At least nothing obvious.

There had to be a way to get inside from up here.

He checked the nearest skylight. Below the grime-encrusted pane was a big open space all the way to ground level, a drop of eight meters, if not more. Though there was some grid work near the ceiling, it was dubious he could use it to get anywhere safe.

From this higher portion of the roof, he had a much better view of the flatter third, and now noticed the vent near the front of the building was larger than he'd thought.

He moved down to it and realized he was wrong about something else. It wasn't a vent, but a hatch more than wide enough for a person to use.

He slipped his fingers under the lip and searched until he found the latch. Unfortunately, without some specialized tools, he couldn't release it. His fingers weren't designed for the twists and turns they would need to make.

Not ready to give up, he checked the hinges, and smiled. A little wiggling, and the short metal rod that had held the first hinge together was sitting in his hand. The second hinge took more effort, but soon its pin also fell free.

He raised the unhinged end of the hatch to peek inside. Light glowed from below, revealing a shaft a bit larger than the hatch opening. Mounted to the side across from Quinn was a ladder.

He raised the hatch higher and backed in, belly up, legs first until his feet were pressed against the wall next to the ladder. Carefully turned until he was facing downward, brought his whole body into the shaft, and lowered the hatch, which had been resting on his shoulders, into its frame.

Slowly, he rotated around the walls of the shaft until his hands were on the ladder. Keeping his left foot pressed against the opposite wall, he lowered his right leg so that it dangled below him. Now, when he released the left, the dangling leg would have only a short distance to travel to the ladder, preventing it from smashing against the rungs.

Before he could execute his plan, he heard someone walking in the room below. He froze and stared down the shaft. A man walked into view, going left to right, and disappeared. Ten seconds passed before Quinn heard a door open and all went quiet.

He released his foot, descended the ladder until he was

dangling from the last rung into what turned out to be a hallway, and quietly dropped to the floor.

To his right, five meters away, was a set of stairs heading down, and to his left, doorways along either side. Only one door was open, the one at the far end, and from it drifted the faintest sound of movement.

Quinn crept toward the noise.

CHAPTER
TWENTY EIGHT

DRAKE PACED THE main warehouse floor, phone pressed to his ear. "What the hell do you mean they're not there?"

"I'm standing in his room right now," Havel said. "There's no one here. And there's no one in their other room, either."

Drake had called Havel during the drive to the warehouse and sent him and Imrich to the St. Regis Hotel, sure that Sandstrom had been involved with St. Amand's kidnappers. The timing was too close to be coincidence. And given that they weren't in their hotel rooms now, Drake was more convinced the whole meeting had been some kind of setup.

"Did they even check in?" he asked.

"Yes. And they *were* in the rooms. Or someone was. All the beds have been used."

"Find out where they went!"

"Imrich is checking video now. I'll call you back as soon as we know something."

Drake hung up and turned to Georgi. "So?"

"They're on their way," Georgi said.

"How many?"

Georgi hesitated.

"*How many?*"

"Four."

Drake stared at him. "Only four?"

"The team we sent to Napoli wasn't due back until tomorrow. I called them, and they're on their way now, but it'll be at least three hours until they get here."

Drake felt the urge to toss his phone into the wall, but he resisted. St. Amand had a robust security team of fourteen men. Even with the six that had gone to Naples, the eight remaining should have been more than enough to deal with any trouble. Now three of those eight were either missing or dead, and Havel and Imrich were chasing down Sandstrom, leaving Drake with only three. And none of them, including himself, had been able to keep their boss from being taken.

"Neno, there should be a Taser in Bianchi's office. Bring it to me. I'll be in talking to our guests. Nikola, watch the front door and make sure no one comes in who shouldn't. Georgi, you're with me."

The ground-floor office space covered the same footprint as the floor above, but instead of a central hallway with offices on both sides, the ground floor's hallway ran along the outside wall of the building and had rooms only on the warehouse side. Because of this, the lower rooms were twice as large as those above. And it was in one of these empty storage rooms that they'd left the prisoners.

The first thing Drake noticed when he entered was that the man had wiggled closer to the girl. He'd probably been trying to wake her up, but it appeared he'd failed.

Georgi grabbed the man by the hair and yanked him into a sitting position. Drake had to admire the prisoner's spirit, as not once had the man's eyes left Drake's since he walked in.

"Where did they take him?" Drake said.

The man said nothing.

Drake nodded, and Georgi pulled the man's head back and punched him in the face. For a second, the man's gaze strayed, but as soon as he'd absorbed the punch, it returned to Drake.

"Where did they take him?"

Another punch. Another stare down.

"Where did they take him?"

As Georgi brought his fist back to deliver another blow, the man finally spoke. "You'll have to be a little more specific."

"The man you and your friends kidnapped," Drake said.

The man parted his lips in a bloody smile. "You mean Mr.

St. Amand? I have no idea."

Drake's eyes narrowed. They knew who they had. That was not good. "Again," he said to Georgi.

Georgi smashed his knuckles into the man's face.

"Where did your friends take him?" Drake said.

The man spat a wad of blood onto the floor. "Dude, I wasn't in charge of knowing the destination."

Georgi looked at Drake, waiting for the go-ahead to hit the guy again, but Drake shook his head. "You work for Sandstrom, don't you?"

The man almost laughed. "Sorry, that's classified."

Drake was right. This *did* have something to do with Sandstrom. "What is he? CIA?"

This time, the man did laugh. "You're not even close."

Drake's lips pressed together. In his experience, the majority of people were weak. Most would have given up what they knew by now. This guy showed no signs of doing that anytime soon. Clearly, it would take more to break him.

Drake walked over to the woman and rolled her onto her back with his foot. She looked a little like the woman who'd been with the Chinese tourist whom he'd scared off outside the office. It had been dark and he'd been more focused on the man, but she was tiny like that woman.

A swift kick to her head might rip it right off, but there was no need to go to that extreme yet.

He set his boot on her ribs. "Where did they take him?"

"You're kind of slow, aren't you?" the man said. "See, the more you hurt us, the less likely your boss stays alive. You kill either of us and I guarantee that'll be the case."

Drake pressed down on the woman. A long groan escaped her mouth. She twitched and tried to roll out from under him, but Drake held her in place.

"Where did they take him?"

"I. Don't. Know," the man said.

Drake shifted his weight back to the foot on the woman, but before he could push down, the man jumped to his feet and launched himself at Drake.

Drake tried to move out of the way, but the man caught

him in the waist with his shoulder and they both fell to the ground. Before the prisoner could regain his feet, Georgi jumped on him and pinned him to the ground.

Drake scrambled up, seething. "You think this is a game?"

He had Georgi roll the man onto his side, and Drake kicked the guy in the stomach.

"*Where* did they take him?"

Unbelievably, the man laughed again. Drake gave him another kick, but this seemed to only increase the man's joy.

Drake took a step back, breathing deeply. If a kick wasn't going to work, maybe a jolt of electricity would. He looked toward the door, wondering what the hell happened to the Taser.

"Go find Neno!" he ordered Georgi.

Georgi hesitated. "Are you sure you don't need me to stay here?"

"I can fucking handle him. Go!"

Georgi shoved the prisoner and hurried out of the room.

Drake crouched down just out of the man's reach. From the way the guy was holding his ribs, Drake was sure the guy wouldn't be getting back on his feet anytime soon. "Last chance before things get really fun. Where did they take him?"

The man locked his gaze onto Drake's. "Who were we talking about again?"

IN MOST CASES, Orlando liked to observe a location for at least a half-hour before moving in, but she and Daeng didn't have that luxury this time.

They made their way to the corner of the building in which Jar's phone was located. Orlando used the gooseneck camera to look around the corner. The area was still unoccupied, the SUV in the same spot it had been on the video.

She and Daeng crept around the corner and slunk down the side to the door she assumed the others had used to go inside. She sent Daeng to check the SUV while she tried the door handle. Locked—two deadbolts and the knob. All would be easy enough to pick, but best to find a less conspicuous place to enter.

Daeng clicked his tongue, so she snuck over to see what was up.

He pointed at the front tire. It was flat. He pointed at the back one. Flat, too.

"The others?" she whispered.

"Same."

She ran a finger over the rubber and discovered the cut on the sidewall, right where an experienced saboteur would have made it.

"Quinn," she said.

Daeng's grin was cut short by the sound coming over the comm of someone entering the room Nate and Jar were in.

When Orlando and Daeng heard flesh hitting flesh, they sprinted to the door, no longer thinking about finding a less conspicuous entrance. But as Orlando pulled out her lockpicks, she heard the squeal of rubber and the roar of an engine.

She glanced toward the road and saw headlights from a vehicle still hidden from view.

"Hide," she said.

Daeng sprinted toward a stack of crates on a loading dock at the back of the building, Orlando right behind him. He ducked behind the boxes and she slid in next to him just as a sedan raced into view.

The light swung through the parking area, illuminating the loading dock before swerving back toward the side of the building. There, the sedan screeched to a stop.

With the gooseneck, Orlando peeked around the crate. The sedan had parked at an angle near the SUV, and all four of its doors were now open. Three of the men who'd been inside approached the SUV, while the fourth man stood guard, scanning the parking area.

The first to reach the SUV crouched next to one of the tires, then said something to his friends. They checked the other tires, and the four of them huddled. When they broke, two headed to the building's entrance and knocked loudly on the door, while the other two turned on flashlights and began searching the parking area.

The sounds of Nate's interrogation continued over the

comm. Though he seemed to be handling it well enough, things could get a whole lot worse in a hurry. Quinn might've been in position to do something, but with no way to communicate with him, they couldn't count on it.

Orlando and Daeng needed to act.

One of the men at the door said something in a loud voice. It opened, and he and his companion crossed inside. Meanwhile, the two searchers were following the building back toward the loading dock.

She whispered into Daeng's ear. After they pulled out their guns, she mouthed, "Three, two, one."

They swung out in unison from behind the boxes, their guns pointed at the searchers. When one of the men saw them and started to bring up his weapon, Orlando said, "Don't."

The guy's partner, who had been looking the other way, twisted around. The first guy hesitated, then tried to whip his gun the rest of the way up.

The *thup* of Orlando's gun was quieter than the sound of the dead man's body falling to the pavement.

His friend was smarter, but only to a point. He dropped his gun, but started running toward the building's entrance.

Orlando put a bullet through his calf before he'd gone five steps, sending him crashing to the ground.

She and Daeng rushed over to make sure the guy didn't yell for help or do anything else to draw the attention of his colleagues inside. But it seemed he was too consumed by the pain to do more than lie there, writhing and groaning.

Daeng clamped a hand over his mouth anyway, while Orlando checked the wound. He wasn't going to bleed out, but with a shattered tibia, he was in for a long recovery period.

She used her knife to cut off the bottom half of his pant leg, then used it as a makeshift bandage. She administered a quarter dose from one of the two remaining syringes.

She and Daeng loaded the unconscious man and his dead friend into the back of the SUV, in case anyone else showed up. They gave the sedan's tires the same treatment those on the SUV had received and then moved over to the building.

This time nothing interfered when she picked the locks.

QUINN SNEAKED DOWN the hallway until he was just outside the open doorway. Pressing against the wall, he inched forward and chanced a peek inside. A man was behind a desk, looking into one of the drawers. He shoved it closed and opened another one.

From the sudden smile on his face, Quinn guessed the man's search had ended. As he reached into the drawer, Quinn pulled back out of sight.

The man's steps tapped across the floor, toward the door.

The moment the man appeared on the threshold, Quinn launched himself and smashed his shoulder into the guy's chest, slamming the man into the doorframe, and sending whatever the guy had been holding clattering to the floor.

Before the guy could react, Quinn grabbed him by the head and yanked it down, hurling the guy's face into Quinn's knee. Cartilage crunched. But the man could barely get a yell started before Quinn had him in a headlock, cutting off his voice and the blood flow to his brain.

In quick order, the man was unconscious.

Quinn carried him into the office and laid the guy on the floor. He took the man's gun and used power cords to tie him up. He considered gagging him, too, but with the broken nose, doing so might kill the guy.

He popped the mag out of the man's weapon and removed the bullet from the chamber. He pocketed the ammo, and tossed the now useless hunk of metal into a rubbish bin.

When he exited the room, he looked around for the item the man had dropped, and spotted it a couple of meters from the door.

A Taser.

He had a pretty good idea who its intended victim was.

As he snatched it up, he heard someone on the stairs at the other end of the hall. He shoved the Taser into his pocket, slipped back into the office, and hid behind the door.

Steps in the hallway now, one person heading toward Quinn's position.

"Neno, let's go," a male voice said near the door. The person stepped inside. "Drake's waiting—"

His colleague lying on the floor stopped him. "Neno?"

As the man hurried across the room to his colleague, Quinn fell in behind him and tapped him on the shoulder.

The man whirled around. "Who—"

Quinn punched him in the larynx. Gasping, the guy backpedaled into the desk. Quinn matched him step for step, then whipped the grip of his gun into the man's head.

The man fell sideways onto the desk. Quinn caught him and lowered him to the floor, next to his buddy.

With no broken nose to worry about this time, Quinn removed the man's suit coat and stuffed one of the sleeves into the guy's mouth. In the desk, he found a set of military-grade handcuffs, and used them to cuff the man's hand above his head and around one of the heavy desk's legs. It would take at least two people to move the damn thing, so the guy wasn't going anywhere fast.

Quinn returned to the doorway, wondering if someone else might show up, but this time the hallway was quiet.

He stepped over the threshold to the stairs.

HAVEL FINISHED HIS fruitless search of the rooms Sandstrom and his men had been staying in and headed down to the lobby. He found Imrich sitting in a quiet area, looking at his phone.

"Their IDs are gone and no computers, either," Havel said as he walked up. "I have a feeling they're not coming back."

"I'm pretty sure you're right," Imrich said. He'd been tasked with using St. Amand's data expert, Lorenzo Conte, to break into the hotel's security system.

"You found something?"

Imrich held up his phone. On the screen was an image of what looked like the hallway outside Sandstrom's room. When Imrich played the video, Havel saw he'd been right. A couple of seconds into the footage, Sandstrom and his companions walked into the hallway from the elevator area. They stopped and talked for a moment, then went to their separate rooms.

"What time was this?" Havel asked.

"Just after they were dropped off."

"So, when did they leave?"

Imrich selected another file and hit Play. It was the same hall, only empty. Havel waited, but when nothing changed, he said, "You're wasting time. Show me when they came out."

"This is when they came out."

"What are you talking about?"

Imrich played a third clip. "This is the exact time when you went into their rooms."

The hallway remained unoccupied.

"That's the same clip you just showed," Havel said.

"It is not. Not like you mean."

"Then Lorenzo must have gotten the times screwed up."

"He didn't. He says it is a ten-second loop."

"A loop?" Havel looked at the screen again, hardly believing it.

"Yes. It began not very long after Sandstrom entered his room."

Havel's anger grew. "Those bastards covered their tracks so we wouldn't figure out when they left. There must be other cameras. They couldn't have looped everything."

"There are, and they didn't. Only the *they* who created the loop weren't Sandstrom or his men."

Imrich was the perfect partner most of the time, but there were moments such as this one when he relished doling out information slowly, like a badly directed stage actor.

"Goddammit, just tell me," Havel said.

Imrich played a fourth clip. This was a different hall, without any of the decorative elements seen elsewhere in the hotel. At the very start, two women in hotel uniforms walked through the frame. A moment after they disappeared, a luggage cart rolled into view at the far end of the hall, being pushed by a man not in uniform. An outside service worker, perhaps, using the cart to transport equipment or something similar. The large box on the cart supported this theory.

The feed went dark before the man got too close.

"Turn it back on," Havel said.

"It is on."

"What?"

Imrich said nothing. A few moments later, the hallway

reappeared, only without the man and the cart.

"The camera was deliberately turned off," Imrich said. "There's another camera that got him turning into a service hallway near the back of the building, but then it went out, too, until he was gone."

"All right, I agree that's strange, but are you trying to tell me Sandstrom was in that box?"

"There is no other way he could have left. Lorenzo has scanned the footage from all the potential exit routes right up until a few minutes ago. Sandstrom doesn't show up in any of them."

"But there are three of them," Havel argued. "They couldn't have all fit in there."

"The man with the cart made three trips."

"Shit." Havel paused. "If that is how they got out, did they go voluntarily? Or were they kidnapped, too?"

"That, I don't know."

"What about outside cameras? Did they get into a vehicle? Did they walk away?"

Imrich touched the screen again. "The outside camera at the service entrance also went dark, but only once, *after* the cart finished its third trip down. Lorenzo used that time frame, and found footage from a security camera on a building across from where the alley behind the hotel lets out."

The new clip showed a van exiting the alley and turning onto the road.

"It's a Mercedes-Benz Sprinter cargo van, either dark gray or dark blue, most likely," Imrich said.

Hovel groaned. "So, we need to drive around until we find a dark gray or dark blue Sprinter? That sounds like fun."

"I am just telling you. It is better to know than not, yes?"

"Yeah, yeah." Havel pulled out his phone. "Drake's not going to like this."

NATE BLINKED.

His head had been ringing since the second time he'd been hit in the face, but that was nothing new. He'd had concussions in the past, and he'd likely have more in the future. What concerned him more was Jar's condition.

They had agreed she should act like she was still unconscious when the men returned, and she'd done an excellent job of that, even when the head asshole threatened to crush her under his foot. What Nate wasn't sure of was whether she was still acting or had actually passed out again.

He couldn't let the guy harm her again, and had already decided if the man tried, Nate would give him a real-sounding story that would hopefully buy Orlando enough time to get them out.

At the moment, the asshole was pacing at the other end of the room, talking on his phone in what Nate thought was Italian. Nate didn't try to understand what was being said, as it took his full attention not to drift off into a fog. But he heard a familiar name and his ears perked up.

Sandstrom.

The conversation did not seem to be making the asshole happy.

Good.

When the man hung up, he stared into the distance for half a minute, his face hard, before he turned toward Nate.

Nate braced himself.

DRAKE DIDN'T KNOW what to think. Sandstrom was missing. But was he responsible for Mr. St. Amand's kidnapping, or had he been taken, too? If the latter, then who in God's name was behind this?

He took a breath and looked over at his prisoner. The man's face was a mess of sweat and blood and bruises, and yet the guy stared back at him with resolve, like he would never break.

Goddammit.

Drake's job had changed from protecting Mr. St. Amand to bringing him back alive. The only way to accomplish that was to go through the bastard wavering on his knees in the center of the room.

A knock on the door.

Georgi, finally.

Perhaps an electric jolt would loosen the prisoner's lips. And if that didn't work, Drake could try the device on the woman.

He sneered at the prisoner. "I think you will talk now."

He walked over and yanked the door open, but it wasn't Georgi. It was Andrey and Vasil, two of the four men who had come to beef up their forces.

"Mr. Drake, I think the building may have been compromised," Andrey said.

"Compromised. What are you talking about?"

"Someone slashed the SUV's tires."

Drake blinked in surprise. "Did you see who did it?"

"No, sir. Happened before we arrived. But Penko and Darian are outside looking right now."

Drake glanced down the hallway toward the building's entrance, wondering if it had been a random act of vandalism, or remnants of Bianchi's organization wanting to retaliate for their boss's death.

"Search the building," Drake said. "And if you see Georgi, tell him to get his ass back here."

After Drake closed the door, he glanced at the prisoner, pulled out his phone, and called Havel.

"I need you two to get here as quick as you can."

QUINN PRESSED HIMSELF against the wall at the bottom of the stairwell, the opening to the ground-floor hallway only a hand's width away.

Though he didn't hear anything, he sensed someone was there. He peered into the corridor by way of his cell phone. Sure enough, near the midway point, a man leaned against the outer wall. No gun visible, but Quinn wasn't going to count on that.

Quinn picked up a couple of small pebbles that had been swept against the wall. His plan was to gently toss one against the wall opposite the stairwell entrance. If the man came down here, Quinn could remove him as a concern.

Three sharp knocks echoed down the hall.

"Who is it?" the man in the hallway barked.

Quinn stuck his camera out again as a muffled voice

answered from outside. Names, it sounded like.

The man inside opened the main door and let two men in. Both had guns in their hands.

There was a short conversation between the three of them, then the first guy pointed down the hall in the opposite direction of where Quinn was. The man pulled out his own pistol, while the other two hurried down to one of the doors and knocked.

When the door opened, the person inside leaned out just enough for Quinn to see his profile.

It was St. Amand's driver. The same son of a bitch who'd been tied up in the back of the SUV when the crash occurred.

The conversation at the door lasted a few more seconds, before the pair of new men headed back down the hall toward the entrance, moving fast. When they reached the guy at the door, one of the two slowed enough to say something to him while the other continued on.

Heading straight toward the stairwell entrance.

Quinn retreated up the stairs, and slipped inside an empty room close to the swanky office. He closed the door but kept the knob turned so the latch didn't engage.

He heard the man enter the hallway and jog toward the office, alone.

As soon as he passed Quinn's position, Quinn slipped out of the room and moved in behind him.

The man entered the office, and stopped dead upon seeing his two unconscious colleagues on the floor. Unlike the last guy Quinn had put down, this one turned around.

"Hi, there," Quinn said, smiling.

He twisted the man's gun out of his hand and pointed both guns at the man's chest.

"Speak English?" Quinn asked.

A nod.

"Good. You see that seat over there?" Quinn indicated the chair behind the desk.

Another nod.

"Sit in it. But no sudden movements. Understand?"

The man turned and walked toward the desk. He stared down at his friends as he passed them.

"You don't cooperate, you can join them," Quinn said.

The man rounded the desk and sat.

Quinn stepped behind him and stuck his sound suppressor against the back of the guy's head. "You're going to want to struggle. Don't."

As Quinn applied a choke hold, the man stiffened and started to raise his hands in defense, but he fought the urge until the last second. By that time, it was too late. Soon his body sagged forward as he slipped under.

Quinn used extension cords to tie the guy's arms and legs to the chair and headed back to the ground floor.

Using his phone again, he checked the lower hall. The original guy was still there, but not the one who'd entered the building with the man Quinn had just taken care of. That was a problem. He didn't need the missing man showing up when he was in the middle of disabling the guy's colleague. But Quinn couldn't wait for him to reappear, either.

The guy in the hall was facing the main entrance, his body tense, his back to Quinn.

Quinn set the extra gun he'd just obtained on the floor, and pulled out the Taser. Its settings told him it was fully charged. Taser in one hand and his gun in the other, he eased into the hallway.

He didn't know the specs of the Taser, but figured if he was no more than ten meters away from his target, it should work fine. Which meant he had about twenty meters to traverse unnoticed before he could use it.

He crept along the back wall, his eyes glued to the man by the door. So far, there hadn't been even a twitch.

Fifteen meters to go, and still no reaction.

Ten, and the same.

If Quinn could go another five, even if the guy did finally realize he had company, Quinn could rush forward and hit the guy with the flying electrified wires before the man could do anything about it.

But Quinn had gone only two more meters when the front door began to swing open.

The guy stepped backward in surprise, his weapon rising.

The shift in position also moved Quinn into the man's peripheral vision.

He jerked his head toward Quinn as Quinn rushed forward, both Taser and gun pointing at the man. When the guy reached back for the door, Quinn hit the Taser's trigger.

The man's eyes widened at the tiny spikes soaring his way. He tried to dive out of the way, but one wire hit him in the center of his chest and the other speared his rib cage.

Body dancing to the electric shock, he fell to the floor.

Whoever was on the other side of the door was now able to push it open again.

Quinn trained his gun on the entrance and kept coming.

Orlando dove through the opening and rolled on the floor, before popping to her feet and sweeping through the corridor with her gun.

When she saw Quinn, she whispered, "Hey, babe." She glanced down at the still shaking man. "Where did you get the Taser?"

"Are you alone?"

Daeng stepped inside and nodded his chin. "Quinn."

"Tell me you found St. Amand already," Quinn said.

"Yeah," Orlando. "Cute use of your phone."

"You did read my note, too, didn't you?"

"Yep."

"Then...what the hell are you doing here? You're supposed to be headed to the rendezvous."

"Steve's handling the rendezvous. Thought you might need our help." She pulled out a syringe and stuck it into the man on the floor. When she pulled it out again, she said, "How many are left?"

"The driver's in a room down there. And there's at least one other somewhere in the building."

"Only one?" she said, eyebrow raised. "I thought there would be more."

"There were. I've been busy."

"Yeah, um, so have we. Took care of the two that were outside."

"Well, there are three upstairs that aren't going to be

giving us any problems. Not that we're keeping—"

A door near the stairwell opened. Quinn turned and saw it was the missing guy. The man whipped his gun up, but before he could get a shot off, Orlando and Daeng pulled their triggers.

Thup. Thup.

The man dropped dead where he stood.

"Looks like we're even," Orlando said.

"How do you figure even?" Quinn asked. He motioned at the guy he tasered. "I have four."

"He's more a shared takedown, isn't he? I'm sure we distracted him for you. So, which room was that driver in?"

DRAKE PACED NEAR the door. A night that had started out so great with the enriched Sandstrom deal had gone to shit. There were going to be some *very* uncomfortable conversations after everything was set right again. Mr. St. Amand would likely demand a complete overhaul of the organization. Drake was pretty sure his position would be safe, but who knew?

The only sure bet was that his boss was going to be furious.

A dull thud from the hallway. Someone knocking on the door?

He checked the time. Havel had said it would take him and Imrich at least twenty minutes to get to the warehouse, so it couldn't be them yet. It was probably the two men searching outside.

Hoping they'd found the troublemakers, Drake strode to the door, but as he grabbed the handle, he heard voices speaking not in Bulgarian but English. And one of the voices sounded female. There were *no* females in Mr. St. Amand's security team.

He quietly turned the handle and opened the door a crack.

Four people were at the entrance. The Caucasian guy who'd been with Drake's two prisoners in the SUV, the Asian guy who'd been outside the office building the night before, and another Asian woman. The fourth person was Nikola, lying on the floor, twitching.

All of a sudden, the Asian guy and the woman shot at

something behind the Caucasian guy, the sound squelched by suppressors. Almost as loud was the thud of something falling to the ground out of Drake's view.

They had taken out another one of Drake's men. How many of his team had they dealt with? Georgi and Neno should have returned a while ago. Had they been eliminated? And what about the two men Andrey had left outside?

What Drake knew was that his already small security team was down at least one, and none of those still in action were with him.

In the hall, the trio had turned and was now walking toward the room where Drake was. Two of them, he could handle. He was less confident about his odds with three, especially since they'd shown they were talented enough to get this far.

He spun around and sprinted to the door that opened into the main warehouse space. If he had more time, he would have shot the prisoners in the head, but his ass was the only thing he cared about at the moment. Any gunfire would bring the others running.

He pulled the door open, closed it quietly behind him, and ran toward the other side of the vast room. He hadn't been in this part of the building yet, but there had to be another exit somewhere.

While the way out remained elusive, he did find a stairway to a basement filled with old generators and other machinery. He discovered a covered spot on top of one of the machines, from which he could watch the entrance. If they came down, he would be able to pick them off before they could even begin looking around.

He aimed his gun and settled in.

QUINN STOOD TO one side of the door, while Orlando and Daeng stood on the other. Quinn pushed the door in with his gun, and they each scanned the part of the room they could see.

The only people in the room were Nate and Jar. They were in the center, Nate on his knees and Jar lying on the floor.

Quinn rushed in first, the other two right behind.

"He left maybe thirty seconds ago," Nate said, his voice weak. He nodded toward the rear corner. "Through the door back there. Hurry!"

Quinn signaled Orlando to check their friends and ran to the rear door.

He jerked the door open and ducked to the side. When no bullets flew, he rushed through the opening in a crouch, and stopped behind one of the pillars holding up the roof.

The room remained still.

The space was huge and dim, lit only by the light seeping in through the skylights high above, but that was enough for him to see there was no sign of the driver anywhere.

He rejoined Orlando, Nate, and Jar.

"He's gone for the moment," he said. "The sooner we can get out of here, the better."

Orlando nodded. "Daeng's getting the car."

"There are at least three others," Nate said.

"Seven, actually," Orlando said. "And were, not are."

"Oh…okay. Good…good."

Quinn crouched next to his partner. Nate's face was bloody and swollen. "How are you feeling?"

"I'll be fine."

Orlando was helping Jar sit up.

"Excellent," Quinn said. "You're awake."

"I would prefer to be asleep," Jar said.

Nate grinned. "Did you just crack a joke?"

"No. I am speaking true."

"Do you think you can walk?" Orlando asked.

"I…do not know."

Quinn and Orlando helped Jar to her feet. When they let go, she wobbled enough that Quinn put his arm back around her. "Just lean on me. Nate, you need help?"

"I don't think so." Nate rose gingerly to his feet. "Let's get out of here."

Quinn and Jar led the way through the corridor and to the building's entrance, with Nate coming next. Orlando brought up the rear, on the lookout in case the driver showed up, but their exit went unmolested. Less than a minute after they stepped outside, Daeng drove a sedan into the parking area.

Jar looked like she was in serious pain, so they put her in the front passenger seat where she'd have more room, and reclined it until the back was almost in Quinn's lap.

"I'll call Misty," Orlando said, pulling out her phone. "And have her arrange for medical to be waiting."

Daeng glanced in the rearview mirror. "North?"

"North," Quinn said. "We have a plane to catch."

CHAPTER
TWENTY NINE

HAVEL AND IMRICH were five minutes out from the warehouse when Lorenzo called. Since Imrich was driving, Havel put the call on speaker.

"Tell me you found the van," he said.

"I found the van."

Lorenzo described how he pieced together the van's route from dozens of security cameras throughout the city. "It made steady progress to the north, until it neared Piazza Euclide."

Havel and Imrich shared a glance. That was the vicinity where the security team had tried to rescue Mr. St. Amand. "Is it still there?"

"No. It entered a dead zone and was in it for approximately ten minutes before I saw it again, only a few blocks from where it disappeared."

"What were they doing there?" Havel asked, more to himself than anyone else.

Lorenzo answered, "I have no idea."

"I realize that. But do you know where they went next?"

"North. Out of the city."

"Out of the city?"

"Yes. Into the countryside."

"Okay, and?"

"And there are not very many cameras in that direction so who knows?"

"Who knows?" Havel said. "That is *not* the right answer. Are you saying you don't know where it is at this moment?"

"The direction, yes. And the vague area. But precisely? No. There are many ways it could go from there."

"I don't care how many ways. You need to find it fast!"

"I'm not sure I can. Like I said, there aren't so many cameras outside the city."

"So, you're saying you'd prefer me to tell Mr. St. Amand directly that you can't do it?" It was an empty threat at the moment, but Lorenzo didn't know why they were interested in the van.

"That...won't be necessary."

"No. It would be my pleasure. Let me get him on the line."

"I'll-I'll find the van," Lorenzo said, his tone over-the-top helpful. "Don't worry. I'm sure I'll get back to you very soon."

"See that you do."

"Oh, I almost forgot. I pulled a good image of the driver. Will that help?"

"It's a start. Send it to us."

"Of course."

Havel disconnected the call.

Two minutes later, Imrich turned the sedan into the warehouse parking lot. Two of the organization's vehicles were parked near the building's entrance, which was open.

Havel didn't like that at all, but he was equally troubled by the tires of both vehicles being completely flat.

"Stop," he said, and pulled out his gun.

Imrich hit the brakes, the sedan's headlights illuminating the disabled SUV and sedan.

"Do you see anyone?" Havel asked.

"No."

"Okay," Havel said. "Take us to the entrance. Slowly."

Imrich rolled across the lot until he was four meters from the open door and stopped.

Havel stared through the opening at a long, dark lump lying on the floor of the lighted corridor.

"I think that's a body," Imrich said.

It definitely was.

Havel pulled out his phone and called Drake, but after four rings the call went to voicemail. "Stay with the car," he said.

"I'll check it out."

He didn't want to go in alone, but he didn't want to risk having their tires slashed, too. He eased out and snuck over to the entrance.

A body, all right. Nikola. But he wasn't dead. Havel could see his chest moving up and down. He could also see two wires pinned to his torso, leading to a Taser near his feet. The device would have hurt like hell, but it shouldn't have knocked him out.

Havel stepped inside and scanned the room. There was another body to the right. It looked like Vasil, only there was no chance he was still alive. His shirt was covered in blood, and his eyes stared at nothing.

Havel tried waking up Nikola, but no luck, so he checked the rest of the rooms along the hallway, then went upstairs. In the office where Bianchi had been killed a few nights earlier, he found three more men. These were all alive, but had been tied up and gagged.

He attempted to revive them one by one. Andrey and Georgi didn't respond, but after a few shakes and a slap, Neno blinked.

"What...Havel?"

"What the hell happened? Where's Drake?"

Neno narrowed his eyes. "Someone jumped me." He blinked again. "We've got to warn Drake. We've got to—"

"I can't find him. Where did you see him last?"

"Can't...find him?"

"Neno, goddammit. Snap out of it. Where was Drake the last time you saw him?"

A pause. "Downstairs. One of the rooms."

"Which room?"

"The...the third one from the end."

Havel freed Neno's hands. "Help the others."

"The others?"

Havel headed back downstairs. Neno would figure it out soon enough.

Havel knew from his earlier search that the third room from the end was empty. All the rooms were. But on his first visit, he'd just glanced inside. This time, he took a longer look around. There were several dark, wet spots near the center of the room that looked like blood.

Drake's? He hoped not.

At the back of the room was another door. He opened it slowly and peeked out. The main warehouse space. No lights, only shadows and darker shadows, and a deep, heavy quiet.

Did that mean no one was there, or that someone was lying in wait?

No way he was just going to walk in. He cursed under his breath, then did the only thing he could think of doing.

DRAKE HAD NOT moved in the near ten minutes he'd been in his basement hiding spot. He'd even remained still when his phone vibrated a few minutes earlier, worried that the others would come down the stairs while he was pulling it out, and he'd miss his chance to gun them down.

He figured the only reason his now former prisoners' friends hadn't reached him yet was that they were searching the ground level first. He was so confident of this that when he heard a voice shouting something upstairs, he didn't at first realize it was his name.

"Mr. Drake!" the voice yelled again.

He cocked his head.

"Mr. Drake! Are you here?"

It sounded like…Havel.

He scrambled off the machine and hurried to the stairs.

"Mr. Drake!"

He moved quickly up the steps and stopped near the top, in case it was a trap. He waited for the voice again, and when it didn't come, he took a deep breath and climbed the final steps.

He was alone. He hurried to the still open door of the room where he'd been interrogating his prisoner.

It was also empty.

Where was Havel? Drake was sure he hadn't been hearing things.

He peeked into the hall, and spotted Nikola lying in the

same spot as before. He could now see a second body down the hall. He couldn't tell who it was, but it had to be the one the prisoners' friends gunned down.

He sprinted to the half open main entrance.

A third car was outside, headlights on, engine running. For a moment, he thought the guy leaning in the passenger-side window, talking to someone inside, was one of the others. But then the guy straightened up and turned toward the warehouse.

Drake stepped into the open doorway. "Havel?"

The man jumped, and brought his gun halfway up before he stopped. "Mr. Drake?"

Four minutes later, Drake, Havel, and Imrich were on the road, heading north.

CHAPTER
THIRTY

AIRFIELD KA14 WAS located ten kilometers off the main road, in a meadow nestled between olive tree orchards. It was funded and maintained through the joint collaboration of several intelligence agencies, including the CIA, MI6, the German BND, and the Italian AISE. The facility was completely automated and had no personnel, save a three-man maintenance crew that checked the facility once a week, to top off the fuel refilling station and to make sure that the landing lights, weather station, and runway were all in working order.

Only aircraft that had been authorized to use the field would have the codes needed to gain remote access to the field's systems. Sensors and hidden cameras would note any unauthorized landings and send an alert to a duty officer at AISE in Rome. If it was determined the plane posed a threat, the duty officer would dispatch an intercept team and activate the runway's built-in deterrents. This consisted of rows of steel posts, set every fifty meters along the runway, that rose via hydraulics to a meter aboveground and made the airstrip useless.

When Howard arrived at 12:50 a.m., the airfield was completely dark. He parked near the small, fenced-in hut that contained the facility's automated systems, positioning the back of the van toward the runway. This would make the transferring of the prisoners easier.

The drive up from Rome had been uneventful. He'd encountered a bit of traffic as he left the city, but after that it had been smooth sailing. He stretched in his seat, working out the kinks of sitting so long in one place, and then grabbed the syringe pouch Orlando had given him, and climbed out.

As he walked to the back of the vehicle, he slipped the pouch into his pocket and drew his gun. He'd heard movement during the last ten minutes of the drive, and guessed at least one of his passengers had woken. He doubted they would have had time to untie themselves, though. He opened the door carefully and pointed his weapon inside.

All four men looked sound asleep.

Howard wasn't buying it.

He flicked the calf of the one on the far left, one of Sandstrom's men. The man didn't move, nor did he tense even in the slightest. Keeping his eyes and gun on the cargo area, Howard took a few steps back, placed the pouch on the ground, and removed one of the syringes.

The needle slipped right through the man's pant leg and into his calf. Howard depressed the plunger until half the contents had been delivered.

There were unwritten rules in the secret world, rules some people ignored, but not the people who worked for Quinn. One was to not cause unintentional harm to an adversary—or friend, for that matter—when it could be avoided. To this end, Howard exchanged the used needle with a replacement in the kit. He then injected the second man, Sandstrom's other associate.

The syringe now empty, he exchanged it for the final full one and moved on to prisoner number three, Sandstrom himself.

When Howard grabbed the older man's calf, he felt the muscle contract a little. He prepared himself for Sandstrom to put up a fight, but the man barely moved as the needle slipped in.

Not awake yet, then. Just starting to, Howard figured.

Which meant the noise he'd heard earlier could have been made only by contestant number four, Christophe St. Amand.

Howard changed the needle and approached St. Amand like he had the others. When he moved his hand toward the man's leg, however, he stopped short of touching it. St.

Amand's calf shifted.

Howard pulled his hand back. "Good morning, Mr. St. Amand."

The arms dealer showed no sign of having heard him.

"Come on, now. I know you're awake."

St. Amand continued his act.

"All right, we can pretend you're still out. You'll be really under in a moment anyway."

For a moment, nothing, then St. Amand's eyes opened. "There is another option."

"See, I knew you were awake."

Howard raised the syringe like he was a nurse checking for air bubbles.

"You know who I am," St. Amand said. "So you know I can make you a very wealthy man."

"Are you trying to buy me?"

"I'm trying to show you there are solutions you may not have considered."

Howard lowered the syringe. "How wealthy?"

"How does a hundred million euros in your bank account by the time the sun comes up sound?"

"A hundred…million? Seriously?"

"Seriously."

"You weren't lying when you said wealthy."

"I was not. All you have to do is let me go."

"What about your friends here?"

"I don't care what you do with them. The deal is for me."

"A hundred million for just you."

"Yes."

Howard's eyes narrowed. "How do I know you'd actually do it?"

"You have my word."

Howard snorted. "All right, say I do take you at your word. The way I hear it, you kill anyone who sees the *real* you. Which, obviously, I have. So maybe you transfer that money to me, but then have me killed at the first chance and take the money back."

"With the money will come a job, working for me. You

clearly have talents I could use. I don't kill my employees."

"What kind of job?"

"You would be one of my top advisors. It's the highest position in my organization."

Howard glanced down the airstrip. "I can't deny it's tempting. I only see one issue."

"Whatever it is, I'm sure I can take care of it."

"Unfortunately, Mr. St. Amand, you can't. See, I'm not an amateur thug you can just buy off. I'm a professional. My friends are professionals. And when professionals like us take a job, we finish it."

Throughout the conversation, Howard had been moving the syringe closer to the man's leg. He jabbed the needle into St. Amand's thigh and shoved down on the plunger.

St. Amand's eyes widened.

"I do appreciate the offer, though," Howard said as he pulled the needle out. "It's flattering. But arms dealing is not my idea of a career upgrade."

Whether it was because of where the Beta-Somnol had entered St. Amand's system, or from sheer force of will, St. Amand didn't fall unconscious quickly.

"You are all dead," St. Amand said. "I will get out of this. I will find you. And I will kill you all myself."

Howard smiled. "You really don't know who you've been dealing with, do you? A part of me wishes you would somehow get free and try to take us down. That would be fun."

Eyelids growing heavy, St. Amand said, "Who are you people?"

Howard patted him on the leg. "Get some sleep. It might be the last you have for a very long time."

St. Amand tried to speak again, but in seconds he was out.

"THAT'S IT," ORLANDO said, pointing at the narrow dirt lane that served as the entrance to airfield KA14.

Utilizing standard mission practice, Daeng killed the lights and took his foot off the accelerator, so that the sedan slowed without his having to tap the brakes and signal their intentions to anyone behind them.

After making the turn, Daeng kept the car at a near crawl, due to ruts and potholes purposely designed into the dirt road.

"Jar, you okay?" Quinn asked. He was sitting behind her and couldn't see her.

"I will…be happy when we…stop," she said.

"Not long now," Orlando told her.

"Anything?" Quinn asked Nate, who was watching out the rear window.

"No. It's quiet."

Quinn checked the time—1:42 a.m. They'd cut it close.

"Up there," Orlando said. "See where the road Ys?"

They were driving by starlight and the dim glow of a quarter moon, so it took Daeng a moment before he said, "Yeah. I see."

"We want the left fork. After that, there'll be another turn to the right and that will take us in."

The road became smoother after the final turn, allowing Daeng to increase their speed. About a minute later, they passed out of the orchard and into the meadow containing airfield KA14.

The van was parked near the runway, but there was no other vehicle around.

"What's going on with the doctor?" Quinn said. "Wasn't he supposed to be here?"

Orlando was tapping a text into her phone. She said nothing until a reply came in seconds later. "Misty says he's ten minutes out."

Quinn grimaced but said nothing. The delay meant the doctor would have only a few minutes to check Jar before the plane was due. Quinn wanted them to load up and get the aircraft back in the air as quickly as they could.

Daeng parked next to the van, and everyone but Jar got out.

Howard, who had been sitting in the open passenger doorway, hopped down onto the grass, smiling. "I was wondering if you were going to make it." He shook hands with Orlando and Quinn.

"Any problems?" Quinn asked.

"St. Amand was awake when we got here. Tried to bribe me."

"How much?" Orlando said.

"A hundred million."

"Whoa."

"Euros."

"And you didn't take it?" Quinn asked.

"Thought about it, but I knew there'd be too many strings attached."

Howard shook with Daeng. When he took Nate's hand, he said, "You look like you've had a fun night."

"I've had worse," Nate said.

"Jar?"

Nate nodded back at the car. "Resting."

While Orlando checked on the prisoners, Quinn and Daeng consolidated their equipment into the gear bags for easy transfer to the plane, and Nate made sure Jar didn't need anything.

It was another five minutes before Quinn heard a car approaching through the orchard.

The doctor.

Finally.

BEFORE DRAKE, HAVEL, and Imrich made it out of the city, Lorenzo called to let them know he'd located the van again.

It had continued heading north so they were still on the right track. Lorenzo texted them directions as he pieced together the van's path.

After they'd been traveling for about an hour, he called them. "It's disappeared."

"What do you mean, disappeared?" Drake said.

"It-it was on the highway, but it never showed up on the next camera."

"Could he have just slowed down?" Havel asked.

"Or stopped for petrol?" Imrich suggested.

"No petrol stations in that area. And the gap between the camera I saw it on and the one I didn't is only a kilometer."

"He must have turned onto another road, then," Drake

said. "Find it!"

"The few roads that are there aren't major ones. I haven't been able to find any cameras. But…"

"But what?"

"Ten kilometers east of where the van disappeared is an AISE airfield."

Drake felt his blood go cold. "Is there a way for them to get there from where you lost them?"

"There is."

A VOLVO SEDAN inched out of the orchard, its headlights off, and rolled to a stop.

Quinn tensed. "Do we know what kind of vehicle medical's arriving in?"

Orlando poked her head from around the van. "A Volvo. Is he here?"

"Looks like it." He glanced at Daeng. "Let's not take a chance, though."

Daeng unzipped the gear bag, pulled out one of the pistols they'd just packed away, and handed it to Quinn.

"Suppressor?" Daeng asked.

"Definitely," Quinn said. Though the airfield was isolated within the trees, sound could carry.

Daeng gave him the attachment, then pulled out another gun and suppressor for himself.

Nate crept over to them. "I'll take one."

By the time all three of them were armed, the Volvo had begun moving toward them.

"You two, stay out of sight," Quinn said.

He stepped from behind Daeng's car so the driver of the other vehicle could see him. When the sedan was about a car length away, it stopped again, and the driver's window rolled down halfway.

From inside, a male voice called in Italian, "I'm looking for Mrs. Blanca. Do you know where I can find her?"

Quinn relaxed. This was the first part of the recognition code Misty had given them. He replied with, "Mrs. Blanca couldn't make it, but she told me to expect you."

The car rolled forward again until it was next to Quinn. The man who climbed out was short and thin, with a full head of salt-and-pepper hair and a frown. "Dr. Ricci," he said, extending his hand.

"Thanks for coming, Doctor," Quinn replied, purposely not giving his name.

"You have someone who's in need of assistance?"

"Right over here."

The doctor retrieved a bag from the trunk of the sedan and followed Quinn to Jar. Quinn left him to examine her and walked over to Orlando.

"Any word on the plane?"

"Relax," Orlando said. "If it was going to be late, Misty would have let us know."

He looked at his watch. "It's almost late now."

"It'll be here."

"ARE YOU SURE this is the right way?" Drake asked.

Lorenzo had directed them onto a dirt road that cut through a grove of olive trees. It was in such bad condition, Imrich had already banged a tire against the wheel well several times, and had almost driven them into a tree as they bounced out of a particularly large hole.

"The information I have says it is."

When they reached the split in the road, Lorenzo told them to go left, and half a minute later, when the road splintered again, he had them turn right.

When Drake spotted the end of the grove, fifty meters ahead, he said, "Cut the light."

Imrich switched the headlights off.

Drake let him drive on for another twenty meters, then said, "Stop. We'll walk in from here."

They exited the vehicle quietly and left the doors open to avoid any excess noise.

The road rose a bit before dipping back down toward the last of the trees. When they reached the crest, Drake noted a glow rising from the field beyond the grove.

He grinned. His biggest worry was that Mr. St. Amand and

his kidnappers would be gone.

But if there was light, there was hope.

QUINN WAS ABOUT to check the time again when something started to hum inside the fenced-off hut. A few seconds after, two parallel rows of dim blue lights switched on along both sides of the runway.

"Told you," Orlando said.

"If I never had any doubts, you'd never have anything to complain about."

"Oh, I'd have plenty."

Quinn looked over at the sedan. Nate, Daeng, and Howard were standing a few feet behind Ricci, who was bent half inside the car, working on Jar.

"Daeng and Steve, you'll help Orlando and me with the cargo."

The two men lingered at the sedan for a moment longer, and then moved to the back of the van. Quinn approached Nate.

"You okay to help Jar onboard?" he asked.

Nate nodded. "I'll be fine."

Quinn wasn't so sure about that. Nate was pretty banged up. Ricci should be looking him over, too, but there would be no time for that.

"How's she doing?" Quinn asked the doctor.

Ricci glanced at him, annoyed. "I've barely had time to look at her."

"I know that, but you need to know that as soon as that plane lands, we need to get her aboard and get out of here. And unless you'd like to come with us, you'd better get her in shape to travel. So, how is she?"

The doctor frowned. "Without an X-ray machine I can't be sure, but I would guess that at least two of her ribs are cracked. I don't think there's any internal bleeding, however. Then there's the concussion, of course. What the hell happened to her?" Before Quinn could answer, Ricci said, "Forget it. I'm not supposed to ask, and I really would rather not know."

"Can she walk? Or do we need to carry her?"

"I…I can walk," Jar said.

Quinn looked at the doctor, who reluctantly nodded.

As Quinn was turning back to Nate, he heard the low hum of an engine somewhere in the olive trees. He whipped his gaze to the entrance road. For a second, he saw light among the trees, then it blinked off.

"Nate," he whispered.

"I saw it."

Quinn looked over at the van, and saw the others also looking toward the trees. He pointed at his ear and motioned for one of them to get him a comm.

To Nate, he said, "Stay here and protect Jar and Dr. Ricci."

"No way. I'm coming with you."

The doctor glanced at them. "What's going on?"

"Nothing. Just worry about your patient."

"I don't want to get in the middle of anything."

"We don't want that, either."

The doctor blew out a breath and turned back to Jar.

"Someone has to stay with them," Quinn whispered to Nate. "And you're not one hundred percent."

"When did that ever matter?"

Howard ran up and gave Quinn a set of comm gear.

As Quinn inserted the earpiece, he glanced at Nate before saying to Howard, "You stay here and watch over Jar and the doctor."

"Okay."

Quinn flicked on his mic. "Orlando and Daeng, circle around and come through the orchard on the left. Nate and I will head straight in."

"Copy," Orlando said.

Quinn said to Howard, "When that plane arrives, if everything's clear, get Jar onboard."

"What about him?" Howard said, nodding toward the doctor.

"Him, too."

Quinn and Nate headed for the trees.

DRAKE SCANNED THE airfield from inside the last row of olive trees.

He could now see dozens of dim blue lights running in paralleling lines down the length of a wide field.

Landing lights. Bordering a runway.

He worried that the plane was at the far end, getting ready to take off, but he didn't see an aircraft anywhere. Either they hadn't left yet or were already gone. But if they were gone, then why were the lights still on?

Parked near the midpoint were three vehicles, two sedans and the van Lorenzo had been tracking. No movement around them.

Havel tapped him on the shoulder and pointed at the sky to the southeast.

A dark shape was low on the horizon, dropping toward the end of the runway.

The plane was arriving. There was still time.

He'd seen what these people did at the warehouse, and was under no delusion that he, Havel, and Imrich could take them down. But he could not let them fly away with his boss. Mr. St. Amand must still be in the van. If Drake could take control of the vehicle before the others moved Mr. St. Amand, he could still fix this mess.

After Drake whispered his plan to Havel and Imrich, the three of them made a beeline for the van.

QUINN AND NATE had almost reached the orchard when Quinn noticed movement fifty meters to their right, toward the entrance road.

Three dark shapes were sprinting across the clearing.

He activated his mic. "They're heading toward the van. Howard, stay with Jar and the doc. Orlando and Daeng—"

"On our way," Orlando said.

Staying low and quiet, Quinn and Nate spread apart and headed on an intercepting course with the intruders. Quinn was close enough now that he could discern some of the men's facial features. The two in the back, he'd never seen before. But the leader was St. Amand's driver.

That son of a bitch must have nine lives.

It soon became clear the three men would reach the van

before Quinn and Nate.

"Now," Quinn whispered into his comm.

THE VAN WAS only twenty meters away, and still no movement ahead. Drake was beginning to think he'd actually pull this off.

But then behind them, a voice yelled, "Stop!"

The urge to look back was great, but he kept his focus on the vehicle as he shouted at the others, "Cover me."

He heard the muffled *thups* and continued to run, but had no idea if they had come from his men or the kidnappers. It didn't matter. The longer Havel and Imrich engaged the others, the more time Drake would have.

As he reached the van, a bullet smacked into the hood, half a meter away. He juked around the front fender and got the van between him and the shooters.

Staying low, he tugged the driver's door open and crawled inside. The vehicle had a push-button start. What he didn't see was the key fob that would make it work. He tried pushing the button anyway, figuring that if the others had stolen the van, they would have rigged the ignition.

The engine rumbled to life.

Jubilant, he reached to put the vehicle in drive, but stopped. He needed to make sure Mr. St. Amand was in back.

He twisted between the seats to see into the cargo area.

QUINN HEARD THE driver shout something to the other two. While the man kept running for the van, his companions turned and started shooting.

Having anticipated the possibility, Quinn had slipped several paces to his left after yelling at them to stop. Their bullets flew through empty air.

Nate's shots, however, did not.

The nearest shadow dropped and lay unmoving on the grass. The other spun from a hit to his upper body but didn't go down. He got off two shots in Nate's general direction before Quinn put a bullet through the side of his head.

Quinn looked over at Nate. "You hit?"

"Still in one piece."

Beyond Nate, Quinn could see movement at the van, something going on with the driver's door.

"Come on," he said, and ran for the vehicle.

Instead of heading for the cab, he motioned for Nate to follow him to the back, where the rear doors had been left open in anticipation of transferring the prisoners to the plane.

When Quinn put a foot on the bumper to climb in, Nate grabbed his arm.

Nate must have also realized St. Amand's driver was the one up front, because the look on Nate's face said, "This one's mine."

Quinn moved out of the way and let Nate enter first. As Quinn joined him, the van's engine started.

Nate was within arm's length of the front when the driver looked back.

"Hi," Nate said, pointing the gun at the man's head.

The driver made a move toward his weapon, but Nate shot the man in the knee, causing the man to scream and grab his leg instead of his gun. Nate reached across, removed the pistol, and tossed it outside.

"I admire the never-give-up attitude," Nate said. "But you shouldn't feel bad for failing. You were playing out of your league and didn't know it."

He looked back at Quinn, who was staring at him.

"What?" Nate asked. "I'm sure ACORT wouldn't mind having someone else from St. Amand's organization to talk to."

Quinn nodded. "I think they'll be very happy."

CHAPTER
THIRTY ONE

AN ANNOYED BUT understanding Ricci joined them on the flight back to the States. Not only were his skills needed for Jar, he had to prevent St. Amand's driver from bleeding to death. In addition, Quinn couldn't rule out the possibility more of St. Amand's men were on their way to the airfield.

While the doctor worked, the rest of the team fell asleep not long after leaving Italian airspace. Quinn didn't wake until right before the plane touched down at Pope Field in North Carolina. There, the prisoners were transferred to a waiting team of military personnel, who would take them to whatever hole in the ground ACORT had arranged. Ricci, after a final check of Jar and Nate, was escorted to a vehicle with the promise that his flight back to Italy would leave within the hour. After the team's plane was refueled, it took off again, heading to DC.

Quinn, Orlando, Nate, and Daeng sat on either side of a table near the back, eating the breakfast that had been brought onboard for them at Pope. Howard had chosen to go back to sleep on the fold-down bed, across the aisle from the one Jar rested on.

Quinn picked at his food more than ate it. It wasn't the job that was on his mind. Even after the on-the-fly adjustment to their mission parameters, they'd completed everything to the great satisfaction of the Office's client.

Misty had called them as soon as they lifted off in Italy. "Director Otero sends his thanks and praise for a job well done.

And so do I. Thank you, all of you. I think it's fair to say the Office has returned with a bang."

What occupied Quinn's thoughts was Nate. After a tense start, they had fallen back together well, like there had never been any issues between them at all. He had tried, when he could, to make sure Nate understood how sorry he was for the way things had gone down with Liz's killer, and how Quinn had acted after Liz's death. He wasn't sure if Nate fully believed him. More concerning, he wasn't sure if Nate would still be his and Orlando's partner after they deplaned in Washington.

"I, um, I want to make sure you understand how thankful we are," Quinn said, "how thankful *I* am, that you decided to help us."

"You're welcome," Daeng said.

"I wasn't talking to you. I mean, I'm glad you're here, too, but…"

Daeng grinned. "But I wasn't the one who made a surprise guest star appearance."

"Exactly." Quinn looked at Nate. "I mean it. Thank you."

Nate glanced down at his food and nodded a few times before saying, "You're welcome."

Quinn wanted to follow up with something like, "Does this mean you're back?" But he couldn't think of any way to say it that didn't sound like he was begging or had expectations. He was also afraid of what the response would be.

It was Daeng who broke the silence. "What do you think is going to happen with Sandstrom and St. Amand?"

"I don't know, and I don't care," Orlando said. "That's not our gig. The only thing I care about is that they're locked away for good."

"What about the Freedom Day thing, though? Doesn't that worry you?"

"Not anymore," Orlando said. "The guy who'd been organizing it and the munitions supplier are both out of commission. I'm betting that over the next few weeks, there will be a series of quiet raids that gut whatever organization is left."

Quinn knew she was right. Just like he knew, if Sandstrom's plot hadn't been uncovered, the country would be facing a disaster. Not that Quinn thought the insurgents would've succeeded, but that kind of attempt would've changed things dramatically for the worse. Even with the country's internal disagreements, the US was full of people who'd rather build something than tear it apart, but it wasn't immune to the acted-out fantasies of a few deranged individuals. Actions like that left scars, and one from Freedom Day would have been particularly deep and painful. It was why those in the position to thwart such behavior had to remain vigilant.

It was why Quinn and the others did what they did.

NATE HAD A lot to think about. While no one had asked him what he was going to do now, he knew they wanted to. He'd rather put off figuring that out, but he owed his friends an answer. And by the time the plane began its descent into DC, he had one.

"Here's the thing," he said, leaning forward. "I'd…I'd like to come back."

"To work?" Orlando asked.

"Yeah. But I'm going to need some time."

"You can have whatever you need," Quinn said. "Just come back when you're ready."

"That's not what I mean."

Nate looked out the window. How was he supposed to explain his plan?

You don't have to tell them everything, Liz said. *They want you no matter what. Just say what you have to, and nothing more.*

She was right. She was always right.

When he turned back, they were all waiting.

"What I mean is, there'll be times when I'm available, and times when I'm not. And when that happens I just need you to say okay and use someone else."

"We can live with that," Orlando said. She glanced at Quinn. "Can't we?"

Quinn was eyeing Nate with the slightest of suspicion.

"We can live with that," he finally said. He held his hand out across the table. "Welcome back."

He knows, Nate thought. *He knows what I'm going to do when I'm not with them.*

Liz smiled reassuringly. *What if he does?*

Nate took his former mentor's hand. "Thank you."